"It's a pleasure to see Temperance returning to what she does best, peeling back the layers and using her forensic brilliance to expose a shocking cover-up. . . . *A Conspiracy of Bones* offers page-turning proof that Kathy Reichs won't be giving up her forensic-anthropologist-in-distress throne anytime soon."

—David Morrell,
author of *Murder as a Fine Art*

A CONSPIRACY OF BONES

KATHY REICHS

PUBLISHED BY SIMON & SCHUSTER

New York London
Toronto Sydney New Delhi

SIMON &
SCHUSTER
CANADA

Simon & Schuster Canada
A Division of Simon & Schuster, Inc.
166 King Street East, Suite 300
Toronto, Ontario M5A 1J3

This Simon & Schuster Canada edition February 2021

SIMON & SCHUSTER CANADA and colophon are trademarks of
Simon & Schuster, Inc.

For information about special discounts for bulk purchases,
please contact Simon & Schuster Special Sales at 1-800-268-3216
or CustomerService@simonandschuster.ca.

Manufactured in the United States of America

10   9   8   7   6   5   4   3   2   1

Library and Archives Canada Cataloguing in Publication

Title: A conspiracy of bones / Kathy Reichs.
Names: Reichs, Kathy, author.
Description: Simon & Schuster Canada edition. | Previously
published: 2020.
Identifiers: Canadiana 20200293176 | ISBN 9781982168469 (softcover)
Classification: LCC PS3568.E49 C66 2021 | DDC 813/.54—dc23

ISBN 978-1-9821-6846-9
ISBN 978-1-9821-3935-3 (pbk)
ISBN 978-1-9821-3936-0 (ebook)

For Carolyn Reidy and Kevin Hanson
You never stopped believing in me

"It is far harder to kill a phantom than a reality."

—Virginia Woolf,
*The Death of the Moth
and Other Essays*

1

Reactions to pressure vary. Some people are ductile, able to stretch. Others are brittle, powerless to bend. Physicists talk of stress-strain curves. One thing is certain. If the burden is too great, or the loading too rapid, anyone can snap.

I know. I reached my breaking point the summer after my boss was murdered. *Moi.* The igneous rock of emotion. And I'm not talking about just the nightmares.

To be fair, Larabee's death wasn't the immediate or sole trigger. There was Andrew Ryan, my longtime lover and cop-partner in investigating homicides in Quebec. Succumbing to pressure, I'd agreed to cohabitate with Ryan on both the Montreal and Charlotte ends of our geographically complex relationship. There was Katy's posting in Afghanistan. Mama's cancer. Pete's news about Boyd. My diagnosis, then surgery. The migraines. A world of stressors was chafing my personal curve.

Looking back, I admit I spun out of orbit. Perhaps going rogue was an attempt to steer unsteerable forces. A bird-flip to aging. To the renegade vessel threatening havoc in my brain. Perhaps it was a cry for Ryan's attention. A subconscious effort to drive him away? Or maybe it was just the goddamn Carolina heat.

Who knows? I was holding my own until the faceless man sent me over the edge. His remains and the subsequent investigation punched a black hole in my smug little world.

My mother spotted the changes long before the enigmatic corpse turned up. The distractedness. The agitation. The short temper. She blamed it all on the aneurysm. From the moment of its discovery, Mama was convinced the little bubble would burst and my own blood would take me out. I scoffed at her critique of my behavior, knowing she was right. I was ignoring emails, the phone. Declining invitations in favor of solo bingeing on old Hollywood flicks. Hell, I'd watched my favorite, *Annie Hall*, four times.

I didn't tell Mama about the nighttime visitations. Twisting montages filled with dark figures and vague dangers. Or frustrating tasks I couldn't complete. Anxiety? Hormones? The headache meds I was forced to ingest? Irrelevant the root of my irritability. I was sleeping little, constantly restless, and exhausted.

It didn't take Freud to recognize I was in a bad place.

So there I was, wide awake in the wee hours, talking myself down from a dream about a storm and snakes and Larabee sealed in a body bag. Ole Sigmund might have offered a comment on that.

I tried deep breathing. A relaxation exercise starting with my toes.

No sale.

Nerves on edge, I got up and crossed to the window. Two floors below, the grounds spread out around my townhouse, dark and still save for the lank twisting of a leaf in the occasional half-hearted breeze. I was turning away when my eyes caught a flicker of movement beside the pine on my neighbor's front lawn.

Peering hard, I made out a silhouette. Bulky. Male?

On the grounds of Sharon Hall at midnight?

Heart pumping a bit faster, I blinked to refocus.

The silhouette had blended into the shadows.

Had someone actually been there?

Curious, I pulled on a pair of discarded shorts and my Nikes and went downstairs. I wasn't planning to confront the guy, if there *was* a guy; I just wanted to determine his reason for being outside my home at that hour.

In the kitchen, I switched off the alarm and slipped out the back door onto my terrace. The weather was beyond Dixie summer-night warm, the air hot and muggy, the leaves as droopy and discouraged as they'd appeared from upstairs. Spotting no prowler, I circled the building. Still no one. I set off on one of the paths crisscrossing the estate.

It had rained as I'd eaten my microwave-pizza dinner at ten, and moisture still hung thick in the air. Puddles glistened black on the gravel, went yellow as my fuzzy shadow and I passed under quaint-as-hell carriage lights blurred by mist.

The tiny pond was a dark void, woolly where the

water met the bank. Murky shapes glided its surface, silent, aware of their tenuous state. The homeowners' association fights an endless, often creative battle. No matter the deterrent, the geese always return.

I was passing a black Lego form I knew to be a small gazebo when I sensed more than heard another presence. I stopped. Stared.

A man was standing in the smear of shadow within the gazebo. His face was down, his features obscured. Medium height and build. I could tell little else about him. Except two things.

First, I didn't know him. He wasn't a resident, and I'd never seen him visit.

Second, despite the stifling heat, the man was wearing a trench coat. When he raised an arm, perhaps to check a watch, the fabric flashed pale in the gloom enveloping him.

I glanced nervously over my shoulder.

Crap. Why hadn't I brought my phone? Easy one there. Because the damn thing was dead. Again.

Fine. Why hadn't I at least lit the porch light? Go home and call 311 to report a prowler? 911?

I turned back. The gazebo was empty. I checked in both directions along the path. To the right, the left. The man wasn't on it.

The mist began to morph back into rain. Listless drops tested for foothold on my face and hair. Time to head in.

Suddenly, beyond the circle drive, I caught a wink of gray. There, then gone.

Shot of adrenaline. Was Trench Coat targeting me? Casing the layout of Sharon Hall? If not, what was he doing here in the rain in the middle of the night? And why so elusive?

Or was my wariness a product of paranoia, another gift from my overburdened stress-strain curve. Either way, I was glad I'd left pepper spray in my shorts pocket after my previous run.

Perhaps roused by the unsettling dream, images of Larabee's last moments unspooled in my head. The gray-green pallor of his skin. The eerie glow of the surgical-trauma ICU. The impartial pinging of the monitors recording their bloodless peaks and valleys. The screaming silence when the pinging stopped. Later, in an interview room smelling of sweat and fear, the slouchy indifference of the brain-fried tweaker who'd sent the bullets into my longtime boss's belly.

Stop!

Aloud? Or just in my mind?

I lengthened my stride, footfalls crunching softly in the stillness.

A full minute, then a trench-coated form, far up where the path emptied into a residents' parking area. The man was walking with an odd swinging gait, his back to me.

Suddenly, noise seemed to ricochet from all around. Rustling leaves. Shifting branches. Snapping twigs. Night creatures? Trench Coat's geeked-out pals looking to fund more meth?

I had no valuables—carried no money, wore no watch. Would that anger them?

Or were the sounds the invention of overwrought nerves?

I patted the pepper spray at my right hip. Felt the

canister. Pink and nasty. A molecule of the price I'd paid had been donated toward breast-cancer research.

Momentary indecision.

Head home? Continue on the path and observe the man? Confront him in the parking lot? There were streetlamps there, overwhelmed but trying their best.

I slowed. Trench Coat was now just ten yards ahead.

My brain chose that moment to unreel a block-buster tableau.

When I approached, the man would pull a knife and try to slit my throat.

Jesus!

Why was I letting this guy fluster me? In my line of work, I encounter far worse than a dude dressed like Bogie in *Casablanca*. Outlaw bikers who chainsaw the heads and hands from their murdered rivals. Macho pricks who stalk and strangle their terrified exes. Drunken bullies who wall-slam fussy infants. Those lowlifes don't dissuade me from focusing on my job. Quite the reverse. They inspire me to work harder.

So why the drama over a man in a belted coat? Why the sense of threat? It was doubtful the guy was a psycho. More likely a harmless geezer overly sensitive to damp.

Either way, I owed it to my neighbors to find out. I'd use the hedge as cover and follow him for a while. If he acted suspicious, I'd go inside and dial the cops. Let them decide.

I wriggled through a gap in the bushes, moved along their far side a few yards, then paused to scan the parking lot.

The man was there, standing under one of the

struggling lamps. His chin was raised, his features vaguely discernible as dark blotches on a smudgy white rectangle.

My breath froze.

The guy was staring straight at me.

Or was he?

Unnerved, I pivoted to search for the opening in the shrubbery at my back. Couldn't find it. Dived in where the darkness seemed less dense. The tunnel was narrow, barely there, or not there at all. Twigs and leaves snagged my arms and hair, skeletal fingers clawing me back.

My breathing sounded louder, more desperate, as though fighting entrapment by the thick vegetation. The air was heavy with the scent of wet bark, damp earth, and my own perspiration.

A few feet, then I was free and hurrying back toward the pond. Not the way I'd come, a new route. More shadowed. Less open.

Imperceptibly, a new odor entered the olfactory mix. A familiar odor. An odor that triggered a fresh wave of adrenaline.

I was catching whiffs of decomposing flesh.

Impossible.

Yet there it was. Stark and cold as the images haunting my dreams.

A minute of scrambling around a stand of azaleas and philodendron, then I detected a thawing in one slice of the darkness ahead. Within the slice, angles and planes of shadow shifting and tilting out on the lawn.

Trench Coat's minions lying in wait?

I was almost to the edge of the garden when a

rip-your-face-off snarl brought me up short. As my mind struggled to form a rational explanation, a high-pitched scream sent every hair on my arms and neck upright.

Hand shaking, I pulled the pepper spray from my pocket and inched forward.

Beyond the shrubs, out where the lawn met the eastern wall of the property, two dogs were locked in winner-take-all combat. The larger, the scraggy consequence of some Lab–pit bull affair, was all hackles, bared teeth, and gleaming white sclera. The smaller, probably a terrier, cowered, tense and timorous, blood and spit matting the fur on one haunch. Neither animal was familiar to me.

Unaware of my presence, or not caring, the Lab-pit braced, then lunged for another attack. The terrier yelped and tried to flatten itself even more to the ground, desperate to reduce the amount of mass it presented to the world.

The Lab-pit held a moment, then, confident that rank had been established, pivoted and trotted toward a dark mound lying at the base of the wall. As the terrier slunk off, tail curled to its belly, the Lab-pit sniffed the air, scanned its surroundings, then lowered its head.

I watched, spellbound, curious about the cause of the fight.

A flurry of thrashing and tugging, then the victor's snout rose.

Clamped in the dog's jaw was the severed head of a goose, ravaged neck glistening black, cheek swath winking white like the smile of an evil clown.

I watched rain fall on the bird's sightless eye.

2

A week passed. Almost to the minute. Nothing much happened. Freaked by the dueling dogs and murdered goose, I hadn't reported the intruder. Or peeper. Or whatever he was. Never saw him again.

I'd hit a rough patch of late. Healthwise. Personally. Professionally. The last self-inflicted. I could have been more diplomatic. Or kept my mouth shut. Who knew my comments would come back to bite me in the ass? Right. Don't they always? Mostly, I focused on those problems.

And seriously? A prowler in a trench coat? Was that not the oldest cliché in the book? Had the man been there at all? Or was the whole incident an aftershock of my migraine-induced nightmare?

A pair of fuzzy orbs congealed into headlights that drilled my car's rear window. The interior brightened, nudging my thoughts back from wherever they'd been.

11:10 p.m. I'd just dropped Mama at her new digs and was stopped on Sharon Amity at the intersection with Providence Road. While waiting for a green, I peeked at myself in the rearview mirror.

Hair knotted at the nape of my neck, not great but OK. Remnants of mascara, blush, and gloss gamely trying to mask the exhaustion.

Mama hadn't commented. Or had she? I'd paid little attention.

Silk tunic, a little bohemian but not over the top. Couldn't see the black skinny jeans, baggier these days. Tory Burch sandals. "I Stop for Red" toes.

The outfit, the L'Oréal, the OPI polish. I was making an effort. Reengaging with the world, as Mama would say. Did say. Repeatedly. Between checking to see if my pupils were equal.

Mahler's Symphony no. 2 in C Minor tonight. *Resurrection*.

Ironic.

I couldn't wait to get home.

Don't get me wrong. I enjoy the concerts. But I rank the postperformance cocktail klatches with Mama's friends on par with a colonoscopy. Though, in fairness, the old up-yours confers a health benefit.

My mother, Katherine Daessee "Daisy" Lee Brennan, is a widow with cancer and a boyfriend who spends his weekdays running a dry-cleaning empire out of its Arkansas headquarters. My sister, Harry, lives a thousand miles away in Texas. And is crazy.

You get the picture. I'm usually Mama's default date.

Which is fine. But why agree to the après-theater gatherings? Simple. My mother elevates the art of passive-aggressive to previously unimagined heights. And I always cave.

The traffic signal changed. I accelerated. The headlights behind me shrank, winged left. Sharon Amity became Sharon Lane. No reason. Ahead, Sharon Lane would T-bone into Sharon Road. Confusing street names are Charlotte's way of messing with out-of-town drivers.

Shadows skipped across the windshield as I passed under a lattice of willow oaks arching high overhead. Snatches of the evening's conversation replayed in my head. The same tired conversations as always.

"Your mother looks great!" Meaning not dead.

"The chemo is going well."

"How's Pete?" I heard your ex is dating a hot yoga instructor, a brain surgeon, the heiress to an international shipping line.

"He's good, thanks."

"Our prayers are with Katy." Thank God it's your kid in a war zone, not ours.

"She's good, thanks."

"My nephew just finalized his divorce and is moving to Charlotte. You two must meet." Let me rescue you from your pathetic life.

"I'm good, thanks."

Tonight new topics had entered in, queries inspired by my current fiasco.

"Are you still teaching at UNCC?" Are you being forced to fall back on your day job?

"A few graduate courses."

"Dr. Larabee's death was a terrible tragedy."

"It was."

"How do you like the current ME?" Rumor has it you're embroiled in a shitstorm with your new boss.

"Excuse me, I think Daisy is signaling that she'd like to leave."

These sessions made me wish I still drank. A lot.

I crossed Wendover. The road narrowed to two lanes. I hit a speed bump, the car bucked, dropped.

My iPhone lit up. No chime. I'd had it on silent during the concert, forgotten to flick the little lever.

I glanced down to where the mobile lay on the passenger seat. A gray box indicated a received text. I figured it was Mama, concerned my embolization had blown. Or that I'd been kidnapped by Somali pirates.

Minutes later, parked in my drive, I tapped the screen and flicked to the Messages app. The text had arrived at 8:34.

I opened the app, the message.

Four images.

A frisson of current sparked under my sternum.

My townhouse was blessedly cool and smelled faintly of plaster and fresh paint.

"Birdie?" Tossing my keys onto the counter.

No response.

"I'm home, Bird."

Nothing. The cat was still pissed about the renovations. Fine. I had my own issues.

I locked the door, set the alarm, and crossed the kitchen without turning on a light. Passing through the dining room and then the parlor, I climbed the stairs.

Nineteenth-century deeds refer to the tiny two-story structure as the annex. Annex to what? No living soul has a clue. To the mansion, now condos, presiding over the grounds of Sharon Hall? To the converted carriage house beside it?

I don't give a rat's ass. I've lived in the annex's Lilliputian rooms for more than a decade, since my separation from the would-be swain of the shipping-line heiress. Throughout my tenancy, I'd changed nothing but light bulbs.

Until recently. And the process—building codes, permits, homeowners' association hysteria—had been horrendous. And still there were issues. Jammed windows. A lunatic electrician. A no-show painter.

Reaching the top tread, I glanced right toward the door leading into the new square footage. As usual, my chest tightened, just a hiccup, enough to get my attention. The same flinch experienced by victims of home invasion?

I'd made the decision to live with Ryan. We'd agreed to shift between cities, commute as work demanded and freedom allowed. We'd bought a condo in Montreal. I'd agreed to construction of the addition here. Enough space for a roomie.

So why the mental cringe? Why the refusal to actually move into the space? Nothing more fear-some than bad wiring and the wrong shade of gray lay beyond the door. Two desks, two bookshelves, two filing cabinets.

Two toothbrushes in the bathroom. Two kinds of bread in the freezer.

Everything in pairs.

My life subdivided. I'd been there. It hadn't worked out.

Get a grip, Brennan. Ryan's not Pete. He'll never betray you. He's handsome, smart, generous, kind. And sexy as hell. Why the reluctance to commit?

As usual, I had no answer.

In the bedroom, I threw my purse onto the bureau, myself into the rocker, and kicked off the sandals. Then I plugged in my phone so the damn thing wouldn't die within seconds.

I view crime-scene and autopsy pics all the time. They're never pretty. The ashen flesh, the unseeing eyes, the blood-spattered walls or car interiors. Though I'm accustomed, the sad tableaus always affect me. The stark reminders that a human life has ended violently.

These hit me harder than most.

I swallowed.

The first image showed a man lying supine in a body bag, arms straight and tight to his sides. The bag had been unzipped to his waist. I could see nothing beyond his rolled sleeves and belt.

The man had died in a blood-soaked ecru shirt. A pair of shoes was tucked by his head, made of the same rich brown leather that had held up his pants.

Above the bloody collar, the man's face was a horror show of macerated flesh and bone. The nose and ears were gone, the orbits dark and empty.

Sightless as the dead goose by the garden wall.

The grim flashback elicited another visceral shudder.

The next two images were close-ups of the man's hands. Or would have been had either survived. His forearms were mangled from the elbows down, the radii and ulnae ending in jagged projections below the point to which the creamy sleeves had been rolled. Severed tendons glistened white in the hamburger mash.

The last image zeroed in on the man's midsection. The shirtfront had been displaced to one side. His abdomen gaped wide below ribs resembling the bleached wreckage of a boat's shattered bow. What remained of his viscera was almost unrecognizable. I spotted a few organ remnants, some threads of liver and spleen, nothing positioned where it should have been.

The message was tagged with no name or number, filtered through a spamlike phone exchange. I knew there were apps and websites that would accommodate a texter's desire for anonymity. Tricks to hide one's identity using throwaway email accounts. But who would do that? And why? And who would have access to such a mangled corpse? To my mobile number?

Joe Hawkins? Such a breach of protocol seemed way out of character. Joe was the oldest death investigator at the Mecklenburg County Medical Examiner's Office. Oldest in every sense. Hawkins was stitching Ys when the MCME had a single pathologist and one assistant. Probably when Custer went down at the Little Big Horn.

If the sender was Hawkins, what was his motive? Yeah, the vic was a mess. But we'd both seen worse. Much worse. Was Hawkins an ally in my current conflict? A neutral leaking intel to a comrade in peril?

Was Hawkins giving me a heads-up? Since the faceless man would be difficult to ID, was he suggesting the case might require an anthropology consult?

For years, I'd been the sole practitioner serving the region. In the past, the task would unquestionably have fallen to me.

Until Larabee was killed and Margot Heavner stepped into his scrubs.

Word of explanation. Since North Carolina has a statewide medical examiner system, the hiring decision was made by the chief ME in Chapel Hill. The Mecklenburg County Medical Examiner's Office, the facility for which I consult, is one of several subsidiary offices and serves the five counties surrounding Charlotte. Thanks to trigger-friendly gun laws, my fellow state citizens shoot one another with glorious enthusiasm. Therefore, following Larabee's murder, the chief needed a replacement fast.

The salary isn't stratospheric, so Heavner had been one of only a handful of applicants. From her perspective, Charlotte's climate dazzled in comparison to that of North Dakota. From the state's perspective, she was willing to work cheap and start right away.

Bingo! Dr. Margot Heavner, forensic pathologist, author, and showboat extraordinaire.

Heavner began freezing me out the minute she landed. No pretense at subtlety. From day one, she made it clear that hiring Charlie Manson would be preferable to working with me.

You guessed it. There's history between us.

Six years back, Heavner published a book titled *Death's Avenger: My Life as a Morgue Doctor*. The opus, intended for a general audience, was a collection of case studies, most fairly mundane, intended to paint its creator as the greatest pathologist since the invention of the scalpel. Fair enough. Shine a light on the profession, inspire the next generation.

And shine she did. For a few weeks, Heavner was everywhere. Talk shows, print, sidebar ads, social media. I was good with it. Until Dr. Morgue did a series of interviews with a right-wing sleazeball named Nick Body.

Blogging and podcasting on the internet, and from there onto scores of AM radio stations, Body spews whatever trash he thinks will boost ratings and readership. Antivaccination, government mind control, U.S. military involvement in the Twin Towers and Beirut barracks attacks—everything is fair game, no matter how hurtful or absurd. Ditto any sensationalized tale of violence and personal devastation.

Heavner didn't restrict her conversations with Body to the topic of her book. In more than one, she discussed the case of a murdered child. A brutal killing for which no perp had been convicted.

I definitely wasn't good with that.

When asked by a journalist for my opinion of Heavner's behavior, I was sharp in my criticism. Maybe he was goading me with loaded questions. Maybe it was the fact that I was working three child homicides and feeling overly protective of victims. Maybe I was tired. Whatever the cause, I didn't hold back.

Heavner was furious. Threatened a lawsuit for slander or libel, or whatever, but didn't follow through. The feud never went public. No one cares about the bickering of science nerds. But in our little nerd circles, the gossip was rife.

That year, at the annual meeting of the American

Academy of Forensic Sciences, a colleague in entomology, Paulette Youngman, advised me to let the
quarrel go. Was it Dallas? Baltimore? The venues all
blur in my mind. Paulette and I were on break from
a multidisciplinary workshop on child abuse when
Heavner passed in one of her signature Diane von
Fürstenberg wraps.

"You're right," Youngman had said. "The woman
has no scruples."

"She discussed an open homicide to hawk her damn
book."

"It doesn't matter."

"It does matter if she's compromised the case and
there's no justice for the child. And he wasn't the only
one. She talked about other missing kids. I could hear
Body salivating through the speakers."

Youngman swirled the ice in her soda, then set
down her Styrofoam tumbler. "Ever hear of *Ophio-
cordyceps camponoti-balzani*?"

"I think I have a colony under my sink."

"It's a fungus that grows out of the heads of ants in
the Brazilian rain forest. They're called zombie ants."

"Sounds like another crackpot Body conspiracy
theory."

"But this is true. The fungus mind-controls the
ants."

"Mind-controls them into doing what? Voting
Republican?"

"It takes over the ant's brain, then kills the host once
it's moved to a location suitable for fungal success."

"Fiendish."

"It's fungus."

I was lost. "Your point?"

"Heavner's morality has been hijacked by a need for fame and public adulation."

"She's become a zombie pathologist."

Youngman shrugged.

"So I should just let it drop?"

"In the end, the ant always loses." Youngman tipped her head, reflecting fluorescent light off the unfashionable black glasses riding low on her nose.

For a long moment, neither of us spoke. Youngman broke the silence.

"Did Heavner's book make the *New York Times* bestseller list?"

"Not even close." I'd checked.

Youngman grinned.

I grinned back.

In the intervening years, I've often thought of that conversation. Assumed the whole ant-fungus metaphor was a by-product of viewing too many projected images of battered children.

But here it was, six years later, and Heavner had found a location where she could flourish. Dr. Morgue was running the MCME. And I was persona non grata, my life in disarray.

I looked at the clock. Almost midnight. Call Hawkins?

Not a chance he'd be awake.

A quick toilette, and I crawled into bed.

Of course, I didn't sleep.

In the dark, images looped and swirled, denizens of my subconscious begging for attention. Heavner. Hawkins. The faceless man. A defect in my left posterior communicating artery now packed with tiny platinum coils.

At some point, Birdie came and curled at my side.

Didn't help. My mind was a hazardous-waste dump of doubt, distress, and unanswered questions.

Chief among them: Who was the doomed ant, who the fungus facing a prosperous future?

3

I was awakened by a mockingbird doing animated a cappella outside my window. Birdie was gone, presumably off resuming his snit.

The clock said 6:27. The sky was easing from pewter to pearl. The room was a collision of shadows sharpening at the edges.

I tried rolling over.

A conversation sluiced into my drowsy brain. An old woman, voice quavery, as though uncertain of wanting her message delivered. Or terrified.

I still hear the old woman's words in my head. *Bloodsucking trash. Using my sweet baby's death to glorify her own self. Lord Jesus knows it's wrong.*

Hardin Symes. That was the dead kid's name.

I later learned that the caller was Bethyl Symes, Hardin's grandmother. I'd heard of Nick Body, of course, the fiery provocateur. I'd never listened to a

Body broadcast or read one of his blogs. I'm not his demographic.

But Bethyl was a regular. And she was incensed that Heavner had made a piss storm, her words, of her grandson's murder. Exposed her family's aching heart to the world.

Because of Bethyl, I tuned into the Heavner interview and subsequently launched the missiles that kicked off the feud.

I never heard from Bethyl Symes again.

Agitated, I got out of bed, did some questionable grooming, mostly teeth, then descended to the kitchen. After brewing coffee, I filled the bowl of my judgmental cat. Then I snagged the *Observer* from the back stoop and settled at the table to scan stories I'd already seen on the internet.

Why the dinosaur approach to news? Loyalty to the kid who's been tossing papers onto my stoop for the past three years, winging them from his bike with NASA precision. Derek. Derek claims he's saving up to attend Harvard. Maybe I'm a sucker. The story also gets him a ridiculous holiday tip.

A pileup on I-77 had taken the lives of an Ohio family en route to Charleston for their annual beach week. New condos were going up in South End. The DOJ was opening an inquiry into the finances of a local member of Congress.

Nothing on the faceless man. My real reason for looking.

Another coffee, then I pulled my MacBook Air from my carryall and ran a quick online search. Found no mention of the discovery of human remains near Charlotte.

I puttered until eight. Dishes. Email. A load of laundry. Then, knowing he was a dawn riser, I dialed Hawkins's mobile. He answered after one ring.

"Shoot." Hawkins's normal greeting.

"Is a thank-you in order?"

"For what?"

"Did you text me last night?"

"Nope."

Surprised, I explained the photos. "Any idea who sent them?"

"Nope."

"Is the body at the MCME?"

"Yep." To say Hawkins is taciturn would be the understatement of the millennium.

"What's the scoop?"

"Guy was pig feed."

"I was guessing dogs." One glance at the texted images had told me the mutilation was due to animal scavenging.

"Wild hogs."

"Where?" When talking to Hawkins, I often adopt his brusque manner. Not a conscious choice, the clipped rhythm just sucks you in.

"Cleveland County."

I left an encouraging pause. As usual, the ploy didn't work.

"Body dump?"

"Unclear."

"When did he roll in?"

"Yesterday."

"The autopsy will take place on Monday?"

"This morning. I caught it."

"It's Saturday. Why the urgency?"

"No idea."

"Who's doing the cutting?"

"Heavner."

"What do you know so far?"

"Stiff's got no face, no belly, no hands."

I could hear a television in the background. Hawkins was at home, wherever home was. In all our years together, I'd never asked where he lived. He'd never volunteered.

"So no visual ID and no IAFIS." I was referring to the Integrated Automated Fingerprint Identification System, the FBI's national database of prints and criminal histories. Sometimes you're lucky and get a cold hit.

"Nope."

"Unless the guy's carrying a license in his pocket, Heavner will need a bio-profile to give to the cops."

"Social Security card would do." Clattering overrode the rise and fall of the TV dialogue. Hawkins was either cooking or building something.

"I'll let you know if I hear from Heavner." Saying the words made my stomach curl in. I knew Dr. Morgue would never call.

She didn't.

Not all morning while the autopsy was under way.

At ten, I went for a long run, pushed myself hard, came back drenched and almost trembling with muscle fatigue. There was no voice message on my mobile. No flashing red light on my answering machine.

I know. More stegosaurus technology. There's zero reason for keeping the landline. No noble delivery boy. Just habit. Like my old prescription meds, expired and useless but never thrown out.

As the hours ticked by, I kept seeing the images. Kept asking myself who might have sent them. Came up with no plausible candidate. Or explanation.

Heavner didn't phone at midday, when she and Hawkins probably broke for lunch.

Birdie was still pouting. Mama didn't check in to see if my head had exploded. Or ablaze with new travel ideas. Though each was the surviving spouse of a long-term marriage, she and the dry-cleaning tsar were planning the mother of all destination weddings. At least, Mama was.

Ryan didn't ring with news from Montreal.

Time was I could always visualize Ryan's whereabouts. The Crime contre la personne squad room, eight floors below my lab in the Édifice Wilfrid-Derome on rue Parthenais. His condo at Habitat 67, all angles and glass and views of the Saint Lawrence River, Vieux-Montréal on the opposite shore. Since his retirement—another stressor for my curve—I can't pinpoint him with any precision.

Slidell had also gone radio silent. Erskine "Skinny" Slidell, a combo of bluster and paunch and bad polyester, was for decades a detective with the Charlotte-Mecklenburg Police Department homicide squad, thus Ryan's equivalent in Dixie. Not in the sheets, just in the murder probes. Like Ryan, Slidell had also retired and shifted to PI work, though he continued as a volunteer with the CMPD cold-case unit. I was never sure of Slidell's whereabouts lately, either.

I heard from no one. Saw no trace of my cat. The annex was filled with a silence so total I wondered if the previous week's migraine had caused a mini-stroke resulting in hearing loss.

By one o'clock, I was suffused with enough manic energy to summit Everest solo.

OK, Brennan. Showtime.

Grabbing a Diet Coke and the laptop, I double-stepped up to the spiffy new addition.

Light was slicing through the slats of the plantation shutters. The gray shutters that were supposed to be white. I made a mental note to phone my contractor first thing Monday. Cursed when I remembered he'd taken off for Puerto Rico to help his brother rebuild after Hurricane Maria. Revised note. Call the painter.

The air was infused with the sweet smell of freshly sawed wood. OK. That was sort of nice.

One of the two desks was new, the brainchild of some chichi designer who'd probably dubbed the style Italian Modern Chic. Slab-of-glass top, stainless-steel legs. I'd found the stark lines jarring at first. Had to admit, the thing was growing on me.

Two pictures hung above the gleaming glass, below the point where the new roof angled down to meet the new wall. Ryan, second from the right top row, taller than most in his police academy graduating class. Ryan in a Sûreté du Québec officer's dress uniform, arm wrapping the shoulders of his daughter, Lily, now several years dead from a heroin overdose.

Atop the gleaming glass, illuminated by an off-angle slash of daylight, a Canadiens bobblehead signed by Guy Lafleur. Beside the bobblehead, a lamp that looked like a twisted hunk of wing from a Nebulon frigate.

I settled at the other desk, old and familiar, a flea-market find the chichi designer would have labeled Salvation Army Reject. Wiring dangled from the ceiling and jutted from the wall above me, a stark reminder of the electrician, as incompetent and unreliable as the painter. The two phone confrontations that would brighten my Monday.

Diplomas waited on my desktop, ready for hanging. Northwestern University MA and PhD degrees. An American Board of Forensic Anthropology diplomate certificate.

Beside the diplomas, framed photos sat on the patina-glazed oak. Mama and Daddy smiling over two blond-plaited girls in pinafores. Pete and I holding an infant Katy. Ryan and I outside an auberge in the Quebec countryside. Larabee and I on an AAFS panel.

Daddy. Larabee. Both dead. Pete and I, metaphorically so. The chronology of a shattered life?

Christ, Brennan. Give it a rest.

Ryan and Slidell, retired and in partnership. PIs, not cops. Heavner in charge and myself exiled from the MCME. The reconfiguration of my well-ordered world was blowing my arterially compromised mind.

Call it a character flaw. A product of aging. I'd only owned up to the weakness in the past few months.

I dislike change.

Thus, my reluctance to relocate to this new space.

But I was here now. With everything related to the faceless man. New investigation. New era. The rest of my files and documents I would bring up piecemeal.

Goaded by my irritation with Heavner, I opened the laptop, went to Google, and entered the name "Hardin Symes."

Not much came up. But enough.

There was coverage of the child's disappearance and the massive search that ensued. The tragic outcome. All reports were consistent on the basics.

Seven-year-old Hardin Symes lived with his mother, grandmother, and two sisters in an apartment on East Indiana Avenue in Bismarck, North Dakota. On August 19, 2012, Hardin was snatched while playing alone on the complex's front lawn. Neighbors reported seeing a dark-haired man forcing a child into a car. Five days later, Hardin's decomposing corpse was found by hunters fifteen miles from where he'd lived.

A 2014 article in the Bismarck *Tribune* reported on the trial of Jonathan Fox, the suspect charged with Hardin's murder. The defense argued that all the evidence was circumstantial and that public statements made by the ME had prejudiced the defendant. The jury ended up deadlocked, and the judge declared a mistrial.

Of particular interest was a story that appeared on the three-year anniversary of Hardin's death. Seventeen months before Hardin had been taken, eight-year-old Jack Jaebernin had disappeared from his home in the same neighborhood. Jack's father said a dark-haired stranger had invited his son to a local park to catch frogs. Though he'd been warned not to go, the boy went anyway. That night, a family out hiking found Jack's beaten body in a forest twelve miles away. An autopsy showed he'd been strangled or smothered.

The parallels were striking. The two boys had lived just blocks apart. They'd disappeared within a year and a half of each other. They were roughly the same age. Both were dumped in wooded areas at approximately the same distances from their homes. And, most telling, Jonathan Fox had rented a unit in the same apartment complex as Hardin Symes's family.

Though the Bismarck police were convinced they'd arrested the right guy, Fox was never retried. In 2015, the department's cold-case homicide squad began sifting through boxes, looking for sufficient evidence to nail the bastard.

I found no follow-up on the investigation. Apparently, nothing had come of reopening the file.

I googled Jonathan Fox. Learned the following.

Fox was a seventh-grade dropout who'd worked in Bismarck as a front-desk clerk at a local motel. After being tried for the murder of Hardin Symes, he moved to Baltimore.

In 2016, Fox was convicted of killing Chelsea Keller. Chelsea was ten years old. She disappeared from the front lawn of her home. Her body was found in a forest eighteen miles away. In 2017, Fox was stabbed to death at the Western Correctional Institution in Cumberland, Maryland.

I sat back, feeling a sharp warning twist in my gut. The same twist I'd felt when Heavner had run her mouth with Body.

In the end, Fox's ass had been slammed to the wall.

But I'd been right. Heavner's remarks had been used by Fox's lawyer at trial. And the strategy had worked.

But the gut twist had been triggered by something more than inappropriate comments about a murdered child.

After checking some old notes in a filing cabinet in the downstairs guest room/study, I googled the name "Nick Body" and got the link to his radio show, *Body Language*. Once there, I clicked on the Archive button and entered the date I'd just retrieved: September 4, 2012.

Reluctantly, I ponied up the required fee. Answered the nonoptional profile questions. Then I opened the audio file.

The interview was as I remembered. Body queried Heavner about her book, steering the conversation toward cases with the most gore and anguish. Heavner was an enthusiastic participant, her nasal whine almost as nauseating as Body's gravel-through-a-sieve bark.

Ten minutes in, Body jumped the lane and asked about Hardin Symes. A momentary hesitation, then Heavner hopped on board, revealing details that should never have left the autopsy room. Opining on the depravity of the doer.

Then the betrayal that had shot my outrage into overdrive. Six years on, it still did.

Heavner told the world that Hardin Symes had been autistic. The revelation allowed Body to segue to one of his favorite topics.

Prearranged? Doesn't matter. The disclosure was wrong, a violation of professional ethics.

Body spent the rest of the broadcast ranting about the evils of vaccination. His reasoning followed the usual two-pronged path of stupidity. He denied there was any scientific proof of a causal connection between vaccines and the reduction or eradication of diseases such as smallpox, polio, measles, or rubella. And he spewed the usual idiocy that vaccination can cause autism.

Heavner, a medical doctor, offered no objection.

Heavner's disclosure about Hardin Symes was improper and callous. She hurt Hardin's family. She compromised the prosecution of his killer.

Heavner's failure to contradict Body's antivax tirade gave credence to the ludicrous. To the dangerous.

These were offenses I could not accept.

I spoke out.

Still nothing by four.

Screw it.

Agitated as hell, I grabbed my keys and headed for my car.

The MCME facility is located on Reno Avenue, just west of uptown. Saturday-afternoon traffic was light. I was there in ten minutes.

Upon arriving, I knew that something was up. The parking lot held too many vehicles. A couple of vans had logos for local TV broadcast affiliates.

Neurons sending out a low-level buzz, I swiped my security card and drove through the gate.

4

Margot Heavner was standing on the steps of the MCME building. Steps I'd mounted countless times. I watched her, shocked and dismayed.

Dr. Morgue was dressed in aquamarine surgical scrubs. Fresh from a postmortem? Or for the I-play-a-TV-doc optics?

Journalists were thrusting boom and handheld mics at Heavner. Not many, five in all. She was finishing a prepared statement or answering a question.

". . . male, five foot eight, medium build, possibly Asian." Heavner's hair and makeup looked suspiciously good for someone coming straight from an autopsy.

"Age?" Asked by a bored-looking reporter from WSOC, the local ABC affiliate.

"Not old, not a kid."

"That describes more than half the population." Wisecracked by a freelancer who looked like a lizard, if a lizard could squeeze into size-forty short cargo pants. I'd met him. Gerry something.

"The body exhibits advanced putrefaction and severe animal damage."

"Like what? Rats?" Unlike my paperboy, Gerry wouldn't be going to Harvard.

"Feral hogs, Mr. Breugger." Adding, as though fearful she might not be believed, "They're a huge problem in North Carolina."

"Feral hogs?" Fessie Green, five minutes out of Clemson and working the *Observer* crime beat. Green sounded like she'd soon be the color of her surname.

"Pigs gotta eat. These pigs chose to eat a corpse." Heavner pointed to a chinless elf who weighed maybe twelve pounds.

"What do you mean, possibly Asian?"

"The features are ambiguous."

"Meaning what?" The elf was persistent.

Heavner's finger went to a bright young thing from FOX 46.

"Will Dr. Brennan be working the case?"

"My office is in contact with local, state, and federal authorities. Together we will get this unfortunate gentleman identified and returned to his loved ones."

The adrenal buzz gave way to heat, a flush that crawled up my throat and spread across my cheeks.

"How'd the guy die?" Gerry.

"I'm not at liberty to discuss cause of death."

"You thinking murder? Suicide?"

"Same answer."

"You organized this party. What *can* you discuss?"

"My office will provide further information as it becomes available." Heavner hesitated, probably for effect. Then, doing earnest and forthright, "In the interest of the soonest possible closure, there are a few details I'm willing to share."

My fingers tightened on the car keys forgotten in my hand.

"Oddities that might mean something to someone reading or hearing about them."

Gerry tried to interrupt. Heavner ignored him.

"The man carried no credit cards, license, or any form of identification. He had no wallet, but a roll of cash totaling over two hundred dollars. The only other item in his possession was a can of Swedish chewing tobacco, brand name Göteborgs Rapé. His shoes appear to be of European origin. His clothing is high-end. The shirt is ecru linen with small ivory buttons. The pants are tan, a wool-cashmere blend. The boxers are made of high-quality black silk."

A pregnant pause. A nuanced gaze.

"The labels had been removed from every garment. The tobacco can yielded not a single print. The roll of cash was made up of both euros and dollars."

Heavner awaited their eager reaction. They only stared at her, confused. Then the elf launched a somewhat listless volley of questions. Others tagged along.

"The labels were cut off?"

"That appears to be the case."

"What's that mean?"

"I don't know."

"Why no prints on the can?"

"I don't know. The outer surfaces are smooth, and the can was protected from the elements inside a pants pocket."

"Did the man die where his body was found?"

"I can't comment on that at this time."

"Why not?"

"If the guy was mugged, why leave the two hundred bucks?"

"Why, indeed."

"How'd he get out to this creek?"

"That, too, is a mystery. Thank you for your patience." Heavner flicked a wave, turned, and disappeared through the glass doors at her back.

The FOX 46 reporter spoke into a camera, probably handing over to her anchor.

My bullshit monitor was banging like a kettledrum.

Heavner had called a presser. Before I'd arrived, she'd explained where the body was found. Was she really engaging the media in the hope someone would come forward? Was I again being paranoid? Misjudging her motives?

Or were my instincts correct? The grisly allure of feral hogs and a faceless corpse. The high drama of missing labels and strangely absent prints. Was Dr. Morgue at it again? Had her performance been Act I in a limelight-grab leading up to a new book launch?

Screw that.

Ignoring a voice screaming that this was a bad idea, I entered the front door, dropped my purse in my office, threw on a lab coat, and hurried through additional security and down the bio-vestibule to the large autopsy room.

One table was occupied. I crossed to it and drew back the blue paper sheeting covering the body.

The faceless man lay naked on the stainless steel, his flesh jarringly pale under the cruel fluorescents.

Wasting no time, I pulled my iPhone from my pocket and, beginning at his head and working toward his feet, started snapping pics. When I'd finished with the corpse, I moved to the counter and took a series of shots of the man's clothing and belongings. Then I laid down my phone and pulled on latex gloves.

Hawkins arrived as I was digging a swab kit from a drawer. He looked his usual zombie self—tall and skeletal, with dead-black hair oiled back from a face centering on a bony nose, gaunt cheeks, and wire-thin lips. I couldn't have guessed his age. Sixty? Eighty? For years, the joke at the MCME was that Hawkins had died in the eighties and no one had noticed.

Cocking one quizzical brow, Hawkins watched without comment as I scraped a sample from the open thorax of the faceless man.

"You really didn't text me pics of this guy?" I asked, voice low.

"Nope."

"Any idea who might have sent them?"

Hawkins wagged his head no.

"Who had access to him?"

"A few folks."

I knew that was true. I'd been running through a mental Rolodex of suspects. An MCME pathologist. Another death investigator. A first responder at the scene. A tech manning the transport vehicle. The kids who discovered the body. But none of those felt right. And the sender had to be someone with access to my mobile number.

"Appears the boss lady's angling for a spot on *Dateline*." Hawkins also spoke mezza voce.

"Not if I can block her." Placing the swab in a tube.

"Maybe I can smoke out your mole."

"You'll ask around?"

"Diplomatically."

I glanced at Hawkins. "I don't want to jam you up."

"Won't happen."

I'd barely tightened the vial's cap when a voice spoke at our backs, nasal and whiny. As I slipped the sealed specimen into my pocket, Hawkins discreetly palmed my mobile from the counter.

We both turned. I forced myself to smile.

"What are you doing here?" Heavner was wearing an expression like she'd just soiled her Gucci's in dog shit.

"I was driving nearby and caught the start of your press conference." Not wanting to out whoever had sent the text. "Hearing you had a decomp, I diverted over."

"My understanding is that you consult to this office only upon specific verbal or written request."

"Dr. Larabee and I—"

"I am not Dr. Larabee."

I said nothing.

"Do you seriously think this office cannot function without you, Dr. Brennan? That I am incapable of determining when specialty expertise is required?"

Our eyes met for a long, cold moment.

"Should I require your services, I will contact you. Now, please leave."

I did, chest burning as though I'd just run a marathon.

As I walked to my car, Paulette Youngman's words came zinging from long ago. The ant always loses.

*   *   *

I'd just entered the annex when my landline rang.

After checking caller ID, I picked up the handset.

"Sweetie, are you all right?" Mama, vowels broader and more honeyed than Scarlett at Tara.

"Of course, I'm all right."

"Why aren't you answering your mobile?"

"I'm having battery issues." True, but unrelated to her query.

"Where are you?"

"Home."

"Are you feeling poorly?"

"Not at all. I'm going out later." Regretted as soon as the words left my lips.

Surprisingly, Mama didn't pounce. "Sinitch arrived today." Mama's fiancé was named Clayton Sinitch. For some reason, she never used his first name. "He'll be here until Wednesday."

"That's nice."

"I suppose so." Wistful, begging me to inquire.

I didn't. "Do you two have big plans?"

"I must do something about the man's feet."

"His feet."

"They smell like soup made from dirty shorts."

No way I was touching that.

"I'm thinking I should buy one of those foot-odor products they sell at the grocery. Maybe shake some into his shoes when he's in the shower. You'd think soap and water should resolve the situation."

"Mm."

"He's in there now, splashing away. One upside to showering is it gets him naked."

Snapshot image I'll never unsee.

"Sinitch is a lovely man, but some days I still do miss your daddy."

"I know, Mama. So do I."

My early childhood was a happy time. I wasn't abused, or bullied, or made to adhere to a set of crazy-strict religious mores. I never broke a bone, needed surgery, stitches, or counseling. My sister, Harry, and I got along reasonably well. Mama suffered from what would now be called bipolar swings. She'd disappear into rehab for periods but always came home. Then my baby brother died of leukemia, and it all went to hell. Mama fell into a dark place that she couldn't escape for years. Daddy turned to drinking hard, ended up dead on a highway in the family Buick. Decades later, I still missed my father terribly.

"I called because I'm lying in bed and just watched some very interesting television." Mama's tone dropped to a confidential half whisper. "You working on this corpse got gnawed by hogs?"

Point of information. My petite, gray-haired mother has a mind like a spaghetti-bowl highway interchange. Conversations with her swoop and diverge, sometimes loop back, sometimes don't. We were now on the subject of my work. Which, for some reason, fascinates her.

Additional POI. Regardless of the momentary off- or on-ramp, Mama can home in on evasion like a night-vision drone. I didn't bother dodging this question.

"Apparently not," I said.

"Is that dreadful woman still causing you grief? What's her name?"

"Margot Heavner."

"Why on earth is she so hateful to you?"

"Years ago, I offended her."

"How? Poisoned her parakeet? Spit in her grits?"

"Does it matter?"

"Yes," she said firmly.

I laid it all out. Hardin Symes. The Body interviews. The revelation about Hardin's autism. Heavner's failure to counter Body's antivax insanity. My calling her unprofessional.

While I was talking, Birdie padded into the kitchen, sat, and fixed me with a contemplative gaze. Either that, or he was hungry.

Choosing to interpret the cat's appearance as a gesture of rapprochement, I got up and filled his bowl. With the canned stuff he prefers, not the dry crunchers. He sniffed, then stretched, to show his indifference. As I turned away, he abandoned the theater and eagerly dived in.

When I'd finished my story, Mama's reaction was quick and severe.

"I can forgive the man his flat-out stupidity. Lord knows he can't help the IQ he's been dealt. But Nick Body is mean-spirited, unprincipled, and vile as a snake."

"You listen to his show?" Surprised.

"I listen to everything."

"But if you don't like him—"

"I need to be aware of the foolishness flying loose in the world."

I said nothing.

"I once heard Body go full-out about the government training up cats for mind control. Can you believe that?"

My eyes drifted to Birdie. I believed it.

"Another time, he was off to the races on white genocide, saying immigration, miscegenation, birth control, and abortion are being used to cause white people to go extinct."

"Used by whom?"

"He was a bit vague on that. Not to mention population genetics. The man is completely ignorant of scientific facts. He doesn't believe in climate change, insists global warming is a sinister hoax. Like the moon landing. And fluoridation of the water supply."

I tried to change the subject. Mama was on a roll.

"Did you know that the little weasel rarely shows his face in public? No one knows where he lives or what he does when he's not contaminating the airwaves with his drivel."

"I've read that."

"He spews his hogwash, then transmits the files through servers in Bosnia, Borneo, Belarus, and who knows where else so that the original IP is untraceable."

Final POI. My mother is a crack-bang genius with computers and manipulation of the World Wide Web. Partly my doing. When she was in one of her funks and checked into a rehab facility, I bought her a laptop to engage her mind. To my surprise, she jumped onto the internet with gusto, subsequently enrolled in and completed scores of courses on various cyber skills. Now there's no stopping her.

I glanced at the clock: 5:20 p.m.

"Mama, I should go."

I could picture the tightening at the corners of the Dior-tinted lips. Then, "Darling, here's my counsel, take it or leave it. You say Heavner had no scruples about wagging her chin with this circus-clown fool of a blowhard. You say she's now blocking you from a job you've been performing for decades. Do it anyway."

"Sorry?"

"Beat Heavner at her own game. If you're feeling up to it, that is."

"Her own game?" I was lost.

"Good lord, Tempe. You're brilliant, but you can be thick." Mega-patient sigh. "ID the faceless man on your own. If you succeed, it'll irk the patootie out of your new boss. Maybe impress the big enchilada in Chapel Hill."

"But—"

"And investigating will give you something to do besides stewing at home all day. As long as it won't compromise your condition, of course."

Nope. Didn't touch that.

"You still there?"

"I am."

"The shower cut off. I should spritz myself up. You'll consider what I said?"

"Yes." Anything to avoid thoughts of Clayton Sinitch fadoodling my mother.

Consider it I did, turning and twisting the idea a zillion different ways.

Accept my fate and focus my professional energies elsewhere? Fact is, I get plenty of requests. Though, to be honest, not enough to fill the financial gap left by my loss of income at the MCME. I still drew a salary for my teaching at UNCC, and payment for my consulting

to the Laboratoire de sciences judiciaires et de médecine légale, the LSJML, in Quebec, but the purchase
of the Montreal condo and the cost of construction at
the annex had me stretched pretty thin. Ryan would
help, of course, but there was no way I'd allow him to
pay more than his share. More stressors for the curve.

So. Follow Mama's suggestion and forge ahead with
the faceless man on my own? Clearly, I was already
invested. Otherwise, why had I taken the photographs
and blood sample?

In addition to Hawkins, I had at least one other ally.
But who was the anonymous texter? And why had he
or she sent me those images?

Going rogue could turn out to be the final career
slayer on my home turf. On the other hand, what did
I have left to be slain?

At five forty, I grabbed the handset and dialed
Chapel Hill. The office of the chief medical examiner
was closed for the day. Of course it was. I left a voice
mail for the big enchilada.

By six, I was fizzing to the fingertips with agitation.
Finally, the call I was expecting.

An hour later, I was sitting in a back booth at Sassy's
Chili Shack, a grubby fifties-style diner behind a patch
of weedy gravel on Wilkinson Boulevard. Sassy's looked
like it might have started life as a Hell's Angels clubhouse. The patrons looked like card-carrying gang
members or wannabes. Shaved heads. Flamboyant
facial hair. Sleeveless denim, lots of leather, studs, and
dangling keys. You get the picture.

Though I like dives, Hawkins's go-to spot is not my fave. The dump smells of cigarette smoke and beer-marinated wood, and the menu offers little but chili and 'cue.

Hawkins sat across from me, looking like an upright cadaver in glasses. He was working a combo plate involving a lot of dead animals. I was sipping a Perrier with lime. An eyebrow raiser with the tattooed and bearded barman.

An eco-friendly Harris Teeter sack lay on the table between us, the parrot-green fabric discordant in the murky light. Inside it, I could see the top of a large brown envelope. A rectangular bulge I hoped was my phone.

I let Hawkins finish eating before asking if he'd floated queries about the mysterious texter.

"Gotta be cagey," he said, meaning no.

"What's in the bag?" Unable to control my curiosity a second longer.

"Copy of Heavner's file."

"Holy shit. Seriously?"

"Calm down. It's just the prelim. Nothing finalized."

"What's your take?"

"I'm thinking suicide."

"Why?"

"No trauma, no signs of a struggle, vic lying straight. Except for the work of the hogs, I'm saying."

"No note?"

"Nope."

"Heavner leaning that way?"

"She wants a murder."

"Did she run a tox screen?" Not questioning the odd comment.

"Standard only."

"Where was the body found?"

"Cleveland County, near Earl, a hop north of the state line."

"Why'd Charlotte catch the case?"

"Guess the locals didn't feel up to the challenge. No face, no hands, no gut."

"Rural area?"

"Mostly farmland and woods."

"The Cleveland County sheriff worked the scene?"

"Such as it was."

"Who found the body?"

"Couple kids figuring to fish. Guess that won't be high on their list for a while." Effusive for Hawkins, maybe a record.

"How'd he get there?"

Hawkins shrugged and lifted both hands. A move that made me think of a praying mantis.

"Was any vehicle parked in the area? Bike? Motorcycle?"

"Not that I heard."

Hawkins knocked back the dregs of his coffee and flicked a finger at the bag. "Photocopied what I could."

"I can't thank you enough."

"Your phone's in there, too."

"I owe you."

"Gotta keep it on the down low."

"Subterranean."

The cadaver eyes locked onto mine.

"No way it came from me."

"No way," I said.

5

Back behind the wheel, in the patch of gravel hosting nothing but old beaters and tricked-out bikes, I checked my watch. Which was hard to read in the slanty amber-violet of early dusk.

8:02. Too early for my dinner date, too late to go home.

The Harris Teeter bag lay on the passenger seat, taunting me with its purloined intel. I lifted a handle and dug out my phone and the brown envelope, which felt disappointingly thin. Unsealing the flap with one index finger, I slid free the collection of paper-clipped sheets and flipped through them.

Photocopies. An incident report from the Cleveland County Sheriff's Department. A morgue intake form, case designated MCME 304-18. Preliminary autopsy notes, very brief. A few crime-scene pics. A speed-read of the docs suggested that, lacking some fine citizen stepping forward, hope of an ID was as bleak as I'd feared.

I scooped the swab-kit tube and a Sharpie from my purse and added the case number. Through the clear plastic, I could see the white wadded gauze with its plastic dowel. I hadn't initialed the tube's small white cap, normal protocol for a tech collecting a sample.

Ignoring the alarm again pinging in my brain, I returned the envelope and the tube to the bag and headed out.

Several zip codes later, I pulled into a small shopping center in a far more privileged section of town. Wine shop, nail salon, mom-and-pop brokerage firm. Tasteful lanterns oozing warm yellow onto well-behaved flora in window boxes and stone-sided planters.

I parked outside a tiny walled courtyard outfitted with scrolly wrought-iron tables and chairs. A sign on the brick announced *Barrington's* in hushed script. I crossed the courtyard and entered through a bell-tinkling door.

The sole commonality between Barrington's and Sassy's was the presence of food. OK. And dimness. At the chili joint, the low lighting was due to cutting corners on utility bills. At Barrington's, the candles and sconces were carefully orchestrated for gastronomically appropriate ambience.

My fellow townsmen love to make lists of the Queen City's finest. The best microbreweries. The top gyms. The tastiest noodle shops. My colleague and friend Lizzy Griesser is a Charlotte expat living in Virginia. Lizzie keeps up with local news and takes such reviews seriously. Thus, the night's venue. In the category of fine dining, Barrington's regularly blows the competition out of the skillet.

The restaurant has only fourteen tables. All of which are filled most nights. When Lizzie finalized the date for her bimonthly pilgrimage south, she phoned immediately. That booking had taken place in mid-May.

The hostess led me to a two-top deep in one corner. I'd just hooked my purse strap and the handles of the Harris Teeter bag over the seatback when Lizzie arrived.

How to best describe Dr. Elizabeth "Lizzie" Griesser? She checks all the boxes that should make her pretty by twenty-first-century Western standards. Bright hazel eyes. Full lips. Button nose that turns up just the right amount at the tip. Somehow the combination doesn't quite work. Instead, her features seem painted on a canvas oversized for proper scale.

Lizzie is older now. Her eyelids droop, and her jawline sags a little. But she's not unattractive. Far from it. She's just, well, odd.

My friend dropped into the seat opposite mine. Which made her appear shorter than her actual five feet nine inches. Lizzie's frame is also a bit outside the curve, her legs contributing far more than their share to her height.

"Am I late?"

"Just got here." I smiled, maybe a little too broadly. Nerves. The pinging id. "How's your mother?"

"Makes me wish I'd taken a job in Missoula."

"There's a lab in Missoula?"

"I could start one. Get me a hat and a bandanna, screw cowboys while wearing my boots. But wait. Isn't Montana the state that elected that jerk to Congress? The one who body-slams reporters?"

"In its defense, the place has a lot of big sky."

"And must be far cooler than here. Damn."

"The Lut Desert must be cooler than here."

"Look, Tempe, I'm not a gusher, but I really appreciate your taking an interest in Mom. Your visits are truly above and beyond."

"It's just around the corner from my townhouse." Not exactly. "And she's an interesting lady."

"She's ninety-nine and thinks I'm still in school."

Lizzie completed her doctorate in molecular biology in 1972. When I hit the local forensics scene, she was working in serology at the CMPD crime lab. One winter day, we shared a tuna salad sandwich and a laugh over the peculiarity of names. Lizzie's mother was called Temple. Tempe—Temple. We found the coincidence funny.

Over the years, Lizzie and I consulted on dozens of the same cases. Though she was at least a decade my senior—a guess, she'd never say—the collegial camaraderie morphed into friendship via dinners, movies, and shared tales of parental woes.

Eventually, Lizzie's father died, and her mother began to forget. How to brush her teeth, find the pharmacy, use the remote. Temple Griesser was currently a resident at Sharon Towers, Charlotte's oldest assisted-living and retirement community. Lizzie was now employed by a private DNA lab in Richmond. I dropped in on Temple as often as I could.

The waitress came and introduced herself as Suzy. Suzy asked our preference in water, then filled our glasses from a pitcher awash in lemons. After issuing menus the size of window shades, she queried our wishes from the bar.

"Mom's happy enough," Lizzie continued when Suzy had gone. "Oblivious to everything but her cactus collection."

"I've learned a lot about succulents."

We took a moment to peruse that evening's offerings. To sip our lemony drinks.

"How about you?" Lizzie laid down her menu. "How's your maternal situation?"

"Mama is engaged to be married."

Lizzie's brows shot to her hairline. Which, like them, was silvery gray.

"Don't ask," I said.

Suzy returned with Lizzie's martini, my Perrier. She ordered the duck, I went with the chicken. Unless it's winter—rabbit potpie season—I always do. I'm a sucker for the garlic smashed potatoes.

We were finishing our meal when I finally made my play. Setting down my fork, I broached the subject that was causing the pinging.

"There's something I want to roll past you."

"Shoot."

"First, some background." I told her about my conflict with Margot Heavner.

"I'm sorry about Larabee," she said when I'd finished. "He was solid."

"He was," I agreed.

"Word is Heavner's a she-beast."

She is. I didn't say it.

Lizzie waited as I reached behind me for the brown envelope and the tube and placed both on the table. She'd noticed the green bag the minute she'd arrived, hadn't asked.

"A body was found Friday out in Cleveland County. Hogs had devoured the viscera, hands, and face."

"So no visual, no prints."

"Exactly. Heavner may run DNA, but that'll mean waiting into the next eon for results. And what are the chances of getting a cold hit?"

"The vic carried no form of ID?"

"None."

"Doesn't sound good." Guarded. Lizzie was getting the first hint where I was headed.

"It doesn't."

"A mugging gone wrong followed by a body dump?"

"The guy had two hundred dollars on him."

Lizzie said nothing.

"Some personal items suggest he might not be local." I finger-tapped the envelope. "It's all here."

Lizzie made no move toward Hawkins's illegal plunder. "Let me guess. Heavner's icing you out."

"She is."

"You do plenty of consults. Why lose sleep over this one?"

The same question I'd asked myself. "I'm not sure. I mean, the guy could have kids, a wife, a"—undirected, one hand rose into the air—"a cocker spaniel."

"Come on, Tempe. We both know the game. Every death leaves a hole in someone's life."

The hand dropped back to the table. "Fine. Full disclosure. I think Heavner's going full-on Dr. Morgue again."

"Exploiting the situation to get her face on TV?"

"She called a presser, played up the"—I hooked air quotes—"'mystery' surrounding the case."

Lizzie leaned back and ran a hand down one cheek. Her knuckles were knobbier, her skin more liver-spotted than I recalled.

Several moments passed. Suzy cleared our plates, brought mugs, and filled them. I added cream. Lizzie added nothing. Stirred anyway, still considering the implications of what I was asking.

I braced for the blow-off. Instead, "Where would you float it?"

"I'd have to figure out where to show it around."

Our eyes met. I could almost hear the gears clicking in her head.

"It's a long shot," she said.

"To Uranus and back."

"Won't be worth a frog's dick in court."

"I know."

"Joe Hawkins?" Gesturing again toward the envelope.

I didn't confirm or deny.

"Who took the sample?" Meaning: it was collected covertly, so can the swab be trusted?

"I did." Meaning: yes.

"Going off script could get you permanently canned," Lizzie said.

"I don't see Heavner featuring me on future rosters."

Until then, the ugly prospect had only hovered, black and fluttery, at the periphery of my perception. Voicing the words brought the concept into stark reality. After decades, I'd be permanently out at the MCME.

"We'd be talking hypotheticals," Lizzie said, voice low.

"I'd owe you big-time."

Lizzie shotgunned the last of her coffee. Crossed her arms and sat still as a bonsai. Seconds passed. A full minute. Then, "You're gonna love yacking prickly pear and aloe with Mom."

The comment sounded just the wrong side of a promise.

I kept the papers. Lizzie took the tube.

It was past eleven when I got back to the annex. Pumped on adrenaline and coffee, which I'd been advised by my neurologist to avoid, I knew sleep wasn't on the radar.

After changing into a clean tee and boxers, propped against bed pillows, I began going through Hawkins's ex officio dossier.

I approached the contents chronologically, starting with the incident report from the Cleveland County Sheriff's Department. *Case number*: 18-36-4129. *Date*: June 29, 2018. *Time*: 1121. *Location*: Earl, NC. *Lead Detective*: Ben Spevack, Criminal Investigation Division. *Incident Type*: Death investigation. *Decedent's Name*: Blank. *Eyewitnesses*: Blank.

A hand-scrawled summary stated the following.

At approximately 0645, June 29, 2018, Ardis Goncalves, age 14, and Jaden Fazio, age 13, arrived by bicycle at a point where Lick Branch cuts south off Buffalo Creek, east of NC-198, just north of the South Carolina state line. The boys had gone to the location for the purpose of fishing. Upon arrival, they spotted two feral hogs at the water's edge, threw rocks, approached when the hogs ran off. Observing a dead body, the boys pedaled to the Fazio home. At 0736 Dodie Fazio dialed 911 to alert the authorities.

The decedent was initially observed by first responder Sheriff's Deputy Cory Jenkins to be clothed, of medium build, with dark hair, lying supine, with feet toward, head oriented away from the creek. No appearance of projectile, sharp or blunt instrument, or vehicular trauma. No signs of defense wounding on lower arms. (Hands not observable.) Mutilation of face, midsection, and hands due to hogs. Blood staining on clothing, soil and vegetation under head, and midsection suggestive of massive bleeding. No attempt made to move body to observe lividity.

Decedent was wearing cream-colored shirt, brown pants, black shoes, no socks. No jewelry, wallet, or keys in vicinity. No drugs or weapons. No suicide note. No signs of foul play. Decedent is believed to have reached the site on foot.

I leaned back, skin twitchy. What were my instincts telling me now?

I reread the summary, more slowly. No epiphany. But I was more wide awake than ever.

Shocked that Hawkins had managed to sneak them, I shifted to the photocopy of Heavner's preliminary autopsy notes.

DECEDENT

Case Number: MCME 304-18. *Name*: Unknown. *Next of Kin*: Unknown. *Location Last Seen Alive*: Unknown. *Vehicle Involved*: Unknown. *Reporting Agency*: Cleveland County SD. *Case Type*: Unidentified fresh body.

EXTERNAL EXAM

Body Condition: Intact save for significant postmortem damage to face, hands, and abdomen due to animal scavenging. Feral hogs reported at body location. *Rigor*: Full: *Livor*: Posterior, purple, fixed.

Body Length: 68.5 inches. *Weight*: 158 pounds. *Hair*: Black and abundant, cut short. *Eyes*: Unobservable. *Nasal Cavities and Other Facial Features*: Unobservable. *Ears*: Clotted blood on external ears, otherwise unremarkable. *Teeth*: Anterior damaged and incomplete (postmortem), posterior natural, in good repair. *Glasses/contacts*: Unknown.

Small raised brown mole below right nipple.

No evidence of disease, congenital abnormality, or medical intervention.

INTERNAL EXAM

Heavner noted that the man's heart weighed 270 grams and was grossly unremarkable. His pericardial sac was free of fluid and adhesions. His cardiac vessels were patent and followed the usual distribution with no evidence of atherosclerosis or thrombosis. His lungs were normal, his airways free of obstruction or foreign debris.

The man's brain weighed 1,360 grams and was grossly unremarkable. His adrenal and thyroid glands, immunological system, musculoskeletal system, and skin were grossly unremarkable. Ditto the one remaining kidney.

The liver, spleen, pancreas, gall bladder, appendix, stomach, intestines, and left kidney were not present for observation or weighing.

Radiographs were taken. Aortic and inferior vena cava blood samples were retained for toxicologic analysis. Microscopic analysis to follow.

Heavner's notes concluded with:

The body is that of a well-developed, well-nourished adult Asian (?) male appearing compatible with an estimated age of 25 to 35 years.
CAUSE/MANNER OF DEATH: *Undetermined.*

Bottom line. Heavner hadn't a clue who the guy was or what had killed him. Yet there she was, talking him up to the media. Would an interview with Nick Body be next?

Leaving Barrington's, I'd felt psyched. Certain I could slap a name on the faceless man. Certain that if he'd been murdered, I could help nail the bastards who did it.

While I had been en route to the annex, bubble-wrapped in the dark stillness inside my car, Lizzie's question had arrowed back, tough and unbending.

Why did I care so deeply about this case? Was I really driven by a desire to do right by the victim? To return his body to those who'd loved him? To gain justice for his death?

Or was the truth somewhat less admirable? Was I on a personal crusade to destroy Margot Heavner? To punish her for supporting Nick Body and the malice that he and his kind represented?

Was my goal purely selfish? Was I dragging colleagues into my private drama to irk the patootie out of my new boss and impress the big enchilada in Chapel Hill?

I turned to the photos on my phone.

Had been scrolling a while when I spotted an image that froze my breath.

6

'd examined the photos over and over. Then transferred them to my Mac and sharpened each pic individually with Photoshop. I'd zoomed in and out on varying details. Tried black-and-white, different hues, saturations, and levels of contrast. Compared what I was seeing against Heavner's notes.

By three a.m., my head was throbbing, and my eyes felt like hot balls of gravel behind my lids. Not a migraine but painful enough. I'd steeled myself for one quick run through the faceless man's clothing and possessions, then lights out.

Didn't happen. The fourth of those images had jolted me alert. A close-up of a tattered scrap of paper. I stared, puzzled and confused.

An online search had provided a partial answer. But no clue to the meaning of that answer.

The images had stormed unchecked throughout the three hours of sleep my hyper-jazzed brain had allowed. The blood-soaked clothing. The gutted body. The scrap. I awoke, still headachy and exhausted.

Strong gusts were spitting leaves and other missiles against the black rectangle that was my window. The mockingbird was playing elsewhere. Or hunkered down, awaiting sunrise or calmer headwinds.

I thought about lying in bed all day. About abandoning my illicit crusade for the faceless man. About sucking up to Heavner, maybe dropping by on Monday with a toe-in-the-water attempt at détente. Then I remembered her tone and the look of loathing on her face. And her self-serving interviews with Nick Body.

I got up and put on my running gear. Slipped out into the warm, windy predawn blackness.

Shapes bobbed on the choppy surface of the pond, heads tucked, necks forming inverted U's against the buffeting blasts.

Skin-puckering flashbacks. Glinting teeth. Bloodied feathers. Sightless eyes.

A trench-coated silhouette.

I left Sharon Hall, ran past Queens University and on to Freedom Park. The place was deserted, all night creatures still burrowed deep in their nests, dens, and holes—the opossums, foxes, junkies, and drunks. The only sounds were my footfalls, the pummeling air, and the twitching branches and vegetation.

By the time I headed home, windows were glowing, and headlights were slicing the slowly yielding darkness. To the east, a buttery crack was wedging open the meeting point between earth and sky.

After a long, hot shower, I fed Birdie, then brewed coffee strong enough to revive roadkill. Armed with my notes, I dialed Hawkins.

Got the recorded voice I expected.

Left a message.

Next, I sent a text to another area code.

Talk when you're awake?

Ten minutes later, Ryan phoned.

"*Bonjour, ma chère.*"

"Hey," I said.

"Feeling all right?" Besides Mama, Ryan was the only person who knew of my recent diagnosis. Sometimes I regretted looping him in.

"It's an aneurysm, not bubonic plague."

"I'm happy to pop down early."

"I'm fine. Stop asking."

"Got it. Are you up with the birds because you miss me so badly?"

"Something like that."

"My toes go all sweaty when you talk mushy."

"Happy Canada Day."

"*Merci, madame.*"

"Doing anything special to celebrate?" Polite for: Why have you gone incommunicado?

"Yesterday I was at Fer a Cheval, a hunting and fishing camp near Mont-Laurier."

"In pursuit of?"

"Walleye and trout."

"Catch anything?"

"A cold. I'm home now."

"Bad weather?"

"Chilly and rainy."

"It's July."

"Thus, the absence of snow. No matter, I'm jammed with work."

"Business is still booming?"

"I've got a builder convinced his lawyer is defrauding him out of billions, a single mom wanting the entire life story of a nanny applicant, and parents terrified that their son may be shacking up with his former high school biology teacher."

"How old is the teacher?"

"Thirty-seven."

"And the kid?"

"Nineteen."

"He's legal to shag the vicar's *grandmère* if he wants. Assuming she's mentally competent and willing."

"So I've informed them. I'm also doing some digging for the SQ."

Since police detectives are restricted in ways private investigators are not, they sometimes turn to PIs when a case has dead-ended. Ryan didn't elaborate, so I didn't ask.

He went on, "I saw LaManche while riding up to the squad room Friday morning. He mentioned some joy waiting in your lab."

"We talked on Thursday. The case isn't urgent, probably old cemetery remains."

"How's Daisy?"

"Chemo-peachy."

"Let me guess. She's considering nuptials in Uganda. Maybe hiring mountain gorillas as waiters."

"Ushers." Though currently she's too busy banging Sinitch to dream up harebrained travel possibilities. I kept that to myself.

"Got big plans for July Fourth?" Ryan asked.

"My stockpile of sparklers is quite impressive."

"Did you lay in Valium for the birdcat?"

"It's not Birdie's favorite holiday. Assuming he doesn't need therapy, I may bring him along when I fly north."

"My toes go all—"

"My relationship with Heavner has become a real train wreck."

Ryan knew our history. "And?"

"I'm considering something that may send it right off the rails."

I heard faint moaning up the line between Charlotte and Quebec. The hypothetical preacher's granny?

"Are you still there?" I asked.

"I'm listening."

I laid down the full version, holding nothing back. As I spoke, I could feel my voice tighten, thread by thread. Ryan didn't interrupt.

I started with the mysteriously texted images, concluded with the leaked dossier and Lizzie Griesser.

"You don't know the source of the pics?"

"No clue. I suspect someone was giving me a heads-up."

"Why?"

"If I knew that, I'd probably know who sent them. Anyway, I spent hours with those and with my photos. None is first-rate. I had to snap mine quickly with just my phone. But it's obvious Heavner's wrong on some points."

"Such as?"

"In one shot, I can see the left upper posterior dentition."

"The molars."

"Yes. Every occlusal surface is worn. In another shot, I can see the superior portion of the right pubic symphyseal face. The hogs yanked the two pelvic halves apart, gnawed one, bypassed the other in favor of the viscera."

"Very accommodating."

"The angle's not perfect, but magnified, I can read the age indicators."

"It's Johnny Appleseed."

"Do you want to hear this?"

Chastened silence.

"The man was older than Heavner implied, I'd say in the thirty-five-to-fifty range, probably the upper end of that. And other than black hair, I can't imagine how she concluded he might be Asian. His features were toast, but the hogs had yanked his scalp back far enough to expose most of his frontal bone—his forehead, orbital ridges, and the area above his nose. The upper nasal aperture, interorbital distance, and orbital shape all suggest the man was Caucasoid. White."

Ryan blew out a long breath. Disinterested? Disapproving? I didn't care. I pressed on.

"Also, one shoulder, one hip, and both upper arms have dark blotches I'd bet the farm are hematomas."

"Bruises."

"In varying stages of healing."

"Meaning the guy had either fallen or been struck on more than one occasion. How could Heavner have missed something like that?"

"Who knows? In her defense, the body was pretty mangled, and the lividity was spectacular." I was referring to the purple discoloration caused by blood pooling in a corpse's downside.

Ryan started to speak. I cut him off before his question was out.

"But that's not all. Along with the money and the chewing tobacco—"

"Snus." Pronounced with Ryan's version of a Scandinavian lilt.

"What?"

"You said he had an empty tin of Göteborgs Rapé, right?"

"Yes."

"That's a brand of snus." Lilty.

"I know you'll explain that."

"It's a spicy, smokeless tobacco. Sometimes comes in little paper packets."

"To stick in your gums."

"Yes. You don't chew it or spit it. I think snus is illegal in some parts of Europe. But the Swedes are apeshit over the stuff."

"Right." I didn't ask how Ryan knew that. Or why anyone would want to suck on tobacco. "Along with the snus"—appropriately lilting—"and the cash, there was a scrap of paper in one of the man's pockets. Looked like part of a blank page torn from a book. One Russian word was scribbled on it. I don't know how to say it, so I'll forward the pic."

I put Ryan on hold, clicked over, and fired off the image. Seconds later, I heard the text ping in.

Законченный.

Ryan didn't try voicing it, either.

"Meaning?" he asked.

"'Finished.' According to three separate internet translation sites. One suggested the word could also mean 'ended.'"

"*Note d'adieu*?" He used the French phrase for suicide note. No lilt.

I shrugged. Wasted effort. Ryan couldn't see me. "Or it could refer to the book from which the page was taken. An affair. A trip. A job. A—"

"I get it." Pause. "Is that writing running sideways down the right edge?"

My reaction, too. "I'm not sure. It's too smudgy and faint to make out. Think it could be some sort of code?"

"Or blood. Spaghetti sauce. Hog poop. A—"

"Touché."

"What's on the flip side?"

"I was hurrying and didn't turn the scrap over. I'll ask Hawkins to snap a shot."

"If Heavner learns about the photocopies, Hawkins's ass will be on the line."

"Only Lizzie and you know."

"And what happens when you start poking around?"

"You're a detective, right?"

"For years, it said so right on my badge."

"I'm hoping you can provide pointers on detecting discreetly."

"This case is that important to you?"

"Maybe. I'm not sure."

A long, empty silence hummed down from Canada. Then, "First off, I wouldn't go diming Detective Spevack out in Cleveland County."

"What would you do?"

Having come from the pocket damp, the scrap had been spread on a drying tray while the autopsy proceeded. The reverse side had not been examined. Hawkins was going into the MCME early Monday morning and agreed to inspect and photograph the back.

I started with my single close-up of the front. Felt the same spark of excitement. The staining definitely looked like lettering.

Barely breathing, I returned to Photoshop and enlarged the image again and again. Thought I could make out an E, maybe an 8 or a 3. Couldn't be sure. Magnification caused the shapes to blur and go grainy.

I used tools to sharpen the edges and reduce background noise. Then, by creating a brightness/contrast layer, I worked to whiten the paper while darkening the writing. Maybe writing.

An hour later, I sat back, pulse humming even more.

No hog poop. No doubt.

AΛG HonΓd NE R48.

Code? Shorthand? In English? Another language? Meaning what?

I studied the string, wondering if the sequence was complete. Were the gaps intentional? Or had information been lost to the elements? To the pocket?

I tried googling a few of the letter sequences. Got nothing useful. Honored. Nebraska.

Wind beat at the annex like an angry landlord come for overdue rent.

Why the underlining of R48? I googled the number-letter combo. Got the following.

A road in South Africa.

An expressway in the Czech Republic.

A risk phrase meaning danger of serious damage to health by prolonged exposure.

HMS *Wrangler*, a British World War II W-class destroyer.

A diagnosis code for dyslexia and other symbolic dysfunctions not elsewhere classified.

That cleared it up.

I thought about a suggestion Ryan had offered before disconnecting. A comment he'd made. Until then, I'd been unaware of friction between Slidell and Heavner. Had to admit. The revelation didn't displease me. Not that it takes much to irk Skinny, whose ego is the size of a small African nation.

Ryan's idea made sense. During his tenure with the CMPD, Slidell had notched far more solves than any of his colleagues. And his role as a volunteer with the cold-case unit gave him access to resources that I didn't have.

I picked up my phone and hit speed dial.

Four rings, then, "Yo."

"It's Temperance Brennan."

"Hell-*ooo*, doc. I got caller ID. Besides, who else would nag my ass on a Sunday?" To say diplomacy isn't Skinny's strength is like saying plague was a minor health issue in the Middle Ages.

"I'm sorry to—"

"Anyone tip you what Sunday means? Like, watching NASCAR, maybe tying some fishing lures, or enjoying a little sheet time with my lady?"

"You fish?"

No response. In the background, a woman asked who was calling. Verlene, the live-in girlfriend. Another mind-blowing development.

"I'm phoning concerning a situation with Dr. Heavner." Cool. "Ryan thought you might be interested."

"Yeah?" I heard rustling, then the commentator's voice and the roaring motors grew fainter. "I was wanting another brew, anyways."

I described the faceless man, providing less detail than I had for Ryan. The dossier, the photos, the Russian word, the code.

"You want to fuck Heavner up," Slidell summarized when I'd finished. "Expose her for the rodent turd she is."

Sounded about right. "I want to get this man ID'd."

"How's that my problem?"

"Ryan admires your"—I sought the right word—"skills."

"You asking to hire me?"

"Maybe." I wasn't.

I heard a refrigerator door open, close. The *whoosh* of a pop-top. Swallowing followed by an expressive belch.

"First thing I'd do is figure out how the vic got onto Poston's patch."

"He's the Cleveland County sheriff?"

"Bill Poston. A real wankwad."

I had no idea what that meant.

"Find out if Poston has people canvassing the hood, looking for wits, searching for a vehicle, whatever."

"The incident report is pretty basic."

"That's 'cause it's Old MacDonald and the E-I-O squad out there. But you take my meaning. See if Poston's looking for a driver who picked up a hitchhiker, a snoopy neighbor who spied a stranger on foot, a mysterious car off-loading a rolled rug."

"Apparently, Sheriff Poston wants no part of the case. Shortage of funds and personnel, blah, blah, blah." Hawkins had shared that earlier.

"Your guy didn't fly out to that creek."

"If I start asking questions, word will get back to Heavner."

Following another pause to refresh, "I guess I could make a few calls."

"That would be helpful."

"But my opinion? Right now, you got jackshit. If Poston's not on it and Heavner's playing games, you're dead in the water."

We both waited out a long, staticky intrusion.

"What the hell was that?"

"My phone has issues."

"You ever think of maybe getting a new one?"

"All the time."

When we'd disconnected, I went back to my pic of the scrap. Found no more inspiration than when I'd first pondered the Russian word and the almost illegible code.

Frustrated, I made myself a salad, picked out and ate the feta and turkey, threw the rest in the trash. Every few minutes, I glanced at the clock. Slidell didn't call.

As the afternoon wore on, the wind diminished. I couldn't pinpoint the exact time. It was the absence of noise that eventually caught my attention. The silence seemed more deafening than all the grating and creaking.

At six, antsy and having no better ideas, I pulled out the photocopy of the Cleveland County incident report. After rereading the description of the body location, I got online and opened Google Earth. Alternating between bird's-eye and street view, I zoomed in and out, studying the locale.

The area was mostly woodland and fields. A railroad paralleled NC-198 just to the west. Another two-lane ran to the west of the tracks.

Could the faceless man have arrived by rail? Might he have been a modern-day hobo hopping free rides? Was his body tossed from a boxcar? Did trains still have boxcars, or had cargo containers replaced them entirely?

Smaller roads cut from the larger highways, most dead-ending amid farm buildings or looping into empty cul-de-sacs. Some were paved, others weren't. Some had names, some didn't. One track led to a fair chunk of acreage enclosed in chain linking. Just one small, ramshackle building. Didn't seem much point to the fence.

My eyes followed the snaking brown line labeled Buffalo Creek. The smaller thread marked Lick Branch. The white dashes indicating the border between North and South Carolina.

A few businesses straggled along the sides of the blacktops. Some churches. A pest-control company. A farm-supply store. A garage and auto-salvage operation.

Directed by an impulse my conscious mind didn't grasp, I zoomed in on the latter. Considered the name. Studied the layout.

My breath escaped in a little rush.

I grabbed my jotted notes.

My eyes ran laps between the screen and the page. Check. Check. Check. Check.

Current spitting from nerve ending to nerve ending, I punched a key on my phone.

7

"**Y**ou better not be wild-goosing my ass."

"I can't be certain, but everything fits."

I'd called Slidell to share my idea. He'd responded like a yellow jacket smoked from its nest. Which I'd expected. But he'd listened, then agreed to go with me to Cleveland County. Which I hadn't expected.

Predictably, Slidell insisted on driving. He'd pulled up in a spit-polished, fully tricked-out silver Toyota 4Runner. The interior was junk-free and crammed with cloying sweetness oozing from an air freshener clipped to an AC vent.

Buckling myself in, I'd complimented his new wheels, masking my shock with reasonable success. As long as I'd known him, Slidell had vehemently disparaged Japanese cars. His series of Fords and Chevys, both personal and official, had been rolling landfills, stacked with the unimaginable and smelling of forgotten fast food, sweaty gym gear, stale tobacco smoke, and Skinny himself.

It was now eight twenty on Monday morning. We were on I-85, barreling west from Charlotte. The temperature had already climbed into the eighties. We were drinking tepid coffee purchased by Slidell at a Greek diner that reliably earned C+s on its annual health inspections.

"You said it yourself," I added. "The guy didn't fly out to that creek."

"Run me through this again."

"OK. Picture it in your mind. A—tent symbol—G. Then H-O-N—hangman symbol—D. NE R48. Got it?"

"I ain't brain-dead."

Not totally, I thought.

I said, "I think the tent symbol is an upper-case A missing the crossbar. So AAG. There's an auto-salvage yard about a half mile from where the body was found. Art's Affordable Garage. I think the hangman symbol is a partial upper-case R. So HonRd. The garage is on Honeysuckle Road."

Slidell started to speak, but I cut him off.

"The cars are parked in four clusters, with wider access lanes running between. I think the rest of the code refers to the northeast, NE, cluster, fourth row, eighth slot. And yes. There's a vehicle parked there." At least, there was when the Google image was captured.

We exited the expressway onto S-11-65, a state road squirming through the northern part of Cherokee County, South Carolina. I watched a fireworks factory, a towing service, a whole lot of soybeans and cows flash by my window.

Slidell was quiet. Contemplating the code. Or the faceless man. Or last night's lamb chops. Yellow slashes clicked up his Ray-Bans, dark splotches as we passed underneath trees.

"So this mope hikes out to the woods to off himself but leaves directions how to find his ride?"

"We don't know it was suicide," I said. "That's Hawkins's opinion."

"I dimed the place." Slidell reached for his cup, and the slashes veered wildly. "Got a recording saying they're closed for the Fourth. Apparently, Art's a patriotic guy."

"And affordable. Did you phone Cleveland County?"

"They told me to piss off."

"They did not."

"They said Art's a moron, have at it. They're waiting for word from Heavner."

We rode in silence again, Skinny slurping, me wondering what his issue was with the Cleveland County sheriff. Or if he'd offended one of Poston's deputies. Maybe all of his deputies.

Every now and then, my eyes flicked sideways, checking the validity of my first impression. Slidell wasn't toned, far from it, but he'd definitely lost weight. And the bags under his eyes looked a little less packed. Credit to the lovely Verlene?

Slidell turned north onto NC-198. We'd just reentered the Tar Heel State when my cell chimed an incoming text. I raised my shades to my head to better see the screen.

The message contained a photo and three words: *Back of scrap.*

I tapped the image.

Printed text. Unlike the jotted code, remarkably sharp. I used two fingers to enlarge it.

"It's from Hawkins." Mumbled.

Slidell shoved the Ray-Bans higher onto his nose. Said nothing.

"Looks like I was right about it being torn from a book." Mostly to myself.

"The scrap with the tips on how to find Art?"

"Mm."

Though the letters were clear, the words made no sense. The alphabet was Roman, not Cyrillic, but the language wasn't any I spoke. Not English, Spanish, or French.

I felt the 4Runner purring around me, knew we were rolling through the landscape I'd eyeballed via the Google Earth satellite view the night before. Paid no attention.

Foreign yet somehow familiar.

Suddenly, a synapse. Another. Then a blizzard.

Jesus. Could that be it?

Slidell must have sensed the change of tension in my spine.

"What?"

Words were careening at me. Symbols.

"Yo. Doc? You sick? No hurling on the new upholstery."

"The book isn't in English."

"You saying your vic was Chinese after all?"

"It's written in Latvian."

"That like the place your ex is from? What's his name?"

"Pete. And yes. Latvia is one of the Baltic republics. Until '91, it was part of the Soviet Union."

"Thanks for the geography lesson." Tip of his head. "What's it say?"

"I recognize the language, but I can't give you a word-for-word. Except for a few English borrow phrases."

"Now we're getting somewhere."

"There's mention of NATO, of a Gulfstream-*Privatjet*, of an *amerikāņu firma*, of Estonia, and of 27–29 *septembri*. Those translations are obvious."

No response.

I scrolled down. Teased out a word here and there.

My fingers halted as two recognizable bits hit hard. I swallowed.

"There's reference to *biologiske un ķīmsko ieroču* and to *dekontaminācijàs specialisti.*"

"Right. I get it. You're bilingual."

"Biological and chemical weapons and decontamination specialists."

The Ray-Bans slowly swung my way, Slidell's brows floating well above the rims.

"What the hell's that mean?"

"Biologic—"

"I heard what you said. What's it mean?"

"I don't know."

Our gaze held for as long as Slidell felt comfortable with his eyes off the road. When he refocused, I went back to prying what I could from the text.

Nogrimšanas diena uz kuģa . . .

"There's a phrase that translates something like 'on the day of the sinking, aboard ship.'"

"Aboard what ship?"

"Hold on." Checking my memory by going online. "The passenger ferry *Estonia* sank while crossing the Baltic Sea to Stockholm on September 28, 1994." I paraphrased. "Eight hundred and fifty-two people died."

Slidell flashed me a glance. Then the dark lenses swiveled back, and his face shut down.

I tried wrestling more from the text, gave up, vowing to seek help from Pete. Born in Riga, he was fluent in Latvian.

"That it?"

I looked up. Slidell was pointing at an unpaved road T-boning in from the right.

"Slow down," I said.

He did.

The sign was twisted off-angle from the pole but readable. *Honeysuckle Road.*

"The garage is a couple hundred yards down, after a curve to the left." I gestured a wide arc.

Slidell made the turn.

The road cut like a dull yellow wound through the scrub vegetation bullying up to its edges. Starlings watched mutely from utility lines overhead. Our tires hummed on the hard-packed clay.

Running along each shoulder, had there been shoulders, were the remnants of ancient wood fences. Vines wormed and coiled around the crossbars and posts, filling every millimeter of open space, turning the tumbledown structures into thick, green walls. After the openness of the highway, the narrow corridor felt close and confining.

Slidell cursed as the 4Runner bounced and lurched

over potholes deep enough to bottom out in Antarctica. An eon, then the curve, and the tight passage opened up.

The clearing was large, at least an acre across, ringed by forest rising dark and leafy against the impossibly blue summer sky. The ground was bare and the same dried-mustard color as the road.

The 4Runner ground to a stop. Slidell scanned with cop eyes. We both did.

No voice shouted a warning. No mongrel charged out to challenge our presence.

The garage lay off to the left, a big metal box with a flat roof and two sliding bay doors on the road-facing side. Beside the bays, a customer entrance with a window on the upper half, covered on the inside by closed venetian blinds.

Cars and trucks were parked between us and the garage, maybe fifty in all, arranged in rectangles. The northeastern cluster was the farthest away.

Off to the right, past the southeastern rectangle, squatted a trailer that had probably rolled off the assembly line sometime in the sixties. Toothpaste-aqua below, pus-gray above, the exterior was as dinged and rusty as a retired battle tank. The windows, one on the end and one on the side, had cracked panes barely hanging on to their frames. The wheels were gone, and weed-wrapped cinder blocks supported the corners.

"Looks like Affordable Art ain't big on security." Slidell's eyes were still roving.

It was true. There was no chain linking, no gate, no barrier of any kind. Not a single security camera in sight.

We both got out, leaving the doors wide. The air was hot and still and smelled faintly of skunk.

"Yo!" Slidell yelled.

Several starlings winged off.

Slidell cupped his hands to his mouth and tried again, louder.

More startled birds.

I strode to the customer entrance and tried the knob. Locked. I knocked. No answer.

I looked at Slidell. He shrugged. We met at the northeast rectangle. It was organized like a pair of parallel centipedes, the vehicles parked headlight to headlight, with a driveway between the two double rows.

Slot 8 was the last in the uppermost string. In it was a black Hyundai Sonata. Slidell said it was a 2014 model. The plate said it called West Virginia home.

Slidell tried the doors, found all four locked. Reaching below the left front wheel guard, he ran his hand over the top of the tire. Withdrew a set of not-so-cleverly hidden keys. Used the fob to disengage the locks.

I took surgical gloves from my shoulder bag and handed a pair to Slidell. He rolled his eyes, I think, but pulled them on before sliding behind the wheel. I gloved and dropped into the passenger seat. The car's interior smelled of overheated plastic and vinyl. The seat felt like a griddle burning my jeans.

Slidell found nothing on or under the dash, nothing in the center console. The glove box was empty. The back seat was empty.

"What kinda clown drives around with no ID?" Slidell, gruff. "No registration, no proof of insurance."

"Think it's a rental?"

"No paperwork on that, either."

Slidell used one key to start the engine, then checked the car's GPS history. Found no record of previous trips.

We got out and circled to the rear. Slidell used the second of the two keys to open the trunk.

Standard jack and spare. Standard folding windshield sunshade. Not-so-standard neon-green duffel.

"Come to Papa, sweetheart."

Slidell snagged the handles and dragged the duffel closer to the back bumper. The *whuurp* of the zipper triggered another avian flurry.

Gesturing a take-it-away palm, Slidell stepped sideways to make space for me. Or to give himself more room to sweat.

A starling chose that moment to land on the car to our right. Tilting, head down and tail up, it observed us with two shiny black eyes.

Momentary flash of a beheaded goose.

Forcing the image back to its mental repository, I leaned in and began pulling items from the duffel.

Not sure what I expected. What I found were a screwdriver with an insulated handle, a butter knife with the blade filed into a shiv, a portable cell phone charger, a flashlight, binoculars, toilet paper, and an empty plastic bottle with a screw cap. I handed each to Slidell. He arranged the collection on the trunk floor. Considered.

Then, "Looks like a surveillance kit?"

"For?"

"Stakeouts, break-ins, whatever."

The tools had been lying on a stack of neatly folded clothing. Slidell watched as I inspected the garments. Tan pants with soil in the cuffs; one silk tie, paisley print; two long-sleeved cotton shirts, one denim, one white; two pairs of boxers, both black silk. All labels had been removed, with a single exception. The tie had the letters I-T-O stitched into the lining. The labels had also been cut from the duffel.

Beneath the clothing was a folded copy of *Moskovskij Komsomolets*. I can't read Cyrillic but recognized the logo and knew the newspaper was a Moscow daily with a large circulation. I checked the date. The edition was ten days old.

Beneath the paper was a six-by-nine spiral, the kind I often use for recording case notes.

Quick glance at Slidell. His brows were raised as high as mine.

I lifted the notebook and opened to the first page. Handwritten on top were two Latvian words: *Nogrimšanas traģēdija*. Below the words, a name: Felix Vodyanov.

"It translates 'sinking tragedy.'" I pointed to the heading.

"The rest in Latspeak?"

I skimmed. Nodded.

"That it?"

I ran my hand around the bottom of the duffel, felt a small rectangular object, and pulled it out. A thumb drive. Across one side was a line of Cyrillic text: Медицинские.

"What's the writing?"

"I don't read Russian," I said.

Using my iPhone, I shot pics of the drive and the articles taken from the duffel.

"Could be your vic is this Felix Vodyanov?"

"Many Latvians have Russian names."

"Maybe the worm's KGB."

Comedic delivery is not Slidell's forte. I looked up to see if he was kidding. Wasn't sure.

"The KGB ended with the dissolution of the Soviet Union." I didn't point out that had happened in '91, thus the Latvian independence. "An operative planted in the States would probably be with SVR, Russia's external intelligence service."

"You seriously thinking the guy's some sort of spy?"

"I'm not thinking anything. I'll go online for a translation." Picking up the thumb drive. "Can you run the plate?"

We were punching keys when the double click of a pump-action shotgun froze us both.

8

"One move buys you a butt load of twelve-gauge."

"I'm a cop—" Slidell started.

"Turn around. Real slow."

We did.

The man was bushy-haired and tall, maybe six-five. The stub of a cigar rested in one corner of his mouth. A Remington 870 rested in his hands. Which had fingers long enough to wrap an asteroid.

The man looked us over impassively. His stubble was dark and abundant, his eyes the faded blue of over-washed denim. I put his age at somewhere between forty and fifty.

"I got no vehicle come from the likes of you." Cigar bobbing a little.

"Let me guess." Controlled. Even Slidell wouldn't pick a fight with this guy. "You're Art."

"And you'd be?"

"Police."

"Pass me a flag. We'll have us a parade."

I sensed Slidell stiffen.

"Detective Slidell and I would like to ask you some questions." To ease the tension, I voiced the cliché.

"Don't talk to cops." All glare and defiance. And shotgun.

"It will take just a moment."

The pale blue gaze went past me. Slight frown as Art took in the Hyundai with its open trunk. "That your car?"

"No," I said.

"Ain't my inventory."

"That's why we're here." I slanted a quick side-eye to Slidell. His attention never wavered from the man with the gun.

"How'd it get onto my lot?" Art sounded a little less confident.

"Last Friday, a body was found beside Buffalo Creek, just past your property line," I said.

"Got no knowledge of that."

"We don't know the man's name. But this may be his Sonata."

Art stared, cigar firm in his teeth. Something new in his eyes. "How'd this fella get his self killed?"

"Cause of death is unclear. The medical examiner—"

The cigar dipped a hair as Art swallowed.

"Look. Either you green-light me to toss this car now, or I come back with a warrant this afternoon. Meanwhile, I bide my time checking your business licenses, your taxes, your gun permits. You living in that dung heap?" Slidell cocked his chin toward the trailer. "I get real bored, I might make a few calls, get inspectors out to verify your little slice of heaven meets fire and health codes. You really want to go that route?"

Typical Slidell bluff. But Art bought it. Nodding once, he lowered the barrel of the Remington. Didn't even ask for a badge.

Slidell's phone was still in his hand. He waved it at the assemblage spread across the trunk. "This shit goes with us."

As I began repacking the duffel, Slidell stripped off his gloves, unpocketed a notebook and pencil stub, spit-thumbed to a clean page, and jotted the Hyundai's tag and license info. Walking toward the 4Runner, he punched keys with one clammy finger. A momentary pause, a click of a conversation, then he disconnected. Butt-leaning the quarter panel, he waited.

Art watched me, now so close I could smell his sweat and the calamine he must have smeared on a rash. I'd just zipped the duffel when Slidell's cell exploded into lyrics about a goodhearted woman. He answered, then shoulder-tucked the phone to write. As I joined him, he was assuring someone named Carla of a beer in her future.

"The car's registered to a John Ito." Pocketing the mobile.

"Ito." Not the name I expected.

"India. Tango. Oscar. The same letters stitched into the tie lining."

"Not Felix Vodyanov."

Slow wag of Slidell's head.

"Ito sounds Japanese." Heavner was right, and I was wrong?

Shoulder shrug.

"OK." At the end of a long breath. "Anything else?"

"Morgantown address. I'll check it out when we get back. Seems Ito's licensed and insured in West Virginia."

"Maybe there's no connection to the faceless man."

"Right. Your stiff's carrying Latvian intel on doomed ships and biochemical weapons. The same jabberwocky's in the trunk of that car." Thumb jabbing the Hyundai. "No connection there."

Unable to fault Slidell's logic, I said nothing.

"Assuming Affordable Art's being straight, and he and I will definitely be discussing his veracity, either Ito parked here on the sly and walked out, or his killer slipped in and ditched the car."

"Both scenarios suggest knowledge of the area."

"Not bad, doc. I'll brief Poston. Ask if he knows a John Ito. Tell him the vehicle's all his."

I peeled off my gloves, feeling unexpected empathy for the Cleveland County sheriff.

Slidell insisted we "stop for slop" en route home. The detour to Hog Heaven added an hour and a half to the trip. The barbecue was good, the hush puppies outstanding. It was almost two by the time he dropped me at the annex.

I called Pete straight off. Couldn't do it from the car since my damn phone had died. His voice mail informed callers that he was away until the middle of the month. The sound effects were either a gun salute or cherry bombs. Patriotic as Art.

I left a request for help with a Latvian translation. Kept it vague, hoping to tickle his curiosity.

Ninety minutes later, my partially charged mobile rang. Thinking my ploy had worked, I answered blindly.

"Who the hell do you think you are?"

The shot of anger caught me by surprise. I lowered my hand to disconnect.

Saw the name of the caller.

"Dr. Heavner." Heart rate up a notch.

"What the shuffling fuck?" Lab noises in the background. The metallic clanking of a bay door. The grinding of a transport van in reverse. The fast, resolute click of heels on tile.

"Can I help you with something?"

"Did we not discuss this? Did I change my mind and request a consult? Did I imply, in any way, at any time, that I desired your assistance?"

"Do you?" Carefully neutral.

"You have no idea how vehemently I do not."

"I'm sorry to hear that."

"Tell me it's bullshit." So furious she was practically spitting her words. "Tell me you did not go to Cleveland County asking about one of my cases."

"I was asking about a car."

"My John Doe is none of your business."

"So the body is still not ID'd?"

"Are you hearing my voice?"

"Did you try CODIS? NDIS?" I was asking about the Combined DNA Index System, the FBI's database, and the National DNA Index System, the part of CODIS containing profiles contributed by federal, state, and local forensic labs. It took a while, but sometimes you got a cold hit.

A long second of silence as Heavner weighed options.

"I have no obligation to tell you anything, Dr. Brennan." Oh, so measured now. "But as a professional courtesy, and to persuade you to desist, I will share that we believe the man's name is John Ito. But due to your meddling, you already know that."

"You still think he's Asian."

"I do."

"Based on?"

"It would be unethical for me to reveal personal details about a deceased."

It took everything I had not to point out that she'd done exactly that. On air. And not to argue that her assessment of the man's ancestry was incorrect. But Heavner couldn't know that I'd shot pics of her case. Or that Hawkins had leaked me the file.

"Of course."

"We should have confirmation shortly." Curt. "I trust you'll keep this information to yourself."

"As would any professional." Reckless. But my patience was rubbing thin.

Three beeps, then empty silence. Heavner knew I'd been alluding to both the present and the past.

I sat a moment, wondering. Was Heavner right, and I was utterly wrong? She'd done the autopsy, explored every inch of the man's anatomy. I'd seen only the jpgs texted to me and my own hastily shot cell-phone pics.

I went to the guest room/study and pulled every image up on my laptop. Printed some.

For the next hour, I reexamined the mutilated cranio-facial features. Took what measurements I could and calculated indices—ratios between one dimension and another.

Birdie joined me at some point. Hopped onto the desk and performed complicated hygiene involving inter-toe spaces.

Finally, I sat back, more firmly convinced than ever. MCME 304-18 had no ancestors in Yokohama, Shanghai, or Pyongyang.

I checked the time. 4:40. Still no call from Slidell. Or Pete.

Mainly to keep busy, I got online and researched John Ito. Google. Facebook. LinkedIn.

The name was not uncommon. A financial adviser in Hawaii. A music professor at Carnegie Mellon University. A student at UNLV. An independent farming professional in Ontario. Whatever that meant.

What interested me most were the photos. Every John Ito was Asian.

I inputted the word combination *John Ito West Virginia*. Got nothing.

Then I tried the name Felix Vodyanov.

Found not a single link. Anywhere.

Curious, I went to Truthfinder.com, a site claiming to have the goods on every living being in the western hemisphere. After entering Felix Vodyanov as the name and West Virginia as the geographic location, I checked the box indicating male gender and watched, simultaneously fascinated and horrified, as the screen whiz-zipped through data sets. Mug shots, online profiles, address information, sexual offenses, traffic offenses, arrest records, phone numbers, court records, felonies, relatives, misdemeanors, birth records. You get it.

Nothing.

Leaving the geographic location blank, I tried again.

Zip.

I was thinking about that when my mobile rang. This time, I checked caller ID. Slidell.

"Yo."

"Detective."

"Curiouser and curiouser." The Lewis Carroll reference surprised me. Probably coincidence, though four-syllable words were impressive for Slidell.

"I'm listening," I said.

"Did some follow-up on this guy, John Ito."

Sounds of crinkling, then chewing. Farther distant, what I took to be squad-room noises. Phones. Keyboards. Voices. I made myself wait.

"The address listed on the car registration is phony."

"Seriously? You ran it that fast?"

"Nah. I just threw up a pin, watched where it came down on a map."

Throw one up your ass, I thought.

"It's an abandoned airfield on the outskirts of Morgantown," Slidell said.

"To register a vehicle, you have to have a valid driver's license or state ID of some sort, right?" I asked.

Skinny refilled his mouth and chewed. Doritos, I guessed, based on the wet crunch. Mid-mastication, "And proof of insurance. The DMV checks all that."

"Then isn't it hard to register a car with a fake ID?"

"Hard but not impossible."

"You're talking about ghosting?" I was referring to a type of identity theft in which the profile of a dead person is stolen. Usually the "ghoster" is the same age as the "ghost," had that person lived, so that birthdates on the fake documents are believable.

"You know the right sources, you can get the job done," Slidell said.

"You think John Ito is an alias?"

"I got a guy working on it."

"When will you know?"

"I could ring him every few minutes the next couple of days, see if that gooses his nuts."

Easy, Brennan.

"I did some digging on Ito and Vodyanov." I described my internet searches.

A few seconds of squad-room noise, then, "You busy right now?"

"Nothing that can't wait."

"Get your ass down here."

The Charlotte-Mecklenburg Police Department operates out of the Law Enforcement Center, a concrete-and-glass complex stretching along East Trade Street in the heart of uptown. Thanks to the brief presence of the 2012 Democratic National Convention and a security budget of $50 million, the ground floor, once an open lobby, now looks like the bridge of a starship charting the outer reaches. Circular wooden barrier. Bulletproof glass. Monitors displaying the building's every millimeter, inside and out.

After signing the register, I swiped my security card

and rode to the second floor. Directly across from the elevator, signs with arrows indicated *Crimes Against Property* to the left, *Crimes Against Persons* to the right. Above the arrows, the hornet's-nest symbol of the CMPD.

I passed through a doorway and turned right into a corridor remarkably bereft of detectives, two in shirt-sleeves and ties, one in khaki pants and a navy golf shirt featuring the intrepid wasp logo. Khakis carried coffee. All three carried a whole lot of firepower.

I proceeded past interview rooms running along the right side of the hall. A second sign ID'd a section on the left, *2220: Violent Crimes Division*. Homicide and assault with a deadly. I entered.

For years, Slidell held title to coveted real estate at the back of the squad. Now he was stuck in a corner by the copy machine. His volunteer status with the cold-case unit scored him the space.

I wormed through the maze of cubicles, accompanied by the same symphony I'd heard via phone thirty minutes earlier. Slidell was seated at his desk, a phone shoulder-clamped to one ear. As I approached, he cradled the receiver.

"Yo, doc." He stood. "Got something's gonna curl your shorts."

Slidell headed for the elevator. Like a well-trained puppy, I followed. We ascended without speaking, Slidell's eyes glued to the digits lighting up to mark our ascent.

"We're going to the crime lab?" I recognized the floor he'd chosen. Had been there many times.

"QD." Slidell used the acronym for Questioned

Documents, one of five specialty sections in the CMPD crime lab. But why?

A woman was waiting when the doors hummed open. Tiny, with tightly cropped black hair and cocoa skin. I didn't know her, figured she must be new.

"Mittie Peppers." Smiling with teeth too small for her mouth. Made me think of Chiclets lined up on her gums.

"Temperance Brennan." Smiling back. We shook hands. Peppers's grip could have crushed dandelion fluff.

"She's been looking at the notebook," Slidell said. To Peppers. "Brief her."

"I prefer to show her."

"We ain't got all day."

"It won't take all day." Not a single Chiclet in sight. I liked this woman.

Peppers chatted as we walked down a corridor that was totally empty. "I'm a bit nerd forward. My heart's with digital—the internet and cybercrime—but I also work traditional QD evidence. Are you familiar with document examination?"

"The analysis of handwriting, typewriting, inks, counterfeiting."

"Here we mostly look at forged or altered checks. Occasionally threatening letters, bank robbery notes, yada yada. But indented writing isn't uncommon."

"Wait." My eyes whipped to Slidell. "You found indented writing?"

"Near the mumbo jumbo about the sinking ship."

"Ferry," I corrected. Needless, but I was jazzed. "So a sheet was missing from above that first page?"

"Thought I spotted grooves, angled my flash across 'em. Called up here."

Peppers used her ID to swipe us through a set of security doors, again to enter the Questioned Documents section. Inside, she went directly to a blue-and-gray box with a flat white top and the letters ESDA on the front. Looked like a small photocopier except for a large roll of clear Mylar sheeting to one side.

"Can we stick to the basics?" Slidell, not at all subtly checking his watch.

Peppers ignored him. "I used a technique called electrostatic detection. Sounds high-tech, but it's not rocket science."

My mind translated the letters on the machine. Electro Static Detection Apparatus.

"The specimen needed some humidification. Not much. It was an outer page, and the trunk environment wasn't too dry." Peppers hit a button, and the apparatus began whirring lustily. "Vacuum pump." Loud enough to be heard over the noise.

I nodded.

Peppers placed a paper on the platen, stretched Mylar across it, and snipped the edge free from the roll. After hitting a second button labeled *corona*, she ran a long, rectangular wand back and forth above the Mylar.

"The corona sends high-voltage static charges onto the paper." Not shouting but close. "The positive charges from the wand are preferentially attracted to the indentations. I'm simplifying."

I nodded again.

After turning off the corona, Peppers tilted the platen and shook black powder from a canister onto the

Mylar. "The toner is similar to that used in dry-process photocopy machines. It's negatively charged."

I nodded again, feeling like a bobblehead. But I didn't want to yell.

"The areas of the document containing the higher static electric charge will retain more of the toner, resulting in dark deposits in the indentations."

A few seconds of shaking to distribute and clear off the excess toner, then she killed the vacuum pump. The room went mercifully quiet. "Take a look."

I stepped closer.

On the paper, in squiggly black script, were the words *Crime Scene Do Not Enter*. I looked a question at Peppers.

"I couldn't use the real evidence to demo the process for you, so I made this mock-up. When finished with my actual analysis, I photographed and preserved the detective's specimen."

Chiclet smile. Not returned by Slidell.

"Have a look."

I followed Peppers to a side counter. The notebook page was there, solo now, covered with a sheet of adhesive-backed clear plastic. Through the plastic, I could read the Latvian words *Nogrimšanas traģēdija*. The name *Felix Vodyanov*.

Beside the words and name, three lines of writing not visible before. Fierce capitals and numerals.

I read them.

And felt a chill wash over my body.

9

The first line was a sequence of ten digits beginning with 704. The Charlotte area code.

The second line was also a telephone number.

The room had dissolved into a soundless whiteout. All I saw were those tiny black numerals, the grayness of the page roaring around them.

My mind was a maelstrom. Confusion. Disbelief. Fear.

For a moment, I felt I was floating. Then the stab of dread. Another migraine? No, this was different.

I blinked. Turned. Slidell and Peppers were watching me, identical frowns on their faces.

"That's my mobile number." Barely audible.

"It is," Slidell said flatly.

"Sonofabitch." Not my best. But I felt violated. As though a stranger had hacked my email or pawed through my underwear drawer.

"You put yourself out there for any of this social-media hooey? He Harmony? Snatch Match? Some egghead chat-room jabbering bones?"

I have years of practice in ignoring Slidell. In letting his callous commentary roll over me. Usually, the experience works to my advantage. Not at that moment.

"Holy Jesus Christ Almighty!" I exploded.

Slidell raised placating palms. "Look. This wanker had your number. John Ito or whoever the fuck left that car. There's lots of ways that could play."

"Don't ever ask me a question like that again." Anger had totally routed the fear.

"Does the third line mean anything?" Peppers asked.

I looked at the letter-number combo. JCOLE1013. Shook my head no.

A small silence. Then Peppers handed Slidell two prints. "I'll keep the original page here, preserve it properly."

Slidell grunted and headed for the door.

"Is he always this pleasant?" Tipping her head toward Skinny's retreating back.

"He's a boor but a good detective. Thanks for doing this."

Downstairs in the squad room, the boor checked one of Peppers's pics, then punched keys on his landline. The tinny sound of a connection came through the speaker. One ring, then a message, the words low and warbly, as though spoken underwater.

"Leave it. Short like this."

A long beep followed by expectant silence.

Slidell disconnected with an irritated jab.

"Can you get someone to trace the number?" I asked.

A one-shoulder shrug.

"Why not?"

"The phone's probably a burner, scored at a Walmart, chucked into a dumpster the next day."

"Voice mail is still working."

"Waste of time."

I knew the basis of Slidell's resistance. He was an outsider now. Enjoyed squad-room space only because of his long tenure and his volunteer work with the cold-case unit down the hall. He could call in only so many favors.

I was about to say something snarky. Which would have sent us into one of our death-battle spirals. Instead, I took a deep, calming breath and dropped into the chair opposite Slidell's.

"The owner of the Hyundai had two numbers—"

"The owner of the notebook."

"The one you just dialed," I said, gesturing at Slidell's phone. "And mine. The Hyundai's owner may or may not be John Ito. Or Felix Vodyanov."

"Or Buck Baker's great-aunt Maude."

I hadn't a clue who that was. "The Hyundai's owner may or may not have turned up dead and become hog feed in Cleveland County."

Slidell arranged himself more comfortably. Loosened his already loose tie, hooked a heel onto an open desk drawer, tipped his chair onto its rear legs, and began rocking slowly back and forth. But he was listening.

"You get any calls from unknown numbers lately?" he asked.

"I get dozens of calls from unknown numbers. Telemarketers trying to sell me insurance or roofing repair. I don't reply to the voice mail."

But I followed Slidell's thinking.

Pulling my iPhone from my purse, I scrolled backward in time, checking the red listings indicating missed calls. Yesterday. Saturday. Wednesday.

Friday. June 22. Area code 681.

I switched to Google. Verified the call's origin.

"A week ago Friday, someone rang me from a West Virginia exchange. I opened my voice mail to check that date. "The caller left no message."

"The Hyundai was registered in West Virginia," Slidell said.

Our eyes met, mine seeking permission. Slidell nodded. I tapped the number. Put my phone on speaker and laid it on the desk.

Two rings, then a voice, robotic, perhaps mechanically distorted to disguise the speaker.

"Record your name, the date and time, and a brief message."

I looked a question at Slidell. He gave a thumbs-up.

"I'm sorry I missed your call. Please try me again. You have my number." Disconnect. To Slidell. "Reach out to the local guy?"

"Sure." Flipping me the second of Peppers's prints.

I read the recovered number, dialed. Got the same recording as Slidell. Did as instructed.

"I need to speak with you concerning a mutual friend. You know where to reach me." Disconnect.

My gaze slid back to Slidell. He was studying Peppers's photo, fingers drumming riffs on the desktop.

"Any hallelujahs on this third line?" he asked.

JCOLE1013.

I manipulated in my head, moving letters and numbers like pieces on a board. Separated the alphabetic from the numeric. Set the first pair of digits apart from the second. Split off one letter at a time. One numeral. Recombined them in various ways.

At one point, I heard Slidell lean back and resume his precarious oscillation.

JCOLE? A name? Wasn't there a hip-hop artist named J. Cole?

10-13. A date? October 2013?

Across from me, Slidell was playing the same game.

The squad room quieted as detectives drifted off to dinner, to interrogations, to promising or tenuous leads. Overhead, the fluorescent bars buzzed softly. Across from me, Slidell's chair groaned in undulating protest.

Abruptly, the grating stopped, and the chair's front legs smacked the tile. "Who was that kid went missing?"

I looked up. Slidell's eyes were on the print, brows angled into a bushy V.

"What kid?" I asked.

"Maybe four, five years ago." Maybe 2013.

Like many in my line of work, I carry a roster of heartache in my brain. A wrenchingly painful catalog of dead and lost children. There was no need to thumb through the names. Slidell's reference roared home instantly.

"Jahaan Cole."

One or two brain cells sizzled cruel. A face popped. The same face displayed on endless posters and news broadcasts. A child with caramel skin, laughing eyes, boisterous dreadlocks bound with bright pink beads.

"Wasn't Cole nine when she went missing?" Slidell asked.

We both did the math. Born 2004. Vanished October 10, 2013.

JCOLE1013.

My mouth suddenly tasted like ash.

Jahaan Cole was last seen leaving home to return a book to a neighborhood library stand at the end of her block, Laura Ingalls Wilder's *Little House on the Prairie*. When Jahaan failed to return home, Brightie Cole phoned 911 to report her daughter missing. The book was found the following day on a rural highway eight miles from the Cole home. Jahaan's hair bow turned up five weeks later.

The media staged their usual circus. With nothing new to report, they eventually folded their tents and scurried off.

Nine months after Jahaan's disappearance, fragmentary remains came to the MCME. The news machine kicked back into gear. Until I determined that the bones were those of *Vulpes vulpes*. A red fox.

Six months after the fox fiasco, I traveled with a recovery team to a farmer's field in Gaston County. When I close my eyes, I can still feel the weight of the afternoon heat on my skin. Smell the mowed hay and see the moths swirling in the dusty sunlight.

Again, breathless anticipation. The bones were human but those of an elderly male. There was a brief flurry of coverage, then the cameras and mics moved on to other tales of grief. While disappointed at the lack of closure, I was gratified that there was still hope for life.

The case was now colder than a glacial lake. Features aired on the anniversary of Jahaan's disappearance.

The media contacted me requesting interviews. The old photo was trotted out. A few calls would come in, lead nowhere. Jahaan Cole remained an MP. Missing person.

"Why the fuck would John Ito jot your number and notes about a missing kid?" Slidell said quietly.

I ran my tongue over my teeth. Swallowed. Had the faceless man known something about the child that he'd wanted to tell me?

I had no answer.

Something startled me awake.

I'd been dreaming, another complex scenario involving tangled shadows and murky figures. It took me a moment to disengage and figure out where I was.

Birdie? Running an arm over the covers without finding a cat.

Heart banging, I listened for noises on the first floor. Down the hall. Heard nothing but the familiar settling of the annex.

Digits glowed teal on the bedside table. 2:47. Sleep had been elusive. And brief. I doubted it would come again.

Still, I tried.

Turning my back to the clock, I closed my eyes.

And saw the photos I'd snapped in the autopsy room. Those texted to me from an unknown source.

John Ito? Felix Vodyanov? Someone else?

The pummeling questions started anew.

How had the faceless man died? Had he hidden the Hyundai at Art's salvage yard, hiked into the woods, and taken his own life? Had he met someone on the banks of Buffalo Creek? Had that person killed him?

If the faceless man had been murdered, who did it? How? Why? Had the killer driven the Hyundai? If so, why leave it at Art's? Did the faceless man and his killer arrive together? If so, how had his killer departed? Did his death have anything to do with the *Estonia* disaster?

Round and round, in endless loops. Question after question. No answers.

I pictured the duffel locked in the Hyundai's trunk. The spiral with its notes about biochemical weapons and a ferry disaster. The peculiar assemblage of tools. The delabeled clothing. The thumb drive with its Cyrillic identifier.

Would the thumb drive provide the breakthrough I was hoping for? Names? Addresses? Passwords for email accounts? Selfies snapped with a cell phone?

Files on top-secret SVR espionage operations? On Russian moles in the CIA?

Sweet Jesus in a romper. I was spending way too much time with Skinny.

Slidell had taken the lot. I'd agreed with his reasoning. The Cleveland County sheriff, if interested, would send the duffel and its contents to the CMPD forensic lab for analysis. A quick dust for prints, then he'd probably transfer the car to Charlotte as well. Slidell was simply speeding the investigatory process.

Slidell's apparent about-face had surprised me. Why the sudden willingness to help with the faceless man? Animosity toward Sheriff Poston? Or did the change in attitude have to do with me?

The notebook had yielded an impression containing

two numbers: one with a West Virginia area code and one for my mobile. The West Virginia number had dialed my phone within the past ten days. Was that it? Was Slidell motivated by some paternalistic notion that I needed protecting? The thought didn't please me.

Had someone told Slidell about the aneurysm? The migraines? If so, who? That thought didn't please me, either.

I got up and walked through the turquoise-lit darkness to the bathroom. A cold drink of water, then I stood, arms crossed, not moving, not listening, as facts and questions collided in my head.

The West Virginia number had called my iPhone on June 22. The date of my migraine nightmare and midnight walk. The night I'd been anxious about the trench-coated man.

But had Trench Coat actually been there? Or was he merely a headache aftereffect?

No. The man was real.

Had my instincts been correct? Had Trench Coat been watching me? Following me? Was he John Ito? Felix Vodyanov? Were the owner of the Hyundai and Trench Coat the same man?

Was the man prowling the grounds of Sharon Hall the faceless man found dead at Buffalo Creek? If so, he'd called me a week before his death. Why? Had he followed me home? Why? Clearly, the man wanted to make contact. To talk about what? The *Estonia*? Biochemical weapons? That made no sense. I knew nothing about either.

The page with the phone number impressions also contained a reference to a missing child. To one of my cases. What did the man know about Jahaan Cole's disappearance?

Was that the reason for Slidell's unexpected interest? Though inactive, Jahaan Cole's file remained open. One of Slidell's rare failures. As a cold case, she was firmly on his turf.

That didn't tally. We'd only learned of the indented code this evening, long after leaving Affordable Art's. Something else had motivated Skinny.

Questions. No answers.

Sinking to the floor, I sat with knees up, shoulder blades to the vanity.

Jahaan Cole had gone missing long before the arrival of Margot Heavner. Back in the Larabee years.

I pictured my former boss, scrawny thin and overtanned from thousands of hours of long-distance running. Gray and still in the trauma surgical intensive-care unit.

Larabee and I had shared little of our personal lives. We didn't hit the bars at day's end or play on the same softball team. But we'd worked well together. His death had left me feeling like I was dangling over the edge of a gaping hole.

Tears burned the backs of my lids. I didn't fight them. Hoped a good cry would vent the emotions thrashing inside me.

No go. I just sat there, blinking into space, mind ricocheting from question to question.

Did I regret my criticism of Heavner? My condemnation of her interviews with Nick Body? I'd taken so much blowback for that.

At least one easy answer. No, damn it to hell, no!

Heavner had leaked privileged information on a radio show hosted by a narcissistic crackpot. Information that had hurt the victim's family and may have prevented the killer's conviction.

Snatches of the exchange slithered free from the dark corner in which I'd stored them. Heavner discussing Hardin Symes's autism. Body spewing bullshit about the hazards of vaccination. Body hyping the alarming number of child homicides and disappearances.

My eyes flew open. Until that moment, I'd forgotten. Or buried the memory so deeply it could find no slither room. I'd listened to Body interview Heavner one other time, more than a year after Hardin's murder. Don't recall my reason. Perhaps to see if Dr. Morgue was still abusing her office. In that broadcast, Body mentioned Jahaan Cole in a similar tirade about missing children. No lurid details, just one of many examples to support the ludicrous notion that the U.S. government was snatching kids.

Sitting on the cold tile, I felt chilled all over.

Margot Heavner hadn't once challenged or contradicted Body.

And something else infuriated me.

Hardin Symes's murder was an open case.

Jahaan Cole's disappearance was an open case.

The faceless man was an open case.

Heavner was exhibiting the same self-serving disregard for his privacy that she had for the others. And reaching beyond her area of expertise. The man wasn't Asian. Heavner was mistaken.

In my gut, I knew that the man on my front lawn

was the man logged into the morgue as MCME 304-18. That his body had been scavenged by hogs near Buffalo Creek. That the Hyundai was his. That he was not John Ito. Felix Vodyanov? Maybe, but gut instinct was far from evidence.

That man had my number and had tried to contact me. Perhaps concerning Jahaan Cole. I had to learn who he was.

Screw Heavner. Her warnings. Her threats. I'd pin a name on this man if it killed me. Get him home to whoever was out there wondering where he'd gone. Then I'd resign.

Returning to bed, I found Birdie stretched out on my pillow, paws in the air.

I displaced the cat. He curled in the crook of my knee.

I fell asleep picturing my report on MCME 304-18 on Heavner's desk, my employee ID and keys lying on top.

10

Three days passed with nothing much happening. Ryan was asked to investigate the theft of a horse named Neville. Neville had gone missing from a vineyard outside Bordeaux. He offered to decline the case, suggested a visit to Charlotte instead. Though his words were sincere, his tone suggested a real desire to get involved. And earn the fee, which would be substantial. I told him to accept. It meant he'd be going to France.

Katy Skyped from Bagram. Not sure why she was back at that airbase. She couldn't elaborate but confirmed that she was still scheduled to rotate stateside in October. Reassured me she wouldn't volunteer for another war-zone deployment.

My sister, Harry, flew to Iceland with a guy named Mookey. Mama went to the mountains with Sinitch.

My blood continued flowing through the proper arterial pathways.

The heat wave steamrolled on over the Carolinas, suffocating mountains, piedmont, and low country with temperatures and humidity more suited to Darwin or Bangkok.

For me, Independence Day was flags and sparklers and the Colonel's chicken with friends at Lake Norman. A brief respite from days of tension and frustration.

The faceless man began his second week on a stainless-steel gurney in the morgue cooler. Still nameless.

Heavner didn't call. Ditto Slidell. Pete.

The annex remained unnervingly quiet. My only progress came with the thumb-drive photo I'd snapped and then forgotten thanks to Art and his shotgun. The Cyrillic word Медицинские translated to "Medical." I had no idea the significance of that.

Friday, everything changed.

It started with an early-morning email from Lizzie Griesser. A one-line message. *Cactus time!*

I clicked open the attachment. And actually did an arm-pump in the air.

Of course, Slidell didn't answer his phone. He returned my call at nine thirty.

Before I could share my news, he let fly.

"Don't chew my ass. I didn't check in because I been busy."

"You ran the name Felix Vodyanov?"

"No missing-persons report. No BOLO. No criminal record. No military. No passport or visa info. No prints. Nothing in any database I checked."

"No dental or medical dossiers."

"Are you listening to me?"

"Did you reach out—"

"To Timbuktu and back. Local, state, federal. It's like the asshat doesn't exist."

"Is that unusual?"

"Eh."

"Could it be Vodyanov's a foreign national?"

"There's no record of anyone with that name entering the U.S. But my guy came through on the thumb drive. Gonna cost me a bottle of Stoli." Slidell paused. Messing with my head? "The thing had one file, not password-protected, not encrypted."

"Not a list of Russian sleeper cells."

"A list of prescription drugs." I heard paper rustle. "Depacon, Zoloft, Seroquel, couple others."

Depacon is an anticonvulsant sometimes used as a mood stabilizer. Zoloft is an antidepressant. Seroquel is an antipsychotic. "Vodyanov must have had mental issues," I said.

"The thing also had info on a doc."

"Name?"

"A. Yuriev. He's licensed but does mostly homeopathic wellness and stress-management crap."

"Where does Yuriev practice?" I was surprised my voice sounded so calm.

"You're gonna love this. He's on staff at some sort of Buddhist monk spa outside Winston-Salem. A joint called Sparkling Waters."

"An ashram?"

"Advertises itself as a spiritual retreat and healing center. Whatever. Yuriev don't sound Indian to me. I'll drop a dime."

"No." Too quick. "We should drive up there."

"He'll pull that doctor-patient crap."

"That's why we should go. Catch Yuriev off guard."

No response.

"We have to give it a try. Felix Vodyanov could be the first break in the Jahaan Cole case."

"We don't know who wrote the code for the kid in the notebook."

"You got any better leads?"

Again, he said nothing.

"I have something that could resolve whether Vodyanov is the faceless man."

"What?"

"I'll explain on the way."

A stretch of decidedly dubious silence. Then, "This better be good."

Slidell tossed the printouts sideways. I caught them as he put the SUV into gear and gunned from the annex.

"You're blowing my mind, doc. For years, you been preaching that DNA's only good for comparing."

"Until recently, that's been the case. An unknown sample was useless in the absence of a 'possible.' A name. We had to know whose home or family to go to. Whose toothbrush to collect."

"Yeah, yeah. I know the drill." Circling a wrist. "Cops bag leftovers from a scene, a vic, or a suspect, then some lab rat compares the sequencing from that stuff to sequencing from stuff obtained from a known person. The profiles match or they don't." More wrist. "A billion to one this, a billion to one that."

"Yes. Comparative results are stated as statistical

probabilities that the materials came from the same individual or a related individual."

"So what's this face you got from Lizzie whoever?"

"Lizzie Griesser."

"She produce those pics?" he asked, gesturing at the pages in my lap.

"And the profile."

"Yeah?"

Interpreting this as interest, I took a moment to simplify in my head.

"The power of DNA is expanding beyond mere comparison. Lizzie and her colleagues have identified SNPs, single nucleotide polymorphisms—"

Slidell's Ray-Bans swung my way. "Don't do it, doc."

"Think genes that affect facial features and shape, skin, eye, and hair color, that kind of thing."

"You saying what I think you're saying? They can tell an unsub's race?"

"They prefer to think in terms of biogeographic ancestry."

"Starting with just blood, semen, spit, sweat—the usual?"

"Yes."

"I'll be damned." Clearly not interested in the specifics of methodology.

"Using algorithms and mathematical modeling—"

Slidell shot me another *lose the jargon* frown.

"—which are beyond my ability to explain, they generate a composite image of the unknown subject."

"Like those little beauties." Another thumb jab at the pages I'd printed.

"The technique is called DNA phenotyping."

"It works?"

"It's been used to successfully ID suspects in several cases that I know of, including serial killers in Louisiana and California and a double murderer right here in North Carolina. The NCMEC is starting to use images from Lizzie's lab for their internet postings." I was referring to the National Center for Missing and Exploited Children.

"News flash. They've been putting up sketches of unidentified kids for years."

"Facial approximations derived solely from skull features. Usually in black-and-white. The DNA-based reconstructions are more detailed, more lifelike, and in color."

"Why isn't every coroner and cop shop in the country jumping on this?"

"It's pricey."

"That why you leaned on your BFF?"

"Lizzie and I support each other professionally." Curt. Though, in fairness, Skinny was right.

I lifted the top sheet and studied the face for the hundredth time. It was realistic enough, though overly symmetrical in the way of all computer-generated portraits.

The man stared straight ahead, features devoid of expression. His eyes were bluish gray and close-set, his nose prominent and narrow throughout its length. His upper lip was unusually long, the philtrum strikingly deep.

The man's skin was pale, his brown-black hair

cropped short in back and above the ears, details observable on the corpse. Though facial hair is anybody's guess, Lizzie had gone with medium brows and clean-shaven jaws and cheeks showing moderate shadowing.

Below the image, colored bar graphs put the man's skin color in the very fair to fair range, his eye color in the blue to green range, and his hair color in the brown to black range, all with greater than 90 percent confidence. The program was equally certain the man had no freckles.

A box to the upper right of the face contained a map highlighting countries in northern and eastern Europe. Colored boxes below the map identified probable ancestry as *European: Eastern: 76.37%; European: Northern: 20.98%.*

The faceless man was definitely not of Asian heritage.

"Want me to explain how they arrived at the profile?" I asked Slidell.

"No."

Alrighty.

Ninety minutes of humming highway, then we pulled into a small parking lot off a street called Sally Anne Lane that cut south from NC Business 40. We were just east of Winston-Salem. I think. Lost in thought, I hadn't paid much attention.

Sparkling Waters Ashram looked like a cross between a resort in Goa and a summer camp in Sheboygan. Brightly painted buildings with elaborate wood trim and peaked roofs sat among live oaks and pines, reasonably well-trimmed hedges, and gravel walking paths. Most buildings were single-story; one rose three floors. In the distance, mud-green water was doing its best to fulfill the promise of the facility's name.

"Can't accuse them of slacking off on security." Slidell was eyeing the twelve-foot-high fence surrounding the grounds. A dome-roofed guardhouse stood sentry at its only gate.

Through the fencing, I could see people sitting on vibrantly colored Adirondacks or on the lawn, others strolling the paths. They wore light summer clothing, yoga gear, or colorful robes or saris. Most were alone. One was in a wheelchair and accompanied by a man in white with the demeanor of an orderly or nurse. I admired the collective stamina. The mercury was at 92°F and climbing.

Slidell and I followed arrows pointing toward *Administration*, which turned out to be a one-story pink cinder-block box on the parking lot side of the fence. Kashmir carpets on the floor, Hindu and Buddhist art on the walls. A real mishmash. Buddha, Shiva, Vishnu, a portrait of Ganesha seated on a neon throne. Made me think of the small stone version of the elephant-headed god at home in my dresser drawer.

A receptionist looked up when we entered. A name bar on her desk said *E. Desai*.

"May I help you?" E. Desai was saggy-breasted and middle-age loose in the arms. Her eyes were brown, her hair black and slicked back into a lank braid. Though her feet weren't visible, below her sari I knew were sensible sandals.

"We're here to see Dr. Yuriev." Slidell badged her, returned the holder to his pocket in one quick move.

"Is he expecting you?" E. Desai's teeth were artificial and spectacularly white. She showed a lot of them while awaiting a response.

"He'll see us."

"May I ask what it's about?" Dentition showing no sign of subsiding.

"No." Slidell, face sweaty and flushed with heat.

That caught her by surprise. Taking advantage, I unfolded and laid the composite on her blotter.

"Do you know this man?"

E. Desai looked down, and for the first time, the smile seemed to falter. Eyes resolutely not on us, she turned one shoulder, punched keys on her desk phone, and whispered, "I'm sorry to interrupt, but a police officer is asking to speak with you."

Pause.

"A certain guest." Very low, hand cupping the mouthpiece. Then words I couldn't make out.

E. Desai was cradling the receiver—gingerly, as though it might break—when I felt a change in the air pressure at our backs. We turned.

A man stood eyeing us dispassionately. Through the open doorway framing him, I could see a carved and painted wooden desk. On it, a bronze of Rabindranath Tagore, the Indian philosopher and poet. Facing it, a pair of mahogany chairs upholstered in red velvet. Behind it, a chair whose back brought to mind a male peacock in full display. Behind the chair, ivory inlaid shelving displaying a collection of brass and silver objects. An Agra rug on the floor. Stacked silk-covered cushions in one corner. The office appeared designed to persuade visitors they were actually in turn-of-the-century Jaipur.

The man's gaze shifted from Slidell to me and back. Remained expressionless as he directed a question to his receptionist.

"Were you shown proper identification?"

E. Desai nodded, lips now tightly compressed.

"I'm Dr. Aryan Yuriev." Yuriev was short, with curly brown hair, an off-angle nose and upper lip, and a chin showing a whole lot of attitude.

"How may I help you, Detective . . . ?" Voice rising in question.

Slidell snatched the composite from the desk and held it up. "I'll make it quick. You know this guy?"

Yuriev glanced at the sketch for a full half second. Then, "Do you have a warrant, sir?"

"Do I need a warrant?"

"You surprise me, detective." Not looking surprised. "We both know I'm not at liberty to discuss a guest." Realizing his mistake. "Had that man been a guest here."

"And you're thinking your 'guests'"—using air quotes—"enjoy doctor-patient privilege?"

"The ashram provides many services for those seeking spiritual healing. Among them is medical care should the need arise. That is my function. And as a licensed physician, my interactions with those I treat are strictly confidential."

"How about I refresh your memory?" Slidell's tone was taking on a familiar edge. He suspected Yuriev was lying. "The name Felix Vodyanov mean anything?"

Yuriev said nothing.

"Felix Vodyanov. You wrote him script for—" Slidell curled upturned fingers in my direction.

"Depacon, Zoloft, Seroquel," I supplied.

Yuriev continued to stare coolly.

Slidell waggled the sketch. "Suppose I tell you the guy's dead. That put a new spin on your doctor-patient bullshit?"

Hearing a sharp intake of breath, I reoriented subtly. E. Desai was still avoiding eye contact, but a red blossom was spreading on each of her cheeks.

A few beats as Yuriev decided his course. Behind me, E. Desai had gone very still.

"Sparkling Waters is a private facility, detective. You have no warrant. I have explained my position, and now I am asking you to leave. Should you not comply, you will be trespassing, and I will call security to have you escorted from the grounds."

"We're going. But take it to the bank, asshole." Slidell now sounding dangerous. "I'll be back."

"An occasion to which I look forward with relish." Flash of unhealthy gums, then Yuriev placed his palms together, bowed slightly, retreated into his office, and closed the door.

Slidell and I were crossing the parking lot when a voice called softly. "Wait."

We turned. E. Desai was hurrying toward us with all the grace of a startled wombat. I was right about the sandals. Birkenstocks.

Slidell checked his watch. A mannerism to redirect frustration. We both knew it was noon.

E. Desai closed in, breathing hard, face now homogeneously red. I could smell her patchouli cologne and the perspiration it was meant to conceal.

Slidell crossed his arms, spread his feet, and eyed her impatiently. A sheen of sweat made his face look like shiny red plastic.

"It's him," she said, casting a quick look behind her. "He was a guest."

"You're certain?" My pulse tripping.

E. Desai nodded, eyes wide. "Is he really dead?"

"What can you tell us about him?" I asked.

"I don't interact with the guests." Slight dip of her brows. "Was his name Vodyanov? Oh, dear."

"When was he here?"

"More than once. Last year, for sure."

"He just come for the monk junk? Or was something more wrong with him?" Slidell, sharp. The sun was directly overhead, a hot white ball in a sky hosting very few clouds.

"I don't interact—"

"Why was Yuriev treating him?"

"I don't know. I swear."

"Do you have contact information for Mr. Vodyanov?" I asked gently.

She shook her head.

"A phone number? An address?"

Another head shake.

Slidell shifted his weight and fist-jammed his hips. A dark green crescent circled each underarm. The rest of his shirt resembled wilted lettuce.

"You should talk to Asia Barrow." Lowering her voice to the same hush she'd used on the phone. "She was his primary counselor."

"Was?"

"She's doing something else now." Furtive glance over one shoulder. An evasion? A lie?

"Do you know where Asia lives?"

"I do." Dragging sweat-soaked strands from her forehead. "I can't tell you how."

"Why Asia?" I asked, handing E. Desai my card.

"If anyone knows anything about your person, it would be Asia."

11

Slidell dropped me at the annex, then blistered off to the Law Enforcement Center, on fire to review the Jahaan Cole file. Knowing he'd be at it for hours, maybe days, I went alone to see Asia Barrow. Skinny had argued against it, of course. I'd promised to be careful and keep in touch.

The address E. Desai gave me was in Mooresville but not the pricey lakefront area favored by bankers and lawyers making the daily slog uptown for the privilege of owning Catalinas and riding mowers. The unfashionable rural part, too far east of I-77 to be of interest to anyone not conversant in John Deere.

From the interstate, the nice Waze lady speaking through my cell phone directed me onto a two-lane winding through fields and scruffy woodland. A farmhouse here, a trailer there. A complicated transformer station. Thirteen miles, then she sent me onto a road with no markings at all. I drove through what must have appeared on a Google Maps satellite view as a knobby green finger of forest. Ten minutes, then I was informed that my destination was on the right.

A rusty mailbox leaned at an angle never intended by its installer. No number, no name. No red flag to be raised for outgoing correspondence.

I looked ahead and behind me. Saw only pavement shimmering like sand in a desert mirage. Not a vehicle in sight.

Bad idea? Probably.

I made the turn.

The driveway was dirt with sporadic patches of gravel. I passed below a mix of pine and hardwood for a long two minutes. Suddenly, the road dipped, changed its mind, and turned sharply uphill.

The few loner clouds were now buddying up into larger clusters. As I crept forward, wishing the intrepid Waze lady was riding shotgun, shadows mottled my windshield, staccato moments of darkness and light filtering through overhead needles and leaves.

Another eon, or thirty seconds, then I crested a hill.

And braked hard. Foot shaky on the pedal, I reached for my water. Drank. Rescrewed the cap.

A structure squatted at the back of an oblong clearing measuring about sixty yards by twenty. It was small, more shack than house. The green paint, faded and peeling, made me think of the anoles that molt and leave their skins stuck to the annex pillars. Blue-and-white curtains hung, limp and dejected, in windows to either side of a sagging front door. The windows were screened and open. The door was screened and closed.

A covered porch stretched the length of the building, adding a certain *je ne sais quoi* to the architectural style. Not so the junk piled along it. Newspapers. Scooters and bikes. A console TV designed to fit into a corner. An old window air conditioner. Stacked Tupperware tubs, their contents resembling shadowy creatures intent on escape.

A chrome-and-leather chair sat to the left of the door. Beside the chair, a floor-model ashtray, the kind once placed outside elevators and in hotel lobbies.

On the lawn, had there been grass, was a scattering of items that hadn't made the cut for the porch. Tires. An ancient Frigidaire washer. A blue toilet with a Hoover upright rising from the bowl. A plastic playhouse molded into the shape of a castle, cracked and coated with mud.

To the right of the house, beside the driveway access point at which I'd stopped, stood a small shed. A muted droning suggested it housed a generator. A black Chevrolet Silverado was parked outside, rear bumper tight to the east-facing wall. The truck, old and dinged, fitted well with its shabby surroundings.

The plastic bottle popped loudly in my hand. Startled, I released the grip I wasn't aware I'd tightened.

Why such apprehension? The place was depressing, sure, but menacing?

Feeling a bit foolish, I turned off the engine.

But was it foolish? What did I know about Asia Barrow? I'd been directed to her by a stranger who didn't seem overly bright.

According to E. Desai, Barrow had been the life coach assigned to the faceless man, Felix Vodyanov. His treatment by Yuriev, combined with the thumbdrive list of meds, suggested Vodyanov had a condition requiring mood regulators, antidepressants, and anti-psychotics. Barrow had left Sparkling Waters for reasons E. Desai chose not to disclose.

Not exactly a road map to the Zodiac killer.

After texting Slidell, I got out and quietly closed the car door. My footsteps chafed across dusty soil that, following a rain, would surely be a sea of mud. Above the whir of the generator, I heard a wind chime, not the usual melodic tinkle, more a metallic clanking, like engine parts begging for oil.

As I approached the house, a red-tailed hawk swooped up and looped low in the sky, framed by a cloud whose belly was the color of a bruise. The avian air show did nothing to calm my nerves.

At the base of the stairs, I called out.

No voice. No movement. No barking dog.

Five treads up to the porch. Seeing no doorbell, I opened the screen and knocked.

Nothing.

I knocked again.

Still no response.

The air was so hot I felt I was standing in a kiln. Wiping sweat from my face, I stepped to the right, around the air conditioner and the TV. Eyes shaded with both hands, I leaned close and peered through the screen.

In a sliver of space between the curtain and the window frame, I could see a multicolor flicker reflected in a wall mirror. The mirror was centered in a pig's belly. The pig was laughing and dancing.

A television was on. Someone was in there with Porky.

Crossing back to the door, I knocked again, harder.

"Who the hell are you?"

I whipped around.

A woman stood halfway between the shed and the house, arms cocked at her sides. Her hair was short and, given the deep brown shade of her skin, bleached several shades lighter than desirable. Her shorts were baggy, her Judas Priest tee several sizes smaller than desirable. A cigarette pack bulged in one rolled sleeve. White cotton socks hung loosely around the tops of her boots.

"I'm sorry to disturb you. I'm looking for Asia Barrow."

The woman eyed me suspiciously. "What do you want with her?"

"I'd like to ask her a few questions."

"About what?" I put the woman's age at mid-forties, her muscle tone somewhere in the Rambo range.

"A visitor to Sparkling Waters."

"Well, that takes major-league balls." Glaring hard.

"Are you Asia Barrow?"

"Who gave you this address?" Slight accent but with a Southern overlay. Georgia?

"Ms. Desai."

"That moron." Exasperated head shake.

"She claimed to know you."

"She's my goddamn cousin." Beat. "This about that lying wankass says I broke his arm?"

"No. I—"

"I ain't saying nothing to no one. Now, I think you'd best get back in your car and drive on off my property."

"I'd like to talk to you about—"

"You representing Sparkling Waters?"

"I'm not an attorney."

"You don't look like a cop."

No way I'd explain my actual profession or tell her I worked with the ME. Word could get back to Heavner.

"You were employed at the ashram?" I asked.

"Until the cocksuckers fired me."

"May I ask why?"

"You may ask, but that don't mean I'll tell you." Barrow hooked her thumbs in her belt loops. Which dragged her waistband low enough to show serious abs.

"Do you know a man named Felix Vodyanov?"

No response.

I pulled the composite from my shoulder bag and held it up. "Is this Mr. Vodyanov?"

Nothing.

"I believe he was under Dr. Yuriev's care?"

"Do I need to haul out my shotgun?"

"Your cousin said Mr. Vodyanov was someone you counseled."

"That the term she used?" Scornful headshake.

"Close enough."

"My cousin has goat shit for brains." Cocking her chin at the sketch. "He in some kind of trouble?"

"A body was found last week in Cleveland County. ID hasn't been confirmed, but we believe the deceased is this man."

A moment of silence, followed by a long exhalation. "How'd he die?"

"Cause of death remains uncertain." Hoping she wouldn't follow up on the *who the hell are you?* line of inquiry.

"I figured the dude would end badly."

"Why do you say that?"

"The crap he was into."

"Can you elaborate?"

"You really think he's dead?"

"Is this Felix Vodyanov?" Raising the sketch.

"My guy registered under the name F. Vance. But yeah, that's him."

"I do," I said.

Barrow's shoulders slumped slightly. Then she straightened and began striding in my direction. "This sun's frying my brain."

I stepped sideways, allowing Barrow room to pass. She opened both doors and held the screen wide. I followed her into the house.

The interior was as hot and cramped as expected. But the air smelled clean and slightly exotic, like Pine-Sol and spices and sandalwood incense.

"Lemonade?"

"That would be nice," I said.

Two doorways faced the front room. Through the right one, I could see a small galley kitchen. Through the left, a tall wooden dresser and part of a bed.

The flooring was linoleum throughout, gray and blue. Maybe chosen to match the curtains. More likely due to a Home Depot sale.

Barrow gestured toward an upholstered grouping far too large for the small space in which we stood. Then she crossed to the kitchen.

Avoiding a quilt featuring a rather angry-looking parrot, I sat on the sofa and scanned my surroundings. The curtains needed attention; otherwise, the place was spotless.

My knees were jammed tight to a steamer trunk serving as a coffee table. From the kitchen came the sound of a faucet squeaking on, then off, the *whoosh* of a refrigerator door, the *clink* of ice hitting glass.

Behind me were bookshelves holding everything but books. Statues of horses, dogs, elephants. Three or four manifestations of Ganesha. Magazines. Framed photos, most featuring the same two little girls at varying ages. A collection of what appeared to be journals or logbooks, dated by year.

Opposite the couch and the trunk between which I was wedged were a round metal table and two rattan chairs. On the table was a potted geranium whose DOD must have been years in the past. Its black, leafless stems reached out like spidery claws. Irrationally, I felt a new wave of foreboding.

Barrow reappeared, set two glasses on the trunk, then crossed to the shelving. Pulling one of the dated journals, she returned and dropped into the larger of the oversized chairs.

"Thank you," I said. "Your home is very cozy."

"It's a rental, and it's shit. I don't like tethers."

I had no response to that.

We both drank. Several moments passed. Barrow ran a thumb across the condensation on her glass. The nail was naked, the cuticle red and ragged. I waited, allowing her to set the pace.

"Felix Vodyanov, F. Vance, whatever. He was a repeat customer at the ashram." Barrow's eyes stayed on her lemonade. "Showed up more than once during the four years I worked there. VIP, so he got special treatment."

"Special?"

"Separate quarters, room service. That sort of thing. Ask me, he came for more than just cleansing and yoga."

"Meaning what?"

Shoulder hitch. "Dunno. He was a quiet guy. Stayed to himself. But then, Hitler liked dogs."

"That's an odd comment," I said.

There was a wide patch of silence. Then, "I think your guy was into some seriously messed-up shit."

"Go on."

"He was Russian. Had an accent. Subtle, but if you listened, you could catch it."

"How do you know it was Russian?"

"Dr. Yuriev's half Indian, half Russian. I made the mistake of showing interest in the Russian bit once, you know, to schmooze him up. He yammered on and on about the glories of Rimsky-Korsakov, Dostoyevsky, the motherland. I never did it again. Anyway, he and your guy sounded alike. And I think Yuriev was the reason he chose the ashram."

"Can you explain the Hitler reference?"

Barrow gulped lemonade. Backhanded her mouth and set down the glass. "When he was at Sparkling Waters, Vodyanov was my main responsibility. I spent a lot of time with him, one-on-one. He knew things."

"Things."

"I keep a sort of diary. Been doing it since high school. Nothing fancy, just random ideas strike my fancy. Or happenings I might want to recall later on."

Silence as Barrow thumbed through the journal, found the entry she sought.

"Ever hear of a ship named the *Estonia*?"

"A passenger ferry that sank in the Baltic in '94." The disaster that had interested the owner of the Hyundai. The owner of the notebook.

"That's the one. Real shame. Almost nine hundred people died." Barrow ran a finger down the page. "Vodyanov—you say that's his name, I'll call him that—knew that this boat was carrying some serious juice." The finger stopped. "Here it is. Advanced Soviet space and laser technology. Whatever the hell that is. Vodyanov claimed the boat was sunk to prevent the transfer of that cargo to the West."

"Go on." Voice calm, pulse not.

"I never got the whole story, but it was clear Vodyanov was privy to classified info."

"Such as?"

Barrow's eyes dropped back to the journal. The finger traveled, mining information. "He knew that the wreck wasn't found for five days, even though it could be seen by helicopter." More mining. "That some sort of multinational military exercise was going on in the Baltic during the entire episode." More. "That two submarines, one Swedish and one Soviet, followed the *Estonia* when it left Tallinn for Stockholm. Don't ask me where those places are." The finger shifted to the next page. "That after the boat went down, the U.S. and Israel began developing this laser crap and something else." Movement, then a finger jab to the paper. "Infrared-beam weaponry."

"Vodyanov talked about this?"

"A couple, three times. Before Yuriev got his meds sorted."

"What else?"

"I didn't write everything down. But hold on." Long pause. "He said that right after the sinking, divers hired by the Swedish government spent hours breaking into cabins searching for a black attaché case belonging to a Russian space-technology dealer. I didn't record the guy's name, but Vodyanov knew it. He said that the case was found in a cabin usually used by one of the ferry's missing captains. And that this dealer's name was on it."

It was as if a barrier had lifted and Barrow was finally able to unburden herself. She talked in bursts as she pried Vodyanov's comments from the words scrawled on the pages before her.

"Here's a kicker. Did you know that most of the victims are still down there? Instead of trying to retrieve the bodies, the Swedish government hired a marine-salvage firm specializing in, get this, neutralizing underwater nuclear waste. Vodyanov knew the name of the outfit. I didn't put it in here. He said they spent $350 million trying to bury the ship in concrete. To this day, no one's allowed to dive anywhere near it."

Barrow's eyes rose, then drifted off over my shoulder. I wondered if she was visualizing her former charge, perhaps corpses rotting on a sea floor.

Assuming Barrow was finished, I said, "I'm curious. Why did you feel compelled to record Vodyanov's statements?"

"I was convinced the dude was some sort of Russian operative. I figured what the hell? The story might come in handy someday."

"You thought he was a spy bec—"

"Are you not listening to me? He was talking about the

transfer of secret Soviet space technology to the West." Speaking slowly, emphasizing each word. "About an attack to prevent that from happening." Voice rising. "About the murder of nine hundred people. About a cover-up to keep those people at the bottom of the ocean. The guy knew way too much about it. And that isn't all."

The pig clock chose that moment to grunt. Repeated the sound twice. Three o'clock.

I waited for Barrow to continue. Instead, she sat back and ran a hand through the ill-advised hair. "Hell, I don't know."

"What is it you're not saying?" I urged gently.

"It's not my business." Visibly uneasy now.

"The more information I have, the better my chances of determining what happened to this man." Indicating the composite.

Barrow's gaze dropped to Vodyanov's face. Lingered a moment, then, "I need a smoke."

Before I could react, she pushed to her feet, shoved the diary back into its slot on the shelf, and *clomped* out the door. I collected the sketch and followed. Barrow had already lit up when I joined her on the porch.

"You're troubled because you believed Vodyanov was a spy yet you didn't report it?"

Barrow drew deeply. Snorted, shooting smoke from both nostrils. "Funny. I was about to say telling you all this could cost me my job. Guess not."

Deep drag.

"Vodyanov wasn't allowed a computer, tablet, cell phone, nothing like that. Ashram rule. Leave your technology at the door when checking in. One day, I was in his room. Sometimes I had to monitor his sleep.

Never knew why. I was reading email on my laptop when the guy woke up and begged for a few minutes online. Shit, he was calm, lucid, his drugs or his cleanse or whatever was working."

"What was he taking?"

"Above my pay grade. Dr. Yuriev dealt with that."

"Was that standard?"

"Yeah, I guess. Anyway, this was before I learned, you know, the *Estonia* stuff. He seemed so sad and lonely, I figured what the hell."

"I understand."

"A couple days later, I went to clear my browser history." Barrow drew smoke into her lungs, exhaled. "Ever hear of the deep net?"

"Yes."

"Vodyanov had gone to it. I admit, I got curious, cruised around. Stumbled onto some pretty grim sites." Barrow sent her ash flying with the flick of a thumb. "Looked like the dude was into two things."

I expected secret government facilities, maybe nuclear reactors. What she said shocked me.

"Missing kids. Child porn."

"Do you recall specific websites?"

Barrow shook her head no. "Made me want to puke. I deleted every link. And the browser. Put nothing in my diary."

"Did you confront him?"

"What for? He was supposed to be unplugged; I broke the rules and wired him in. I wiped the whole incident from my mind. Tried to, anyway. Vowed to never let the asshole con me again. Didn't matter. Shortly after that, he was gone."

"This occurred during his final stay?"

"Nah, an earlier one."

"When was he last at Sparkling Waters?"

She considered. "I keep in touch some. I hear he was last there late May, early June."

"Do you know where Vodyanov lived?"

Barrow mashed her cigarette against the heel of her boot. Held the stub in one palm, considering. Then, without a word, she yanked the screen open and disappeared into the house.

Time passed. I sweated. A lot. I was certain I'd been dismissed when Barrow reappeared, holding the door with one hand while thrusting a yellow Post-it at me with the other.

"You didn't get this from me."

"Thank you." Quick glance, then I slipped her offering into my shoulder bag.

"Any way I spin it, spying, trafficking, child porn, comes down to the guy was bad news. My conscience is clear. Now I got work needs doing."

"One last question."

Barrow didn't retreat.

"If they weren't simply spiritual retreats, why do you think Mr. Vodyanov made visits to Sparkling Waters?"

"I never asked the reasons folks needed to get away from their lives. Still, some shared. Usually, it was alcohol, drugs, stress at work. Vodyanov told me he suffered from taphophobia."

I raised questioning brows.

"The dude had spells when he was terrified of being buried alive."

12

The drive back to the highway felt as dismal as the drive in from it. More so. The clouds, no longer satisfied with forming small alliances, were expanding and muscling out the sun. Rolling and bumping over the driveway and then the narrow road, I felt enveloped in gloom—gray forest, gray road, gray sky through gray vegetation. Monet might have titled the landscape *Study in Depression*.

Rush-hour traffic had the northbound lanes of I-77 congealed into one enormous clot. Fortunately, I was heading south, toward Charlotte. Still, it was five forty when I finally parked at the annex.

Walking from the car felt like passing through a steam bath. I estimated the barometric pressure at about a billion.

First off, I fished the yellow Post-it from my purse and, seated at the kitchen table, googled the address. Was a bit surprised.

If Barrow was correct, Vodyanov had lived in a part

of Charlotte I skirted on one of my driving routes to UNCC, a largely Latino area with a robust gang presence. MS-13, Sur 13, subsidiaries of both. Disputes between rival entrepreneurs often sent corpses toes-up through the doors at the MCME.

I dialed Slidell. Got his voice mail and left a message. *Call me.*

Minutes dragged by. A half hour.

I fed Birdie, then paced. Undecided. Knowing the wise decision.

I picked things up. Put them down. Returned to the table. Plucked a daisy from a vase, triaged petals, returned it to its pals. Ran my palm over a place mat. Felt roughness and spit-cleaned the morsel with one thumb. Paced some more.

My stomach growled. I ate a carton of yogurt. A peach.

The annex was silent save for the tinkle of Bird's tags against his bowl. The metronome ticking of the mantel clock.

Unable to stay still, I crossed to the window overlooking the patio. The world outside was bathed in eerie plum light. The clouds, now bloated and bruised, were organizing for serious action.

Agitated, I called Slidell again. With the same result.

Was he ignoring me?

Snap decision.

Even with rain, it would be light for another three hours. I had a vague sense of Vodyanov's hood. Had gone there for the occasional burrito or enchilada.

I left a different message for Skinny. This one included the address.

Quick trip to the head, then I grabbed my purse and set off.

Ignoring the navigational advice emanating from my mobile, I drove to the intersection of Central Avenue and Eastway Drive, then turned left. Gloomy due to the impending storm, yet too early for streetlamps programmed for summertime dusk, the area seemed unnaturally dim and shadowy. I passed a check-cashing operation, an auto-parts store, strip malls containing bodegas, taquerias, tattoo parlors, gun shops, and other small businesses, all with bars on their windows and doors. Most were padlocked and dark. Only the occasional fast-food joint still blazed neon.

Unfamiliar with the maze of streets surrounding the main drag, I now followed the Waze lady's robotic instructions. A couple of right turns, a left. The area became less commercial and more residential. I passed a lot of spray-painted graffiti, largely in Spanish. On one crumbling wall, the word *Malditos* in lime green.

Another right, and I was crawling down a narrow street packed shoulder to shoulder with unadorned boxes rising three or four stories. Grotty air conditioners jutted from windows, and rusty fire escapes snaked the brick. The iPhone voice told me my destination was on the right. Pulling to the curb between two pickups that had to be at least twenty years old, I scanned for Barrow's Post-it address.

The digits 2307 overhung the front entrance of the last box in the row, smaller than its brethren. The first floor housed what looked like a comic-book shop. Lots of ads featuring dragons and superheroes. Metal grates covered the shop's single window and door. Darkness beyond told me that business was closed for the day. Maybe forever.

Number 2307 was situated on a corner and had a small, unlit street skimming past its left side. A narrow walkway separated it from its neighbor to the right. A grass parkway separated it from the curb at which I sat.

Assuming rental units would be on the upper two floors, I checked those windows for signs of life. Only two were lit. Both were covered by yellowed shades. Behind the shades, small silhouettes lined the sills, a plant, a bird figurine, bottles of lotion or shampoo.

I got out and locked the Mazda. From far off came the thrum of unseen cars on Central Avenue. Closer, a rhythmic squeaking. I searched the sidewalk in both directions.

The pavement was deserted save for a lone woman pulling a handcart with one bad wheel. She stopped to stare at me, face unreadable in the prestorm gloom. I hurried to 2307.

Access was through a graffiti-splattered brown metal door to the right of the comic shop's front entrance. Six buzzers, three with names: #1 Ramos, #5 Garcia, #6 Vance. Based on Barrow's comments, I was betting on Vance to be Vodyanov. If Vodyanov had actually been a tenant.

I stood, considering options. Push random buttons? Phone Slidell? Retreat and call it a day? I was tired and hungry. Any second, the sky would unload.

I was pulling out my mobile to speed-dial Skinny when the door opened and a man hurried out. He was small and wiry and dark. Startled eyes took me in, then the man pushed the door wide, nodded, and hurried on his way, cleated heels ringing steely on the pavement. I mumbled a thank-you to his back and slipped inside.

The air felt damp and sticky against my hot skin. I smelled onions and grease. I glanced around.

The place was like any other dingy walk-up I'd seen. Grimy green tile on the floor. Cracked and peeling paint on the walls. Empty cans and unwanted flyers lining the point where one met the other.

I hesitated a few wild heartbeats, then headed for the staircase. It was narrow and poorly lit, with most fixtures lacking a bulb or two.

Rounding the second-floor turn, I heard a TV playing behind one of three gray metal doors. The cadence of canned laughter suggested a sitcom. I guessed tenant Ramos was catching some tube.

I continued to climb, my shadow crawling along the wall beside me like a fuzzy black slug. The higher I went, the more oppressive the heat.

Reaching the top floor, I paused again. Same setup as below. Three gray metal doors. Deep breath, then I crept down the hall. At unit 6, I stopped to listen for signs of a presence inside. Heard only the thrumming of my own pulse.

Now what? Vodyanov was in the morgue, not here. I had no key. Try the neighbor, Garcia, in unit 5? Ramos? Perhaps one or the other was the caretaker.

I was conceding what a spectacularly stupid idea this had been, on so many levels, when a thunderous *clang* sent adrenaline into every cell in my body. My eyes cut left, right. Nothing.

I was turning to leave when a voice froze me in place. "Just you hold it right now."

A woman crouched at the top of the stairs, right foot on my level, left foot below on the top tread. Short and skinny and swathed in something floral resembling a tent, she was wheezing and leaning on the banister. The exposed wrist sported enough bangles to stock a Target jewelry counter.

Before I could answer, the woman palm-pushed the upraised knee with her free hand, also bejeweled, hauled herself fully into the hallway, and shuffled toward me, bracelets jangling in rhythm with her steps.

"What you be doing there?" The first two words came out "wha-choo."

"I'm sorry if—"

"*Qué chingados!*" What the fuck. Breathy, with a tense edge of anger.

Close up, I could see that the woman's makeup was cheap, overdone, and losing out to perspiration. Her skin was mahogany, her hair polychromatic, combining shades favored by apricots, cherries, and merlot. "Are you Mrs. Ramos?"

"And if I be?"

"Are you the caretaker?"

The woman sniffed, insulted. "Owner."

I pulled the composite sketch of Felix Vodyanov from my bag and held it up. "Is this man your tenant?"

The mascaraed eyes narrowed, almost disappeared above the overly rouged cheeks. "You be with immigration?"

"No."

"The cops? Don't matter. I don't be lovin' not the one not the other." Her speech had such an odd cadence I couldn't place her. It sounded like a mélange of Jamaican patois, gangsta rap, and Spanish slang.

"I work with the medical examiner."

Blank stare.

"The coroner."

The eyes reemerged, wider. "The guy's dead?"

"Possibly."

"*Maldito.*"

"When did you last see him?"

"Couldn't say. His rent came as cash in envelopes under my door. He was reliable, I'll give him that."

"What can you tell me about him?"

"What is to tell? Tenants pay, I don't ask their business, you understand what I'm sayin'?"

"Did he have a vehicle?"

"Never saw one."

"How long was he here?"

She gave the question some thought. Or pretended to. "Maybe two years."

"How did he find this place?"

"I never knew, and I didn't ask. We're listed like everyone else."

I went at it from a different angle. "Do you run background checks? Require potential tenants to fill out applications?"

"I be renting flats here, not managing Trump Tower."

"You say this man lived in the building two years." Indicating the sketch. "Did you—"

"Not sure he did."

"What do you mean?" Trying to mask my frustration.

"I barely saw him. Don't know if he actually slept here. Just sayin'."

"Through that entire two-year period, the two of you never talked?"

"Maybe a few times." Drenched in the saccharine light of the hall sconces, the clown face turned wary.

"I'd like to see the apartment," I said.

"*Ni de coña.*" Not a fucking chance. My knowledge of street Spanish was coming in handy.

"How much to let me in?" Tone hushed, though we were alone.

"Violatin' tenants' rights could jam me up." The woman's hand rose, palm up, bracelets clanking. I dug five tens from my wallet and laid the bills on it. The hand stayed level. I added two more.

The woman produced a ring from somewhere deep within the flowery folds, fished out a key. After inserting her selection into the lock, she turned the knob and pushed the door in.

"Can't hurt if the guy's dead. Help yourself. Less clearing for me." With that, the woman jangle-shuffled down the stairs.

Using one arm, I eased the door back as far as it would go. The displaced air smelled of mildew and old wood. And something else. Something that triggered a tumult of images. Larabee's lifeless face the night he was shot. Tubes. Pinging machines.

After slipping on latex gloves, I leaned in and slid my hand along the wall. Felt a switch and flicked it.

An overhead fixture turned the room a jaundiced

ocher. Glancing up, I saw one of those amber bulbs shaped like pine cones. A large stain circled the bulb's chipped ceramic fixture, its color alarmingly similar to that of dried blood.

My eyes made the rounds.

Facing the door was a single window with a torn and discolored shade pulled all the way down. Below the window, a collapsible metal table held a hot plate, a kettle, a small fry pan, a can opener, a dining kit composed of plate, cup, and bowl, all red, and a trio of clear plastic utensils. No ramen noodles, cans of Dinty Moore, or boxes of Kraft dinner. Not a crumb or particle of food in sight.

A battered dresser, down one leg, leaned at a cockeyed angle against the right wall. A twin bed sat opposite against the left, a single pillow and a rough wool blanket piled at the foot. A ratty orange carpet covered the floor space between.

Satisfied no one was home, I stepped into the unit.

The heat inside was even crueler than that in the hall. I vowed this would be a quick in-and-out.

Flanking the dresser were doors opening onto a tiny bath and what I assumed was a closet. No TV. No phone.

I checked the bath. Toilet sans lid, pedestal sink, shower hung with a translucent plastic curtain. Not a single product or personal item.

I returned to the main room. Ran a hand over the top of the dresser. The glove came up grease- and dust-free. One by one, I checked the drawers. Empty. No lint, no fibers, no hairs.

Tent Woman may have been right. The shabby space held nothing to suggest anyone lived in it.

I stood a moment, looking around. Since entering, I hadn't shaken the sense that something was off. What? Like a name you can't recall, the troubling impression skulked below the surface, untouchable.

I circled the dresser and opened the second door. The closet was roughly three feet square. Wire hangers held two items: a long-sleeved white shirt and a pair of tan chinos.

I ran my hand over the shelf, then along the rod. Again, the latex was clean.

A third article dangled from a wall hook near one of the closet's rear corners. I stretched forward and lifted it free.

Other images detonated. A dark silhouette in the shadows at Sharon Hall. A face staring from within a pale cone of light.

Recognition sent my heart rate spiking.

The garment in my hand was a faded gray trench coat. Identical to the one worn by the man on the night of my migraine dream. The faceless man. Felix Vodyanov.

Trench Coat was real!

Confiscate the thing? Hell, yes. The owner had granted permission to take what I wanted.

A clap of thunder startled me back into action. One last sweep, then adios.

I looked under the shade, below the metal table, behind the dresser and commode. Found all surfaces and objects spotless.

Was that the detail my subconscious had logged? A dingy, empty apartment, yet every inch immaculate?

I dropped to my knees to check beneath the bed. The odor was stronger close to the floor. I turned to sniff the orange rug. It reeked.

Sudden recognition. I was smelling hospital anti-septic, the kind I'd inhaled for hours in the intensive-care unit the night Larabee died. The kind strong enough to destroy materials containing DNA.

Second shocking realization.

The apartment and all its contents had been wiped clean of prints and everything that could identify its occupant. Vodyanov had wanted to destroy all traces of himself. And was sophisticated enough to know how to do it.

But why?

I was snapping pics when the jingle of faux silver again caused me to jump. Pivoting, I noted floral pat-terning filling the gap between the door and the jamb. In one move, I was on my feet and out into the hall.

"You're spying on me."

"Don't you go getting all up in my face," Tent Woman shot back.

"Talk to me about the occupant of this unit."

"Got nothin' to say." Overridden by a peal of thun-der louder than the first.

"Perhaps I *should* drop a word to ICE." Unkind, but my patience had run thin.

The woman's mouth opened, but no sound came out.

"Two years," I said. "You must have learned some-thing about him? His name? His hometown? His occu-pation?"

Two bony arms floated high in surrender, revealing that the tent actually had sleeves.

"*Dios mío.* I barely saw the guy."

"Look, Mrs. Ramos. It is Ramos, right? I'm not try-ing to cause you trouble. I couldn't care less who lives in this building."

"*Qué chingados.*" Apparently, she liked the expres-sion.

"Seriously," I said.

The arms dropped, the shoulders. Then, grudgingly, "It's Ms., not Mrs. Señor Estúpido kicked eight years back. I kept his building and name."

Unsure if that called for condolences or congratu-lations, I said nothing.

"We don't do intros here, you understand what I'm saying? People come, people go, everyone they keep to themselves. I speak with your guy a couple of times. Heard him now and again through the door."

Meaning she'd eavesdropped. As she had with me. I didn't say it. "Was he speaking on a phone?"

"Hell if I know. Could be he had someone in there. I don't provide chaperone service, if you catch my meanin'. What I *can* say is sometimes he talked foreign."

"What language?"

"Not English or Spanish."

"Can you recall anything he said?"

Blank stare.

"When he spoke English."

"Mostly he'd whine about needing security. Like this place is Guantánamo or something." A scrawny finger came up. "But wait. One thing stuck with me. Once, he said his life would soon be over."

"When was that?"

"Six, maybe seven months ago." The digits spread,

palm facing me. "That's all I know. I didn't ask no follow-up."

"Did you ever see him with anyone?"

Ramos shook her head no. "No shocker. The guy was scared shitless."

"Why?"

The Revlon eyes crimped in disdain. "He believed the government was trying to get him."

"The U.S. government?"

"Coulda been the Bosnians for all I know."

"He actually said that?"

"Yeah. In his blubberin' about privacy. I mostly didn't listen."

"He seemed genuinely afraid?"

"Terrified. Look, I got a window needs unjamming before this storm hits. Otherwise, I'll be spending my night moppin'."

"Thank you, Ms. Ramos. You've been helpful."

"So, what? I can go ahead and rent out the room?"

"I'd hold off a bit longer."

"Sonofabitch."

"I understand the inconvenience. I'm sure the wait list is longer than my arm."

Ramos flipped me a heartfelt bird.

The storm broke as I was sprinting to my car. The downpour was everything the clouds had promised.

Drenched, I *wheeped* the locks and threw myself behind the wheel. While palming rain from my face and hair, I glanced through the passenger window at 2307.

Above a Marvel poster featuring Doctor Strange, I could see Ramos backlit in a second-floor window. She was talking on a mobile phone. As I watched, her eyes came around in my direction. She stared. Continued speaking.

Paranoia?

Or was she discussing me?

13

The downpour was so fierce I pulled into the Wendy's at the Eastway Drive intersection. Figured I'd wait for the storm to let up, then grab a Dave's Double meal before heading to the annex. Others had done the same. The occupants of those vehicles looked like woolly ghosts through the wall of rain and the fog-clouded windows.

With drops pounding the roof and hood like stampeding hooves, I turned on the interior light and reached for the small pile of clothing I'd dumped beside me, still puzzled. Vodyanov had taken everything of a personal nature. Why leave garments in the closet? Had he planned to return? Forgotten them due to a hurried departure? Decided he no longer wanted them?

Once home, I'd do a thorough search, but to pass the time, I dug latex gloves and a compact LED penlight from my shoulder bag. First, I checked the pockets of the shirt and pants, remembering Hawkins's score at the autopsy. Found nothing. I noted that all labels had been removed.

Next, I stretched the trench coat full length across the passenger seat and onto my lap. I'd used it as a makeshift umbrella during my sprint from 2307, and it now felt heavy and damp.

The fabric was gabardine, styled in the fashion made popular by the British military during World War II— double-breasted with a wide collar, epaulettes, raglan sleeves, a gun flap, and a top-stitched belt outfitted with D-rings. The design looked familiar though somehow foreign. Again, I looked for labels. All were gone.

I ran a palm over the coat. Felt no lumps or bulges. A quick inventory revealed five pockets. Two on each side by the hip, one interior and one exterior. One on the inside at the breast.

Lightning sparked, then darkness snapped back. My eyes flew up.

Beyond my windshield, the world was swallowed in a green-gray opacity as dense as the sea. Across the shiny black pavement, a shimmering rectangle I knew to be the restaurant. A nanosecond, then thunder boomed.

Aided by the penlight's powerful little beam, I searched the coat's breast pocket. Seeing zip, I slid a hand inside. Felt nothing.

I moved on to the back-to-back right hip pockets. The one on the outside held only lint and small particles of what might have been gravel or coarse sand. The one on the inside was totally empty.

I shifted to the left pair. Spotted zilch in the outer

pocket, was probing its counterpart when, deep down, the bright little oval cast an odd shadow. Peering closer, I detected an irregularity in the base of the pocket, a rip roughly two inches long. In the blackness beyond, a pale flash caught in the beam.

As I stared, the rooftop stampede dropped in intensity. I glanced around. The world was reemerging. Get my burger and fries and head home? Turn the coat over to Slidell for an official police examination?

No way. The wild lightning had nothing on the adrenaline jolting my nerves. I needed to know if something had wriggled through that torn seam.

Barely breathing, I inserted and gently seesawed a finger. Eventually, the gap was large enough to shine my light through.

Three items winked white, caught in the rough fibers of the lining. Using a thumb and a fingertip, I teased them free and laid them on the damp gabardine.

Paper scraps, one wadded, two folded together.

Ever so gingerly, I opened and inspected each.

Slidell finally phoned at ten fifty-five. Before he could launch into his tirade, I described what I'd discovered on one of the folded papers. And during my subsequent cyber-looping. He listened, anger grudgingly yielding to curiosity.

"You're sure it's BRES?"

"Yes. And I found info online. Brown and Root Energy Services. There wasn't much, but one site reported that following the *Estonia* sinking, the official divers hired to work the ferry were employed by Rockwater. Rockwater is a subsidiary of BRES. The divers had to sign lifetime contracts requiring secrecy about what they did at the wreckage."

"That don't—"

"According to more than one site, Rockwater wasn't the low bidder for the job."

"Meaning maybe the fix was in."

"If it's true. And if it is, who knows the significance? If any."

"But this interested your guy, Vodyanov." A pause as Slidell considered the ramifications. "So what's this other mojo?"

"MKUltra was written below the acronym BRES."

"Sounds like some kinda candyass detox swill."

"It's an abbreviation of a code name for a CIA mind-control program." I knew this because of my many years working in Montreal. The hush-hush dirty secret of McGill University and the Royal Victoria Hospital still cropped up in occasional conversations.

"Gimme a break."

"Under Project MKUltra, experiments were done on human subjects in order to develop more effective interrogation and torture techniques."

"We're talking volunteers, right?"

"Unwitting U.S. and Canadian citizens."

"Go on." All levity had vanished from Slidell's tone.

"The CIA sought to manipulate the mental state of subjects by secretly administering drugs and other chemicals, especially LSD. They also used hypnosis, sensory deprivation, isolation, verbal and sexual abuse, and various forms of torture. Have you seen the TV show *Stranger Things*?"

"No. Why?"

"Never mind."

"We're talking ancient history, right?"

"The program began in the early 1950s, was officially halted in 1973."

"You're shitting me."

I summarized what I'd learned, using notes I'd taken from various websites.

"MKUltra was organized through the Scientific Intelligence Division of the CIA and coordinated with the Special Operations Division of the U.S. Army's Chemical Corps. The program consisted of some one hundred forty-nine subprojects that the CIA contracted out to universities, research foundations, hospitals, prisons, pharmaceutical companies, places like that."

I struggled a moment to decipher my own writing.

"Research was done at eighty institutions, including forty-four colleges and universities. One hundred eighty-five private researchers participated." Cherry-picking facts. "The program operated using front organizations, although top officials at some institutions were aware of the CIA's involvement."

"Wait. Slow down. You're saying the government was into mind control?"

"I'm not saying. According to the U.S. Supreme Court, the program was tasked with, and I quote, 'the research and development of chemical, biological, and radiological materials capable of employment in clandestine operations to control human behavior.' Unquote."

"That's messed up."

"Not to mention illegal. Reasons the program was finally shut down."

"So why was Vodyanov poking at that?"

Having no response, I briefed Slidell on my visit with Asia Barrow.

"Barrow thinks your vic was a spy?" Not the harangue I expected for going solo to Mooresville.

"Yes."

Buoyed by Slidell's uncharacteristically calm demeanor, I described my visit to Vodyanov's apartment and outlined my conversation with Ramos. I'd already explained the coat with the booty in the lining.

"So this landlady says your vic told someone he'd soon be dead. And that he was terrified the government was trying to put him down?"

"Yes."

Empty air while we both chewed on that.

"What's on the other scraps?" Slidell spoke first.

"One's a crumpled paper that's very thin and badly crinkled. There are black markings, but if that's ink, it's too faded and smudged to make anything out."

"Another job for Mittie Peppers."

"Good idea. The third appears to be a list of codes or shorthand. Mostly letters and numbers."

"Like JCOLE1013."

"Yes." And no.

"Any idea what they mean?"

"None."

A moment as we both contemplated the same grim possibility. Other kids? Neither of us voiced the thought.

I hesitated, unsure. Decided to chance it, now that I was certain the man had been real. "Can I get your take on something?"

Silence, not encouraging, not discouraging.

I told Slidell about the trench-coated prowler on the grounds at Sharon Hall.

"You're convinced it was your faceless vic, Vody-anov." More statement than question.

"I am."

"That he was watching you."

"We know he dialed my mobile the week before he died."

"Or someone with access to his phone."

"Yes."

"I'll get the scraps and shoot them up to QD first thing Monday. In the meantime, buy some shoes, hit the spa, do lunch with the girls."

"Meaning?"

"Don't go rogue-ass cowboy on me over the weekend."

I hated the thought of losing so much time. And I hated Slidell acting bossy and paternal. But the long day had my mind moving like sludge, and disparate thoughts were now taking forever to connect. An oncoming migraine? I focused on focusing. Nope. No rogue-ass blood misbehaving in my brain. Or eyes. My vision was crystal-clear.

"Spas are good," I said, noncommittal.

After disconnecting, I trudged upstairs and dropped into bed.

The last sound to register was the mantel clock announcing midnight with twelve soft bongs.

*   *   *

I popped awake at five fifteen. The annex was dark and still. Birdie was gone.

I knew I'd been dreaming, but no memories lingered. Only the unsettling sense that somewhere out there, someone was watching me. A feeling so intense I got up and crossed to the window.

The grounds of Sharon Hall were silent and empty. No crouching silhouettes, no unfamiliar shapes. Just multilayered shadows, shifting now and then in a light breeze.

Paranoia again? A nightmare hangover?

I returned to bed and forced myself to relax, muscle group by muscle group. Did one of those counting mantras in my head. Punched the pillow, turned it to the smooth side, turned it back again. Kicked free the covers and sheets. Thought about dolphins. Sea turtles. Willed sleep to come.

Images of Vodyanov kept playing on the backs of my tightly closed lids. Faceless at Buffalo Creek. Cold and lifeless on a gurney in the morgue. Trench-coated at my home.

Vodyanov had been at Sharon Hall. I was convinced of it now. The prowler wasn't a nocturnal illusion generated by my migraine-stressed neurons.

When the window started going translucent, I gave up. The clock said 6:10.

I shrugged into shorts and a tee, pulled my hair into a pony, and laced on my Nikes. Right out the door, I knew running was a bad idea.

Contrary to my expectations, the storm had been

powerless in breaking the grip of the heat. Just past dawn, and the porch thermometer was already registering 84°F. Due to the rain, the air felt hothouse muggy.

Forty minutes of pushing, then I returned to the annex, exhausted, flushed, and sweaty. After a long shower, I made coffee and cinnamon toast and settled at the table. The exercise helped some, but I still felt restless and tense. I considered turning on CNN as a distraction. Decided talking heads debating the mess in Washington were the last thing I needed.

As I ate, my eyes landed on the clothing I'd dumped by the sink. On the cutting board on which I'd spread the scraps to dry.

Would squinting at paper qualify as rogue-ass cowboying? What the hell. I had nothing else to do.

I got up, washed buttery crumbs from my hands, and carried the board to the table. Then I retrieved a hand magnifier from the guest room/study, the penlight from my purse.

First, I checked both sides of the BRES/MKUltra note. Saw no other writing. No telltale hint suggesting the provenience of the scrap. Looked like part of a blank page torn from a notebook.

Next, I skimmed the codes. RABUK19-smear-3. DALIHP2580. UATNOM1793.

I wondered. Was that Vodyanov's MO? Jot cryptic reminders, clear to himself but obscure to others? Code for the location of a vehicle? A missing child? A secret government operation?

Had Vodyanov shoved the reminders into the coat pocket, planning to discard them later? Had the scraps worked their way through the torn seam and become lost? Was he unaware of their fate? Had he simply forgotten them?

I snapped a few pics with my iPhone. The screen went black, seconds later came back on. I checked to see if the images had been properly saved. Found they hadn't. Cursing, I repeated the exercise. This time, the shots were there. Definitely time for a visit to the Apple Store.

I was pouring more coffee, the last thing I needed, when Birdie strolled into the kitchen. An appraising glance, then he padded to me and began loop-rubbing my ankles. I filled his dish and returned to the table.

Though still creased and faded, and now stuck to the board, the third scrap had improved somewhat overnight. The paper was much thinner than the BRES or code scraps, almost translucent. But the black marks now looked ordered, the patterning intentional. Like printing.

I flicked the button on the penlight, picked up and maneuvered the magnifier. The black smudges and dots sharpened.

"Yes!" Shouted with such feeling that Birdie coiled for action.

The scrap appeared to be part of a delivery receipt. The smudges and dots were definitely ink, perhaps made by carbon paper. Under magnification, they organized into a blurry address and a partial name. The last letters of the name were *ov*.

Securing the light in position with a folded place mat, I grabbed a pen. Then I raised and lowered the lens, scribbling digits and letters as they came into focus.

In less than five minutes, I had a few versions, depending on my take on one letter and one digit. Obvious fact. The address was not that of the Charlotte building owned by Ms. Ramos.

But I was familiar with the zip code.

Excited fingers clumsy on the keyboard, I entered my first interpretation into Google Earth. Got an error message suggesting I try again.

I did. Twice.

On my third attempt, Mother Earth rotated, and the screen zoomed in. I switched to street view. Saw a rural two-lane. Woodland. A property enclosed by chain-link fencing.

Pay dirt.

14

I'm lousy with auditory cues—names, verbal instructions, lyrics. But give me a visual—a map, a crime scene, a face, a photo—and my mind logs data with uncanny precision.

I recognized the layout right away. The rural highways with spurs shooting into farms and cul-de-sacs. The shoulder-straggling homes and mom-and-pop businesses.

When given the correct address, Google Earth had swooped me to a view of heavily wooded acreage enclosed in chain-link fencing. By zooming in, I could see a driveway leading from the blacktop, via a gate, to a clearing surrounding a humpy rock formation. Not far from the hump, a small, ramshackle building. I remembered my reaction upon first stumbling across the property. Why bother with a fence?

I was rolling by eight. Didn't bother phoning Slidell. It was Saturday morning. My nerves weren't up to one of his harangues. Besides, this was strictly a scouting mission.

I followed the same route Slidell had taken. West out of Charlotte, a dip below the border, then back up to Cleveland County, North Carolina.

This time, my navigation system wove me through a tangle of meandering side roads off NC-198. Not far from Art's Affordable Garage and Buffalo Creek. Not close to anything but the occasional frog, deer, or squirrel. Feral hog?

An hour and a half after I left the annex, the trusty Waze lady directed me onto an unmarked road. Minutes later, she announced my arrival. I did a slow drive-by, scanning the setup. Saw pretty much what I'd observed during my cyber-recon: trees, a short driveway, a whole lot of twelve-foot fencing, the galvanized steel darkened by weather and time. And one additional tidbit. A keypad beside the gate that looked shiny new.

Two passes, roughly half a mile in each direction, revealed absolutely no signage. To either side stretched impenetrable conifer, oak, and beech, their massive branches reaching high to form sun-choking canopies overhead.

The road seemed abandoned by time, save for one shack and two mobile homes on the side opposite the chain linking. The windows of the shack were covered with plywood, the walls with spray-painted graffiti, all pictorial, none skilled.

The owners of the mobile home to the south were also long gone. All glass was broken, and the door was missing. Tangled kudzu wrapped the trailer's every inch like a leafy green quilt.

The mobile home to the north told a different story.

The exterior was white with brown striping. The siding and windows appeared recently washed. A wooden ramp enclosed by banisters and picket rails led, through one right-angle turn, to a do-it-yourself wooden stoop at the trailer's side door. A red awning jutted from its rear. Below the awning, two molded-plastic chairs and a small table, all Crayola yellow.

Noting the possibility of neighbors, I returned to the fenced property, pulled into the drive, and got out. And felt I'd stepped into the Amazon basin.

I held a moment, listening. The forest was eerily mute. No whining locusts or chirping birds. No creaking branches or shifting leaves. It seemed every living thing was burrowed in, trying to stay cool.

I glanced up. The sun, still low, sizzled behind a gauzy smear of morning haze. The old adage popped into my brain. Mad dogs and Englishmen. No argument here. I wouldn't be lingering outside long.

The gate was roughly five yards from the road. I walked to it, aware of the gritty crunch of my sneakers on the gravel. Of the possibility I was being observed. Of wilderness in every direction. Of feral hogs.

A security camera mounted high on a metal beam kept vigil like an unblinking alien eye. I saw no buzzer or intercom box, nothing to allow communication with what lay beyond.

I held absolutely still, straining for a hint of human activity. Heard no generator, sprinkler, or mower. No slamming door. No dialogue floating from a radio or TV. No voice ordering me to halt.

If people were back there, they were damn quiet.

I looked up again. The camera stared down. Though

it appeared relatively new, I couldn't tell if the system was functioning or not.

I scanned my surroundings. Noted no utility or phone lines. No mailbox. No address marker. On the gate, a sign saying *Private Property Keep Out*. A spiffy fresh keypad.

Beyond the gate, the driveway tunneled through hardwoods and pines for about thirty feet, then a jungle of leaves, branches, and kudzu choked off the view. I spotted no tire tracks or oil stains in the gravel. No trash cans. No dog poop or litter. Just vegetation so dense it seemed to soak up every pixel of daylight. My frustration came out as a heartfelt curse.

Stepping from the gravel, I moved north through the scrub bordering the shoulder. Insects billowed from the weeds in frenzied clouds, making me regret my decision to forgo socks.

I caught no glimpse of anything among or beyond the dark trunks and shadows. The fence, though weathered, was well maintained. Beams similar to the one at the gate rose at regular intervals along its inside perimeter. Twenty feet tall, they held nothing. Rectangular discolorations on the outside of the chain linking beneath each beam suggested the possibility of missing signs. Now I was getting somewhere.

A sortie south yielded the same picture. And more bites.

Back in the car, waiting for the AC to kick in, I scratched and debated my next move. A casual internet search of the address had yielded no links. My visit to it had proven spectacularly unproductive. Not sure what I'd expected. A mailbox marked *F. Vodyanov, KGB*?

I was itchy and irritable. My shirt was damp and stuck to my back. Still, before declaring the trip a bust, I decided on one last effort.

It seemed I was expected. Or the occupant had been tracking my moves.

As I shifted into park, the trailer door opened and a man hop-stepped onto the stoop. The stump of a thigh projected from one leg of his grubby camo shorts. A faded red tee hung loose on his rib-shadowed chest. A blue bandanna covered dreads perhaps not rewoven since Da Nang.

Dreads watched me climb from my car, eyes unreadable. The sheathed knife on his belt sent a more obvious message.

"Good morning." I smiled my warmest smile.

Dreads nodded, a barely perceptible angling of his chin. Which grazed his ZZ Top beard across the dog tags hanging from his neck.

"I'm Temperance Brennan." In case he cared about names.

The only sound was an undulating hum coming from inside the trailer. I guessed an oscillating fan.

"Hot enough to grill steaks on the blacktop." *Jesus, Brennan.*

No hint of a smile.

"I'm curious about your neighbors." Jabbing a thumb over one shoulder.

Dreads continued to appraise me.

"A man died not far from here a little while back. I'm trying to determine who he was."

"Why?"

"I'm helping the medical examiner." Sensing that mention of the police might be a deal breaker. "I wonder if you know the owner of the property across the road."

Dreads didn't move for a full thirty seconds. From where I stood, I could see his tongue doing something with his front teeth.

"We have reason to believe—"

"I knew someone would show up one day." Accent definitely not local. New York?

Before I could ask his meaning, Dreads gripped the banister with hands missing four digits and a thumb, collectively. A palm-foot maneuver brought him swinging down the ramp.

"Name's Duncan Keesing." Nodding toward the Crayola grouping. "Park it there."

I did. Keesing followed, hopping like a pogo, then tossed a flip phone onto the table, dropped, and scooched his chair to face me.

"You're not here to beef me about the cat?"

"No." Surprised. Keesing didn't strike me as the Mr. Whiskers type.

"VA gimme a prosthetic. Hurts like a bitch."

"I'm sorry."

"Say you got a nameless stiff?" Keesing's face remained immobile behind the beard, but his eyes roved curiously over me. Odd, russet eyes.

"That's correct."

Keesing tapped the dog tags on his chest with an intact middle finger. The nail was long and yellow, with a black crescent cap. "The day I buy it, the cops'll know exactly who's gone down."

"That's very clever."

"In Nam, your unit had to leave your sorry carcass, they kicked these little beauties into your teeth."

"Yes." Not sure that was true.

"It's the only reason I keep a phone." Tapping the device. Which looked like it was manufactured in the eighties. But probably worked better than mine. "Got no one to call me. But I get to feeling poorly, I can SOS."

"I hope that never happens."

"Keep my number right there on the lid. It's ten digits now. That's a lot to remember."

"Smart." It was handwritten in Sharpie. I wondered, didn't ask, why he might need to call his own line.

"You think your dead guy's the nutjob from over yonder?" Chin-cock toward the fenced acreage.

As had become my routine, I pulled the composite sketch of Vodyanov from my purse and held it up.

"Yes, ma'am." Keesing nodded. "That's the fella."

"His full name is Felix Vodyanov. Can you tell me anything about him?" Slapping a mosquito that was lunching on my arm.

"No, ma'am."

"Did you two ever speak?"

"We chewed the fat now and again." Studying the sketch. "Vodyanov, eh? Sounds right. I called him Igor."

"Why?"

"He talked like a Russki."

"You never asked his last name?"

"No need to know."

"Have you visited the property across the road?"

"Negatory."

"Do you know why it's protected by security cameras?"

"Negatory."

"How long have you lived here?"

"Going on twelve years."

"Why did you refer to Vodyanov as a nutjob?"

"The guy was fucked up, pardon my French."

"Can you be more specific?" One of the dead mosquito's pals was circling my ear. I waved it away.

"Hell, I don't know. Maybe my words was harsh. We've all got our demons."

I gave Keesing silence, hoping he'd feel compelled to fill it. He did.

"The guy would drop by, usually at night, like he had nowhere else to go or didn't want to be alone. Not often, just now and again. Guess he'd see my light burning, figure an old hermit gimp was safe territory."

Keesing dropped his gaze, perhaps reliving the horror of his injury. Perhaps his path to a solo life in a trailer at the back end of nowhere.

"Go on," I encouraged.

"Sometimes he'd talk a blue streak, all wound up and shaking. Sometimes he'd sit and brood. For a while, I thought he might be a drinker. Never smelled a drop. I got a condition. Might be he had one, too. Made him unsteady."

"Vodyanov exhibited mood swings?"

"That's it." Pointing what remained of an index finger. "He'd either be flying high or draggin' ass."

"When chatty, what did he say?"

"Bunch of twaddle." Slowly wagging his head.

"Such as?" Exasperated. The bugs and oppressive heat and humidity were getting to me.

Keesing's shoulders hunched, and his good leg began dancing a jig.

"I'm sorry," I said, more gently. "Please take your time."

Keesing pressed both damaged hands to the jittering knee. "He claimed the government was into bad doings. Said he had proof."

I felt my pulse accelerate but didn't push.

"He said the CIA had secret labs all over the country. That they was trying to figure ways to control people's minds, to get them to crack under pressure. Ask me, they should've squeezed the Vietcong on that when they had the chance."

A long mosquito moment. Annoyingly, Keesing seemed OK with being used as a food source.

"Did Vodyanov ever discuss specifics?" I asked.

"Mostly, he'd ramble. Could be the guy was a junkie." The stub of finger rose again. "But wait. Once he named names. Most I didn't catch, but a couple stuck, 'cause of my having been to those places. Philadelphia and Montauk. Yep, those I remember. And there was one sounded like some kinda sci-fi movie." Pause. "Stargate. That was it."

"Did he ever mention MKUltra?" With absolutely no inflection.

"Sounds right. Once he was all on about the government creating a disease to wipe out the Chinese. Something about mixing measles and mumps to create a superbug."

"SARS?" I used the acronym for severe acute

respiratory syndrome. A deadly outbreak hit China and the Far East in 2003. Beyond that, I knew little.

"Bingo. He said it smacked the Chinese and Canadians, but—here was the thing boiled his nads—the U.S. had very few cases and no fatalities."

Why would Vodyanov be privy to information about the SARS epidemic? I made a mental note to do some digging.

"Another occasion, he was in a dither about the government hiding secret military bases. Places that lit up bright on some kind of maps. Didn't seem likely to me, what with my experience serving." Lowering both his head and his voice, Keesing added, "The dude also had intel on ops involving kids."

"What intel?" Little tingle at the base of my skull.

"I was never clear on that, didn't want to listen. Something about vaccines and holding kids in special camps to train 'em up for something. Maybe sex." Repulsion sneaking into the rust-colored irises. "Sounded devo, so I tuned out."

"Did he say—"

Keesing stopped me with a raised palm. "No, ma'am. Don't want to talk none about hurting kids."

I decided to switch topics.

"Was Vodyanov living across the road?"

"Hell if I know. Truth be told, I wished he'd just leave me alone."

"Why?"

"He was nuts."

"When did you usually see Mr. Vodyanov?"

"At night."

"He drove?"

"Roger that."

"What type vehicle?"

"Lots of different ones."

"A black Hyundai Sonata?"

Shoulder shrug. "Maybe. I don't know much about cars."

"Did you ever see anyone else entering or leaving the property?"

"Look, lady. I'm no snoop and no snitch. I mind my own p's and q's. Mostly, I'd half listen. Not sure why. I guess I felt for the guy. He seemed kind of lonely."

"When was the last time you saw Vodyanov?"

"Two, maybe three weeks ago. Came to tell me he was sorry. I figured he was referring to how he'd deep-sixed the signs along this stretch of the road. Hell, I was good with it. Makes it hard for folks to find us out here." He seemed about to continue, caught himself, and fell silent.

"What is it you're not saying?"

"It's probably nothing." Keesing scratched his neck. Crossed his arms. "The guy was section eight all the way."

I raised both brows in question.

"A loony tune."

My eyes drifted past Keesing to the far side of his trailer. Fell on a barrel with a picture of a crab in an aquarium painted on one side. Pink shells at the base of each claw. Or maybe they were eyes. Between the charring and the flaking, it was hard to know.

"Did you do the art?"

"Yes, ma'am."

"Very nice."

A renegade puff of wind shifted the leaves overhead, throwing spiderweb shadows across Keesing's face. When I thought he'd shut down for good, he spoke, voice again low.

"Your mentioning the barrel does bring to mind one thing. One night, maybe five, six years back, I was out securing the lid against the damn coons. I'd forgotten to do it, had to haul ass back outta bed. If the seal's not tight, come morning, there's trash from here to tomorrow. Anyways, it was late. A car passed. Don't get much traffic this way, so I took note. The car turned into the driveway yonder, idled while the driver leaned out to open the gate."

"Was it Vodyanov?"

"It was pitch-black, so I'm catching mostly taillights and headlights." Keesing swallowed. Swallowed again. "But I swear to God I seen a kid peering out the rear window. A small little face with a tiny hand to either side."

Keesing pantomimed the vision, then dropped his hands and closed his eyes as if feeling pain. Guilt?

I waited.

"I been to hell and back. I know fear when I see it." The russet eyes locked onto mine. "That kid looked terrified."

"Are you sure?" I asked.

"Lady, I ain't sure of nothing 'cept death. But I stand by one thing."

Keesing leaned back and ran a mangled hand down his beard.

"That dude was crazy as a bag of rats."

15

With the conversation still fresh in my mind, I dictated notes onto my phone, then headed out. I was wending toward NC-198 when the lyrics of Les Cowboys Fringants exploded from my mobile.

"*Monsieur le detective*," I answered, sounding more chipper than I felt.

"*Madame . . . l'anthropol—*" A hissing echo garbled Ryan's customary response.

"What's up?" Shocked at how glad I was to hear his voice. It hadn't been that long since we'd spoken.

"Bordeaux this morn— . . ."

"Any luck with the horse?"

"Neville remains AWOL. But I . . . wee garcon who . . ."

"This connection sucks," I said.

"Want me to . . . back?"

"Not sure it would do any good. I'm driving through the boonies. And my phone is circling the drain."

"Sounds like you're . . . iving through Uzbekistan."

"I might as well be."

". . . out so early on a Satur . . . ?"

"I can barely hear you." Braking for a squirrel kamikaze-ing across the pavement. "I'll explain later. For now, may I ask a favor?"

"*Bien sûr, ma chou . . .*"

"I want to know about Project MKUltra."

"The LSD experi . . . McGill?" Static and distance blurred whatever surprise Ryan's tone might have carried.

"Yes."

"I know . . . done at the Allan Memorial Institute . . . Royal Victoria Hospital . . . funded by the CIA and the Canadian government . . ."

Ryan's voice cut out abruptly, and a high metallic buzz took over the line.

"This is hopeless," I said. "I'll be back on the grid soon. Ring me when you have something?"

"I'll need . . ."

A crackling screech. Then the line went dead.

I was crossing the patio when Les Cowboys crooned again. The thermometer now read 101°F.

"Good timing. I just hit the annex. Hold on."

En route home, I'd stopped at my neighborhood Harris Teeter. Balancing my provisions on one knee, I fished out my key, opened the door, and stepped into the kitchen. Air thirty degrees cooler puckered my skin.

"Is the birdcat happy to see you?" Ryan asked.

"No sign of him." Placing the bags on the counter. "He hates hot weather."

"He never goes outside."

"I've explained that to him."

"Got some info for you." Ryan didn't ask my reason for wanting it. I like that about him. "MKUltra was a nasty piece of work."

I poured water from a Brita pitcher in the fridge. My personal crusade. I refuse to contribute to the 50 million plastic bottles discarded in the U.S. daily.

"The Montreal portion of the program, dubbed MKUltra subproject 68, was run by a Scottish-born doctor named Donald Ewen Cameron. The experiments were called mind-control studies. To my thinking, it was torture disguised as medical research."

I finished drinking and began moving around the room, stowing produce in bins, cans in cabinets.

"I was a kid when this all came out," Ryan continued. "The media latched on to the LSD angle, but apparently barbiturates and amphetamines were also in the mix. Patients were subjected to prolonged periods of sensory deprivation and induced sleep. Cameron believed in what he called repatterning and remothering the human mind."

"What the flip does that mean?"

"Cameron thought mental illness resulted from learning incorrect ways of responding to the world. That these learned responses created brain pathways that led to repetitive abnormal behaviors. And of course, Mommy was to blame. I'm not a psychologist, but it sounds like a load of crap to me."

"At best." Finger-hooking my tee away from my chest. Thanks to the glorious AC, the damp cotton felt like cold, wet tissue pasted to my skin.

"Electroshock was used to depattern a patient. Not

the usual three times weekly but twice daily. This was supposed to break all incorrect neural pathways caused by poor mothering."

"Sounds like brainwashing." I began to shiver. Maybe the cold. Maybe not.

"Indeed."

I clicked to speaker, set down the phone, and peeled the damp shirt up and over my head. In the effort, I must have let out a grunt.

"What are you doing?"

"My top was sweaty, so I took it off."

"Can you shoot me a selfie?"

"No."

"Your bra must also be wet."

"How did this so-called treatment work?"

"Is it that little black lacy number?"

"Ryan." Faux stern. "Jesus, we're talking about torture."

"Right. To prepare for depatterning, a patient was put into a state of drug-induced sleep, usually for a period of ten days. After that, the electroshock therapy lasted for about two weeks. Some patients also required more extreme forms of sensory deprivation."

"Jesus."

"Cameron wanted his subjects to lose all sense of space and time, of feeling. If they couldn't walk or feed themselves, or became incontinent, that was acceptable."

I was too revolted to speak.

"After depatterning came the process of psychic driving, or repatterning. Patients were forced to listen to recorded messages, some positive, some negative, about their life or personality. Get this. The messages could be repeated up to half a million times."

"Sounds barbaric."

"That's being kind."

Appalled silence hummed across the Atlantic. Then Ryan resumed.

"The McGill experiments were part of the larger MKUltra project led by Sidney Gottlieb."

"Gottlieb was CIA?" Stowing dried pasta and corn flakes on a pantry shelf.

"Yes. In 1963, the CIA compiled its findings into a manual called the *KUBARK Counterintelligence Interrogation Manual*. It came to define the agency's interrogation methods and training programs."

"A torture manual." Ignoring a subtle *Pssst* from my id.

"Yes."

"You've seen it?"

"It's readily available. Let me read you one passage from the instructions given to CIA interrogators: 'Results produced only after weeks or months of imprisonment in an ordinary cell can be duplicated in hours or days in a cell which has no light, which is soundproofed, in which odors are eliminated, et cetera.'"

"Sounds like something out of *A Clockwork Orange*."

"Except we're talking recent history. Following 9/11, Bush's secretary of defense, Donald Rumsfeld, approved the use of isolation facilities for up to thirty days."

"The celebrated War on Terror." Detergent went under the sink.

"Still cold?" Ryan asked.

"A little. But it beats the inferno outside."

"Are your nipples—"

"I've made progress with the faceless man." Settling at the table.

"Lay it on me."

I summarized my outing to Cleveland County with Slidell. The code leading to the Hyundai at Art's Affordable Garage. The duffel in the trunk. The notebook with its references to the *Estonia* disaster. The confrontation and subsequent outraged call from Margot Heavner. Skipping the reference to Jahaan Cole, I explained the indented printing and Mittie Peppers's recovery of the phone numbers, one of them mine. I shared my recollection of the man at Sharon Hall the night of my migraine nightmare, my suspicion that he'd been the faceless man, and my belief that he'd called me shortly before his death.

Ryan was so quiet I feared we'd been disconnected.

"You still there?"

"I'm listening."

I told him about Lizzie Griesser's phenotype composite. About Dr. Yuriev at Sparkling Waters. About my conversations with E. Desai, Asia Barrow, Ms. Ramos, and Duncan Keesing. That, based on the sketch, all four had ID'd the faceless man as Felix Vodyanov, one of the names in the Hyundai notebook. I described the antiseptic apartment and the strangely secure property in Cleveland County.

By the time I finished, thirty minutes had passed.

Ryan took time digesting what I'd said. Then, "I assume Slidell ran this guy Vodyanov through the system."

"Reluctantly. He found zip."

"Really? Nothing at all?"

"Nada. I tried several internet search engines. Same result."

"Vodyanov talked at the ashram about the sinking of the *Estonia*."

"To Asia Barrow. She's convinced he was a spy."

"Because . . . ?"

"In her opinion, he had way too much inside information."

"The landlady thought Vodyanov was terrified."

"Ms. Ramos. She said he feared the government was trying to kill him."

"The neighbor believed he was crazy."

"Duncan Keesing. I suspect he suffers from PTSD."

"Keesing said Vodyanov discussed MKUltra?"

"Among other things. I've got notes that I'll look into when we hang up."

"After you change undies."

"You're perverted."

"You love it."

I pictured eyes blue enough to laser your skin. I did love it. But right then, I wanted to keep Ryan focused.

"Have you been in contact with Slidell recently?" I asked.

"No. Why?"

"When I first asked for his help, he acted all Skinny. Now he seems to be coming on board."

"Wanting to stick it to Heavner?"

"Partly."

"You need to brief her on what you've found."

"I will. Anyway, Slidell's newfound zeal doesn't stem solely from his distaste for Heavner."

"Oh?"

"A nine-year-old girl named Jahaan Cole vanished here in Charlotte in 2013. Slidell worked the case but never got a solve. You know how that irks him."

"I'm not sure 'irk' is a strong enough verb."

"Right. Anyway, along with the two phone numbers, the QD analysis revealed a third line of indented writing. A coded reference to Cole."

I felt the familiar clench in my gut when he asked, "You're sure?"

"We think so."

"Slidell suspects Vodyanov could be involved in the kid's disappearance?"

"He's reopened the file."

"Based on a one-line scribble." No one does neutral like Ryan.

"Slidell doesn't know yet, but there may be more. Keesing said Vodyanov told him about experiments involving kids."

"What kind of experiments?"

"He said he refused to listen."

"He also said Vodyanov was nuts."

"He did. But this is what really disturbs me. Keesing said he witnessed a car entering the fenced property late one night. A child's face was pressed to the rear window. Keesing said the kid looked terrified."

"It's not much."

"Asia Barrow said she once let Vodyanov use her laptop."

"Isn't that forbid—"

"Yes. But she did it anyway. Afterward, the browser history indicated visits to two kinds of sites. Those reporting missing kids and those featuring child porn."

"You're thinking Vodyanov was a pedophile?"

"I'm not sure what I'm thinking."

"It's worth looking into." Brief hesitation. "Assuming you're feeling up to it."

"Don't go there, Ryan. I'll outlive you."

After showering and pulling on a dry tee and shorts, I quickly ate a ham sandwich, got my Mac, and climbed to the new study. The exposed wires reminded me about my truant workers. I phoned the electrician. No answer. Of course not. I left a message. Same routine with the painter.

Then it was a laptop afternoon.

First, I wrote a long email to Margot Heavner outlining all I'd done and explaining that the faceless man was Felix Vodyanov. Kept it cordial and professional. Exaggerated just a titch Slidell's role in my undertakings.

Then I began with the other terms Keesing had mentioned. And learned the following.

The Philadelphia Experiment was an alleged military test carried out by the U.S. Navy at the Philadelphia Naval Shipyard in 1943. The destroyer escort USS *Eldridge* (DE-173) was supposedly rendered invisible, or "cloaked to enemy devices." The Navy maintains that no such experiment ever took place, and the story is generally considered a hoax.

The Montauk Project was an alleged series of secret U.S. government programs conducted at Camp Hero or Montauk Air Force Station at Montauk, Long Island. The purpose of the research was to develop psychological warfare techniques, including time travel.

The Star Gate Project was the code name for a secret U.S. Army unit established in 1978 at Fort Meade, Maryland, by the DIA, the Defense Intelligence Agency, and a California contractor named SRI International. In 1991, Star Gate and its precursor and sister projects were consolidated and renamed the Stargate Project. Research focused primarily on the potential for psychic phenomena in military and domestic applications—on remote viewing, the ability to see events and sites or to acquire information from great distances. The Stargate Project was terminated and declassified in 1995 after a CIA report concluded that its findings were never useful in any intelligence operation. Though never cited, the Stargate Project inspired the 2004 book and 2009 film *The Men Who Stare at Goats.*

After researching the Philadelphia, Montauk, and Stargate programs, I probed a bit deeper into MKUltra. As I typed, and looped, and read, particles of a theory started to swirl in my brain.

Using a keyword modifier, I tried the term *vaccine*, then SARS.

The particles began to congeal.

I tried the same modifier paired with *Estonia*.

By the time I logged off, my screen was a rectangle of light in a room gone dark.

The theory was fully formed.

16

The idea ricocheted inside my skull like a puck in a rink.

Mind going ninety, I checked more angles. Then, braced for a tirade, I phoned Slidell. Was shocked when he actually picked up.

"I see you're living the life on a Saturday night." Beating Skinny to his own nongreeting game.

"And you're not out tripping the light fantastic, being as you're burning up my phone right now."

"I'm working."

"I'll send your name up for a commendation. Oh, wait. You're not a cop."

"Do you have a minute?"

"Me and Verlene are catching a flick. Some horse-shit about two people hate each other but fall in love with email." Muffled sound, as though the phone were pressed to his chest. Then he was back. "This better be good."

"Have you made any progress on Jahaan Cole?"

"You called to ask me that?"

Taking his response as a negative, "While you've been tied up with the Cole file, I talked to some folks."

"Didn't I tell you to—"

Poking right into the bubble of bluster, I laid down a variation of the briefing I'd given Ryan. Barrow. Ramos. The puzzling fenced acreage minutes from Art's Affordable Garage and the creek where Vodyanov's body was found.

"I went back out there today."

"What? Where?"

"Cleveland County. Scoped out the property, then talked to a neighbor."

"You just got into your car and—"

"Duncan Keesing. A war-damaged Vietnam vet living in a trailer just up the road."

The change in Slidell's breathing cued me to his level of ire.

"A bit odd, but you'd like the guy."

"Son of a freaking bitch!" A hair below outrage.

"Here's why I'm calling. Vodyanov's life coach at the ashram thought he was a spy. He told his landlady the government was out to get him. I doubt it was either."

"What the hell are you talking about?"

"No cloak-and-dagger. No fatwa. Vodyanov was into conspiracy theories."

"Conspiracy theories." Patronizing.

"The stuff's all over the internet. The sinking of the *Estonia* was intentional. Vaccination causes autism. Fluoridated water is a pinko plot. Governments are implanting citizens with RFID chips. The earth is flat. The QAnon nutballs believe in a deep state that's working to undermine the president. There's a world of cockamamie crap out there."

"You're saying this mondo beyondo bullshit is what got your boy killed?"

"I'm not sure anything actually got him killed. Have you talked to Margot Heavner?"

"Don't plan to."

"I wrote an email explaining the Vodyanov ID on the faceless man. Haven't heard back. So we still don't know the official cause of death."

I waited out a pause that felt like a month, certain Slidell would wet-blanket my theory big-time. He didn't.

"Vodyanov looked at child porn and visited sites listing missing kids. Wrote Jahaan Cole's name in his notebook. Drove a scared kid through his gate in the middle of the night."

Slidell has many faults. He's uncouth, judgmental, and short-tempered. But when focused, his mind chews through data like a buzz saw through pine. His summation nailed it.

"So this shitbird was a perv," he went on. "Don't suppose you know who owns that property?"

"No."

Slidell digested that for a few seconds. Then, more to himself than to me, "No judge will issue a warrant based on hearsay."

"We could—" I started.

"There's no 'we.'" Snapped. "You will sit tight while I do some digging."

I rolled my eyes. Pointless, since Slidell couldn't see me.

"I'm serious. If this guy's dirty for Cole, maybe others, I want this done by the book."

"May I continue with my computer?" Chilly.

"Nothing else until you hear back from me. Comprendo?"

"Perhaps if you speak with a bit more condescension," I said.

Dead air.

It's a sick feeling being an exile, unable to go home.

The phone rang again at eight. I was stepping from the shower, reeking of fake citron and ginger. Bathing twice in one day? Not for cleanliness or hygiene. Churning with anxiety, agitation, and frustration, every nerve in my body was going berserk. I thought drugstore herbals and hot water might reboot the system.

Eager to answer, hoping Slidell had gotten a name from some tax roll or deed registration, I skidded and nearly ass-planted on the tile.

It was Mama. She and Sinitch had argued, and her mood wasn't cheery.

"The man refuses to take a position on anything."

"Don't you two have a pact to never discuss politics?" One-handed wrapping my hair in a towel.

"I'm talking about our nuptials. Venue? Theme? Lord in heaven, he won't even weigh in on a destination. Doesn't he grasp that a wedding takes months of planning?"

I was with Sinitch on this one. Didn't say it.

"You sound out of breath, sweet pea. Are you OK?"

"Mama, stop."

"You need to be mindful—"

"The doctor said I may have had this aneurysm from birth. It's unerupted and now packed with tiny platinum coils."

"I'm just—"

"Mama. My arteries are not conspiring to drown me in my own blood."

"So why the headaches?"

"We will figure that out. How about we discuss your chemo? How are *you* feeling?"

Exasperated sniff. "What are you doing?"

"I just finished showering." And just started the day's second seminude phone conversation.

"Would you prefer to call me back? It's nothing that can't wait." Meaning I want to talk now.

"Sure, Mama."

Fifteen minutes later, dried and lotioned, I dialed. She picked up instantly.

"Feeling reborn?"

"Definitely."

"This heat is absolutely beastly." Ice clinked against glass. "I hope you're not leaving your nice cool house."

"Mmm."

"Did you use that lovely Chantecaille energizing cream I gave you for Christmas?"

"Yes. Thanks again." I had no idea what I'd slapped on. "So what's the issue with the wedding?"

"Oh, that. It's nothing. Sinitch is a man, and they do have their ways."

The past quarter hour had obviously involved Southern Comfort.

"And we girls have ours." She laughed, a lilting chirp,

like a kite lifting on a sudden breeze. "Tomorrow I'm preparing an Italian feast for him."

Mama isn't a good cook. When Harry and I were kids, she'd hit the stove now and then. Her sauce always tasted like bright red nothing, her salads like wilted green nothing. But we loved when she tried. It meant she was in a sunny place, as she called her good days. Or that her meds were properly balanced, and she was taking them.

"Good food, fine wine, a little postprandial mischief. He'll be eating out of my hand."

"Try not to kill him."

"Sweet Lord in heaven. Do you think it's too much—"

"I'm joking. He'll be fine."

More swirling ice. The sound of swallowing. Then, low and conspiratorial, "Has anything happened with your faceless man?"

"We have an ID." Sudden thought. "Listen, Mama. I have an internet question."

"*Ma spécialité!*" Too much enthusiasm. Or whiskey.

"I've tried to track an individual and come up blank. Zero on social media, no email address, nothing via the usual search engines. How would you go about finding a person with absolutely no footprint?"

"Do you know anything about him?"

"I have reason to believe he's a conspiracy theorist."

"Like your archenemy."

"Sorry?" She'd lost me.

"The dreadful woman who did the interview with that huckster, Nick Body."

"Right." I'd managed to push Heavner to far background.

"Try the deep web." When I said nothing. "You've heard of it, I assume?"

"Hasn't everyone?" Not that I thought so at all.

"Many hear, few visit."

I knew that the deep web was favored by privacy advocates and whistle-blowers like Edward Snowden and Julian Assange. That it was used to collect information hidden from common users. That Asia Barrow had been disgusted by it. Beyond that, I was clueless.

"Can you be more specific?" I asked.

"The deep web, deep net, invisible web, dark web— it goes by many names—contains World Wide Web content that's hidden and can't be accessed by commonly known search engines. It's crawling with vermin like Body."

"How extensive is it?"

"I've read estimates that as much as ninety-six percent of the content of the WWW is buried in the deep web. Claims that the deep web is five hundred times larger than the surface web."

"You're saying that only four percent of WWW content is visible and accessible via common search engines?"

"I'm not. Others are."

"How does one get to it?"

"You need a specialized deep web browser, such as the Onion Router."

"TOR." There. I knew something.

"Yes. TOR works by redirecting internet traffic through a network of thousands of relays. TOR got its name from the term *onion routing*, which refers to layers of encryption, kind of like the layers of an onion. Isn't that simply too droll?"

"I'm not sure I understand."

"TOR encrypts a user's original data together with the destination IP address and sends the request through a virtual circuit of successive, randomly selected TOR relays."

When I said nothing.

"Picture the relay points as being along big loops. Each successive relay decodes a layer of coding in the original, which is then revealed only to the next relay in the circuit."

"Scrambling and unscrambling so the user's location and IP address remain anonymous."

"There are other deep net browsers. I2P, Freenet. But I prefer TOR."

"You've used it?" My almost octogenarian mother never ceases to surprise me.

"Of course." Amused by my surprise.

"It's more difficult to access the really deep, nasty stuff. That requires knowledge of the URL, usually a password."

A voice called out in the background. Male.

"Hold on." Followed by the same muffled hollowness I'd heard with Slidell. Then, "Showtime, sweet pea."

"I thought your ambush was planned for tomorrow."

"Dress rehearsal. Or should I say undress." With a warm molasses undercurrent I refused to consider.

"Thanks, Mama."

She was right. A few minutes at the keyboard scored the following facts.

The deep web holds 7,500 terabytes of content, compared to 19 terabytes for the surface web, and has more than 200,000 sites. The deep web contains 550 billion documents compared to 1 billion for the surface web, between 400 and 550 times more public information. Ninety-five percent of the deep web is publicly accessible, meaning no fees or subscriptions.

Googling the term *TOR* brought me to a site offering a free download. With some trepidation, I hit the purple tab. The browser was mine in seconds. I connected, tested my network settings, was cleared. The keywords *conspiracy theory* produced a screen listing links, some familiar, most not.

I spent hours swinging from one site to the next. The level of idiocy was astounding.

There was the usual hackneyed rubbish. A lone gunman didn't kill JFK. Paul McCartney really died in 1966. The moon landing was an elaborate hoax, every photo shot in a studio on earth. The 1947 crash in Area 51 near Roswell, New Mexico, involved an alien-operated UFO.

My personal favorite, from a British sportscaster, asserted that anyone holding a position of power was actually a bloodthirsty, extraterrestrial, shape-shifting reptile. A+ for creativity.

Eventually, I stumbled across a reference to Nick Body. Lacking a better idea, I went to his website Body Language and listened to several of his archived podcasts. Hell, I'd already paid the fee.

In one, Body asserted that the FDA and big pharma

were conspiring to keep people sick by withholding cures discovered via their research. In another, he claimed that the accident that killed Princess Diana was a set up by British intelligence acting on behalf of the royal family. In another, he argued that the concept of global warming is based on science distorted for ideological or financial reasons.

In another, he suggested that many of the alleged survivors of mass shootings are actually paid "crisis actors." Such may have been the case, he implied, at the Pulse nightclub in Orlando, the Mandalay Bay Resort and Casino in Las Vegas, the Marjory Stoneman Douglas High School in Parkland, the Santa Fe High School in Santa Fe, the Tree of Life synagogue outside Pittsburgh, and the Borderline Bar and Grill in Thousand Oaks.

I recognized the obscure reference made by Duncan Keesing in an almost unintelligible harangue inspired by Strava, a mobile fitness app used by cyclists and runners to keep track of the distances, speeds, and routes they travel. Several years back, it was discovered that Strava's global heat map feature had inadvertently revealed the location of secret military bases throughout the United States. Body was incensed that the government would conceal the existence of such facilities from those living nearby.

In a particularly revolting diatribe, Body insisted that the Holocaust never happened. That there was no anti-Jewish government policy. That no gas chambers were used. That those killed numbered far fewer than the historically accepted figure of 5 to 6 million.

Listening to Body's voice rasp like sand through

mesh, I tried to imagine the level of gullibility required to buy into the viciousness he was spewing into the world. To understand the mystique of his popularity. The appeal was clearly not his insight or intellect.

I hopscotched through additional podcasts, choosing topics randomly, listening to snippets.

Big oil. The industry was keeping prices high while holding back massive reserves to create the illusion of scarcity.

9/11. The towers couldn't have come down due to impact and jet fuel alone. The U.S. government had assisted with the attack.

Directed-energy weapons. The devastating fires in California in 2018 were started by government lasers.

On and on. Zionists, shadow governments, Freemasons, Illuminati. Each time a different enemy but always one unifying theme. Some person or entity was out to hurt the little guy. Or to take over everything.

Returning to the home page, I chose the link to Body's "General Store." Five "aisles": Survival Gear, Wellness and Health, Security, Educational Media, and Support Our Efforts. I tried Survival Gear. Inventory included storage containers designed to outlast a nuclear winter, water-filtration equipment, countless types of radios, flashlights, dual-panel portable solar LED lanterns, packaged foods, and myriad other items, most of which were available at Home Depot or Amazon.

Body's Educational Media comprised the expected array of antivaccination, antifluoride, anti-climate-change, and antiliberal conspiracy books and DVDs.

Not surprisingly, his own podcasts were available for purchase on CD or as MP3 files.

The Wellness and Health offerings included an assortment of organic herbs, plants, powders, and oils promising far more than they could deliver. The Security aisle listed gadgets guaranteed to make you and your home safe, others that allowed you to spy on others. Knowing it was a money grab, I skipped the final option.

Next, I cruised through Body's blogs. Found more of the same themes.

Disgusted, I was about to log off when I noticed an obscure reference to a URL such as those Mama had mentioned. Within the long string of letters, numbers, and symbols was the word *DeepUnder*. The domain suffix was *.onion*.

I clicked on the link. The site took time to load. The home page had a banner saying *DeepUnder* and a background image of an inverted cone, like a dormant volcano tipped upside down. Centered in the cone was a blinking rectangle demanding a password.

Crap.

I tried *conspiracy*, *Body*, and the usual variations, frontward, backward, and so on. *Body Language*, featured words, and phrases from Body's podcasts and blogs. *Roswell, Area 51, vaccine, global warming, 9/11*, dozens of terms Body had used in his diatribes.

The rectangle blinked on.

Holocaust. Zionists. Strava. Pharma. Twin Towers. Nope.

I was typing in *Moon Landing* when the lights flickered, died, then cut back on. A glance at my phone told me it was going on midnight. Conceding that I had a zillion-to-one shot of lucking onto the password, I gave up and went to bed.

I lay in the dark, conspiracy theories sliding through my overwrought brain. Eventually, I drifted off. Woke two hours later, damp with sweat and tangled in my sheets.

Failure chews at me. When blocked, I can't rest. Can't let it go. I've always been wired this way. When young, I was the ultimate high achiever, the one who had to earn the highest grades, attend the best university, swim the fastest times, win the most tennis matches. Nature? Nurture? Because I was the firstborn?

Though I rarely allow myself to pick at the memory, I know, deep down, that my brother Kevin's death had an enormous impact on the formation of my psyche. Watching, helpless, as the tiny toddler whom I loved so dearly weakened, then died. Witnessing the crushing pain felt by my parents. Suffering the breakdown of my once happy family. I have no doubt that this tragic turning point in my eight-year-old world left scars that still drive me today. Especially with regard to missing and murdered children. I've been there. I know the agony caused by the loss of a child. Sometimes on a conscious level, sometimes less so, that knowledge is the motivator behind my battering-ram doggedness.

I rose, made mint tea, returned to the new study, and tapped the keyboard. My laptop fired to life. The rectangle still taunted.

Frustrated, and lacking a better idea, I tried terms that had interested Vodyanov, apparently another conspiracy theorist. *MKUltra. Montauk. Philadelphia. Stargate. Estonia.*

I tried the address written on the crumpled scrap from the trench coat pocket. The address of Ms. Ramos's building. Felt ridiculous. Those had to do solely with Vodyanov. Not relevant.

The only lights in the room were my screen and its reflection in the window behind me. I tried to think like a conspiracy theorist. Experienced no epiphany.

I glanced at my mobile. Recalled my conversations with Ryan and Slidell. My recent internet search.

Blinding synapse. A folded paper with hand-printed codes.

Holy shit? Could that be it? Might Vodyanov have frequented DeepUnder?

I scrolled through my phone's newly stored images.

Typed "UATNOM1793."

Nope.

"DALIHP2580."

No joy.

My mind played games with the letters. Could UATNOM be Montauk backward and truncated? DALIHP Philadelphia? That made sense.

I tried RABUK1963, a shortened version of the name of the infamous CIA manual along with the date of its publication.

No go.

I focused on the numerals. Instantly recognized the patterning. The pair of complete four-digit sequences were two of the most common passwords in use: 1793, counterclockwise on a digital phone pad, using the corners; 2580, straight down the middle. Another frequently employed combo crisscrosses the keyboard, grabbing the corners.

I tried RABUK1973.

The rectangle disappeared. The page darkened and zoomed, creating the illusion of being sucked down a swirling vortex. For a moment, I felt disoriented.

Deep breath.

I entered a black hole in which belief in treachery, collusion, and deceit was the connective tissue for those who came.

17

The name *DeepUnder* topped the home page in fiery red against a black banner.

Beneath that, in large block letters:

WELCOME! BE OPEN! BE ENLIGHTENED! BE CAUTIOUS!!!

Following that enthusiastic but somewhat menacing greeting, a paragraph explained the purpose of the site.

> *You are one of us. You have come because you seek the truth. We are here to provide it.*
>
> *When governance fails—the politicians, judges, educators, and religious leaders—it is the duty of individual citizens to protect themselves and their families. Knowledge is the key to survival.*

This site provides a format for truth to be shared. Truth about the government, academics, scientists, journalists, corporations, the military, the elite. Truth about collusion and greed. About those who would destroy our health, our country, our way of life. About those who seek to keep the complicity and duplicity from us.

Herein all is revealed and freely discussed. But be warned. The reality exposed herein is truly terrifying.

—The Architects of DeepUnder

"Those are most desirous of honor and glory who cry out the loudest of its abuse and the vanity of the world."

Spinoza? Was the quote a clue into the mind-set of those responsible for the site? Or did the creators simply like the ring of the words?

A series of seven tabs ran along the right margin of the page. "The External Menace." "The Internal Menace." "The Menace Above." "The Menace Below." "The Watchdogs." "The Enemies." "Photos and Archives."

I clicked through the first four options. Each opened a submenu listing further choices.

The first tab linked to conspiracy theories involving the takeover of the U.S. by outside forces. The second linked to theories involving homegrown plots. The third linked to theories about powerful people manipulating events for personal gain. The fourth linked to theories about the destruction of the social order by an uprising of the lower class.

Returning to "The Internal Menace," I chose *Sandy Hook* and found a bulleted list of selections, including two chat rooms. Blocked from the first, I gained entrance to the second.

In 2012, before killing himself, Adam Lanza fatally shot his mother, then murdered twenty children and six staff at the Sandy Hook Elementary School in Newtown, Connecticut. The heartbreaking massacre received wide media coverage.

I found revolting dialogue questioning the authenticity of the incident. In one thread, discussants agreed that the bloodbath had been orchestrated by the U.S. government as part of a plot to promote stricter gun-control laws. In another, those posting were convinced that the incident was "fake news." That the shooting never took place.

I sat in the dark, aware of my breathing, my fingers on the keys, my eyes on the screen. I wanted to slam down the lid and walk away. Instead, I returned to the home page and tried the tab labeled "The Watchdogs." As expected, I was directed to a page listing conspiracy theorists.

Some were strangers. Some I knew. Gary Allen. David V. Icke, the genius behind the shape-shifting lizard-people myth. Alex E. Jones. Jim Marrs.

I tried a few. Each led to a bio page containing links to publications, interviews, photos, and, in some cases, media appearances.

John Robison was an eighteenth-century researcher of secret societies. Steven M. Greer was a ufologist, self-proclaimed contactee, and founder of the Disclosure and Orion Projects. Jim Marrs, an expert on JFK conspiracy theories, loved appearing as a talking head.

Nick Body was second on the alphabetized list. I clicked on his name. A box materialized, stating that the link had been deleted.

I thought about that. How had Body managed to block access to information about himself? No one knew where he lived or the location at which he recorded his podcasts. How did he so effectively remain deep background?

Why such secrecy? Was he manipulating his audience by creating an aura of mystery? Concerned for his personal safety?

The clock said 3:20. My tea was cold, and my neck was stiff.

I felt like I'd spent hours feeling my way through a pitch-black cave, stumbling down steep inclines, around blind corners, through twisting passages and narrow openings. Each time I was about to quit, the home page with its unexplored tabs drew me back.

Final one. Then off to bed.

I placed the cursor on "Photos and Archives" and encountered many unsurprising offerings. The motorcade, the grassy knoll, the book repository. Planes arrowing through a clear blue sky toward two tall buildings. Mummified remains of three-fingered aliens. Bigfoot. Atlantis. Ancient astronauts.

Others were grimmer. Leaked autopsy photos of Anna Nicole Smith, Marilyn Monroe, Tupac Shakur, Elvis Presley. Survivors of the Hiroshima and Nagasaki bombings. Victims of Ebola, Mad Cow, SARS, AIDS.

There were diagrams of bomb shelters, flight plans, underground complexes, bullet-trajectory simulations. Maps showed the projected fallout of nuclear radiation, the spread of smallpox and plague, the dissemination rate of ricin in lakes and streams.

I viewed photo displays from conferences denying global warming, affirming extraterrestrial life and UFOs, promoting New Age philosophies, questioning various celebrity deaths. Other reasons to gather and exchange wisdom included government poisoning of baby products and the creation of the H1N1 flu, as well as the existence of slave camps on Mars.

The convention photos were interchangeable. Speakers at lecterns, diners at tables, people standing or seated, drinks in hand, smiling at the camera. Or not. The occasional subject was identified; most weren't. Many seemed normal. Some looked totally bonkerballs. I recognized a few faces from my romp through "The Watchdogs."

As I was about to log off, mind numb with fatigue, my eyes roved over three images filling the screen.

One picture showed a middle-aged man behind a podium, wispy white hair poorly concealing a shiny pink scalp, glasses the size of bagels. Above his left shoulder, a portion of a banner—*ference on MKUltra and Mind Control 2010.*

The second was a group shot following what may have been a panel presentation. Three men, one woman, all with plastic-encased badges pinned to their chests. I recognized no one.

The third was a candid of maybe twenty people, closely packed and oblivious to the camera. The angle wasn't great, catching mostly profiles and the backs of heads. It looked like an image captured by a mobile phone or camera held high with no attempt at framing.

The men were in off-the-rack suits, the lone woman in a Walmart Women's Plus red dress and fake pearls. A party or reception of some sort.

Farthest from the lens, detached from the crowd, three men stood, visible from the shoulders up. They were deep in conversation, heads tilted, unaware of their part in an iPhone or Kodak moment. Two of the faces were caught full frontal, making me wonder if one of them had been the focus of the photographer's interest. The third stood obliquely, features hidden.

The man on the left was the tallest of the three. Probably mid-forties, he wore military-style glasses and had wavy brown hair side-parted and combed back from his face. A text box had been inserted into the picture below his chin. It said *Yates Timmer*.

The man turned away was short and stocky, with thick black hair that spilled over his collar. A text box gave his name as Nick Body.

Holy shit. There he was, looking younger than in any of the more recent photos I'd seen.

I shifted to the third man in the trio. And lurched forward in my seat.

It was Felix Vodyanov.

A june bug beat against the screen. I pictured it, small and bronze in the moonlight. I'd listened to it for hours, crawling up, falling away, returning with a buzzing *clunk*. Trying over and over to do what? Weren't june bugs supposed to be gone after sunset?

Had it been a single insect? Or had I heard a succession, struggling, failing, being replaced?

The digits on the clock said 8:05. The window showed a montage of greens below a hazy sky.

The beetle was gone.

Had it been real? Or had I dreamed it as a metaphor for my frustration?

It's a sick feeling being an exile, unable to go home.

But at last, I had a lead. A maybe lead.

Totally pumped from what I'd seen online, I considered driving to Slidell's home. It was Sunday morning again. I doubted he'd answer a call from me.

Instead, I snatched my mobile from the nightstand, went to the privacy settings, and switched off caller ID. Then I dialed Slidell. The ploy worked.

"I got this number on every Do Not Call list on the planet. You're now blocked. I'm a cop. I hear from you again, you're going to the can. Share my sentiments with the skeevy-ass outfit that's paying you."

"It's me," I said. "Do not hang up."

Slidell sucked a quick breath. I shut him down.

"Felix Vodyanov knows Nick Body."

"What in the name of sweet Christ are you talking about?"

"I found a picture of them together in 2010."

"The internet wingnut and the dead perv?"

"Yes."

"Where?"

"At a conference on mind control."

"You said Body don't like paparazzi." Dubious.

I told Slidell about the dark web and the Deep-Under site.

"Apparently, someone spotted Body in the crowd. Maybe an admirer, maybe an opportunist hoping to score with the shot. Who knows? I recognized Vodyanov from the composite sketch."

"You're sure it was him?"

"Yes. So the two know each other."

"The link being this conspiracy shit?"

"Vodyanov was into it. Conspiracy theories are Body's lifeblood."

Slidell did the thing he does in his throat.

"They were with a third man identified as Yates Timmer."

"What kinda pussy-ass name is Y—"

"Can you run him? See if anything pops?"

"I'm just heading out to work something."

"A lead on Jahaan Cole?"

"No. I'm looking into maybe D. B. Cooper's buried under Panthers Stadium."

I said nothing.

Long-suffering sigh. Then, "An old woman living near the Cole home called the tip line saying a car circled the block twice around two a.m. the night before the kid went missing. Apparently, the old biddy don't sleep so well. Anyway, her call slipped through the cracks."

"Slipped through the cracks?"

"There's no ref to a follow-up, no interview report. I did some digging. Turns out Granny was eighty-three back then. Shortly after that, her kids parked her in an old folks' home."

"Assisted living." With an appropriate note of reproach.

"Whatever. We're going to have a little chat."

"Have you spoken to her?"

"No. Could be her circuits are scrambled."

Could be hers are sharper than yours. I didn't say it.

"You'll look into Yates Timmer as soon as you're back?"

"Sure. In the meantime, I'm certain you'll have at him on the Weird Wide Web."

I did. As soon as I'd brewed coffee and fed the cat.

I needed no deep-net browser to find Yates Timmer. No password. Links to his website popped up with good old Google.

Timmer was a Realtor with properties to sell. Not ranch homes in Modesto or condos in Fort Wayne.

As I clicked through listings, my jaw literally dropped.

18

Timmer's business was called Homes at the End of the World, LLP. The home page was set up much like that of DeepUnder. Tabs across the top offered four options: "About Me," "Contact Me," "Properties for Sale," "Property Video Tours."

Below the tabs: "I specialize in the Acquisition & Sale of Missile Bases & Underground Structures."

Under that startling statement was a pair of before-and-after aerial shots. On the left, looking militaristically stark, was a Nike missile base built in 1954, decommissioned in 1965. On the right was the same property in 2014, now lushly landscaped with hedge-lined walks, driveway, and pond. A flat, concrete-roofed hill could be seen just breaching the surface at the center of an expanse of unrelentingly green grass.

Beneath the two pictures, a sales pitch.

The properties I represent give new meaning to the word hardscape. *HARD ESCAPE!*

Underground bunkers. Hidden missile silos. Buried command centers. These subterranean strongholds provide the ultimate in safety and privacy. They assure solitude and security in violent and troubling times. Once converted, such complexes are ports in any storm, be it actual war or simply the frenzy of 21st century life. Far from the beaten path, and safe from calamity, they are truly Homes at the End of the World.

Designed by the Department of Defense and constructed with enough reinforced steel and impenetrable concrete to survive a nuclear attack, underground missile bases and silos are some of the strongest buildings in existence. Such structures redefine the words bomb shelter.

And what an investment opportunity! Given climate change and today's highly volatile political situation, both domestically and internationally, these prized and very limited properties are rapidly appreciating in value. Act now, and I can make one yours!

Selecting the tab labeled "About Me" produced a picture of Yates Timmer. Same military-style glasses. But the wavy hair was thinner, the dress more casual than at the mind-control conference eight years earlier. Wearing jeans, a safari bush jacket, and boots, Timmer stood with arms crossed, legs spread, in a tubular tunnel with walls of corrugated steel. Behind him, rocket-shaped coach lights flanked a studded steel door.

A brief bio described Timmer as a retired Army engineer specializing in the niche market of underground military structures. His background included the exploration of nearly one hundred sites and the sale of more than forty properties.

Timmer was described as an expert at converting subterranean complexes into residences, having spent twenty years transforming a missile base into a home he called World's End House.

I clicked on the worldsendhouse.com link.

And found myself looking at the "after" photo featured on the page I'd just left. And an overview of the property's grim history.

World's End House began life in 1954 as part of the Nike Ajax project, a surface-to-air defense system (SAM) developed by the Army Air Defense Command (ARADCOM). Eventually, the Ajax was replaced by the improved Hercules missile, and Nike Ajax bases became Hercules sites. A gradual decrease in Nike deployment began in 1967, and by 1975, with the SALT II Treaty, ARADCOM itself was deactivated.

World's End House is now a twenty-seven-acre estate located forty miles south of Manhattan, Kansas. The missiles are long gone, and the structure has been converted into a home in which Yates Timmer has lived since 1998. Tours are available, and World's End House can be rented for special events.

I took the video tour.

Timmer narrated as the camera moved up and down dizzyingly steep steel stairs, across massive open spaces, past rusty metal entities about whose function I hadn't a clue, eventually into rooms with cheap

paintings, factory-made Oriental carpets, and brightly
colored Rooms To Go furnishings striving to be cheer-
ful within miles of windowless concrete.

Living room, bedroom, institutional-sized kitchen.
As he passed through, Timmer explained the original
function of each. Missile magazine. Personnel safety
room. Mechanical room. Storage area.

After twenty minutes, Timmer reentered the outside world, exiting through a one-foot-thick entry blast
door. Behind him, the camera caught the small mountain of earth now concealing the Cold War relic that
was his home. The lawns and walkways. The perimeter
fence.

The video shifted to a montage of abandoned bases
similar to World's End House. Nike. Titan I and II. Atlas
E and F. Communication bunkers. As the footage moved
from one listing to the next, Timmer spooled through
a sales pitch, touting the desirability of underground
living, discreetly concealing prices and locations.

Some properties were wooded, some barren. Some
had been landscaped; others remained as they'd been
when mothballed by the DOD. But a configuration of
common features linked them all.

A synapse fired red-hot in my brain.

Dots connected. A vision of real estate emerged.

Not waiting for Timmer's closing remarks, I dialed
the number on the screen.

A recorded voice confirmed that I'd reached Homes
at the End of the World, apologized for being unavailable,
and requested that I leave my name and number. I did.

Throwing on sneakers, jeans, and a tee, I grabbed
a long-sleeved shirt and headed out.

*   *   *

Images kaleidoscoped as I made my way back to Cleveland County. The Google Earth bird's-eye view of the acreage down the road from Duncan Keesing. The mound at its center. The security camera and keypad. The overkill fence.

Questions rode with the images. Some old, some new.

Was the site an abandoned military base? The apartment in Ramos's building appeared to have been used solely for storage. Perhaps as a safehouse. Was a converted silo or bunker Vodyanov's actual home? Why?

Keesing said he'd occupied his trailer for twelve years. Was he aware of the history of the neighboring land? If so, why didn't he tell me?

Vodyanov knew Yates Timmer. Had Timmer arranged for him to use the property? Who was listed as the owner with the register of deeds?

Nick Body knew Yates Timmer. Where Body lived and worked were closely guarded secrets. Might the place be Body's home? His studio? Might he record his outrageous podcasts there?

Vodyanov had known Body for at least eight years. The MKUltra conference had taken place in 2010. Both knew Timmer. All three were interested in conspiracy theories. Was that their connection? Or did the link go beyond that?

And. For the zillionth time. How had Felix Vodyanov ended up dead on Buffalo Creek?

And how the hell was I going to get through the gate?

*   *   *

Arriving at the fenced property, I backed into the drive and parked with the front bumper facing the road. Slipping the shirt on over my tee, I climbed out of the car.

Undeterred by Friday's storm, the heat had rolled its sleeves up and committed to a personal best. A record-breaking 105°F was predicted for the afternoon high.

I stood with arms out, in full view of the camera, sweat glands already clocking in. As before, no one questioned my presence.

The gate proved easy. It wasn't fully latched.

A little pressure with one hand, and it swung inward.

Careless? Overconfident? Either way, the behavior was consistent. Vodyanov had kept copious notes and carried them on his person and in his car. He'd left the keys to the Hyundai on the front tire. Acts that showed neither a concern with nor an aptitude for tight security or clever concealment.

Based on the Google Earth capture, I estimated the distance to the clearing at roughly fifty yards, the earthen mound another twenty beyond that.

Before proceeding, I paused to text Slidell. The message failed to send. Either lack of signal or juice in my phone.

Turn around?

Not a chance. My curiosity was like a force field driving me forward.

Keeping my mobile in hand, I started up the drive.

The thick mesh of leaves and branches blocked all

sunlight, lowering the temperature and creating an atmosphere of perpetual dusk. Though far from cool, my skin prickled.

Again, the forest seemed ominously still. No locust whined in the foliage. No creature stirred in the underbrush. No bird took flight overhead.

I spotted no tread mark in the gravel, no rut in the narrow strip of dirt skimming each edge. Nothing to indicate the passage of a vehicle.

In minutes, the driveway ended in an odd hexagon hosting only some very optimistic grass and brush. Where the brush thinned, I could see gravel, here and there a straight ribbon of gray that was probably an old walkway or drive. Off to the left, the remains of a shed, one wall barely upright and leaning precariously, the other three collapsed into a jumble of rusted tin and weathered boards. At the far end of the hexagon, the strange-looking rise.

I paused, recalling Affordable Art and his Remington. The clearing offered zero cover. If someone was present and armed, I'd be an easy target.

I checked my watch. 1:45 p.m.

"Hello!"

Nothing.

"Is anyone there?"

More nothing.

I stepped from the trees. The sudden onslaught of sun caused me to squint.

The closer I got, the more detail I could make out. The mound was shaped like an enormous flat-topped Quonset hut. Though an overlay of soil softened its outer contour, an angular hardscape was evident beneath. My archaeologist's eye said the thing was definitely not the work of Mother Nature. Additional clues were the steel girders surrounding its perimeter. And the camouflage netting stretched across them, the type used by the military in woodland settings.

I had no doubt the mound was man-made. Or the purpose of the camo. Someone wanted the structure and any vehicles parked beside it hidden from aerial view. The ploy had worked. On Google Earth, the setup had appeared as an unremarkable rise in elevation.

I was struck by the same somber thought I'd had at Ms. Ramos's building. If this really was Vodyanov's place of residence, he wouldn't be here. He was lying on a gurney in the MCME morgue. Heavner's morgue.

Blood pumping, I crossed the last few yards and stepped under the netting. The near-blackness forced my constricted pupils into a rapid about-face.

"Anyone home?"

No response.

I crept forward, using the flashlight app on my phone. Stopping every few yards to listen. To shout.

Slowly, my vision adjusted. I made out a wall some distance ahead. In the wall, a dark rectangular outline, maybe a door.

As I moved, objects leaped from the gloom in the glow from my screen. A backhoe, a front-loader, other machinery that might have been meant for farming or construction. A bent bicycle wheel. Stacked metal bins. Dumpsters. Each article threw an elongated shadow version of itself before dissolving back into darkness.

In less than a minute, I reached the wall. The

rectangle was a blast door similar to the one in World's End House.

I illuminated the concrete in small sections. Saw no handle or latch, no buzzer or bell, no camera. Knocking was futile. I knew from the Timmer video that the door was a freaking foot thick.

"Crap!" Swallowed by the suffocating heat and darkness trapped under the camo.

I felt stymied. What had I expected? A little glass box with a cake saying *Eat Me* spelled out with currants?

I spent a pointless moment chastising myself for "wild-goosing," as Slidell would say. Myself took issue, arguing that the trip hadn't been futile. The nature of the property was now clear.

Suddenly, I tensed.

Pressing the phone to my chest, I went totally still.

Ten seconds. Thirty? Had I imagined the sound?

Then I heard it again.

Dear God in heaven!

I wasn't alone.

19

Someone was there!

Something?

Skritch. Skritch.

Reflexively, my free hand flew to my mouth.

The noise stopped abruptly.

The renewed silence was worse. Unseen eyes were watching. Ears listening.

I stood in the darkness, heart banging, mobile mashed to my shirt.

Run? Try resending the text? Maybe here I'd pick up a signal from inside the bunker?

Yes. Reverse order.

I tapped the screen. Felt crosshairs on my back. My illuminated face.

Still no go.

I was cursing again when a shadow detached from the closest dumpster, a cigar-shaped object clamped in its jaws.

An image sparked in my brain. Glistening teeth. A bloody goose head.

A nanosecond, then relief. No gun-wielding psycho had me in his sights. But what? The creature seemed too low to the ground to be a dog. Too large to be a rat. And the Macanudo?

I shone the phone toward the dumpster.

The raccoon froze. Banded eyes wide, it gave a juddery chirp, then scurry-dashed for the safety of the outside world.

The limbic buzz almost caused me to laugh. Almost.

In his panic to haul ass, Groucho had dropped his prize. It lay in the dirt, fuzzy and ill defined. Curious, I walked over for a closer look.

The coon hadn't been enjoying a fine Cuban. Of course it hadn't. It had been rummaging for food. I bent and lifted its discarded booty.

Two bone fragments lay in my palm, their combined length approximately six inches. Each had one end terminating in jagged spikes, the other in a clean-edged break.

Gripping the phone with my teeth, I raised the fragments into the light. Both showed areas of charring, suggesting burning. The splintered end of each was scored and punctured, suggesting scavenging. No way to know which had come first.

The borders of the clean-edged break were pale and unstained, suggesting that trauma was recent. I tried fitting the two pieces together. They aligned nicely. I was holding a mid-shaft section of long bone, its only surviving anatomical feature a sliver of articular surface rimming one AWOL joint. The sliver's wavy texture told me the limb had still been growing when its owner had died.

A grim thought sent a rush of gooseflesh up my arms.

The bone's small size and cross-sectional shape were consistent with those of an immature human tibia.

My mind was fighting that horrifying possibility when my eyes caught a hint of red embedded in a crack running from one shattered extremity. Blood?

Drawing the fragments closer to the phone, I made out a tiny shred of fabric patterned with flowers or dots. Paws?

Had the coon been lunching on the remains of a child? Was I looking at a scrap of teddy bear PJs or superhero briefs?

Mouth dry, fingers sweaty slick, I laid down the bones, switched to camera mode, and took several shots, flash strobing bright in the murky gloom. That done, I slipped the fragments into my shirt pocket and stepped to the dumpster into which the coon had been diving.

Groucho hadn't been messing around. Or, more accurately, he had. Garbage spread out in every direction, strewn like wreckage after a cyclone.

Trash. The detective's best friend.

Up close, I could see that the dumpster was made of steel and green plastic, had wheels, and was accessed through a slanted front-loading lid. The lid was up. Another indication of carelessness. Or *Procyon* dexterity.

I leaned over to peer in. The stench blasted me like a sirocco, a blend of liquefaction, fermentation, rot, and microbes. Covering my mouth and nose, I lit the bin's interior.

Groucho's gang—the abundance of scatter suggested accomplices—had been selective. Left behind were nonedibles and articles too heavy to mine. A woven vinyl and metal chair. A globe with a broken base. A leather shoe. Light bulbs. Empty containers— Windex, Mr. Clean, Clorox, Gatorade. Cardboard boxes. Rags. Lengths of pipe. I snapped a few shots with my camera app and backed away.

Hoping for clues to the occupants or purpose of the bunker, I moved among the items littering the ground. Saw gnawed slices of pizza, pasta curling like ghostly white worms, ziplocks oozing unidentifiable sludge.

At the far end of the mess lay an eviscerated drawstring plastic bag, innards fanning out as a smaller debris field within the larger. Among the bag's displaced contents were foil packets, Styrofoam cups, cardboard baskets, and waxy wrappers from Taco Bell, Burger King, and Bojangles' dinners. Of more interest, a manila file, grease-stained and covered with putrefying beans, fries, bread, meat, and garnish.

I wove my way to the folder and, using a plastic knife, flipped back the cover. Inside were the mangled remains of newspaper clippings, most deteriorated to mushy clumps resembling flattened tofu. Breathing through my mouth, I teased out the only two intact enough to retain legible copy. Each had been cut from a larger page, leaving neither a date nor the name of the paper.

Centered in the first clipping was a head-and-shoulders color shot of a blond-haired, green-eyed boy. Gaps in his front dentition suggested an age of six or seven. The boy was looking straight at the camera, smiling stiffly, a potted palm at his back. I guessed it was a school portrait, first, maybe second grade.

Below the portrait ran the caption: *Timothy Horshauser, still missing after five yea* . . .What remained of the accompanying story was lost to a slurry of ketchup, mustard, and mayo.

The second surviving clipping had fared even worse. The coons and condiments had destroyed half of the picture and the entire article.

Still, I recognized the photo's subject. The caramel skin, the dreadlocks bound with bright pink beads.

Jahaan Cole.

Anger starts like a match flaring in my chest. Spreads like wildfire roaring through dry grass.

I felt the tiny hot flame.

Upper incisors vising onto my lower lip, I spread the file's soggy contents and took shot after shot, blind to my subject matter in the dark. The tunnel was bake-oven hot, the only sound the soft click of my phone. Outside, far beyond the camo, a muted whine, there then gone.

Suddenly, the low-battery warning filled my screen. Crap.

A few more pics, then I carefully regathered the whole slimy mess. Tucking the folder under one arm, I rose, hoping the clipped articles, along with the bone fragments, would be enough to justify a search warrant.

Exiting the camo elicited more pupil retrenchment.

I scanned while walking, hand-shielding my eyes. The clearing was empty, filled with the same silence echoing everywhere but inside my chest.

The sun had dropped and was now skimming the tree line. In the late-afternoon shadows, off to the right, I noticed a blackened cylinder rising to a height of roughly five feet. Its walls were constructed of horizontal steel bands with open slits between. A vegetation-free zone circled the base, a mix of gravel and cinders. I suspected the thing was a home incinerator. Somehow I'd missed it on my inward charge toward the bunker.

The source of the charred bone in my pocket?

I made the short detour. Two yards out, I smelled burnt paper, smoky wood, and melted plastic. Not pleasant but not as bad as the decaying organics I'd left behind.

The raccoons had also worked their magic here, but not with the same enthusiasm as at the dumpster. Or maybe it was a human hand, sloppy while emptying the ashy dregs.

Several blackened hunks lay helter-skelter, too twisted and distorted to identify. Not so a small duct-taped pouch. Though it was obscured by the shadows and covered with soot, I recognized the fabric. Not daisies or polka-dots. Rabbits doing handsprings and somersaults against a field of red.

I dropped to my knees, set the folder aside, and began thumbnailing the end of the tape. Badly heat-seared, the adhesive refused to budge. I gouged deeper, again and again, my perspiration falling as small dark blotches on the acrobatic bunnies.

No go. I kept digging, oblivious to the heat and carnivorous insects. To my surroundings.

Finally, a corner yielded. I tugged gently. Millimeter by millimeter, the sticky tape lifted, taking with it a fold-over flap that covered the pouch's upper border. I shone my light into the interior.

Two incisors and two molars lay along the bottom seam. The small size of the former and the bulbous cusps and slender, divergent roots of the latter told me the teeth had belonged to a child.

I stared, stunned that I'd found even more potentially incriminating material. Had I literally just stumbled across the very proof I needed to obtain a warrant? When does that ever happen?

I wanted to grab the pouch and rush to my car. Instead, I forced myself calm and ran a mental checklist of proper protocol.

Leaving the evidence in situ would be best but far too risky. I'd take the pouch with me. Before removal from the scene, I'd document its provenience. First with establishing shots—the bunker, the clearing, the incinerator. Then the pouch positioned to allow a close-up peek at the contents.

I glanced at my screen. The battery icon was alarmingly short and red. The digits said 3:20.

Hoping enough juice remained, I tapped the camera app and backtracked a few yards into the clearing. I was focusing the final shot when an elongated shadow swept across the frame. Human but distorted. Irrationally, my mind popped an image of the looming Easter Island statues.

I whirled. Saw nothing.

Had I imagined it?

My eyes swept a one-eighty across the trees, the gravelly brush, the fallen-down shed, the incinerator, the debris.

Damn!

I rushed forward, desperate to be wrong. I wasn't.

Disbelieving, I stared at the spot where I'd placed the folder. At the spot where I'd left the pouch. Neither was there.

I'd heard no car engine, no footsteps, no movement at all. How was it possible?

And who the hell would take them?

And why?

Mental cringe at the reaming I'd get from Slidell.

After a fruitless ten minutes searching the area, I aimed my phone for one final shot. It was dead.

Outta here.

I'd just passed through the gate when something hard whacked the back of my skull. I started to pivot, but a kick struck the small of my back. I fell. My phone dropped and slid across the gravel. A second kick struck my side, fast and vicious. Pain exploded in my ribs.

Gasping, taste of dirt in my mouth, vision afloat with black dots, I rolled to my back and looked up. A figure stood above me, a dark silhouette backlit by shafts of coppery orange sun. The silhouette was slender, about my height, a long, thin implement in its hands, a baseball cap on its head. I couldn't tell the gender of the wearer.

I struggled to rise. A foot mashed down on my chest.

"What the fuck are you doing here?" The voice

sounded wobbly, like wind passing through fan blades. That same tiny chime in my hindbrain. Had I heard it before?

Too freaked to be cautious, or disoriented by the blows, I snapped back, "Who the hell's asking?"

"None of your goddamn business." Slurry at the edges. Was the guy drunk? High?

"I'm here officially," I panted.

"You're a fucking liar."

Without thinking, I grabbed the ankle and wrenched sideways. Thrown off balance, Ball Cap hopped backward, arms pinwheeling. I scrambled to my feet and socked him with an elbow to the temple. He collapsed and lay still.

My eyes roved wildly. Saw no one else near.

Ball Cap lay facedown, features hidden from view. I noted cowboy boots, tan with a green floral overlay and turquoise studs, a maroon tee, maybe Gamecocks, faded jeans. A heavy-duty Maglite lay by the guy's right elbow.

No file. No place it could be hidden on his person.

Shit on a stick!

The tee had ridden up, exposing a strip of pale freckled skin. Vertebrae sharp as oyster shells. Bulges in both back pockets.

The pouch?

Frisk the bastard?

I felt fire in my ribs, a lump rising on my occipital.

Oh, yeah.

I inched close, snatched up the flash, and, alert to the faintest sign of returning consciousness, leaned down and dug the contents from the right jeans pocket.

Three keys, one for a Chevy, two probably for doors. The left pocket produced a faux-leather coin purse.

Still no moaning, no movement.

I pulled the purse's zipper tab. Inside was an impressive wad of cash, which I left in place. Folded around the bills, a note, which I opened.

> *You find this, you want to live, phone the number below. Now.*
> *I'm not fucking around.*
> *H. Kimrey*

The number had a 704 area code.

My impulse was to kick H. Kimrey in the nuts. To wake him and demand the folder and the pouch.

A more rational voice overrode the fury.

I stood a moment, watching the skinny chest rise and fall. The punk was breathing. Wary, I squatted to place a fingertip to his neck. Felt a pulsing carotid. Smelled boozy sweat.

Tossing down the Maglite, the keys, and the purse with its cash, I scooped up my mobile and stuffed the note in my pocket. A quick scurry-and-dart search of the surrounding trees and brush, then I dashed for my car.

20

En route home, I charged my iPhone and dialed Slidell. After explaining my day, and the attack by H. Kimrey, I suggested he call Sheriff Poston. Skinny's rhetoric was all I'd imagined.

When I arrived at the annex, the silver 4Runner was moored in the drive. Face crimson, Slidell launched himself from it and stormed toward me. His pants were brown, his socks orange. The ends of a green-and-rust tie hung to either side of his unbuttoned collar. I assumed he'd bumped up the couture for his visit with Jahaan Cole's neighbor.

"I don't believe it!" Practically spitting, he was so irate. "I don't freakin' believe it!"

"Is it enough for a warrant?" I *wheep-wheeped* my car.

"Jesus Christ! You're a defense lawyer's wet dream, you know that?"

"Thus, the need for a warrant," I said.

"You got some kind of hearing disorder? That why you don't capiche what I tell you?"

"Bring it down, detective. I don't want you having a coronary in my yard."

"Or maybe the problem's in your brain." Finger jabbing his temple. "Maybe you got some delusion you're a TV dick gonna get the big solve and a fucking medal from the mayor?"

I didn't acknowledge that Slidell might have a point. That he might have stumbled very close to the truth.

"And no worries about me! My ticker's a beast!"

I crossed the patio and let myself in. Slidell was right on my heels, smelling of temper and sweaty synthetics.

Over the years, I've come to recognize two things about Skinny. He can't stand being defied. He can't stand being bested. Today his anger was springing from twin wells.

"Would you like a cold drink?" Over my shoulder.

"Gimme everything. Now! Maybe, just maybe, I can talk some asswipe judge into overlooking the fact that what I'm writing up wasn't even close to lawfully acquired. As in hot-fingered by a civilian out for a joy ride! You going through some kind of mental thing? Even for you, your behavior lately has been plain nuts."

Another hard-earned insight. When Slidell does outrage, it's best to let him vent. I'd trolled through garbage, found evidence concerning missing kids, maybe the remains of one, lost most of that evidence, taken shots to my head and torso, and driven for almost two hours with sun in my eyes. I was grimy and hot and devoid of patience. And hungry.

"Stop!" Pivoting to face him. Which sent pain spiking up my rib cage.

Slidell glared, jaw muscles doing shotgun flexes.

"Have a seat." Lifting a ponytail that was plastered to my neck. "I'll pour iced tea."

He did. I did. After washing my hands.

We both drank. Then I got latex gloves from my scene kit, donned one, handed the other to Slidell, and laid the note and the larger bone fragment on the table. Not sure why, but I left the smaller one in my pocket.

Slidell eyed the glove, the note, and the bone but touched nothing. "I'm supposed to applaud?"

"Did you run Kimrey?" Ignoring his sarcasm.

Slidell opened a picture on his phone and showed me the screen. It was a mug shot of the guy who'd leveled me.

"That's him," I said.

Hunching a shoulder to blot sweat from his chin, Slidell slid a small spiral from his breast pocket, thumbed his tongue, and flipped pages.

"Thirty-four-year-old Caucasian, home boy, managed to graduate from Northwest School of the Arts back in the day. Kid was some kinda violin prodigy." A pause to decipher his notes. Or triage what to hold back. "String of collars for dealing, soliciting, all small-time, nothing violent. Did a couple stretches at jail north, up on Spector Drive."

I waited.

"The H is for Hollister. Goes by Holly. Known as Molly Holly on the street. Apparently, that's his specialty." Slidell referred to the drug Molly, thought by some to be pure MDMA, or ecstasy, but more commonly a toxic mixture of lab-made chemicals. "That and blow, acid, weed, you name it."

"You alerted the sheriff?" I asked.

"Poston had one of his deputies swing by the property. Your guy was gone. Place was secure, no sign of forced entry, no response to his shouting."

I tried to recall if I'd properly closed the gate. If that was even possible, given that I'd found it open. Had no idea. "Kimrey must have come to and split."

"You hit him that hard?" Impressed?

"I think he was drunk."

"What the hell was he doing out there?"

I had no answer to that. "Have you traced the owners of the property?"

"It's a goddamn holding company. Individual names will be buried in reams of legal bullshit." Gruff but more controlled. Slidell had kicked into cop mode. "Did you spot a vehicle?"

"No. But I wasn't really looking." Remembering the faint, truncated whine. "If Kimrey came by motorcycle, I might not have seen it."

"You're sure this Kimrey snaked the pouch and the folder?"

"I think so."

Slidell's face did something I couldn't really describe. But he didn't lambast me for my ineptitude. "Let's see the pics."

I watched Slidell swipe through the images, expanding some with an index finger and the spitty thumb. When finished, "Send 'em to me."

"I will."

"Kimrey works a patch off Eastway and Central."

"Vodyanov had an apartment in a building near there. Did you get an LKA?" I was asking about a last-known address.

"When I do, there's zero chance I'll be sharing it with you."

"You'll bring Kimrey in for questioning? You have to act fast. He could ditch the stuff. Or destroy it."

"Never thought of that."

Birdie chose that moment to make his appearance. We both watched him slide around the door frame, circle Slidell's ankles twice, then disappear into the pantry. For some reason, the cat is exceptionally fond of Skinny.

"Why clip reports on missing kids?"

Slidell has a habit of thinking out loud. He was doing that, but I answered anyway. "I don't know."

"Why toss them now?"

"We don't know how long they were in the dumpster."

"You're sure the pouch held kids' teeth?"

I nodded.

"They were at the incinerator?"

"Yes."

"Why weren't they toast?"

"Raccoons."

Slidell raised quizzical brows.

"I'm guessing wet garbage was allowed to pile up, then hauled to the incinerator. Maybe some was taken straight out there. Either way, the 'coons hit before the next burn."

"And one of them dragged the bone back under the netting?" Chin cocking at the fragment.

"Seems so."

"Why would this yahoo Kimrey snatch the shit you collected?"

"I don't know." I was saying that a lot.

"Is it human?"

I tipped frustrated palms.

"DNA clear that up?"

"Yes. But you know how long it takes."

Slidell ran a hand down his face and leaned back.

"How was your interview with the Cole neighbor?" I asked.

"Colorful."

"Meaning?"

"Her name's Cootie Clanahan. She hates Trump, loves Pearl Jam, NASCAR, and the White Sox."

"Really."

"And roses. Smelled like I was sitting in a goddamn funeral parlor."

"What did she tell you?" Not touching the odd metaphor.

"She remembers a car circling the block the night before the Cole kid vanished. Says it was a 2007 Ford Mustang, forest green with a hinky front. The old gal's batshit into cars, 'cause of the NASCAR thing."

"Hinky?"

"Had some kinda custom grille work. She showed me in *Road & Track* what the '07 Mustang looks like coming off the line. She subscribes, you believe that?"

"Impressive."

"Gotta admit, she seemed solid. Weird but solid. She also said something got my attention."

I waited while Slidell chugged more tea.

"There's a park at the end of the street where the Coles were living. Clanahan could see it from her front window. I'm guessing she spent a lot of hours with her nose to the glass. Anyway, she remembers a guy hanging around about that same time. Said he looked hinky."

"Odd grille work?"

"You want to practice your stand-up, or should I go on?"

I gestured for him to continue.

"She says she saw this guy talking to Jahaan and some other kids."

"Did she report that?"

"When the cops didn't call her back about the Mustang, she dropped it. Then she moved away. Here's the thing. A couple months ago, a man came to see her. She found it weird that he'd tracked her down so long after the kid went missing, so she made an entry in her diary. I forgot to mention, Cootie's writing her memoirs. That's how she could remember all this detail about the vehicle. The guy claimed to be a cop, but she said he looked hinky."

I refrained from comment.

"I've scoured the file. There's no mention of any follow-up to Clanahan's call. So that part tracks. Nothing about running down a tip on a Mustang. But back in the spring, when she says she was contacted, the case was colder than a nun's tit."

"No one was conducting interviews at that time?"

"No one was doing jackshit."

"Did the hinky cop look like the guy in the park?"

"She wasn't sure."

"OK," I said, not knowing what else to say. "OK."

For several seconds, the only sound was Birdie messing with something in the pantry.

"What's up with the Hyundai from Art's Afford-able?" I asked.

"As I suspected, Poston turned it over to us. Dick-wad's too—"

"And?"

"Forensics found nada."

"No trace? No prints?"

"Wiped clean. Ditto the duffel and the stuff inside. Car's registered to John Ito. Fake name, fake address. Dead end."

"What's happening with the notebook?"

"Peppers is holding it up in QD. Apparently, we've got no Latvian translator, so she's waiting on you for that."

"I'll phone Pete again. He's been out of town. But I'll bet the farm the *Estonia* references are just notes on another conspiracy theory."

Slidell nodded.

"Now what?" I asked.

"First, I tag and bag your bone and drop it by the lab."

"It's probably nonhuman." Locking eyes with Slidell. He got my meaning.

"So the ME don't need to be involved. Then I pry a judge away from his Sunday-night gin—"

"We absolutely have to get into that bunker. Fast."

"Don't get your skivvies in a twist. Assuming I score a warrant, and that's a big-ass assumption, I'm not about to go off half-cocked."

"I've left a message with a Realtor who specializes in these abandoned military structures."

"You're shitting me."

"I'll ring him again. And I'll do more cyber-research."

"I'll run Kimrey to ground. Meanwhile, I want you—" Slidell pushed to his feet, head wagging glumly. "Why do I even bother?"

"Call me the minute you find him."

"Yeah. You're topping my dance card."

After Slidell left, I showered, shampooed, and dug sooty mud from under my nails. The bruise on my left side was congealing like the thunderheads before Friday's storm.

Cleaner, and decidedly more fragrant, I defrosted a Stouffer's spaghetti dinner and ate while googling Timothy Horshauser. His story was given less attention than many child disappearances. But the circumstances were painfully familiar.

On May 22, 2014, nine-year-old Timothy John Horshauser vanished while waiting for a school bus in Uniontown, Pennsylvania. Horshauser's parents were divorced. Janelle Horshauser was an RN raising her son solo. Paul Horshauser was an auto mechanic, remarried and living in upstate New York. "Timmy" went missing while under the care of his maternal aunt, Brigitte England.

As was their routine, England made breakfast for her nephew so her sister could leave for a morning shift at the local hospital. Just past seven a.m., England drove Timmy to the bus stop, then continued on to her job as a seamstress at an alteration business.

Timmy was the first to arrive at the stop. No one recalled seeing him boarding or riding the bus. He did not appear at school that day. He was never seen again.

A massive search turned up neither the child nor his remains. The usual persons were investigated—known sex offenders, teachers, family members, coaches, bus drivers, everyone in the boy's life. No suspect was ever identified or charged.

The clipped article had appeared in the Uniontown *Herald-Standard.* Outside the kid's hometown, there had been minimal statewide and no national coverage.

I sent an email to Slidell, sharing what I'd learned. And reminding him about the papers from the trench-coat lining that he'd forgotten to take.

Next, I researched iPhone blackouts and poor battery life. Found numerous opinions that the poor performance might be resulting from inadequate memory due to storage of too many images. I checked. My geriatric device was juggling 33,207 stills and 297 videos. Pure laziness. I didn't need memories of Halloween 2002 at my fingertips.

But what to do? Put everything in the cloud as most cyber-nerds were suggesting? Many of the photos were of sensitive case material, including several still in litigation. Were my pictures more secure in cyber-space or on my laptop, which I alone controlled? Not knowing the legal restraints concerning image reten-tion, I'd done no cloud backups.

Uncertain about the answer, and wanting to be totally safe, I transferred everything to my laptop for temporary storage. Then I googled instructions on how to delete all data in my phone's library. With great trep-idation, I carried them out.

That done, I turned to the newly stored images on my Mac. I didn't really expect to hear from Slidell. Still, every few minutes, I glanced up to check the time.

With my mobile in camera mode, I'd been unable

to use the flashlight app while under the camo netting. Shooting blind hadn't gone well. Many images were badly framed, out of focus, or too dim to make out the subject. But now and then, I'd nailed it. An empty Campbell's tomato soup can. A crumpled Doritos bag. A child's neon-pink sneaker.

Uptick in my pulse.

Focus.

Maybe because my movement was constricted by the size of the opening. Maybe because the light from my flash was trapped inside the bin. The objects in the dumpster were captured with crystal clarity, still-life trash in an inky sea.

I was working through that series when my eyes fell on a tangled washcloth flaring white amid the jumbled fill. Stitched across it was a line of blue script.

DeepHaven.

The logo or name of a towel manufacturer? A place? Maybe a resort or hotel?

Google produced links to several possibilities. A town in Minnesota. A mortgage company. A family camp in New Hampshire. A series of romance novels.

I explored the camp. Followed links to every business in Deephaven, Minnesota. Looped through Zillow listings of real estate on Deephaven Courts, Deephaven Lanes, and Deephaven Roads across the country. Nothing seemed promising,

But repetition has its rewards. Seeing the name over and over triggered memories of my foray down into the dark web.

DeepHaven. On a facecloth in a bunker near the creek where Felix Vodyanov's mutilated body was found.

DeepUnder. Vodyanov, Yates Timmer, and Nick Body together at an MKUltra and mind-control conference in 2010.

I don't believe in coincidence.

Switching to the TOR browser, I took another plunge down the DeepUnder vortex. This time, instead of choosing one of the tabs, I typed *Nick Body* into the search box beside the black-and-red banner.

The screen darkened, swirled like ink spinning down a drain, then filled with a long list of text. I scrolled through it. Found nothing but links to Body's podcasts and blogs.

A low-level headache sent feelers up the back of my skull. A migraine? Nope. Wrong cranial zip code.

I tried the name *Felix Vodyanov.* The cursor blinked, puzzled or defiant.

Yates Timmer. More swirling. Slowly, the page loaded. Three URLs were listed. *Homes at the End of the World, LLP* and *World's End House.* Familiar with those, I went for the third.

And found myself reading a full-screen infomercial, an ad touting the desirability of underground living and promising the investment opportunity of a lifetime. An Atlas F missile site in upstate New York backlit the bold black message in pastoral greens and blues.

Interested parties were encouraged to contact Yates Timmer by phone. The number was the one at which I'd left my voice mail.

At the bottom of the page, in extraordinarily wee font, was the surprising invitation: *Qualified individuals are invited to DeepHaven.* An address was provided in GPS coordinates: *35°20′00″N 80°59′58″W.* Beside the address, blank rectangles requested a username and password.

Knowing it was the longest of long shots, I checked my images and began with the passcodes scribbled on the folded scrap. *RABUK 1973. DALIHP2580. UATNOM1739.* No winner there. Then, though hopeless, I began entering random combinations. *Timmer, Body, Vodyanov, WorldsEnd. MKUltra. Body Language.*

I'd been at it several minutes when the screen went black. A beat, then I was bounced to the TOR home page. I'd been ejected.

I returned to DeepUnder and entered the password I'd been using. No go.

I unplugged the modem to obtain a new IP address and adjusted settings. Repeated the process several times. With no success.

I'd been barred from the site. Busted? If so, what had they learned about me?

And how? Had my laptop been hijacked? Altered to permit a remote user to spy on me with my own camera? To secretly record me? I'd read about such hackers. And there was that FaceTime bug that allowed anyone to make a group call, add their own number, and gain access to audio and video of the recipient without the recipient's knowledge. Had Apple fixed that? Had I downloaded the update?

I powered down, slammed the lid, and yanked the plug. Irrational, I know. But my frustration and anxiety were stratospheric. And the throbbing in my side and up my neck and occipital wasn't helping.

To calm my frazzled nerves and battered ribs, I took a very long, very hot bath. Then, fingers pruny, body smelling of honey-apple-blossom lotion, I crawled into bed and dialed Ryan.

No answer.

I left a message.

It was too late to call anyone else.

On impulse, I downloaded a new ringtone.

Sleep eluded me for a very long time. Finally, spurred by some impulse I couldn't explain, I got up, crossed to my dresser, and searched a drawer two-handed in the dark. Found the object I was seeking. Smooth and round with a plump belly, long trunk, and one broken tusk.

Returning to bed, I set the little elephant-headed figure on the bedside table and stared into his eyes. He stared back. Ganesha. The god of beginnings. The remover of obstacles.

Somehow, I felt lighter.

When Birdie curled at my knee, I stroked his back and explained why I'd been so tense of late. Tomorrow was Monday, I assured him. A new week. Things would improve. A breakthrough in the case was imminent.

A new beginning.

I was wrong.

Life was about to go from bad to pure hell.

21

I woke to Bob Marley urging me to chill. My eyes flew to the clock.

9:48. Impossible.

'Cause every little thing gonna be all right . . .

I grabbed my mobile. Slidell was already talking when it hit my ear.

"—bench slug says it ain't enough, I should—"

"A judge refused to issue a warrant?" Overenunciating to sound fully awake.

"According to her thinking, which is on par with my cousin Blanton's senile gerbil, undocumented photos, a bone of dubious origin, and a hearsay tale don't constitute probable cause."

"Damn."

"She suggested, not so politely, I come back with more."

"Then we'll do that."

"We? I don't recall you standing there getting your head handed—"

I told him about the washcloth, DeepHaven, the GPS coordinates buried in Timmer's ad.

"I'm sure you looked them up."

"Not yet." I didn't mention my ouster from Deep-Under and the subsequent paranoia that my Mac was now spying on me. "But I'm conversant enough to know the location is just south of Charlotte."

"You think it's some kinda real estate office?"

"If so, Timmer's not putting it out high-profile."

"You say this yak's hawking old missile sites. Maybe a buyer's gotta be vetted to get the inside skinny."

That made sense.

"What's up with Kimrey?" I asked.

"In the wind. I'll get him."

"Find anything more on Vodyanov?"

"Nada. It's like the skank never existed. I checked records for the unit in Ramos's building. You're right. The tenant in number six had no cable, no phone, no internet. Swung by for a chat with the landlady. There's a piece of work. Ramos claims she hardly ever saw the guy. Got the same story from a neighbor." Pages flipped. "Hugo Garcia. Looks like Vodyanov used the place as a drop, maybe a safe house."

"Drop for what? Safe from what?"

"Who the hell knows?"

"Why swab the apartment with antiseptic?"

"Same answer."

I changed gears. "What about Cootie Clanahan's Mustang lead?"

"Got someone helping me dig through DMV

records—licenses, registrations, citations, the usual. The CCU ain't overstaffed, so it's probably gonna take the rest of our lives." I could hear the frustration in his voice.

"How about the holding company that owns the property?"

"Working on that, too."

Thirty minutes later, Marley sang again.

I recognized the number. I'd worked at that end of the line for decades.

"Good morning." Uber-cheerful.

"This is not a social call." Heavner's tone was overtly hostile.

"It's still a good morning," I chirped.

"I thought I was explicit in asking that you refrain from interfering in cases assigned to my office."

"You received my second email."

"It seems I have not made myself clear."

"Did you follow up on the Vodyanov ID?"

"How the hell did you obtain a sample for DNA testing?"

"Did I explain that Detective Slidell and I tossed Vodyanov's car and confiscated personal items?" True but irrelevant. I wanted to divert Heavner. The dodge worked.

"I have no obligation to disclose this to you. I do so to demonstrate the inappropriateness of your behavior." Meaningful pause. "There is no record of a Felix Vodyanov ever having been a guest at Sparkling Waters Ashram. There is no record of Dr. Yuriev treating such a person."

"He probably registered under the name F. Vance." Devoid of chirp. "More than once."

Glacial silence.

"Ask Yuriev. Give him a call."

"Do not tell me how to do my job."

"I'm sorry. I wasn't—"

"Dr. Brennan, your actions amount to more than simple interference. What you are doing may rise to the level of obstruction. I am seeking advice concerning legal action against you. In the meantime, I am lodging ethics complaints with both the American Academy of Forensic Sciences and the American Board of Forensic Anthropology."

"Because I've made the only breakthrough in *your* case?"

"Your actions were unauthorized and may have compromised an official death investigation."

"My input was sought by a member of the CMPD cold-case unit." Not exactly.

"Really?" Disdainful snort. "The only thing cold in this case is the stiff."

"That stiff, as you so crudely refer to a human being, may be linked to a number of child disappearances."

"And to the rabbit assassinated at the Circle K?"

Ignoring Heavner's sarcasm, "How did Vodyanov die?"

Silly question. Even if she knew, she wasn't going to tell me.

"That does not concern you."

"Did you run a full tox screen?" Further questioning was certain to annoy her more, but I couldn't help myself.

"That information is confidential."

"Are you engaging a board-certified anthropologist other than myself?"

"Not needed."

A moment of chilly nothing filled the line. No clanking or buzzing, none of the familiar autopsy-room sounds. I pictured Heavner in Larabee's office. He'd hung a Peter Max poster behind the desk. I wondered what she had gracing the wall.

When angered, one's heart rate, arterial tension, and testosterone production increase, the stress hormone cortisol decreases, and the left-brain hemisphere goes all twitchy. The thought of Dr. Morgue in Larabee's space triggered the whole raucous circus.

"It's been ten days," I snapped. "If you had cause of death, you'd have staged another of your alpha-dog performances. That's your specialty, right? Playing the media for personal glorification?"

"How dare y—"

"You better believe I dare." Blood was exploding into the tiny vessels in my cheeks. "I dare to get this man identified. I dare to pursue even the faintest glimmer of a lead concerning the fate of these missing kids."

Heavner shifted the phone and spoke to someone. A male voice responded. When her mouth returned to the receiver, "There is no point in further discussion."

I drew a hot breath to respond. Heavner cut me off.

"But bear in mind one truth, Dr. Brennan. I *am* the alpha dog."

Abrupt disconnect.

I sat quite a while, face flaming, trying to recover the decades of professionalism I'd mislaid during that brief conversation.

The torture continued all day.

At noon, it was Pete. He was back in Charlotte and

had news that could only be relayed in person. He was solemn and engaged in none of his usual banter or teasing. His tone frightened me. Beyond saying that the topic had nothing to do with Katy, no amount of wheedling could get him to expand. I agreed to dinner the following night.

Then it was Mama. She and Sinitch had booked a trip to Bhutan to work on their spirituality and wellness and to reconsider the concept of weddings. When pressed for specifics, she said they'd be visiting Buddhist meditation centers and undergoing hot-springs therapy. When I asked if these centers could accommodate her chemo regime, she assured me all would be fine. Far from reassured, I phoned her doctor's office. The switchboard directory made me certain my brain was dribbling right out of my ear. I left a message with a bot in a basement cubbyhole entered through a secret door in an abandoned cutlery closet.

Disconnecting, I wondered. Was it my fault? Had I mentioned the ashram to her? Thought not, but couldn't be sure.

I checked my email, hoping for a consult request, which would mean a bit of additional income. Found none. At one point, I considered a trip to the Apple Store but couldn't muster the energy. Another truth about me. I hate malls. And waiting in lines. And there was the budgetary issue. After phoning the painter and the electrician again, I spent time catching up on neglected paperwork.

As the afternoon wore on, a troubling question percolated up through my agitation. Given Heavner's obvious hostility, why had she shared any information at all? Was her uncharacteristic collegiality spurred by an ulterior motive? Dribble Brennan a few crumbs, let her crack the case, then Dr. Morgue can swoop in and grab credit for the solve?

Around five, after placing duct tape over my laptop's camera lens, I logged onto WebMD and typed in the term *taphophobia*. Consistent with Asia Barrow's characterization, the condition was defined as the irrational fear of being buried alive, sometimes the fear of interment resulting from a false pronouncement of death. The site also offered these tidbits.

Taphophobia can originate from childhood experiences involving actual entrapment or from viewing depictions of such situations. Sufferers may avoid enclosed buildings, fearing collapse. Some refuse anesthesia, fearing they'll be wrongly declared dead and buried. Exacerbating factors include other mental disorders and substance abuse.

Felix Vodyanov was being treated for taphophobia? Then why live underground?

After a Foodie Call dinner of lamb korma, much appreciated by Birdie, I tried reading. My theory was solid: escape into a world I could leave whenever I chose. My carry-through was lacking. Anger and frustration had me jittery and unable to focus.

Just past six, Marley announced yet another caller. Blocked number. Thinking my anxiety couldn't possibly increase, maybe hoping to unload on some unsuspecting telemarketer, I answered.

"I'm trying to reach Dr. Temperance Brennan." Male. Unfamiliar.

"This is she."

"I work for the Charlotte *Observer*."

"I already have a subscription."

"I'm sorry. I should have made myself clear. I'm a reporter."

"What's your name?" Wary. I knew most of those on the crime beat.

"Gerald Breugger."

Gerry. The lizard asking questions at Heavner's press conference.

"You're a freelancer," I said. "You're not actually employed by the *Observer*."

"Yes, but they often publish my pieces."

"How did you get this number?"

"I have my ways."

I said nothing.

"I've just had a long conversation with Dr. Margot Heavner."

"Bully for you. Have a good life."

"Please don't hang up."

For some reason, I didn't. An instinct for self-preservation?

"I'm doing a story on the state of forensic science in North Carolina," Breugger said. "My lead-in will be the case of the corpse eaten by hogs out in Cleveland County. I'm wondering if you'd like to make a statement."

"Rethink your use of the term *eaten*."

"Go on."

"I'm done."

"Is it true the body is still unidentified?"

"No comment."

"That cause of death is unknown?"

"No comment."

"That the ME refuses to bring you in on the case?"

"No comment."

"Is it true that Dr. Heavner is filing complaints against you?"

"Who told you that?"

"You know I can't reveal my sources."

"You and your sources can take a flying fuck off my backyard fence."

"I regularly do stories for the *New York Times*, the *Washington Post*, and the *Daily Beast*. I have those numbers right here in my contacts."

The implied threat sent the three-ring emotional circus into hyperdrive. My thumb mashed so hard to disconnect I nearly dropped the phone.

Sitting there, coaxing my pulse back down into the normal range, I was hit by a sudden recollection from Heavner's presser. She'd addressed only one journalist by name. Gerry Breugger.

I was considering the significance of that when Marley sang again. This time, I checked.

Area code 514. I pictured a different desk, a different office, *Dr. Pierre LaManche, Directeur* on a plaque by the door.

"*Bonjour. Comment ça va?*" I answered.

"*Très bien, merci.*" LaManche switched to English as precise as his French. "I apologize for contacting you so late."

"It's good to hear your voice."

"You are unwell?" My boss for decades at the Laboratoire de sciences judiciaires et de médecine légale, LaManche was uncanny at interpreting the subtlest of nuances in my mood.

"I'm fine."

"Ah, Temperance. You sound *peiné*." Pained? Distressed? Either way, he'd nailed it.

"I have a lot on my mind."

"Such a vale of woes in which we ply our trade. But I am an old wagon, all rusty metal and squeaky wheels. You are young. You should be happy."

The sad metaphor did little to raise my spirits. "What's up?"

"A subpoena has arrived for you. Do you recall the Pasquerault case?"

"Of course." Dorothée Pasquerault vanished while walking home from an outdoor performance of the Montreal Symphony Orchestra. Eight days later, her decomposed body was found in a hockey bag tossed up on the shore of the Saint Lawrence River. The concert had been organized to honor the city's three hundred seventy-fifth birthday. Dorothée hadn't lived to see her seventeenth. The investigation resulted in the arrest of her ex-fiancé.

"The trial is scheduled to begin next week. Jury selection is expected to conclude on Tuesday at the latest. Your availability is ordered beginning on Wednesday."

"OK." It was so far from OK I couldn't fathom a device capable of doing the math.

"I have placed the subpoena on your desk."

"Thanks."

"There are several *demande d'expertise* forms there with it. *Pas d'urgence* on those cases."

"I'll reserve a flight."

"*À bientôt.*"

"*Oui*. See you soon."

I returned to the book, again planning to lose myself in 1930s New Guinea. Again failing. The subpoena imposed a new urgency. I had to leave for Montreal no later than Tuesday. Yet Felix Vodyanov remained on his gurney.

The same old questions spun in my off-kilter brain. Had Vodyanov been stalking me shortly before his death? If so, why? How had he found me? What had he wanted to tell me?

An image of the severed goose head congealed on the unread page. I thought of the flock struggling to cling to its turf. A metaphor more apt than LaManche's wagon. Like the geese, I was fighting to save my career. To return from exile.

Was that it? Was my motive purely self-interest? Or did I truly care about justice for Felix Vodyanov? For the kids he may have harmed? Was Vodyanov a victim or an offender?

On and on. Round and round. Slidell's failure to obtain a warrant. Heavner's determination to ruin me professionally. Mama's cavalier, perhaps lethal, attitude toward her chemo. Gerry Breugger's knowledge of Heavner's crusade against me and possible intent to assist in that campaign.

How much did Breugger know? His call, more than anything, had driven home the precariousness of my situation. Should Heavner's charges actually stick, Breugger would be on the story like jackals on a carcass. While dodging his questions, I'd visualized a predator.

What the hell was up with Pete?

And always, when would the next migraine slam me to the boards? Or worse, a vascular assault? If the tiny bubble did burst, how bad would it be?

A stray thought caused a sharp intake of breath. Slidell was right. I was acting much more rashly of late, taking far more risks. Tailing the trench-coated prowler at Sharon Hall. Sneaking illicit photos and samples from the faceless man at the MCME. Interviewing Barrow, Ramos, and Keesing alone. Exploring the Cleveland County property solo. Did this recent recklessness arise from a newborn sense of my own mortality? One day, the aneurysm may burst, so what the hell?

I rolled the idea around, testing to see if the epiphany had legs. Could my "rogue-ass cowboying" be a subliminal reaction to the prospect of my own death? Or was my furious intensity on this case just a variation on my usual commitment to anonymous victims? To the possibility of wronged children or children in danger?

Why all the goddamn introspection? Self-analysis is not a game I enjoy or one at which I excel.

Tossing the book across the room, I got up to pace. Sat down. Got up again to retrieve the book and flatten the pages. I felt useless but too restless to stay still.

By eight, I was absolutely wild with nerves. Slidell hadn't phoned. There were no new leads. Those that we had were going nowhere. The clock was ticking. I imagined I was trapped in a pressure cooker with no steam vent.

Vowing to take no action without consulting Slidell, I got online and entered Timmer's GPS coordinates.

A red flag appeared on a hair-thin road near Lake Wylie, South Carolina, just south of Charlotte. My friend Anne had been listing and selling properties in the area for decades, mostly high-end homes in and around a golf course development called River Hills. Still, she knew the turf.

I hit speed dial.

"I can hardly hear you, Tempe." Hollow air with lots of background noise. "I'm at a Knights game."

"Quick question?"

"Shoot."

"Do you know Lone Eagle Lane? Near Lake Wylie?"

"Donegal Lane?" Shouted.

"Lone. Eagle."

As Anne searched terrain in her mind, an amplified voice gave a stroke-worthy whoop. The crowd noise swelled, receded.

"Yeah. Lone Eagle runs along behind the nature preserve. Accesses some old-style cottages dating back to the postwar years. You pick the war."

"Waterfront?"

"Yes." The din was receding. Anne was moving to a quieter location.

"I'm surprised some builder hasn't slapped condos on the property."

"Developers contact me all the time. The homeowners say they've been going to 'the river' all their lives and have no interest in selling."

"What else is back there?"

"To my knowledge, fuck-all."

"Ever hear of a real estate company called Deep-Haven?"

"Dipshit name from a marketing perspective. But no."

"Any chance a Realtor could have opened an office on Lone Eagle?"

"Anything's possible since those neutron stars collided."

"What?"

"The gravitational waves?"

"Enjoy the game."

"We're losing by four runs. But the peanuts rock. Why the interest in Lone Eagle Lane?"

"No reason."

"Uh-huh. If the old coots have decided to sell, I want in."

I returned to Google Earth and shifted to aerial view. My eyes confirmed what the map, and Anne, had said. Lots of shoreline. Lots of fuck-all.

Knowing the idea was pure insanity, I decided on a drive-by. What could it hurt?

Another courtesy call to Slidell, then, phone and flash at the ready, I set out.

22

Wylie, one of eleven man-made reservoirs strung like clots along the Catawba River, has 352 miles of shoreline meandering through both Carolinas. The Allen Steam Station is located at the lake's northern end, near Charlotte. The Catawba Nuclear Generating Station dominates a peninsula in its southwestern part. I once read an NRC disaster emergency plan that defined plume exposure and ingestion pathway zones. Needless to say, fish from these waters don't figure into my diet.

Despite the presence of gorilla reactors, the lake is a popular residential and recreational area, a schizoid mix of nouveau-riche McMansion and golf course communities, retirement condos, and *Dukes of Hazzard*–type trailers and shacks. Lots of barbecue and boat-supply stores.

Thirty minutes after we left the annex, Slidell turned right from Shopton Road. Yeah, I was shocked, too. He'd phoned back within minutes. Insisted on a tag-team approach. I had no choice. Though, truth be told, I was glad not to be tackling this one solo.

Dusk was yielding to night, and everything around us was monochrome gray. I'd never ventured into the area but knew that the McDowell Nature Preserve and Copperhead Island Park were somewhere to the south, the Daniel Stowe Botanical Garden off to the west, across the water.

A left, then another right. The streets were poorly lit, the homes modest ranches and bungalows. No gates, no guards demanding ID. Driveways ended under carports, or just ended. Bikes lay on lawns that were mowed, not professionally landscaped. Porch lights were coming on. Two boys kicked a soccer ball far down the block. A dog of indeterminate breed yapped and dashed from kid to kid.

A short distance, then my Google Maps app said to go right. Slidell did, at a nonthreatening green street sign: *Lone Eagle Lane*. Below that, a not-so-welcoming declaration: *Dead End*.

Lone Eagle was as empty and still as an abandoned movie set. Slidell eased to a stop. When we lowered our windows, hot air engulfed us like steam off soup. I smelled water, gasoline, algae, and mud. A hint of pine.

On my side loomed a wall of old-growth cypress interrupted here and there by a hut or shed. On Slidell's side, across the narrow pavement, cottages crouched dark and sullen along the shore.

Quick glance over my shoulder. Twenty yards back, an empty lot separated two lakeside homes. Paralleling the lot's right boundary, a concrete slab sloped gently into the water. Waves lapped sluggishly at the slab's far end, audible but invisible in the thickening dark.

"Boat ramp," I said.

Slidell said nothing.

We both logged its position, then the 4Runner crept forward.

I soon realized the street was far from deserted. Conservation, tradition, whatever the reason, lights were shunned on Lone Eagle on hot summer nights. Maybe always.

Despite the self-imposed gloom, perhaps because of it, people were out on their porches and stoops, rocking, talking, smoking cigarettes that sparked like tiny orange fireflies. Anne's old coots. I sensed displeasure at our intrusion.

As we proceeded, the road rose in elevation. I felt hostile eyes tracking our uphill climb. Five houses, eight, twelve. Suddenly, loud as gunfire, my iPhone proclaimed our arrival.

"Jesus H. Christ. They probably heard that in the next county."

I muted the sound and raised my window. Slidell slowed but didn't stop. We both glanced left.

The cottage didn't stand out structurally. One-story frame, window AC units, veranda in front, carport on the near side, chain-link fence enclosing the rear. The first difference involved cars. Unlike the others we'd passed, this driveway hosted a small fleet. The second involved illumination. Behind shuttered windows, every room appeared to be lit. The third involved neighbors. Being last before the promised dead end, there was nothing on the far side but a hill covered with holly and other inhospitable vegetation.

Slidell cruised past, looped around the cul-de-sac, and retraced our path. Pulling onto a narrow dirt strip fronting the cypresses, we observed. Saw no human form at a car, in the yard, or on the porch. But a prism of rainbow colors flickered around the edges and through the closed slats of shutters covering windows facing the dead end.

"Someone's home," I said.

Wordlessly, we got out, crossed the street and the lawn, and climbed the steps. A sign on the door said: *No admittance after presentation begins.*

Seeing no bell, I knocked. Zero response.

I tried the knob. The door was locked. I checked the fence. The sole gate was secured by a very large padlock.

"That's it," Slidell said. "We're outta here."

"I want to know what's going on in there."

"The homeowner ain't exactly inviting us in. And I got no jurisdiction and no cause—"

"This is our only lead to Vodyanov. Maybe to those kids. Let's try a different tack."

One long-suffering look, then Slidell pivoted and headed for the car. I followed, certain he intended to leadfoot it back to Charlotte. Instead, he drove downhill, passed our entrance point, pulled in at the boat ramp, and cut the engine.

"They don't open up willingly, we're done."

"Roger that." I shoved my phone into a pocket, the flash into my waistband, and got out.

It was full night now. No moon. No streetlamp. Around us, only darkness and hot, stagnant air.

A small colony of neurons urged retreat.

Ignoring the warning, I stepped onto the concrete. The surface was slick with algae, forcing me to move gingerly. At my back, Slidell slip-slid and cursed indignantly.

To either side, the land dropped without drama to a narrow ribbon of rock and sand. To call it a beach would be unfair to beaches. Wooden piers ran from the edge of the ribbon out over the water. Most had a rowboat or canoe tied to an upright.

We maneuvered to the side of the concrete, worked our way downward, and, using our flashes sparingly to avoid drawing attention, set off along the shore. Far distant, across the water, lights twinkled with multicolored cheer. Now and then, the muggy air stirred on a rare breeze, carrying the murmur of waves listlessly brushing pilings, the muted hum of a distant outboard motor.

As my eyes adjusted, I could see that the ground was littered with debris. When lit, my beam crawled over dead fish, empty sunblock tubes, the long tentacles of twisted plastic grocery bags.

Ten minutes beyond the ramp, a rocky breakwater jutted toward the shore like a long, arthritic digit. In my scramble across, generations of algae transferred to my person. If Slidell and I did encounter Yates Timmer, we were going to look like creatures from some dark lagoon.

Paralleling the gradient on Lone Eagle Lane, the beach angled upward. Panting and perspiring, we forged on. Though less enthused now, I was determined to see the escapade through to its conclusion.

"This is the goddamn stupidest thing you've ever dragged my ass into." Slidell was breathing hard. I hoped I wasn't dragging his ass into a cardiac event.

The straps of my sandals, grown soggy and gritty, sawed channels into my heels and the tops of my feet. My clothing molded to me like a second skin. How had the distance seemed so much shorter in the 4Runner?

Behind me, I could hear Slidell crunching and wheezing. At any second, I was certain he'd order retreat. Then, without warning, the shoreline cut in, and the bank to our right rose sharply. Google Maps flashed bright and mutely announced we were at the programmed GPS coordinates.

I thumbed on my flash and pointed it toward the water. The pier was bigger than most and had a pontoon boat moored beside it.

As Slidell's beam fell on the pontoon, I aimed mine right. It landed on a narrow flight of wooden stairs. I ran the light up the steps. Could see nothing beyond the top one.

As one, we killed our lights and listened for movement above us. I caught only Slidell's breathing and the blood pulsing in my ears.

Jesus, Brennan. The guy's a Realtor, not Polyphemus. He owns a party boat.

One fiercely unfriendly glance, then Slidell began climbing, cautiously testing before putting his full weight onto each tread. White-knuckling the rail, I followed.

Topside, a zillion tree frogs chirped amphibian gossip. Maybe crickets. I risked a nanosecond of flash. So did Slidell.

A path led from the stairs to a gate, then across a small yard to the cottage. Surprisingly, the back door was ajar. A violet-blue slash cut through the gap, lighting a deck holding a Weber grill and angular shapes that looked like rockers and patio chairs.

The gate was unlocked. Slidell disengaged the lever and strode to the deck.

"Yo!"

Same result as out front. Silence. He shouted again. Still no response.

Slidell palmed the door open. We both stepped inside.

We were in a kitchen lit by overhead recessed cans. Faux-brick tile floor, farm-style sink, stainless-steel appliances. The refrigerator was just to our right. Through a glass panel, I could see containers of Osetra and Beluga caviar, smoked duck, foie gras, and lump crab meat. Enough cheeses to feed all of Wisconsin.

At the room's center was a plank pine table. Eight bamboo place mats, eight chairs, one askew, as though hastily vacated. At the table's center, a ceramic vase with a pink calla lily in its prime.

A clipboard lay on the mat in front of the off-angle chair. I walked over, glanced down, and noted a list of names, all but two checked. Beside the clipboard, a crystal tumbler holding an inch of amber liquid.

Slidell joined me and picked up the glass. Sniffed. "Hell-o."

He extended his arm. I inhaled. ID'd cognac or brandy.

Straight ahead, opposite the back entrance and beside a Wolf range, was a closed door. From beyond it came what sounded like a recorded voice, the cadence suggesting TV or film dialogue.

To the right of the closed door, an open one allowed a view into a pantry. We crossed to it. On the floor were cases of liquor and wine. Macallan. Patrón. Tito's. Rémy Martin. The wines were mostly domestic pinot noirs and French burgundies. Good ones. I knew. Light reds had been my poison of choice.

Godiva chocolates and other delicacies filled the shelves. Walker's shortbread cookies. Jars of olives and tiny cornichon pickles. Boxes of cigars displaying the word *Habana*.

"Looks like someone's planning a party," Slidell said, voice muted.

"That someone's a mighty big spender."

Then a high-voltage shot of adrenaline. In one corner, a stack of cocktail napkins with the word *Deep-Haven* in royal blue script.

"Holy shit."

"What?"

"I'll explain later." As I captured the napkins with my phone.

Beyond the closed door, the cinematic voice droned on. As Slidell moved into the pantry to inventory the shelves, I scurried over and put my ear to the wood. Made out a few words. Maybe *safety*? Maybe *threat*? I was repositioning for better acoustics when a hinge squeaked at my back. I whirled.

A man stood in the doorway, feet spread, fingers fumbling with his fly. A plastic badge on his shirt introduced him as *Bing*. A rainbow tattoo on one forearm showed a snarling reptile and said *Florida Gators*.

A tug, another, then Bing gave up and braced with a hand to the frame. He was large, in a linebacker-gone-to-fat way. A slack jawline and blond fringe struggling to form brows and cover his scalp said Bing's gridiron days were far in the past.

My gaze found Slidell's. His eyes narrowed as he indicated his badge and shook his head. I dipped my chin in acknowledgment of his desire to conceal that he was a cop.

"The door was open." As Slidell listened from the pantry, I spoke up, not wanting to startle.

If my presence unnerved Bing, he gave no indication. Taking me in with bloodshot eyes, he said, "Had to piss."

"Understandable."

The scraggly brows dipped as my algae-stained state penetrated to Bing's brain.

"Walked over along the beach." To distract, I wiggled a finger at Bing's unzipped pants. "You want to . . . ?"

"Sorry." After clumsily achieving success, "I need to verify you're invited."

"Sure."

Bing walked to the table, not stumbling but clearly unsteady. "Name?"

"Flora." One of the unchecked pair on the list.

"You're not . . ."

"I'm a friend of Flora's. She said it would be all right if I came in her place."

A beat, then, "You got ID?"

"I'm sorry. I didn't want to haul my purse. It's really big. You know how women are." Silly woman grin. "I left everything behind in my car. I suppose I could go all the way back to get it . . ."

More puzzled brows. Then a steroidal arm arced. "You can't go in until they're finished."

"So I get to hang with you?" Accompanied by a flirtatious smile.

Blushing, which did not improve his appearance, Bing reoriented the arm, still upraised, in the general direction of the table. I sat.

"They'll be tied up an hour, maybe longer."

"Oh, my."

"Buy a lady a drink?" The dolt actually said that.

"Please, sir." I actually said that.

Bing walked to a cabinet, returned with a second tumbler and an open bottle of Courvoisier. Dropping beside me with a whoosh of cheap cologne and an alarming creaking of wood, he poured us each three inches of cognac.

"I'll bet you played football," I said, eyes roving, discreetly seeking options for an exit plan.

"Defensive tackle." Bing knocked back two of his three inches.

"Wow." Beaming feigned admiration, I pretended to drink.

"I can still bench-press three fifty."

"That's awesome." I had no idea.

Bing tried to rest his chin on his palm. It slipped off. "Oops," he said, grinning.

"Oops," I said, grinning.

Bing drained then refilled his tumbler, leaned close, and placed the gator hand on my arm. "I gotta lock up here tonight. But you want to wait, I'll drive you to your car. Or wherever." The rheumy leer made me want an immediate shower.

"That's so kind." Taking another sham sip. "Your boss must be a really good guy, sharing such expensive cognac."

Bing winked. "It's our little secret."

"I'll bet your job allows you to meet loads of interesting people."

Humble hitch of one shoulder.

"Have you met Felix Vodyanov?" Casual as hell.

The leer cooled. I'd said something wrong.

"I only asked bec—"

"You want more brandy?" Withdrawing his hand.

"This is lovely. But I'm actually more of a scotch drinker."

"Hold on."

As Bing lurched off, I poured my cognac into the lily. A glance at the list revealed my mistake.

"I'm so sorry. I know I shouldn't have used a last name," I said when my glass held Glenfiddich and the bottle sat beside it.

Bing repeated the one-shoulder shrug.

"Flora explained." Contrite. "I forgot."

"It's not a big deal with me. Just, you know, house rules."

"Won't happen again." Mimicking a key turning over my lips.

For several seconds, the only sound was the muffled narration beyond the door.

"Has Felix been here recently?"

"Not lately." Then a comment Bing's brain hadn't fully vetted. "Haven't seen little brother in a while, either."

"Little brother?" Hoping Slidell was getting all this.

"Nick."

Holy hopping shit!

"Of course." Forcing my voice neutral. "Nick's so much fun."

The bleary eyes bugged, and the bull neck turtled out. "Are you fuckin' serious? The guy's an asshole."

"You think so?"

"Fuuuck."

Speaking in a coquettish whisper, I encouraged, "Are we talking about the same Nick?"

"The guy's a tool." The booze was now dulling Bing's mind and slurring his speech. "A fuckin' Russian tool."

Don't overplay.

"What's that old story about Nick and Felix?"

"Yeah." Bing snorted wetly. "They both start out Vodyanov, right? But Nick don't want to sound foreign, so he changes the V to B, since that's how it's written in whatever the hell alphabet Russkis use, and he chops off the end. Vodyanov becomes goddamn Body."

Bing again drained his glass, smacked down the tumbler.

"Yeah." I nodded. "That's the one."

"He probably quit coming because of the fight."

"Body?" Forming the name with my lips but not speaking it aloud.

Bing shook his head no. "Big brother."

"Felix."

"Felix the fall guy." Mocking. "Klutzoid."

"Who did he fight with?"

"Dude named Twist. I wasn't here that night, but things get around."

"When was this?"

"I'm thinking maybe three, four weeks back." Bing's brows dipped again. "Yeah. The twentieth. I wasn't working that Wednesday. Don't get that many days off."

June 20. Two days before Vodyanov's late-night prowl at Sharon Hall.

Another snort. "I heard Felix jumped Twist's ass. Quite a move for the little wimp. Can't say I blame him. Twist's another real sleaze."

"Why do you say that?"

"The dickhead's into kiddie porn. In my book, anyone messes with . . ."

Over Bing's shoulder, I saw the closed door swing in toward the stove. Yates Timmer stood with one hand on the knob, military glasses pointed squarely at me.

"Who is this?"

Bing fired up so fast his chair crashed to the floor. "A friend of Flora's."

"I see." Unruffled. "Her name?"

Realizing he'd never asked, Bing tried to segue. "I was showing cordiality. Like you coach us."

"Did you request ID?" Gaze still on me.

Bing stood mute, mouth agape.

I rose.

Timmer eyed me a few seconds longer. Then, "Have we met?"

"No."

Bing shot me a furious look, or tried to. The sudden movement forced him to step sideways to regain his balance.

"Why are you here?"

"I'm interested in DeepHaven."

"What do you know about DeepHaven?"

"I'm hoping you'll inform me."

"You are an acquaintance of Flora's?"

I nodded.

"Her surname, please?"

I had no answer.

"She knows Felix and Nick." Bing, desperate to justify his actions.

"Detain her," Timmer said.

An entire nation of neurons bellowed retreat.

Slidell stepped from the pantry.

23

"No one's detaining no one." Slidell's tone was even but glacial.

Timmer's eyes hardened behind their Army-style lenses. He turned them on Skinny but spoke to Bing.

"Why are these people in my kitchen?"

Not unexpectedly, Bing was slow to react. "I was watching her. She wasn't going nowhere."

"And the gentleman?"

"I—I didn't know he was here." Sloppy shrug. "He slipped by me."

"Slipped by you." Anger swelled in his voice, threatening to surface.

"I had to take a leak, all right? You told me never to interrupt the pitch. Since I couldn't cut through the living room to the crapper, I went outside."

Timmer looked at me across the bright pink calla lily. At the cognac and scotch sitting on the table.

"I will ask you again, miss. What do you want?"

"I will answer you again, sir. Info on DeepHaven."

"How did you learn of this place?"

"Your catchy logo."

"We don't advertise."

"I viewed your website. Took the tour of World's End House."

"You are interested in underground living?"

"Maybe."

"Visits to this location are by invitation only. You should contact my office during regular business hours."

"I did."

A sliver of a pause, then, "You fraudulently claim to know one of my clients. You enter my property under false pretenses. Somehow I doubt your veracity, Miss—?"

"We're done here." Slidell jumped in before I could answer.

"I could have you both arrested." A hint of aggression in Timmer's voice.

"That would be a very bad idea." To me. "Let's go."

Without warning, Bing launched himself at Slidell in a disorganized, sloppy-jointed, slo-mo lunge. Skinny reacted with more agility than I'd have thought him capable of. In one lightning move, he sidestepped, grabbed Bing's leading shoulder, and, using the forward motion to his advantage, spun and slammed the big man into the wall.

Timmer retreated behind the door.

Slidell held Bing a long, painful moment, crooking one arm high behind his back. Then, "As I said, we're going now."

Bing grunted and nodded, one beefy cheek tight to the plaster. A few beats, then Slidell released his grip. Bing slid to the floor, a glistening trail of drool and snot marking his descent.

With one glare in my direction, Slidell strode past me toward the door.

The return trip along the beach was not an experience I want to repeat. Slidell was furious. At me. At Timmer. At being in a situation not fully under his control. Mostly at me.

"That was one stupid goddamn waste of time."

"It wasn't. We learned several things."

"Yeah? Like I shouldn't listen to any more of your harebrained ideas."

"We learned that Felix Vodyanov and Nick Body are brothers. That Vodyanov got into a fight with a guy named Twist."

Slidell tripped and stumbled forward. I waited as he regained his balance.

"We learned that the fight took place two days before I spotted Vodyanov prowling my front yard."

"If the guy in the trench coat was Vodyanov."

"A week after the fight with Twist, Vodyanov turned up dead."

"Eeyuh."

We continued past yards and cottages still as crypts. Through mud-crusted litter. My breathing was good, my legs strong from the hours of jogging. And the downhill gradient didn't hurt. Beside me, Slidell was struggling.

Then, above Slidell's panting and slogging, I heard a sound. Footsteps? Were Timmer and Bing following us? Others? Cops? Had Timmer called 911?

"What was that?"

We both froze, vigilant for movement ahead, above, or out over the water. I heard a swish of fabric. Knew Slidell's hand had cocked toward his gun.

All was muggy stillness around us.

As we clambered over the algae-slimed outcrop, I worried. Had Timmer deployed his henchmen to discover where we'd parked? Did he have henchmen? Was he planning an ambush at the 4Runner? Or had he simply returned to his movie? Was my paranoia playing more games with my sanity?

Minutes, maybe eons, then we finally reached the boat ramp. The 4Runner sat alone in the dark. No Bing. No Timmer. No henchmen.

Thank Christ.

A surprising puff of hot air brushed my skin as we both scrambled up the incline and across the concrete. When Slidell wasn't venting his indignation over one thing or another, we rode to Charlotte in silence. Which provided far too much time for reflection.

Had Timmer ordered a covert investigation? Surely he wanted to know who we were. It was obvious he hadn't called 911. Was he afraid of a police presence in the cottage? Of an inquiry into the nature of the event and those who were present?

Had we blundered into something more sinister than a pitch for the delights of a subterranean abode?

*   *   *

Slidell phoned early the next morning. Spent time reemphasizing themes he'd highlighted during the previous night's trudge down the beach and the endless drive home. Finally got to the point.

"Vice boys knew the name right off. Vincent Aiello. Online, goes by Twist."

"Good work."

"You know that dark web thing you been talking up?"

"I wouldn't say I've bee—"

"There was a kiddie porn site down there called PlaySchool. Users went in through some sick-as-shit browser—"

"TOR?"

"Sounds right. Keeps your cyber-prowling secret, so word on the street had PlaySchool as a nice, safe hidey-hole for viewing and trading kiddie porn. Vice guys say there were over a hundred thousand users and tens of thousands of posts involving sexual abuse and exploitation of minors."

"You're using the past tense." Hiding my revulsion.

"Two years ago, the feds shut the fucker down. They arrested the creator and head administrator, a douchebag in Philadelphia name of Sammy Lowenstein, a busload of child porn producers, and a couple hundred U.S.-based users."

"Jesus."

"Messed up, eh? On the plus side, they also rescued thirty-two kids."

"How does Vincent Aiello figure in?"

"Your boy Twist was a frequent flier."

"Meaning?"

"He regularly posted content in the forums."

"The FBI snagged Aiello in their net?"

"Yep. Prosecuted him on a number of counts of engaging in a child-exploitation enterprise."

"I hope he stays behind bars till his dick falls off." Repugnance now curdling my tone.

"Unfortunately, all charges had to be dropped."

"Seriously?"

"To crack into TOR, special agents used what the DOJ described as—I'm quoting here—a network investigative technique approved by a federal court. Later, a different judge ruled that the FBI had to reveal the nature of said technique in order to move forward with prosecuting Aiello. The Bureau said kiss my sweet cheeks. The turd walked."

"Bigger fish?"

"Apparently, the DOJ has related probes that are still ongoing."

"Aiello lives local?"

"Dilworth."

"What's he do?"

"You ready for this? The guy's a lawyer."

"Are you kidding?"

"Solo practitioner, does something with patents, works out of his home."

"Any previous arrests?"

"In 2010, he was charged with one count of possessing and three counts of transporting child pornography. That's how he came to the notice of CMPD vice."

"Let me guess. He skated."

"Got everything thrown out because of a technicality. Apparently, they found the stuff in his car without probable cause to search the vehicle."

"Bing said Vodyanov fought with Aiello. Attacked him, actually. That the incident got him kicked out of DeepHaven."

"What'd they fight about?"

"You know what I know."

"What the hell *is* DeepHaven?"

"I thought it might be a real estate office. Now I'm not so sure."

"Because?"

"Why such an odd location? Why no commercial signage? Why so much security? Why use only the first names of clients?"

There was a pause over the line. Heavy. Then Slidell summarized aloud what we were both thinking.

"Aiello's a pedophile. He's living in Charlotte when Jahaan Cole goes missing. The kid's name is in Vodyanov's notebook. Vodyanov gets into a throwdown with Aiello and shortly thereafter turns up dead."

I picked up the thread. "Aiello's into kiddie porn but managed to stay under the radar until 2010, then again for the next six years. He's a lawyer, he's careful, undoubtedly more so since the FBI bust. We need to question him before he gets wind of our interest."

"*We* don't need to do *nothing*. Just because I agreed to your little sortie last night don't mean we're now Starsky and Hutch."

Expected. I pressed on anyway.

"Can you pull Aiello's file? Talk to the feds? To the vice detective and prosecutor from 2010?"

"Sit tight until you hear from me."

"I—"

"No promises. Just be ready when I call."

After disconnecting, the revulsion hung on. I was fixed in place, wallowing in it, when a knock sounded on the door. I looked up. Through the window above the sink I could see a panel truck, through the one in the door a stoop-shouldered silhouette wearing a broad-billed white cap. I recognized the long-lost painter. Fred? Frank?

I let Fred/Frank in. He was in his mid-fifties, with sullen eyes and pockmarked skin that looked like it had spent its whole life in a cellar. As on our earlier encounters, I suspected that neither Fred/Frank's cap nor his matching coveralls had enjoyed the company of detergent in the recent past.

Fred/Frank and I discussed the errant shade of paint. After he showed me the new color and I approved, he trudged upstairs. Several return trips for a ladder, more cans, brushes, drop cloths, and other paraphernalia, and Fred/Frank disappeared into the new study.

Recalling Fred/Frank's fondness for sun tea, I filled my large glass jar with distilled water, threw in a mix of green, hibiscus, and peach tea bags, capped it, and set the jar out on the porch. God forbid I should fall short should Fred/Frank grow thirsty.

By ten, the place smelled like the inside of a chimney at a chemical plant. Unsure if that was normal, or healthy, I decided to vacate.

Throughout the morning, I ran errands. After lunch, I began work on an article for the *Journal of Forensic Sciences.* In the downstairs guest room/study. With the door closed to head off the fumes.

Around two, heavy clomping on the staircase

caught my attention. I peeked out in time to see Fred/
Frank hurrying down the hall.

"All finished?" To his retreating back.

"Got a phone call. Gotta go."

"But—"

I heard the kitchen door open, click shut. Exasperated, I rolled a towel and jammed it along the crack
below the door in the upstairs study. The hasty departure felt worryingly familiar. Why, I wondered, had I
stuck with this guy?

At six, I left to meet Pete for dinner.

His news made thoughts of fickle painters, missing
kids, pedophiles, faceless corpses, and strange bunkers
dissolve like fog on a hot summer dawn.

Pete and I tied the knot young, kept it tied for two
decades. Then came the nurse, the Realtor, the law-
firm colleague. Unable to ignore the affairs, I left. For
years, my simmering anger and his guilt kept us apart.
The resentment and self-blame are gone now. We both
agree. We're better friends single than we ever were
married.

Despite the temperature, Pete was on the patio at
Toscana, our favorite restaurant since back in the day.
He was wearing khaki shorts, a cotton polo, boat shoes,
no socks. Standard dress.

Pete smiled on seeing me. Rose as I crossed to the
table.

"Tempe." He'd been out of town, and we hadn't
spoken in a month. As usual, hearing Pete's voice
stirred memories long dormant. Snuggling in a carrel

in the law-school library, his worn leather jacket soft against my cheek. His hair glinting white-gold under a full Barbados moon. His eyes beaming joy, infant Katy raised two-handed high above his head. His eyes wide in horror, like those of the lady beside him in our bed.

"Hey, Pete." Kicking the memories aside.

"You look terrific."

I didn't. I'd thrown on a sundress, my sole inspiration for coping with the merciless heat.

Pete's arms went around me. My cheek brushed his shirt, and my nose took in his Aramis cologne, a scent he refused to supplant with any other. I relaxed into his chest. For a moment, all was as it once was.

Sweet Jesus! My overloaded stress-strain curve was turning me into a mooning adolescent. The treasonous glitch in my arterial wiring?

Right, Brennan. Blame everything on the aneurysm.

I stepped back. The moment ended. We both sat.

Through long-standing and hard-won mutual agreement, my ex and I strive to keep all conversations neutral. That night, we discussed Katy. Mama. The Hornets' prospects for the upcoming season. When Pete queried my work, I shook my head no. When I asked about his travels, he said they'd involved a Winnebago and parklands. Alrighty.

As we ate, I tried not to glance at my watch. To wonder what was occupying Slidell. Behind Pete's head, a faulty carriage-lantern bulb winked on and off. I absently tracked its sputtering decline. Thought again about the AWOL electrician. Resolved to keep nagging until he finished the job in the new study.

We were sipping decaf espressos when I said, "OK, big guy. What's this news that must only be shared in person?"

Pete's face went all tight angles and bones. A beat, then he set his tiny china cup on its tiny china saucer. It made a soft chinking sound. Long after, I recalled that odd little detail.

"My trip was for Boyd."

Pete's strange response. His somber tone and obvious tension. I felt a tickle of unease.

"For the dog," I said.

"Yes."

When anxious, I often joke. I did so then. "The chow's worried about the rising cost of admission to national parks?"

Unsmiling, Pete took my hand. The gesture, meant to comfort, had the opposite effect.

"Boyd has a brain tumor, Tempe. I took him to a specialist in Raleigh."

"A tumor." The bulb was dead, the lantern across the terrace now a hazy Cyclops eye.

"It's frontal. He's losing vision on the right."

I swallowed. "How will they treat it?"

Pete squeezed my hand harder.

The cold hollowness spread outward. I said nothing.

"He loved being out on the trails," Pete said. "I think Acadia was his favorite."

I nodded.

"Boyd's had a good life."

I'm lousy at expressing emotion. At offering condolence. I spoke the first words to come into my head.

"It'll be fine."

My artless response hung between us on the hot summer air. We both knew it wouldn't be fine. It would be agonizing. Heart-wrenching. Achingly sad.

"I want to see him."

"Of course. We'll—"

"Now."

"Sure."

Pete signaled for the check. Paid. I was too devastated to argue.

I followed Pete to the house we'd shared for almost twenty years. His now. I waited while he used his key to let us in.

We'd barely cleared the door when Boyd came strolling into the foyer, ears at half mast, tongue dangling purple. Seeing me, the dog went into his usual routine, not full-out berserk but pretty excited, circling me and nudging both my hands with his snout. I petted his head and ruffled the fur on his neck. Which did nothing to calm the display.

At Pete's suggestion, we all moved into the family room. I accepted his offer of coffee, too focused on Boyd to consider the consequences of late-night caffeine. As Pete disappeared into the kitchen, I dropped onto the sofa, leaned forward, and opened my arms.

Boyd put his head on my knee, looked up, and rotated his eyebrow whiskers. I gazed into the doleful brown eyes, a million memories colliding in my mind. Fighting tears, I wondered. Did the dog know something was amiss in his head? Did he sense his upcoming decline? His death?

Was I projecting my own angst onto the chow? My newborn sense of my own mortality?

Pete and I took Boyd for a very long walk. I stayed far later than I should have. While starting the car, I noticed the time on the dashboard clock. 11:37.

I wept all the way to the annex.

Another shock awaited me there.

24

The porch light was on, but the usual squadron of moths wasn't fluttering in the nimbus around it. My ears registered no soft ticking of wings against bulbs. The air smelled of petunias and marigolds and freshly mowed lawn. And something else. An acrid tinge overriding the floral mix.

A ghostlike shadow materialized from the darkness at the corner of the house. To either side of it, the ground looked oddly rippled, as though the soil had been gouged, the grass trampled and flattened.

My mind logged all the incongruous cues. Offered no explanation.

"Bird?"

As the cat padded toward me, I checked my surroundings. Still no alarm bells. My gaze fell on the door leading into the kitchen. Dark slashes ran along the edges where the wood should have met the frame.

Had the wind knocked it ajar? For those in my line

of work, security is second nature. Like washing your hands with soap. Or breathing. Plus, there had been break-ins in the past. No way I'd ever forget to lock up.

Seriously, Brennan? Lately you've been acting like a sparrow caged with a Maine Coon.

Pete was with me during dinner and later at his house. Katy wasn't in Charlotte. Mama didn't drive after dark. No one else in town had a key. Who?

I jumped at the brush of fur on my ankles. Squatted and scooped Birdie into my arms.

"Good boy for hanging close to home."

The cat purred and raised his head. I buried my nose behind his right ear.

My pulse quickened.

He smelled like cinders.

Flash image of the incinerator at the fenced bunker.

Alert Slidell?

Detective Delightful would either go radioactive at being phoned so late or set a land record rushing over to protect my ass. Before dialing, I had to know what the hell was going on. If anything.

Another quick glance around, then I eased the door inward and stepped inside. No ski-masked figure lurched from the gloom. Every familiar shape was in its normal position. The sink, the appliances, the table and chairs.

But the smell of smoke was unmistakable.

Nervous energy must have goosed me into squeezing harder than I realized. Birdie *yrrrped* and twisted. With a four-paw brace, he launched from my chest and shot from the room.

Lights?

I knew the layout. An intruder, if there was one, would not. Advantage to me.

Feeling half foolish, half frightened, I crept forward in the dark. The dining room was undisturbed. Ditto the living room, the only movement the gentle swaying of the pendulum on the mantel clock. The only sound its low metronome.

But why so black? Usually, I leave the hall table lamp burning. I'd also forgotten that?

As I inched toward the guest room/study, the air felt wrong. Too heavy, too warm. Had the hot mugginess seeped in through the open back door? And why the smell of burning?

One peek gave rise to alarm.

The room sparkled with a million points of iridescence.

A moment of confusion, then comprehension.

Light from a streetlamp was filtering through a shattered window behind the sofa, sparking shards of glass blanketing the furniture and rug.

Birdie was on an end table, a pale, fuzzy cutout in the shimmery gloom. His nose was raised, his nostrils testing the out-of-place scents of flowers, grass, and soot. On sensing my presence, he focused round questioning eyes on me.

I had no answer for him. A missile hurled through the window? By accident? On purpose? No foreign object lay embedded in the aurora borealis display.

A break-in?

Was the burglar still in the house?

I tried to calm myself to think.

Phone Slidell! The old gaggle of wary neurons urged.

Yes.

Of course, I got voice mail. Left a message.

911?

Not yet.

Why not?

I stood, breath frozen, listening for movement upstairs. Heard footsteps. Rustling. A soft *sssshh*.

No pistol being cocked. No semiautomatic slide being ratcheted back. That was good.

Ignoring the alarmist neurons, I gathered Birdie and locked him in the pantry. Then I grabbed a hammer, retraced my steps, and stole up the stairs. With each tread, the smoky stench grew stronger.

Halfway up, I paused. Was I actually hearing movement? Or were the sounds a new fantasy born of my paranoia? Of my unbearable grief over Boyd?

At the top, my anxiety went suborbital. The thuds and swishes were real and coming from off to the right.

I tried to swallow. My mouth was too dry.

Tightening my grip on the hammer, I tiptoed down the hallway toward the new shared office.

The door was open, the rolled towel kicked to one side. A Coleman LED lantern sat just inside, throwing off-angle slashes of light and shadow upward from its floor-level placement.

The room looked like a nuclear bomb had gone off. The south and east walls remained as scorched uprights backed by mangled exterior siding. Melted wiring dangled from the exposed framing and damaged ceiling.

Both desks were destroyed, my patinaed old oak charred and blackened, Ryan's glass cracked and fragmented. The two filing cabinets were now scorched hulks, their drawers exploded outward by the intense heat. What was left of my reports, printouts, and photos lay scattered across the floor as sodden sludge.

The reek of smoke, seared metal, and liquefied plastic was so overpowering my eyes began to burn, and tears ran down my cheeks. And, underlying the mix, another noxious note. Paint? Turpentine?

I pictured the broken window downstairs. Wondered again about an intruder. Could the added element I was smelling be an accelerant such as gas or kerosene? Was I the victim of arson?

Amid the wreckage I spotted what survived of Ryan's Guy Lafleur bobblehead, my picture of Katy, the Nebulon frigate lamp, all twisted and distorted. My framed diplomas leaned cockeyed, glass shattered, documents torn, every component covered in soot. Propped against what was once the east wall was a blackened metal ladder. Flanking it, along the baseboard, were incinerated cans and remnants of what had been drop cloths and rags.

Also amid the wreckage was my neighbor, dressed in bathrobe, PJs, and sneakers. A mask covered his mouth, and a fire extinguisher jutted from between his arms and his ribs.

"Walter?"

He turned and lowered the mask. "Oh, Tempe. I am so sorry."

"What happened?"

"I looked over and saw smoke billowing from your window." Pointing the extinguisher's nozzle in that direction. "Called 911. That was around seven."

"Thanks." Stunned mumble through fingers pressed to my lips.

"One responder said the fire appeared electrical in origin. A flying spark hit the rags and open paint and turpentine, and *boom*." Dramatized with exploding fingers. "Apparently, the new smoke alarm wasn't functioning properly."

"Did you open the door for them?" Knowing Walter had an emergency key to my place.

"Seriously?"

"Right." The startled hand floating down to my chest.

Disbelieving, I took in the devastation.

"They said it was one of those freak situations where the fire exploded, blew up fast and incredibly hot, then ran out of fuel and died without spreading to other parts of the house. They had a term for it. Flashover? I don't recall."

I nodded, eyes still on the chaos.

"You can relax, though. The flames are totally out, and the walls are cool. I checked. I didn't really trust that crew to be thorough, so I went over everything after the truck left. Twice." Raising the extinguisher. "My grandfather was a firefighter. He always said secondary flare-ups were the real danger."

Sudden horrifying thought.

My eyes flew to my desktop. The AC adapter was there, gnarled and melted. A lump of plastic that was once the mouse. Both were embedded in the charred wood on which they lay.

My computer was gone!

Blind fury ramrodded through the shock. "Sonofabitch! Where's my laptop?"

"Where did you leave it?" Walter, eyes roving.

Ignoring the question, and the gritty crunch of glass underfoot, I darted into the room and began rummaging through the mess. Walter set down the extinguisher and joined in the search.

"I suppose it could be on the lawn," he said, after several fruitless minutes. "They chucked things out the window."

I raced down the stairs, fired through the door, and circled to the back of the annex. Shapes littered the ground, unidentifiable in the darkness. Frantic, I moved from object to object, desperately hoping my laptop had somehow been spared and lay among the jumble.

I nearly cried when I found it, a hunk of blackened metal, melted keys, shattered fiber-optic glass and circuit board. Devastated, I laid down the ruined Mac, hurried back inside, and mounted the stairs. With trembling hands, I began picking up and setting aside random items. Paper scraps. Fragments of pillow stuffing. Hunks of wire.

At one point, Walter again offered his condolences, then took his leave, saying something about later retrieving his lamp. I paid no attention.

How could Fred/Frank have been so negligent? How could I have been so stupid? The small space must have been pyrotechnic. Why hadn't I checked the room following his abrupt departure? Why hadn't I personally tested the smoke alarm? Why hadn't I replaced the bungling twit?

My self-recrimination was such that I didn't hear

the SUV engine. The doorbell. The buzz of my mobile against my ass finally caught my attention. I answered.

"You OK in there?"

"Best day of my life." White-hot with anger at myself.

"You want I should call a SWAT team, or you plan to answer the door?"

I trudged downstairs, let Slidell in, and led him up to the study.

"Holy fucking fuckville."

"Poetic. Add a bleating goat sound to that, and you've got a hit." Mean, but I hated this. Hated Fred/Frank and the equally inept electrician for causing it. Hated myself for letting it happen. Hated Slidell for being in my home. For being a witness to the disaster.

Slidell's nose wrinkled, and his face crimped. "That paint thinner I'm smelling?"

I just glared at him.

"What did you lose?"

"My laptop."

"What else?"

"The Rolex and keys to the yacht."

Slidell ignored my snark. "You got any idea—"

"Bad wiring and fumes," I snapped.

"You keep any valuables in here? Jewelry? Electronics? Stuff you'll need to document for insurance purposes?"

"Isn't my goddamn laptop enough?"

I noticed that the front of Slidell's shirt was sweat-stained in the shape of a newt, the holstered Glock at his hip fully exposed.

"Sorry," I added. "I appreciate your coming."

"It ain't the end of the world." Cocking his chin at the rubble.

"It sure as hell doesn't help our investigation. Everything relating to the Vodyanov case is toast."

"Yeah?"

"What the fire didn't destroy my overly zealous neighbor turned into mush."

"Like what?"

"The MCME file that Joe Hawkins gave me. The photos I printed. My notes. The scraps from Vodyanov's trench-coat pocket. Lizzie Griesser's phenotype sketch and report. I'd just moved it all up here."

"Your pal can print you another sketch."

"That's not the point."

Slidell scanned with professional eyes. Then, "Any chance it wasn't the wiring?"

"What are you saying?"

"You chafe someone's ass lately?"

That scored him another livid glare.

"The fire boys break that window downstairs?"

"I assume so. It's what they do, right? With big manly axes?"

"How's this play? Someone's caking his shorts not knowing what we've found. You being an easier target than a cop . . ." Slidell let the thought hang.

"Arson?"

Slidell didn't answer.

"Who?"

"You tell me."

"How could I have been so stupid?" The overload of adrenaline was making me shrill. "So catastrophically careless?"

"Lose the drama, OK? You have a lot of pics on your phone, right?"

"I was having battery issues, so I transferred everything to my laptop."

"You saved all your shit in the mist or the fog or whatever, right?"

"No."

Slidell's brows floated up.

"Look, I've been a little freaked since Larabee's death. Vodyanov stalking me here didn't help." If he did stalk me here. "Call it paranoia, whatever. I put nothing in the cloud."

"You sent me the pics from your cell?"

"No." The call from Gerry Breugger. The subpoena. The outing to Lake Wylie. The news about Boyd. With so much happening, I'd totally forgotten to forward the images.

Slidell gave the slightest of nods.

"Exposed wires. Flickering lights. Open paint and rags soaked in turpentine or whatever. Christ Almighty! What was I thinking?"

"My opinion, it ain't all that straightforward."

"Wait. You're seriously suggesting arson? That I was targeted?"

"I'm suggesting it ain't all that straightforward."

"Small comfort. I was just as negligent about security. No lock on this door." A shocking consequence hit me hard. "If what you're saying is true, then everything we had could now be in the hands of . . . of . . . *who*? The very assholes we've been tracking?"

"Your laptop was password-protected, right?"

"Of course it was. But I think I was hacked recently. Even if I wasn't, any high school techie worth his binary code can bypass or change a password. Hell, I know how to do that!"

"Reel it in." Slidell gestured with downturned palms.

He was right. I'd made reentry into strident. I closed my eyes and took a deep breath. Before the exhale, another realization.

"I can't remember when I last cleared my browser history. If someone did break in, and if the creep logged onto my laptop before setting the fire, he would have seen my searches on Vodyanov, Body, Timmer, MKUltra, the *Estonia*. My Google Earth visits. My trips to the dark web, DeepUnder, Homes at the End of the World, World's End House—"

"I get it."

"And what about Joe Hawkins? What if the guy saw that file? Joe could lose his job for leaking it to me. Face legal action if Heavner decides to play hard ball. What if the creep downloaded stuff onto a thumb drive or—"

"Gimme some possibles." Slidell yanked his notebook from a breast pocket sweat-stained by the newt's tail.

I had no idea of his meaning.

"Say this wasn't random. Say it is arson. Gimme some scenarios. Who? Why? Even if they're crazy. Just keep talking."

"I tangled with Heavner. That didn't go well." Half joking, half serious.

"Motive?"

"Fear of disclosure as incompetent? Maybe even obstructive? It's been almost two weeks, and still there's no ID on Vodyanov, no cause of death."

"Go on."

"Nick Body?"

"Why?"

"Fear of exposure as a fraud? Of bad publicity?"

"The shitbird thrives on bad publicity."

"Maybe Body learned that you and I are investigating his brother's death. Maybe he knew Felix had something to do with Jahaan Cole's disappearance. With other kids going missing. Or maybe Nick himself was involved with the disappearances. Maybe he was responsible for Vodyanov's death."

"Who tipped him?"

"He and Heavner are old pals. Or it could have been someone at Sparkling Waters. Dr. Yuriev? Asia Barrow? Holly Kimrey jumped me outside the gate to the fenced property. Maybe the place belongs to Body. Maybe Kimrey's paid to do Body's dirty work. Maybe Body hired Kimrey to torch my place."

Slidell scribbled as I spoke.

"Vince Aiello?" I was on a roll, spewing words with no thought. "Maybe Aiello fears three strikes as a pedophile and he's going down. Did you talk to him today? Maybe inadvertently clue him?"

Slidell's eyes rolled up and narrowed. Don't go there.

"Yates Timmer was unhappy that we showed up at his cottage." As understatements go, that one was epic. "Maybe he had Bing follow me here from Lake Wylie last night, though I don't think the guy was in any shape to drive. Maybe Timmer ordered the fire. He could have had someone watching the annex. His goon saw me leave for dinner with Pete and struck."

"Motive?"

"No idea. But Timmer's DeepHaven setup gives off a bad vibe."

Slidell wiggled impatient fingers.

"Too much security, too little transparency for a Realtor."

"What he hawks ain't exactly standard."

"Selling bunkers and missile silos is perfectly legal. Why employ a steroidal bouncer?"

"Any other ideas?"

"Gerry Breugger?"

"Who the fuck is Gerry Breugger?"

"A freelance journalist who called looking for intel on the Vodyanov case."

"Would Breugger go that far?"

"If he thought the story would put a shine on his Wikipedia bio."

"Others?"

I lifted both palms and shoulders in frustration.

"Or maybe it was just turpentine and bad wiring."

A beat as we both looked around. Slidell spoke first.

"I'll send someone to slap plywood on this window and the one downstairs."

"I can do it."

"He'll do it faster."

"Thanks." Detesting my role as a victim.

"You want I should have CSU swing by in the morning? The arson boys?"

"What's the point?" I said.

"Can't hurt to establish someone torched the place. Dust for prints." With little enthusiasm. "Don't touch—"

"I got it."

When Slidell left, I tried phoning Ryan. Was rolled to voice mail.

Exhausted, I ignored my face and teeth and crawled into bed. A cue for my brain to begin trolling for worries over which to obsess. That night, the choices were endless.

At one point, I heard banging, figured Slidell's minions had arrived to secure the window. Birdie joined me when the hammering stopped, probably peeved that his call-of-the-wild portal had been sealed. I reached down to stroke his head.

"So glad you weren't hurt." Mumbled, at last drowsy. "Was our arsonist a cat lover or just a cat burglar? Did you charm him? Or hunker down and sneak outside unnoticed?"

Faulty wiring or an intruder?

Suddenly I was wide awake, struck by a horrifying thought.

Had Birdie slipped out on his own when the downstairs window was broken or the back door opened? Or was he intentionally spared?

If the latter, had leaving Birdie unharmed been intended to send a message? A message saying my intruder could have taken or killed my pet but didn't?

Was there an intruder?

Was there a message?

A message telling me who was in charge?

A threat?

A threat from whom?

Or was my paranoia flaring again?

25

CSU, the crime-scene unit, showed up at seven. Slidell's "arson boys." After they'd finished dusting the guest room/study, I cleaned up the glass. No doubt a death sentence for the vacuum, but I wanted it gone.

Next, using my phone, I emailed LaManche, explaining the fire and the demise of my laptop and asking that copies of the Pasquerault file be sent to the MCME. I'd planned to review all my reports and notes following dinner with Pete. Only one week until my testimony, and I was starting to get anxious.

When CSU wrapped up in the upstairs office, I plowed through the charred chaos. Found not a single readable document or viewable photo. What the fire hadn't consumed the water from the hoses and the foam from the extinguisher had reduced to pulp.

Slidell phoned as I was depositing another five-gallon bag of slop into my outdoor trash bin.

"Aiello's ass is parked in a room down the hall."

"At the Law Enforcement Center?"

"No. I booked him into the Ritz."

"How did you persuade him to come in?"

"Told him his name came up in a cold-case investigation."

"He asked for no details?"

"I promised lots when he got here. Being an upstanding citizen, he agreed. That and the fact I mentioned the old jacket on kiddie porn. Maybe implied I was debating a call to the state bar."

"Will he bring counsel?"

"He mentioned that. I mentioned how I hoped the media didn't get wind of our chat."

"I can be there in twenty minutes."

"I want to sweat Aiello a while, let him take a solo stroll down memory lane."

"What time will you start?"

"Eleven."

"I'm in."

I arrived on the second floor at 10:52. Slidell was not at his desk in the violent crimes division. He was not in the cold-case unit. A detective named Conover thought he'd gone to question a witness. Gave me directions I didn't need.

Hiding my annoyance, I thanked Conover, hurried back up the hall, and let myself into a space the size of my pantry. Leaving the overheads off, I stepped to a lighted rectangle on the right-hand wall.

Through the one-way mirror, I could see the

adjacent interrogation room, a stark duplicate of the one I was in. Same wall phone, same recording equipment, same institutional table and chairs.

No red light glowed on the camera tucked high in one corner. I wondered if Aiello had balked at being taped. The audio was working. Objection or not, Slidell would have insisted on that.

Slidell occupied one chair, his back to me. A yellow legal pad and a folder lay on the table before him, the contents of the latter mostly blocked by his bulk.

The man opposite looked like he'd never visited a gym in his life. Which I guessed had lasted maybe fifty years. His hair was dirty-blond, center-parted, and tucked behind his ears. His bottom lip was fuller than his top, giving his face a perpetual pout.

Aiello shoved a paper across the tabletop, I assumed some type of waiver form. Tossed a pen after. When Slidell leaned forward to collect them, I caught my first glimpse of Aiello's eyes, Coke-bottle green and bereft of feeling.

Slidell was still in good-cop mode.

"OK, Vince. Glad we got all that legal mumbo jumbo out of the way. It's OK if I call you Vince?"

"Could we move this along?"

"I appreciate you coming in. You need anything? A coffee? A soda?"

"I'm good." Pointedly checking his watch. Which was gold and the size of a manhole cover.

Slidell shuffled his papers, selected and studied one. Or appeared to. Smiled, friendly as hell.

"You've lived in Charlotte since—"

"Since 1984."

"You're a lawyer, right?"

"I am."

"You help folks protect their inventions?"

"Yes."

"Tell me about that."

Aiello took Slidell through a brief discourse on the U.S. Patent Act, exclusive rights, trademarks, limited monopolies, for all of which Slidell feigned avid interest. He appeared to take notes. Finally laid down his pen.

"You know how you can never fill up your bathtub? I got an idea for this gadget plugs the overflow drain so's you can have a nice, deep soak. Think that'd qualify?"

Aiello listed the five requirements: patentable subject matter, utility, novelty, nonobviousness, and enablement. Advised Slidell to apply for a utility patent, describing his device as a machine with a new useful purpose.

Slidell listened, overnodding. "Thanks. I'll do that." Then, reading from a printout, "You live alone, right?"

"Last I checked, that's not a crime."

"You own property in Dilworth."

"We both know these things."

"A house on Mount Vernon Avenue. That's near Latta Park, yeah?"

"As I said, I have a busy day. What's this all about?"

"Real pretty park. I used to walk my dog there."

"Please spare me the small talk."

"Will do." Quick flick of a smile. "Tell me what you know about Felix Vodyanov."

"Who?" Clearly surprised at the question.

"Felix. Vodyanov." Slowly.

"Don't know the man."

"I think you do."

"You are mistaken."

Aiello tried to cross his arms on his chest. The parts involved were too large for the arrangement to work. The flabby forelimbs dropped back to the armrests barely containing his torso.

"We'll circle back to Vodyanov," Slidell said. "Talk about his brother."

"Who?"

"Nick Body. You three buddied up through Yates Timmer, correct?"

"I've never heard any of those names."

"That's not the story coming from Timmer's muscle. According to Bing, you and Vodyanov had one hell of a throwdown."

"You said you had questions about a cold case." Still cocky but showing the first cracks.

"He's cold enough."

"What does that mean?"

"Vodyanov entered long-term parking right after the two of you went at each other."

"Long-term parking?"

"He turned up dead."

"I'm sorry for the man's misfortune."

Slidell switched tacks. An old trick to catch a witness off guard. "Twist. That's an odd handle. How'd you get it?"

Seconds passed. Aiello looked like he was counting the concrete blocks in the wall to Slidell's left. Or deciding on a strategy.

"Probably not your dancing skills," Slidell said.

"Boo-hah. The cop does comedy."

"I'm guessing it's a reference to your favorite pastime."

The pouty lips tightened.

Slidell pulled a photo from his file and skimmed it across the table. Through the speaker, the paper made a slithery, hissing sound. Through the glass, I caught a flash of bright pink beads.

"Jahaan Cole." Slidell's words were suddenly curdled with loathing. "She was nine when some degenerate piece of shit yanked her out of her life. You get your rocks off leering at naked kids, *Twist*. You know anything about that?"

Aiello's Adam's apple took a roller-coaster ride in his fleshy throat.

"Look at her!" Slidell finger-jabbed the image.

Aiello glanced down, quickly away.

"What happened to her?"

"I have no idea."

"I think you're lying."

"OK, fine. I heard about her on the news." The Coke-bottle eyes were now round and flat. "Everyone did. Because of past . . . difficulties . . . I was caught up in the hysteria, questioned illegally. I had an alibi. I wasn't in Charlotte when the child disappeared."

Skinny knew the Cole file inside and out. Knew Aiello hadn't been a suspect. I understood his motive.

The chair legs screeched as Slidell popped to his feet and leaned across the table. When he spoke again, nose inches above Aiello's, his voice was low and dangerous.

"That's the cold case I want to talk about, you dumb prick." Sending droplets of spit onto Aiello's face. "Only this one's never going cold on my watch. So. You want we should dive down that hole? Or maybe you're suddenly remembering your pals?"

Aiello raised a hand to wipe the saliva from his skin, reconsidered, and dropped it.

"I'm waiting, asshole."

Aiello held perfectly still a moment before responding.

"Please step away."

Slidell hesitated, then dropped back into his chair.

"Nick Body is a radio personality. But I'm sure you are cognizant of that fact."

"He's a boil on the buttcheek of humanity, but go on."

"Body has a large national audience but avoids the limelight when off air." Aiello was choosing his words carefully. "He fervently safeguards his privacy and allows very few into his inner circle. I am not one of those few."

"You met Body through Timmer."

"I did."

"Timmer sells real estate."

"He does."

"What's DeepHaven?"

"My word, detective. You have done some digging."

"You need I should repeat the question?"

"DeepHaven is a sort of social club."

"For suckers buying into Body's conspiracy bullshit?"

"Nothing like that. Body and his brother are mere members like the rest of us." Another pause for word choice. "DeepHaven is a gathering place for those sharing the same concerns as Yates Timmer."

"Wackadoos wanting to live underground."

"In his day, Edward Jenner was considered a wackadoo. You're familiar with Jenner, of course?" Raising supercilious brows. "Vaccination?"

"Talk about Vodyanov."

Aiello said nothing.

"You need a visual aid on him, too." Sharp. "I got one. It ain't pretty."

"I hardly knew the man."

"You fought with him."

"*He* attacked *me*."

"Was Vodyanov into hard candy, like you?" Slidell's face was red and moving toward claret. "You two pair up to ogle toddlers outta their diapers?"

Aiello's eyes returned to the concrete blocks.

"Why was Vodyanov carrying info on this kid?" Slidell snatched up Cole's photo, glowering hard.

"If you'll calm down and keep your distance, I'll tell you what I know." Again, the arm-cross failed. "But this cannot get back to DeepHaven."

"Those cretins are the least of your worries."

A moment of mental editing. "Felix Vodyanov was delusional and dishonest."

"Explain that."

"Here's an example. He liked custom-made clothing he couldn't afford, so he shopped resale. You know what I'm talking about? Stores where high-end items are sold on consignment?"

Slidell probably didn't but nodded.

"Then he'd cut out the labels so no one would

know." Aiello smoothed down the front of his shirt. "He'd buy cheap tobacco and transfer it to fancy European packaging."

"I got a nephew's pretentious like that. Don't make him a perv."

"Vodyanov was also paranoid. He'd pay only in cash, had no credit cards, no cell phone, constantly created and abandoned internet accounts. He went through aliases like the rest of us go through tissue."

"Where did he live?"

"I don't know. At DeepHaven, one does not query the personal lives of others."

"Yet he told you where he bought his skivvies."

"I certainly didn't ask."

"The guy have a job?"

"He did research for Body's blogs and podcasts. Apparently, little bro was too cheap to support the lifestyle to which big bro aspired."

"Why'd you clock him?"

"I told you. I was defending myself."

"Why'd he jump you?"

"It's a long story."

"I'm listening."

Very deep sigh. "Early last month, people started reporting that someone was looking for me. I had no idea who. Or why."

"People?"

"Neighbors, a client, the gardener."

"Go on."

"One day, I saw a man on the sidewalk outside my home. He was just standing there, staring at the house. It was Felix Vodyanov."

Flashback. A face lit by a streetlamp in a parking lot at Sharon Hall.

"What did he want?"

Aiello's fingers interlaced, tightened so hard they paled. Discomfort with the upcoming part of the story.

"He used to ask me questions about kids. I don't know why he was interested or why he chose me."

"What kids?"

"Missing kids."

Slidell again jabbed the Cole photo, now back on the table.

Aiello nodded. "And others."

"What others?"

"I don't recall names."

"Don't jerk me around."

"I'm not." Aiello was sweating visibly now. His skin looked silky yellow through the filter of the mirror. "More than once, he accused me of kidnapping and molesting children. Of being behind these disappearances."

"What made him think that?"

"The man was insane."

"And there's that pesky arrest record you got."

"I was never convicted." Churlish. "Everyone misunderstands. Viewing images does not equate to hurting children."

"Go on." I couldn't see Slidell's face but knew he was struggling to control his temper.

"For a while, he dropped the whole subject. Then, as I said, maybe six weeks ago, he started this stalking business. When I saw him outside my home, I confronted him. He said he'd come to force me to level with him. To tell him what had happened to these kids. I told him to go screw himself. He tried again at DeepHaven. That's when I hit him."

Slidell looked at Aiello a very long moment. Then, "Don't move."

"I really must—"

Slidell gathered his papers, got to his feet, and crossed to the door. I met him in the hall.

"What do you think?" Wiping his face with a grayed square of fabric yanked from a back pocket.

"He never asked how Vodyanov died."

"You noticed that, too."

"Still, my gut says he's telling the truth."

"But not all of it."

"Exactly." The hands on the wall clock were pointing to the twelve and the five. "Listen, I still have some cleaning up to do. And a file to collect and read before my testimony next week."

"Go." Pocket-jamming the hankie. "I'll trot this wanker through his story a couple more times. See if it hangs together when he's balls to the wall."

A wave of hot, humid air engulfed me when I left the building. Slogged me across the lot to my car.

I was at the MCME in minutes. The lobby was almost empty, not unusual for a Wednesday afternoon in July. An elderly woman slouched in a chair, crying quietly into a lavender tissue. A death investigator stood flipping through papers on a clipboard.

I swiped my card, passed through the bio-vestibule to the secure side of the facility, and went straight to my office. No sign of Heavner. Mixed feelings about that. Part of me wanted to confront her. Another part wanted to avoid another skirmish with Dr. Death.

Once at my desk, I logged onto my computer and checked my email. Nothing from LaManche. I busied myself with other messages and requests, other tasks. The Pasquerault file finally arrived around four. After downloading and printing the relevant portions, I logged off and headed out.

I made a not-so-quick stop at the vet's office to pick up a case of Birdie's preferred food, apparently stored in a warehouse in suburban Dubrovnik. I was back at the annex by five.

After a glass of sun tea, which I'd brought in from outside and placed in the fridge, I opened the Pasquerault file and sorted the components into stacks at the kitchen table.

I was reviewing my skeletal autopsy report when Dorothée Pasquerault opened the back door.

26

Sounds eddied around me, a cacophony of beeping and clanking and humming and ringing.

And voices, most hushed, one forceful, frenzied almost.

I smelled climatized air and disinfectant.

My head pounded. My chest burned. My forearm prickled.

I tried to sit up. Felt pressure on my shoulders, gentle but firm. I lay back.

"She's awake."

Footsteps clicked, hard and fast.

I opened my eyes.

Light scorched my optic nerves like a jolt from a Taser.

A face hovered above me, a landscape of foggy valleys and peaks. Slowly, the geography crystallized into a recognizable pattern.

"You're going to be just dandy, doc." Forced calm belying tension.

I could only stare at Slidell, unable to speak.

"I rang for the nurse." Then, bellowed over one shoulder, "Where's the goddamn nurse?"

"Drink?" My mouth was as dry as an unwatered lawn in August.

Slidell conferred with someone. Got clearance. A plastic tumbler was produced. I sucked on the straw like I'd never drunk liquid before.

Flash synapses. Dorothée Pasquerault backlit in my doorway. Standing at my car, flies buzzing and dive-bombing the fenders and hood.

"Wha . . . time?"

"Almost four."

Jesus Christ. Could that be?

When I tried rewinding a mental tape of the afternoon, my brain unspooled a mash-up of visual, tactile, and olfactory impressions. Images of a jarringly blue path winding through psychedelically green vegetation toward an open blast door leading to a pitch-black void. A tiny green beacon beckoning me through an endless warren of ebony darkness. My fingers brailling over concrete furry with moss, convoluted piping, metal fittings vomiting rust. My nose sorting primordial smells—moldy earth, rotting fabric, and creatures long dead.

Had I gone to Cleveland County? Had I descended into Vodyanov's bunker?

Slidell read my confusion. "It's four a.m., Thursday morning. You were AWOL for almost ten hours."

Was that possible?

"What happened?" I croaked.

"A guy walking his poodle found you outside by the back wall at Sharon Hall. Harcourt, that's the guy, claims Larry, that's the poodle, was sniffing for a leak, nosed you out under a hedge. Thinking you were either drunk or dead, Harcourt called 911. That was around two a.m. Don't ask me why the dog needed to piss at that hour of the morning." Nervous run-on. Slidell was clearly wired. "Harcourt says he's willing to do interviews. Not sure about Larry."

Had I spent that long wandering the grounds or curled up outside? Had I driven to Cleveland County, eventually returned, and passed out by the wall? Had someone taken me there, then brought me back home? Was it all the result of a cataclysmic headache? Meds? I didn't remember taking anything. A sign of deterioration? Of escalating symptoms? A stroke?

I hadn't a clue. My memories were like flakes in a blizzard, battered and spun by the wind, then left to melt in my head. Vivid, detailed, yet surreal. A Hiroshima of garish chaos.

"How did you know?"

"I swung by your place around eight last night to brief you on some news. Found your door wide open, your purse on the counter, your wheels in the drive. I waited a bit, thinking maybe you was out jogging, but that seemed off, even with the lone-gunslinger act you been peddling lately. I called in a BOLO, eventually got word the EMTs had brought you here."

"My cat?"

"Already pissed when I showed up. I fed him."

The curtain *whrrped* on its little metal rings. A

nurse strode into the bay. Her name was Georgia. She looked like El Chapo having a bad day.

Georgia checked a printout, a drip bottle, the beeping machines. Crossed to me.

"ER?" Stupid question.

"That's right, honey. We're bringing you down easy."

"I have an embolized aneurysm and I suffer from migraines. I might have taken something if I felt a headache coming on."

Georgia took my pulse. Her fingers felt strong and cool. "Whatever you knocked back left no trace."

My last conscious memories were fragmentary. The fire. The Aiello interrogation. The Pasquerault file. The heat. The sun tea.

Crap! Might that be it? The jar had remained outside far too long. Might something have contaminated the tea? Might someone have tampered with it? The burglar/arsonist?

"I don't do drugs." Absurd, but I felt an overpowering need to convince Georgia of my innocent role in the overdose.

"Whatever. You're going to live."

Georgia plumped my pillow and straightened my sheet, then hurried off to spread joy elsewhere.

I lay still, every cranial vessel throbbing. It had all seemed so real. So vibrant. How much was true? How much a wild opera scripted by the wayward little bubble in my brain? By chemicals roaring through my veins?

"Feeling better?" Slidell was again looming, but with a fraction less drama.

I gulped the rest of the water. Put the cup on the

table they'd wheeled to my bedside. Sat up and almost gagged. Swallowed.

"I called Ryan. He's—"

"You didn't!"

"Relax. He wanted to fly straight home, but I talked him down. Assured him you're OK."

"I need my clothes," I said.

"You gotta stay the night. There's a nasty lump on your noggin. Docs think you might have whacked your head and got a concussion."

"I'll recover faster at home."

"They say at least twenty-four—"

"I prefer my own bed."

"I scored some new intel."

"Seriously? What?"

"You gotta promise to chill till morning. Otherwise, the added stimulation might refry your wiring."

"Don't do this, detective."

"They're finishing the paperwork to admit you. You'll get oatmeal for breakfast. Maybe Jell-O. I think you always get Jell-O."

I glared as hard as I could. Slidell glared back.

Since my head was exploding, I cracked first. Besides, I had to admit, checking the state of my lumpy noggin was probably advisable.

"What's this big breakthrough?" Petulant.

"Two breakthroughs."

I lifted an impatient palm. Noticed my nails were crusted with dirt.

"Heavner ran a second, broader tox screen."

"And shared results with you?"

"With some persuasion." Slidell rubbed his jaw.

Thumb-hooked his pants. "Vodyanov had enough China Girl on board to kill half of New Hampshire."

Skinny used one of the many street names for fentanyl, heroin's synthetic cousin and the gold medalist in the current opioid crisis.

A little background. The medical community originally employed fentanyl as an anesthetic but quickly realized its effectiveness as a painkiller. Always open to innovation, the drug-dealer community sat up and took notice. Since fentanyl is one hundred times more potent than morphine, many times more so than heroin, why not use the stuff to lower the cost of doing business? Both drugs exist as white powders. Mix in the cheaper, more powerful fentanyl to cut your product and increase supply.

Tragically, this entrepreneurial vision proved deadly. Hard fact: thirty milligrams of smack can kill you; with China Girl, it takes only three.

Why the difference? Basic chemistry. Both compounds bind to the mu-opioid receptor in the brain. But fentanyl is better at passing through fat, a substance surprisingly plentiful in the head. It arrives faster and, once landed, hugs the receptor so tightly that a minuscule amount triggers the chain of effects so pleasing to the body. End result: Fentanyl is now a ruthless predator roaming the streets of America.

Too much for my mind to compute at that moment. But the bleak facts were in there, stored from previous headlines and research.

"OK," I said. "Heavner's got cause. What's she citing as manner?"

"Undetermined."

There are only five choices for manner of death: homicide, suicide, accidental, natural, undetermined. Based solely on the tox report, I couldn't disagree.

I said, "It's unlikely Vodyanov hid his car at Art's, hiked out to Buffalo Creek, screwed up, and OD'd."

"We can talk about this after you rest."

"Now."

"Fine. No argument here. So we're back to square one. The guy probably killed himself, or somebody offed him."

"If Vodyanov committed suicide, the question is why? If someone murdered him, the question is who?" Also why, but my thoughts were going muddier with each beep of the monitor.

"The other development's no surprise."

I'd forgotten there were two. Waited.

"They ran the prints from your place, focusing on the ones lifted in the two studies. Nothing popped. Most were yours, already on file for comparison."

"No hits in AFIS?"

"Local, North Carolina, surrounding states, nothing popped in any system."

"The rest will come back as family or friends. Maybe my workers."

"I'm gonna want to talk to those guys."

"Right."

"And, like you said, if it was arson and a B and E, the perp probably wore gloves."

"You have to admire proper planning."

Slidell ignored that. "The arson guys found no accelerant other than the paint and turpentine. But they found the distribution pattern odd."

"Odd."

"The stuff was really spread around."

"So our perp is probably bad wiring and a careless painter."

Did I really think so?

What did I believe?

Twenty minutes later, an orderly rolled me into an elevator, then down a corridor to a room so predictable nothing registered. With his help, I maneuvered the twenty-mile gap from the gurney to the bed. A blanket covered me. Lights dimmed. Footsteps retreated. Air movement suggested a reangling of the door. Sometime later, tubes rattled and fingers touched my wrist.

An IED could have detonated beside me. I would not have reacted. My body was down for the count.

Not so my blood or drug-pummeled brain. Sensing an opening, the questions and misgivings reengaged with undiminished zeal.

Image chased image. Some from the inexplicably missing ten hours. Pulsating walls. A steel tunnel tightening to form a cocoon around me. My fingers searching the inky blackness, desperate for a handle, a lever, a chain. The flesh melting from my hands, baring the bones, yellow and raw.

Like the bones in the face of the faceless man.

Other images sprang from the recent investigation. A trench-coated Vodyanov. A pigtailed Jahaan Cole. A gap-toothed Timothy Horshauser. A belligerent Aiello. A shard-covered study. A burned-out office.

Had I been targeted? Was I being watched? If so, by whom? Why? What danger did I pose? Did it involve government secrets? Dodgy real estate? Missing kids? Murder?

Was the threat a bombshell revelation that Margot Heavner was incompetent or corrupt? Was it Vince Aiello's exposure as a pedophile? Nick Body's as a fraud? Vodyanov's as an enabler? A trafficker?

The discovery of a killer?

Or was it all the product of my faulty circuitry?

And where did Yates Timmer fit in?

Two weeks had passed since Vodyanov's body was found. Slidell and I had zero to show for our investigation.

In addition to frustration, I felt terrible guilt.

Joe Hawkins had leaked me confidential information. That file may have been viewed, even stolen in the break-in. If there was a break-in. Lizzie Griesser had performed an analysis gratis. Her phenotype report was also destroyed, perhaps viewed or downloaded.

Out of some half-baked mistrust of cyber-security, I'd stored nothing in the cloud. Not a chance Heavner would share her notes, and I wouldn't place Joe at further risk. I could ask Lizzie for another copy of her report, but that might put her in jeopardy.

Sudden frightening possibility.

Had Gerry Breugger burgled my home? Had he torched the annex to cover his tracks? To slow me and Slidell in our investigation? Did the reporter want a story that badly?

The implications were horrendous.

If Breugger made everything public, Joe might be fired, his long career ended in disgrace. Would Lizzie suffer the same fate? Would her employer lose clients due to distrust in the lab's ability to maintain confidentiality?

My career was in free fall. Was I dragging my friends down with me?

I envisioned radiating circles with me at the epicenter. A ripple effect of destruction created by my actions.

Besides hallucinations, could migraines cause panic, paranoia, and feelings of hopelessness? Could the aneurysm or subsequent embolization? Or had I been drugged? Was my heightened anxiety a by-product of a bad acid or Molly trip? Were my fears justified?

Were Slidell and I closing in on someone or something?

A long-hidden government secret?

A real estate scam?

A media fraud?

A child molester?

A killer?

27

Hospitals are the least restful places on earth.
Nevertheless, I ended up having to stay what remained of that first night and the next. Once my medical history was revealed, my neurologist was notified. He ordered an MRI and MRA, an EEG, and other poking and prodding, "just to be sure."

Both nights, I was awakened repeatedly by a pen-light shining in my eyes. Both dawns, some doctor was paged for some color-coded crisis. Constant summonses followed. Carts rattled. Speakers bonged.

At seven a.m. on Friday, anxious to return home to rescue Birdie from my neighbor Walter's care, I started agitating for release.

The wheels ground at the pace of tectonic drift.

At eight, I was disengaged from my drip line.

At eight thirty, breakfast was placed on my over-the-bed table. As on my first morning, no Jell-O.

At nine thirty, the tray was cleared. I inquired about my belongings, not disclosing my intention to bolt.

At nine forty, Ryan walked through the door with a bouquet the size of a Hereford. Mixed feelings flooded through me. Happiness? Humiliation? Resentment?

"Wow," was all I could muster.

"Wow, as in good wow? Or just-shoot-me wow?"

Ryan looked around, finally set the flowers on the windowsill. They were not a good fit. Then he crossed to the bed to kiss me.

"Of course I'm glad to see you. It's just such a surprise." We'd spoken early Thursday, agreed it was just a bump on the head and that Ryan should remain in France.

"Staying put didn't work for me. I had to see your smiling face myself."

My smiling face did anything but.

"What about Neville?" I asked.

"I set some things in motion. Will head back if one of those leads pans out." Big Ryan grin. "So. When are you out of here?"

"Any minute. Or we hatch an escape plan."

Ryan snapped a salute. "I am a police officer. I can condone no illegal maneuver."

At ten thirty, a plastic bag appeared, *T. Brennan, Rm. #1203* penned in Sharpie on the outside. I loosened the drawstring, was relieved to see my keys tucked into one dirt-crusted sneaker. A silent thank-you to Slidell. I was pulling out my jeans when an attending physician appeared. Or a hospitalist. Maybe a plumber. His name tag said Gursahani.

After giving me a cursory once-over and issuing

recommendations for my continued well-being, Gursa-hani informed me that Dr. Bernard, my neurologist, was on his way. And that Bernard would be discharging me.

When Gursahani had gone, I glanced over at Ryan, defiant.

"Don't even think about it," he said, confiscating the bag and dropping into the room's only chair.

Arms crossed, I slumped back on my pillows.

"Want to talk about what happened?" Ryan asked after several moments of silence.

"I don't *know* what happened," I said, too snappishly. I wasn't in a chatty mood.

"Fair enough. How about this?" Gesturing at my eyes. "Lids down."

"Why?"

"So you can tell me what you remember. It will pass the time while we wait."

After rolling them, I closed my eyes. Given a little encouragement, a bedlam of disconnected scenes fired like tracer rounds in my head. Fragmented. Disorganized. I sorted briefly, hoping for some semblance of chronology.

"I was reviewing the Pasquerault file when Dorothée appeared and told me I'd made an error."

"That must have been unsettling."

"You think?" Eyes still closed. "Dorothée and I drove to the bunker in Cleveland County. Everything was the same, yet exaggerated—the colors too bright, the vegetation too thick and tangled, the heat too oppressive, the shadows too dizzying. It was like picking my way through the frames of an overcolored film cranking in slo-mo."

"I get it."

"Dorothée disappeared through the blast door. Though afraid, I followed. It's hard to explain why. Somehow, I couldn't turn back. It was like I was driven by a need to right my mistake."

I paused. Ryan waited.

"Underground, the darkness was so absolute I had to feel my way by touch. Then, in the distance, I saw this tiny green dot. It seemed to be beckoning. But the more I moved toward it, the farther away it seemed. This is making no sense."

"It is." Again wiggling a finger at my now-open eyes. I complied.

"I felt my way through inky-black tunnels into open chasms filled with swirling neon light, pulsating walls, and heaving floors and ceilings."

I swallowed, nauseated by the recalled tumult.

"At one point, I was in a passageway, at first doubled over, then crawling on all fours, then curled fetal. The space was shrinking, and I knew I had to get out. Or wake up. But I couldn't do either."

My lids flew open. I looked at Ryan. "I remember thinking it was like being trapped in an upturned tin of snus. Strange thought."

Ryan repeated the finger command.

"At one point, I saw Jahaan Cole." Eyes shut. "She was talking about her bones. Begging me to do something."

My gut tightened.

"That's enough," I said, weary of spelunking through the nightmare.

"OK," he said.

Twenty minutes later, Bernard came smiling in, all morning cheer and bubbly good spirits.

"How is our patient this morning?"

"Ready to split."

"And split you shall. All your results look excellent. The aneurysm is not misbehaving. There is no evidence of a TIA or mini-stroke. Nothing unusual turned up in your blood or urine."

"What does that mean?"

"Not much. The symptoms you described—hallucinations, a seemingly 'out-of-body experience'—are consistent with the effects of LSD, but acid wouldn't have been detected by any mainstream drug test. Which is all they did in the ER."

I started to interrupt. Bernard ignored me.

"And had you ingested LSD, fifty percent of the drug would have cleared your body within five hours, the remainder within as little as fifteen."

"I don't do drugs."

"I understand. Not my skill set." Meaningful lifting of brows to me, then to Ryan. "Poisoning?"

"Forget the concussion. And the lump. Might the whole thing have been a gorilla of a migraine?" I asked.

"Unusual, but anything's possible. Did you feel a headache coming on? Had you just taken your current prescription?"

"I don't recall either."

"If it was a migraine, what might have triggered it?" Ryan asked.

Bernard shrugged. "It's hard to isolate one factor."

This was getting us nowhere. I was anxious to leave.

"So." Swinging my legs over the side of the bed. "I'm good to go, right?"

Bernard provided discharge advice similar to Gursahani's and took his leave. He'd barely cleared the door when I snatched the bag from Ryan and darted into the bathroom.

My clothes hadn't improved during the hours they'd spent bunched like linguini. Scraping off soil and debris as best I could, I dressed. Then I washed my face and scrubbed my nails. My hands tingled. My vision seemed strange as I watched the final remnants of soil swirl down the drain as muddy runoff.

While rebinding my hair, I caught sight of myself in the mirror.

I couldn't recall ever looking so haggard. My cheeks were hollow, my lower lids baggy, my skin ashen. My hair was a greasy brown coil wrapping my skull. The combination made me look older by at least ten years.

I stared at my face. It stared back. Me, a decade in the future.

Did I have a decade? If so, what did it hold?

To Ryan's credit, he'd given no indication that I looked so awful. If he did so now, I swore I'd level him. At least metaphorically.

Ryan made no comment. Wordlessly, he arm-wrapped my shoulders, collected the bovine flora, and walked me out into the corridor.

I declined the mandatory wheelchair ride to the main entrance, a wildly unpopular move. An argument ensued. Catching the orderly's eye, Ryan shook his head subtly while pushing for an elevator. The man backed off.

At ground level, Ryan called an Uber. Ten minutes later, I let us into the annex. The Pasquerault file was gone from the kitchen table, my shoulder bag from the counter. I found both in the pantry. Another wily effort by Skinny.

To my horror, my iPhone was not in my purse. Red rocket flare in my chest! I'd never had a chance to forward the pics to Slidell. Not quite accurate. I just hadn't done it. Panicky, I searched everywhere, knowing the reaming I'd endure. Finally gave up, certain it was futile.

Ryan had left three messages on my landline, the final one at six a.m. Thursday morning. Slidell had obviously kept him looped in concerning my disappearance and reemergence. While I listened and deleted, he climbed to assess the damage upstairs.

Birdie was as peeved as expected. And ravenous. After issuing double cat rations, I enjoyed a very long, very hot shower. I was taking a lot of those lately. One difference: Ryan slipped in to join me for this one. Helped with the soaping and spraying. Then, thoroughly clean, we retreated to my bed to assess my injuries and remedy my pain. No mixed feelings about that enterprise.

Following our thoroughly satisfying romp in the sheets, Ryan napped, exhausted from the long overnight flight. I dug out a mask and gloves and resumed my excavation in the upstairs office.

Ninety minutes later, I'd confirmed my worst fears. I had nothing to show for all my investigative efforts. A destroyed-beyond-hope laptop, no mobile, no file, no photos, no notes. Nothing concrete linking Vodyanov or anyone in his circle to Jahaan Cole. To any missing child.

All I retained were the memories assembled in my head. But how reliable were those? Would they filter back warped and twisted through a migraine or drug lens?

I am a scientist. I test hypotheses based on items I can observe, measure, weigh, and photograph. I'd been left with none.

Could I rely on my stored perceptions? Could I sort what was real from what was not?

Test run.

I closed my eyes. Experienced another flash flood of psychedelic images.

A resurrected murder victim.

An azure path.

A tiny emerald orb.

Rainbow madness.

Airless captivity.

A pleading child.

Holy shitballs!

I rocketed to my bedroom and yanked open the top dresser drawer.

Yes!

Gursahani and Bernard had both recommended against operating a motor vehicle or heavy equipment for a minimum of forty-eight hours. Out of deference to their training, I allowed Ryan to drive.

By three, we were at UNCC. Though summer

session was in full swing, the lawns and walkways were largely deserted. Finding an ace parking spot was freakishly easy.

Crossing from the deck to the building housing the bio-anthropology lab, we saw no students throwing Frisbees to each other or to their dogs. No undergraduates shooting the breeze or hurrying between classes. Here and there, we passed a grad student stooped under the weight of an overloaded backpack, a faculty member lugging a battered briefcase. Most of the latter I knew, some I didn't. One, a physics professor, wished me an uneventful Friday the thirteenth.

The interior of the Friday Building was blessedly arctic. We rode the elevator to four, and I unlocked the door to the lab. After turning on the overheads, I used another key to open a metal cabinet. Ryan settled in a chair and watched silently.

I removed a small Dremel cutting tool from the cabinet's top shelf, the kind used by most DNA labs, and grabbed a packet of Carborundum sandpaper. Taking my supplies to a workstation, I lifted the protective cover from the microscope, readied a set of glass slides, and sat down. Ryan pulled out his phone and began scrolling.

After gloving, I slipped a small Tupperware tub from my purse and removed its single tissue-wrapped item. The slender segment of long bone looked worryingly less substantial than I remembered.

Placing the specimen on the scope's platform, I leaned in to the eyepiece. With a few adjustments to lighting and magnification, details snapped into focus.

The charring was more superficial than I'd

suspected upon first seeing the fragment beside the Cleveland County dumpster. Tooth marks were apparent that hadn't been visible in the dimness under the camo netting.

I slid the partial tibia its entire length, millimeter by millimeter, noting details. Then I removed, measured, and photographed it, marveling at my foresight in holding the fragment back from Slidell.

"Skinny let you keep that?" Ryan was again watching me.

"Not exactly," I said.

Then it was showtime.

After setting several sheets of sandpaper to soak, I inserted a fine-edged blade into the handheld rotary saw. A quick buzz through the middle of the shaft, then I cut a series of vertical slices. Carefully lining them up on a tray, I began polishing each, starting with rough grit, then easing through sheets with finer and finer coarseness.

When satisfied that my thin sections were adequately smooth and, well, thin, I inserted the first slide under the lens, set the power to 100X, and maxed the brightness, so light would pass through the specimen.

"Explain again what you're looking for." Ryan had crossed the room to stand behind me.

"Human cortical bone—"

"The dense part on the outside."

"Yes. It's made up of Haversian systems, or osteons, each with a central canal surrounded by concentric layers, or lamellae, of compact bone tissue. When magnified, that's the arrangement." I pointed to a poster hanging on the wall by the door.

"Looks like a moonscape of closely packed volcanoes."

"Exactly. Ungulate bone, that of hoof-toed mammals, has a plexiform, or columnar, structure. When magnified, it's more like that." Pointing to a second poster.

"Looks like layers of sausage with bubbles trapped in and between."

I'd never thought of it that way but couldn't disagree. Barely breathing, I reengaged with the eyepiece and fine-tuned the focus.

"Crap."

"What?"

"Sausage all the way."

"Meaning?"

"Based on estimated size and shape were the bone complete, I think it belonged to a young *Odocoileus virginianus*."

"Which is?"

"Bambi."

"A white-tailed deer."

I nodded, emotions circling, unsure where to land. Mercifully, the fragment hadn't come from an immature human skeleton.

"So it's not a kid," Ryan said.

"No. But that's not true of the incisors and molars in that duct-taped pouch."

"Those teeth definitely came from a child?"

"Yes. Damn it to hell!" Way too harsh.

"It's not the end of the world." Ryan placed a calming hand on my shoulder.

"But it is. What physical evidence do I have? This

fragment was my last hope, and it's from an animal. The human teeth were snatched before I could even take pictures. I photographed the folder and the articles on missing kids, but those images are gone with my laptop."

"You have—"

"I have zero!"

The lab hummed quietly. The building.

"I know what you need," Ryan said, tightening his fingers.

"How can you think about sex?"

"Let's go."

Frustrated, I packed up, and we left.

And discovered where the entire population of Charlotte was spending its hot and steamy Friday the thirteenth.

28

The Apple Store at SouthPark Mall was elbow-to-earlobe. Ryan's idea of a cure for my needs, not further afternoon delight. While I was cutting bone, he'd called ahead to the Genius Bar.

I gave my name to the lady in the official blue shirt. A screen listed my queue position as twenty-seven. That number was called, or projected, an hour after our arrival.

Twenty minutes of discussion, then I headed out with a spanking new MacBook Air and the latest-model iPhone, each equipped with every innovation known to the cyber-mind.

God bless credit cards.

Back home, with phone coaching from Apple Support and from Ryan, I downloaded all the old files and photos I had stored in the cloud, most of which were personal, and reinstalled several essential apps. Then I initiated my new phone, which deactivated the old one.

Two hours after starting, woefully lacking in content but functional, I was good to go.

The onward march of civilization.

First off, I left a message for Slidell. *I am home. I have news. Call me.*

"Now," Ryan encouraged. "Open a new dossier on the faceless man."

"What's the point?" Sounding like a sulky kid. "I've got nothing to put in it."

"Yes. You do."

I just looked at him.

"Enter everything that's in your head."

Grudgingly, I had to admit the logic of his suggestion. But not out loud.

"What will you do?" I asked.

"I have a long list of calls to make."

"To a man about a horse?"

"Something like that."

I opened a blank document on the laptop, titled it *Timeline*. Then, working from memory, I began entering data.

TIMELINE

June 22: Midnight. Temperance Brennan observes a trench-coated man at Sharon Hall.

June 29: An anonymous source texts Brennan images of a Cleveland County corpse.

June 30: Brennan reviews her criticism of Margot Heavner. Heavner calls a press conference re ME 304-18 (the faceless man from Cleveland County), erroneously suggests ME 304-18 is of Asian ancestry. Brennan takes pics and a DNA sample from ME 304-18. Joe Hawkins provides Brennan photocopies of docs. Lizzie Griesser agrees to perform an off-the-books phenotype analysis of ME 304-18.

July 1: Brennan finds errors in Heavner's notes (age, ancestry), observes bruising on corpse missed by Heavner. Brennan deciphers coded note found on ME 304-18.

July 2: Brennan learns that back of scrap found on faceless man has reference to sinking of ferry *Estonia*/biochemical weapons. Skinny Slidell and Brennan find Hyundai at Art's Affordable Garage, near creek where ME 304-18 was discovered, duffel in trunk. Duffel contains: (a) more Russian and Latvian notations, some regarding *Estonia*/biochemical weapons; (b) names Felix Vodyanov and John Ito; (c) thumb drive labeled in Russian. Slidell determines John Ito is an alias, Hyundai registered to nonexistent West Virginia address.

Slidell spots indented writing, delivers torn page to Mittie Peppers at CMPD forensics lab for QD analysis. Analysis reveals: (a) Brennan mobile phone number; (b) second phone number, local 704; (c) reference to missing child Jahaan Cole. Brennan and Slidell determine Vodyanov had tried to contact Brennan shortly before his death.

July 6: Brennan and Slidell learn Vodyanov is absent from all databases, has zero profile on internet. Brennan gets phenotype sketch from Griesser. Slidell obtains name of physician and ashram from thumb drive. Slidell and Brennan go to Sparkling Waters Ashram. Aryan Yuriev is uncooperative. Receptionist E. Desai IDs Vodyanov from sketch, says Vodyanov was registered under name F. Vance.

Brennan interviews Vodyanov/Vance caretaker, Asia Barrow. Barrow says Vodyanov/Vance suffered from taphophobia. Barrow reveals Vodyanov/Vance researched kiddie porn, missing kids using her laptop. Barrow says Vodyanov was a Russian operative. Brennan interviews Vodyanov/Vance landlady, Marguerite Ramos. Ramos IDs Vodyanov/Vance, says he was terrified government was out to kill him.

July 7: Brennan finds items in coat taken from antiseptically clean Vodyanov/Vance apartment: list of codes, info on Project MKUltra, receipt that leads to fenced Cleveland County property. Brennan goes to property, unable to enter. Brennan interviews neighbor, Duncan Keesing. Keesing IDs Vodyanov, says he was crazy. Says when high, Vodyanov talked about MKUltra, other covert ops. Keesing witnessed frightened child being driven onto fenced property. Brennan learns more about MKUltra from Andrew Ryan. Brennan emails Heavner. Brennan visits websites, reads Body conspiracy theory blogs, listens to podcasts.

July 8: Brennan visits deep/dark web, site DeepUnder (a) old info and photos about conspiracy theories; (b) photo of Vodyanov with Body and Yates Timmer. Brennan visits site Homes at the End of the World. Brennan returns to fenced property, finds: (a) file with clippings about missing kids; (b) reference to DeepHaven (pic viewed later); (c) child dentition; (d) bone fragments. Attacked. Slidell runs name Holly Kimrey. Sex trade/drug dealer.

July 9: Brennan and Slidell go to DeepHaven (Lake Wylie). Realtor office/club. Meet Bing, Timmer. Learn: (a) Felix Vodyanov is older brother of Nick Body; (b) Vodyanov fought with Vince Aiello, aka Twist, was banned from DeepHaven; (c) Aiello has reputation for kiddie porn.

July 10: Fire at Brennan condo. B&E? Arson? Accidental? Laptop and all materials pertaining to Vodyanov investigation destroyed.

July 11: Slidell interrogates Aiello, patent attorney with two kiddie-porn busts. Aiello says Vodyanov (a) was paranoid; (b) accused him of kidnapping and killing kids, suddenly dropped allegations; (c) resumed stalking him shortly before his death. Brennan has migraine or is poisoned/drugged and disappears for ten hours.

July 12: Heavner tells Slidell that Vodyanov died of fentanyl overdose.

July 13: Brennan makes thin sections from bone fragment found at fenced property/bunker in Cleveland
County. Deer bone.

I scanned the timeline. Mostly, it reflected my
actions and those of Slidell. Lots of digging, little result.

Ryan returned to find me slumped back, frown-
ing at the screen. At his prompting, I explained my
frustration.

"Try a new angle," he suggested.

"Such as?"

"Retrace the movements of your faceless man.
Track what Vodyanov did in the weeks leading up to
his death."

"Sadly, I know very little."

"Hit me with it."

"According to Asia Barrow, Vodyanov had repeatedly checked into Sparkling Waters because of stress
related to taphophobia, was discharged for the final
time in late May or early June."

Something niggled at a corner of my brain. What?
I tried to pry the thought loose. It wouldn't budge. I
continued.

"According to Vince Aiello, Vodyanov's stalking
resumed in late May or early June, continued over the
next several weeks."

"Coincidence?"

I shrugged. Who knows?

"Go on."

"According to Bing, Vodyanov and Aiello had their
fight at DeepHaven on June 20. I spotted Vodyanov

skulking around Sharon Hall on June 22. He was dead of a fentanyl overdose by June 29."

We both considered the dates, looking for a pattern. Ryan spoke first.

"After leaving the ashram, Vodyanov repeatedly tried to connect with Vince Aiello. Resumed harassing him for information on missing kids."

"Yes. And Vodyanov was also watching me."

"Why?"

"To share intel? Ask for intel?"

"Concerning?"

"No idea."

"What could have triggered Vodyanov's desire to contact a forensic anthropologist and a patent lawyer with a taste for child porn? Might something have happened during his last stay at Sparkling Waters?"

"Felix Vodyanov was Nick Body's older brother," I said, having no answer to Ryan's question.

"Nick Body, the egomaniacal provocateur."

"Yes. New angle. How about we take a look at Body?"

We revisited the timeline. Found not the slightest hint to the whereabouts or actions of Vodyanov's younger sibling.

I sat back, thinking about that. About the hours of digging that Slidell and I had done.

Was I wearing blinders? Was I missing one big-ass exhibit A?

I was defining evidence as that which I had. That which I'd lost. Objects. Images. But what about all those tiny facts bearing witness to a life? The personal minutiae stored in millions of archives in dozens of countries?

"Vodyanov left virtually no internet footprint," I said. "Slidell and I both researched the guy. He wasn't in any database."

"Little brother?"

"Same story. Body has a public profile, still he managed to keep his private life hidden. In today's interconnected, digitized world, that kind of anonymity is almost impossible."

Realization. The absence of data can be as important as that which is present. That absence *is* evidence.

I straightened in my chair and tapped the space bar.

"Going to have another go at him?"

I nodded.

First off, I spent a little more time at Body Language. What the hell? I'd already forked over the fee. Body was as nauseating as I recalled. I was switching from a rant on fraudulent voting in the last election to one suggesting that the recent wildfires in California were the result of a government conspiracy to clear land for a rapid-transit system when my new phone chimed an incoming call.

29

"**W**here the hell have you been?"

"They didn't serve Jell-O."

"For shit's sake. For once, can't you just chill?" Slidell's voice sounded like battery acid burning through rust. The stress and fatigue told me he'd been up all night.

"Yes, I am feeling better. Thanks for asking."

My eyes met Ryan's. I mouthed the name Slidell. He gestured that he was going back upstairs and waggled his phone. I nodded.

"Ryan get in OK?"

"Yes. I bought a new mobile and laptop." Reporting my histology caper would have required a confession of withholding half the bone fragment. No way.

"You lost your phone?"

"Or someone took it. It was missing from my purse. Thanks for stowing that and the file, by the way. And for bringing my keys to the hospital."

"Looks like some asshat maybe did torch your place."

I didn't interrupt.

"CSU lifted one print had no business being there."

"Where?"

"Ledge outside the kitchen window."

"You got a hit?"

"Holly Kimrey."

"No shit."

"No shit."

"Have you found him?"

"We will. If the little cretin did set that fire, we're talking B and E, arson, assault, maybe manslaughter, attempted murder—"

"I doubt anyone wanted to kill me."

"You know where you were those ten hours?"

I didn't. "Were you able to test the sun tea?"

"The jar was in the sink. You probably poured or spilled the stuff down the drain, so that won't be happening."

"Are you questioning Kimrey's associates? Other dealers? Sex workers?"

"I don't know how I'd do this job without you." A small, tired pause, then, "We're poking down every hole. Hooking every snake squirms up."

"How can someone just vanish like that?"

"You managed."

"If Kimrey did bust into my place, torch it, I doubt he was acting on his own. Who do you suppose directed him?"

"Can't say. But I can say the little turd links to that bunker you're so hot to toss."

Maybe did toss? I couldn't be sure. Had I actually gone there? Or were my memories fantasies spawned by my own rebellious blood? By a bad acid trip?

"Kimrey mugs you in the boonies, now his print turns up at your crib." Slidell was still talking. "Might be enough for a warrant."

"Have you determined who owns the fenced property?"

"We're working on it. Look, I'm not sitting with my thumb up my ass. While you were sleeping off your concussion—"

"Maybe concussion."

"—or Lucy in the Sky jaunt, I did follow-ups with some of your other pals. Marguerite Ramos ain't getting my vote for citizen of the year."

"You talked to Ramos again?"

"That about sums it up. *I* talked to *her*. This time, she barely said shit."

"I may have loosened her tongue by implying I might alert ICE." I still wasn't proud of that.

"Gee, I'd never think of something so devious."

I held back a retort.

"Ramos says the guy in number six was named Vance. That Vance was a sterling tenant, then he moved on. She thinks maybe Slovakia. She never heard of Felix Vodyanov."

"She told me she spoke to Vodyanov several times. Overheard him on the phone. She said Vodyanov was afraid for his life."

"All of which I stated to jog her recall. Seems the *señora*'s memory is no longer so *bueno*."

"Why the about-face?"

"It gets better. I drove to Mooresville to see Barrow."

"She was more forthcoming with me than Ramos."

"It appears Nurse Ratchet is seeking broader horizons."

"She stonewalled, too?" Not mentioning that Asia Barrow wasn't a nurse.

"The house was boarded up, the generator off, the truck nowhere to be seen."

"Barrow is gone?"

"Yep."

"Did you question her cousin?" This was making no sense. "The receptionist at the ashram?"

"E. Desai quit her job last Tuesday. Called it in."

"Why?"

"Personal reasons. FYI, the E stands for Eunice. Also FYI, the new receptionist makes Eunice look like Alfred Einstein."

"Did you question Yuriev?" Again, not bothering to correct Slidell.

"The good doctor wasn't there. But he's topping my agenda."

"The ashram must have contact information in Desai's personnel file."

"Eunice lives alone in Winston-Salem, has for four years. Or had. The landlord wasn't thrilled to see she'd packed up and split without notice." I started to interrupt. Slidell rolled on. "Her cell phone was also disconnected. On Tuesday, the day she resigned."

"Jesus Christ." Sirens were rising in my head. "So Ramos isn't talking, and Kimrey, Barrow, and Desai are in the wind."

"Eeyuh." Slidell's fallback when frustrated.

"Barrow was renting that house. Said she didn't like being tethered. Maybe she and her cousin just decided to move on."

Slidell said nothing.

"Or maybe something spooked them."

"Thought crossed my mind."

"Have you talked to Yates Timmer? Nick Body?"

"My other headliners, right behind Yuriev."

"You could go back at Duncan Keesing. He's the disabled vet who lives down the road."

"He's OK."

"You saw Keesing?"

"He claims to know nothing about Vodyanov beyond what he told you. Zip about Body. Says he's never heard of Yates Timmer. I believe him."

Guilt pulled like undertow in my chest. The possibility of attacks against me had spurred Slidell more than I'd realized. He was pushing hard.

"Now what?" I asked, tone gentler.

"You said you had news."

"Have you gotten DNA results on the bone I liberated from the raccoon?" I asked, voice carefully neutral.

"What dream you living in?"

"The more I think about it, visualize it, the more I doubt that fragment is human."

"Don't matter. We'll have colonies on the moon before we get a report."

"Any developments on Jahaan Cole?"

There was silence, followed by a sigh. "No."

"You'll keep me looped in about the warrant?"

"Eeyuh."

"Is that a yes?"

"Promise one thing, doc."

I said nothing.

"Stay busy doodling Ryan until you hear from me."

*　　　*　　　*

A good doodle didn't sound all that bad. Certainly kept Mama purring along. But Ryan had his own worries, was now cloistered in the bedroom with his laptop.

No hard-copy files. No stored images or documents. No physical evidence. Cut off from most witnesses.

Eeyuh.

I fed the cat and returned to my groovy new Mac. After logging back on, I downloaded the TOR browser and nosedived into the dark web.

No surprise. I was still blocked from DeepUnder.

I dredged for a while, netted nothing new on Yates Timmer. Nothing at all on Nick Body.

Who was this arrogant loudmouth who always hid in the shadows? I decided to resurface and spend time listening to Body's podcasts and reading his blogs. Some of his rants were more toxic than I'd imagined.

Over the past decade, Body had been particularly vehement on two themes. Plots involving kids. Plots involving medical wrongdoing. Occasionally, his insane theories managed to combine both elements.

I began with titles suggesting misconduct through manipulation of public health.

There were numerous variations on the evils of vaccination. In the old tried-and-true, Body alleged that vaccination causes autism. In a somewhat more creative twist, he argued that Bill Gates was behind a plot to use immunization for population control. In another series of tirades, he insisted that the government was sneaking RFID chips into children via inoculation.

Many of Body's harangues focused on disease. Over and over, he returned to the theme of government conspiracy. A sampling: He claimed that the Ebola epidemic in West Africa was a biological-weapons test performed by America. That SARS was a germ attack against the Chinese. That AIDS was created and distributed by those in power in the U.S. That the anthrax attacks following 9/11 were orchestrated by the government. That banning DDT was a scheme to depopulate the earth by spreading malaria. That Huntington's disease is caused by a microbe and the government is conspiring to suppress a known cure. And, my personal favorite, that chemtrails are responsible for mad cow outbreaks.

Ryan popped in now and then to ask how I was. To offer a drink or a back rub. To say he was sallying forth to forage for a late dinner.

By the time I sat back, the windows were dark and my stomach was growling. I cruised through the annex, checking security and turning on lights. Was just finishing when Ryan returned bearing pizza.

Birdie joined us as I made the first cut. I gave him a tiny slice, Ryan and myself large ones. As we chewed pie and slurped cheese, I shared snippets of what I'd read and heard.

"Body's theories are absurd, his arguments laughably devoid of accurate detail or plausible evidence." My critique.

"Your personal faves?"

I provided a half-dozen ludicrous examples.

"The guy's got millions of loyal followers."

"Sadly, that may be true. And the credulous chumps aren't laughing. What kept you so busy today?"

"Got a tip that Neville is on his way to Marseille."

"You're guessing the horse didn't book his own passage."

"Doubtful."

"I appreciate you making such a long trip, Ryan. But you really don't need to stay here with me."

"I want to be sure you're fully sound before hitting the road."

"Has that ever been the case?"

Ryan waggled a hand. Maybe yes, maybe no.

"I'm cool," I said, smiling.

"A Merry Prankster."

"Riding the bus." Acknowledging Ryan's Ken Kesey reference.

"Seriously. How are you feeling?"

"Perfectly chipper." It was true. Though I should have been exhausted, I felt oddly energized. A by-product of the concussion? Of meds I was given at the hospital? Of drug-laced tea?

"Skinny was crazy until you turned up."

"He's busting ass to determine what happened here. Did he tell you CSU found a print outside the kitchen window?"

"I haven't spoken to Slidell today."

I briefed Ryan on Holly Kimrey. Was concluding when his mobile buzzed.

"Do you mind if I take this?"

"Of course not. And please, go ahead and make flight reservations if necessary. I really am fine."

Still too jazzed for sleep, or doodling, I returned to my Mac and endured a second round of Body, this time focusing on his other favorite theme. Plots involving children.

Some theories had been around for decades. Kids were being kidnapped and killed for their organs, a valuable commodity in a global black market. Kids were being kidnapped and sold as sex slaves, domestic workers, farm laborers. Kids were being kidnapped for sacrifice in satanic rituals. Kids were being kidnapped for use in mind-control experiments run by the CIA.

Many theories were new, some so outlandish it was incredible that even the most gullible could buy in. Kids were being kidnapped and transported to work camps built by NASA on Mars. Kids were being kidnapped and taken to concentration camps set up by FEMA in preparation for the imposition of martial law and the killing of millions of Americans. Kids were being kidnapped and flown to Jonestown, the abandoned camp in Guyana where Jim Jones and members of his Peoples Temple committed mass suicide.

Though the experience was loathsome, I learned one thing, perhaps useful, perhaps not. Margot Heavner's betrayal of Hardin Symes was not an isolated instance of indiscretion. Dr. Morgue's interview was one of many during a particularly virulent two-year period in which Body seemed fixated on the topic of murdered and missing kids. And he didn't hold back. Who. Where. When. Some cases I knew. Others I didn't.

Podcast after podcast. Blog after blog. Always the same message. Like a rabid zealot, Body spewed conspiracy hokum, warning parents of the dangers of losing their children.

By two a.m., I'd had it. Disgusted, I closed my laptop. Birdie and Ryan were already curled together in bed. I joined them and closed my eyes, at last mentally and physically drained.

Still, Body's voice jackhammered through the fatigue. Names: Hardin Symes. Jahaan Cole. Timothy Horshauser. Images: Young faces in grainy print. A neon-pink sneaker deep in a dumpster. Milky-white teeth in a duct-taped pouch.

Questions fluttered like the moths that circled my porch light.

A coded reference to Jahaan Cole in Vodyanov's notebook. Why?

Articles on Jahaan Cole and Timothy Horshauser at the fenced property. Why?

Body raging on *Body Language*, inciting fear about kids. Kindling parental paranoia. Why?

I sat up in the dark.

Could that be it?

The notion was so wild it needed a cage.

I hurried back to the kitchen and reopened my Mac.

By dawn, I was certain the pattern was real.

And horrified it might confirm my suspicion.

30

Slidell was in my kitchen by 8:45. I walked him and Ryan through it.

"You're both familiar with the National Center for Missing and Exploited Children, right?"

"Their site posts info on missing kids." Slidell's face looked like jumbled laundry waiting to be washed.

I nodded. "NamUs?"

"Same deal."

"Doesn't NamUs also list unidentified remains?" Ryan asked.

"Yes. So searchers can try to put names to unknown corpses."

"Jahaan Cole's on both," Slidell said. "So what?"

"And there are many other organizations, some regional, some national," I added.

"Look, I been all over—"

"I spent several hours checking stats, plotting

child disappearances by date, by locale, and so on. I also did an analysis of Body's podcasts and blogs by topic, by airdate, and so on. Then I did some cross-tabulation."

"How could you stomach listening to that douchebag?"

"Fortitude." And a tanker truck of coffee. "From 2012 to 2014, Body was obsessed with the topic of missing and murdered children. I could give you the daily breakdown, but for now, trust me."

"Where you going with this?" Slidell didn't try to mask his impatience. At least, not effectively.

"From 2012 to 2014, Amber Alerts and other reports of missing kids rose sharply in some areas."

"The guy plays off paranoia," Ryan said.

"His harangues both followed *and* preceded the disappearances."

"You suggesting Body goaded his listeners into snatching kids?" Slidell couldn't have sounded more dubious.

"Hear me out."

The laundry rearranged slightly, but Skinny held his tongue.

"I also tabulated child disappearances by geography and by year." I was relying on the KISS principle: Keep it simple, stupid. "During the period Body was pushing conspiracy theories involving kids, most states maintained typical numbers for Amber Alerts, child homicides, MPs. In only two did those numbers rise sharply." I slid a paper across the table so both men could see. "West Virginia and North Carolina."

Four eyes dropped to the printout. Skimmed the

heartbreaking catalog of names. Rolled up. "What are you saying?" Slidell.

"Jahaan Cole disappeared during a time Body was hammering on about kids being targeted. Timothy Horshauser. The others on that list. Children who vanished, never to be found."

"Didn't you say Horshauser lived in Pennsylvania?" Ryan.

"Uniontown is just thirty miles up the road from Morgantown, West Virginia."

Ryan grasped it immediately. "Vodyanov registered his Hyundai in Morgantown under the alias John Ito. He was living in Charlotte under the name F. Vance. He links to both places."

"He had Jahaan Cole's name in his notebook."

Slidell chest-crossed his arms, listening.

"I found baby teeth at the fenced property in Cleveland County. Articles on Cole and Horshauser. I photographed a child's sneaker in the dumpster."

"You making a point or just doing a recap?" Slidell, sharp.

"We know Vodyanov was working for his brother."

"So?"

I swallowed. What I was about to say was almost too appalling for words.

"What if Body had Vodyanov grabbing kids to scare the crap out of people? To create an atmosphere of fear and drive followers to Body Language?"

"That's pretty extreme." Ryan, far more diplomatic than Slidell.

"I'm just putting it out there. Child disappearances spiked in only two states out of fifty during the period

Body was raging on the topic. The very states associated with Vodyanov and his brother."

Our eyes met. Ryan's ice-blue and troubled, Slidell's red-rimmed and bleary. A beat, then Skinny's gaze returned to the page before him.

"I remember most of these North Carolina alerts coming across the wire. West Virginia's off the patch. I'll float queries, try to contact the lead in each case."

"What happened with the warrant?" I asked.

"Still a nonstarter. Judge says all I'm arguing is a dead guy and a place makes me nervous."

"Are you kidding? Kimrey jumped me—"

"Outside the gate. She needs stronger evidence suggesting criminal activity on the property. Of course, I can't mention nothing you got *inside* the gate, it being from an illegal entry and all."

"Any word on who holds title?"

"Expecting that any minute." Slidell rose with a slowness that bore witness to his exhaustion. "Had one amusing moment yesterday."

I waited, far from amused.

"Got a call from Cootie Clanahan."

"Jahaan Cole's elderly neighbor," I explained to Ryan.

"Cootie's been devoting serious thought to my queries. Recalls one detail about the hinky cop banged on her door this spring. She says the guy spoke with an accent. Suspects Swedish, maybe Norwegian."

"Russian?"

Slidell shrugged.

"You think it could have been Vodyanov?"

"He tailed you and Vince Aiello just before he died."

"Why approach Cole's neighbor?"

Slidell shrugged again, a sluggish levering up of one shoulder.

"I've printed a new copy of Lizzie's phenotype sketch. You could show it to Cootie, see if she can ID him," I suggested.

"After I look into these kids."

When frustrated, I am harsh in my self-appraisal. Following Slidell's departure, I sat a while, constructing a mental register of all the ways I'd botched the investigation. Another of all the things I'd done to bring disaster down on myself. Feeling like a loser.

Ryan went off, returned sometime later, and resumed his place in the chair beside mine. For a few seconds, I felt his eyes on my face. Then he leaned very, very close and spoke in hushed tones, almost a whisper. "Anything I can do to cheer you up?"

I felt his lips brush my ear. The heat of his body tight to mine.

"Tempting offer." My voice felt thick in my throat. "But I need to stay focused."

Ryan raised his brows and flicked his naughty-choirboy smile.

I pressed a palm to his chest. The electricity sizzled between us. I didn't push him away.

"I'll be leaving soon," he purred.

"Ah, Jesus, Ryan."

He took both my hands in his and pulled me to my feet. Released one and unbuttoned the top two buttons of my shirt.

"You are a terrible influence." A tiny smile lifting the corners of my mouth, I undid the next two.

We scampered upstairs.

Our little dance in the sheets forced the negativity to run for cover. Once again dressed and back at my laptop, I was able to think more logically.

In my heart, I knew everything came back to the fenced property. That it was critical to gain legal access.

Ryan stayed upstairs to pursue whatever lead he'd kicked loose regarding his purloined pony.

Unsure what tidbit would ring his or her honor's bell, I opened a blank document and entered every detail I could recall from every interview I'd conducted or witnessed. Desai. Yuriev. Barrow. Ramos. Keesing. Bing. Aiello. Then I went back over my notes. Twice. The second time through, I paused on Duncan Keesing.

Keesing witnessed a frightened child being driven onto the fenced property. When was that? Did the date track with the disappearance of any child on my list? If I could show a correlation, might that be the judge's smoking gun?

When questioned by Slidell, Keesing had denied further knowledge of Vodyanov. Drive back out to Cleveland County?

When Harry and I were kids, we spent hours alone together. Especially when Mama was having one of her "bad days." Sequestered in the secret clubhouse cubby off our bedroom, we'd play mind games, taking turns creating long sequences of memory challenges—strings of words, numerals, names of states or vegetables—

then presenting the list for the other to recite back blind. Points for accuracy. Points for speed.

I closed my eyes as I had long ago in that tiny closet. Visualized Keesing's phone. The numbers jotted on the lid. Thanks to all those years of practice, the area code was easy. Ditto the exchange. The next three digits because they formed a pattern: 2-4-6. Try as I might, the last numeral eluded me.

I punched in a ten-digit combo. Got a woman named Tammy. I tried again. Got voice mail for Bill and Irene. On my fifth attempt, a man answered.

"Yeah." Startled, maybe alarmed.

"Duncan Keesing?"

"Who's this?"

"It's Temperance Brennan. I stopped by to see you last Saturday?"

"How'd you get this number?"

"You showed it to me." True, indirectly. "Remember? You said it was your SOS line?"

"Didn't figure you'd be calling it."

"I hope this isn't a bad time."

"Don't know there's ever a good time for bad news."

"Oh, no, sir. This isn't bad news. I just wondered if I could ask you a follow-up question."

Fuzzy air. Then a cat meowed loudly.

"Mr. Keesing?"

"I'm here. Calculating if you're my first time talking on this thing."

"I've been wondering about the child you saw in the car entering your neighbor's gate. Do you know what date that took place?"

"Damn, lady. I told you that?"

"You did, sir."

Another pause, then, "You're talking three, four years ago."

"I know, sir. But it would be very helpful if you could be more precise."

"Helpful with what?"

"An investigation."

"That little one come to harm?" Voice rising.

"I'm not at liberty to discuss specifics."

"That why that fat cop come by my trailer?"

"Mm."

Objects clattered, then the cat let loose a piercing screech.

"Goddammit, Sarge. Git." To me. "I gotta go. All this ringing's got my cat's balls in a twist."

"If you think of anything, would you please contact me?"

"Yeah, yeah."

I gave Keesing my number. He may or may not have written it down.

We disconnected.

I returned to the timeline. The interviews. As before, I kept checking the clock, impatient for a call from Slidell. Again.

I started by focusing on Felix Vodyanov. The victim. The faceless man.

I browsed the interviews, plucking out facts and observations.

Ryan came downstairs around one. Banged around in the refrigerator, then placed two sandwiches on the table. A diet Coke for me, a Grolsch beer for himself.

"Going well?"

"Eh."

"Bounce it off me."

I did. Between bites and swigs.

"Barrow thought Vodyanov was a spy. Ramos thought he was terrified of being killed. Keesing and Aiello thought he was nuts."

"There are things known and things unknown and in between are the doors of perception."

"Rod Serling?"

"Aldous Huxley. Or maybe it was Jim Morrison."

"Right. So. Barrow said Vodyanov, aka Vance, had been at Sparkling Waters more than once. That his issue was taphophobia. That he stayed to himself. That Yuriev alone tended to his medical care and administered his meds."

"Was that unusual?"

"No idea." I rolled a questionable item around on my tongue. "Is this a beet?"

"Yes."

"On ham and cheese?"

"Go on."

"Vodyanov's body was found close to the Cleveland County property. He may have stayed or worked in the bunker. Does taphophobia seem compatible with underground living?"

"Not really."

I pictured my autopsy-room photos of MCME 304-18. The mangled face and belly. The missing hands. The bruising that Heavner had failed to note.

"Vodyanov's body showed multiple hematomas in various stages of healing."

"From falls? Blows?"

"Who knows?"

"How old was Vodyanov when he died?"

"I put him at mid-to-late forties or early fifties."

A thought tapped softly deep down in my subconscious. I tried to haul it up but couldn't.

"What else did others say about Vodyanov?"

"Keesing said sometimes he'd be all wound up and shaking. Speculated about a condition that made him unsteady. Bing called him Felix the fall guy. Klutzoid. Mocked him."

Tap. Tap.

"In the weeks before his death, Vodyanov tried to contact several people. Vince Aiello. Me."

"Maybe this Cootie Clanahan?"

"Maybe."

Tap! Tap!

"Vodyanov's thumb drive listed Depacon, Zoloft, and Seroquel."

"Do those drugs make sense for the treatment of taphophobia?"

I hardly heard Ryan's question. Data bytes were clicking together in my mind.

Bruising. Unsteady movement. Middle age. Mood stabilizers.

In a blinding moment of absolute clarity, the thought broke through.

Jesus on a tightrope!

"What?"

"Just give me a few minutes."

Fingers flying over the keyboard, I got back online and linked from site to site. At one point, I heard Ryan request car keys, the door open and close.

Thirty minutes later, I was so jazzed I couldn't sit still.

I knew the reason Vodyanov had been at Sparkling Waters.

I knew that he'd killed himself.

I knew why.

31

It was then that things kicked into warp speed. Had Ryan stayed, I might have acted with more caution. Perhaps avoided a spectacular mistake.

He didn't. Though his offer was sincere, I assured him my cerebral vessels and all other systems were fully online and insisted he return to France, knowing he was anxious to get back on Neville's trail. Lots of discussion, in English and French, and in the end I won. Ryan's retirement was recent, his career as a PI in its infancy. He needed to establish his reputation. That's the argument he bought.

I dropped Ryan at the airport, outlined my breakthrough on the way. He didn't scoff, didn't shout hallelujah. Just listened, squinting at me and nodding. I think his mind was on the damn horse.

Back home, I began punching Slidell's number every thirty minutes. Was on my fourth volley when the phone buzzed in my hand. I checked caller ID, clicked on, unsure what to expect.

"Mr. Keesing. That was quick."

"Yes, ma'am. I got to pondering. You know, 'bout that young 'un. Your questions grabbed hold of my mind, so I been feeling outta sorts since you called."

"I appreciate your concern."

"I'm taking out the lunch trash, and suddenly it hits me. Duncan, you dimwit. You put that child on your barrel."

"I'm sorry?"

"It ain't worth crap, but I do some drawing and painting. You seen it."

Flashbulb image. Not an aquarium crab, a rear window? Not claws, pigtails? Not shells, beads?

"You painted your memory of the child on your barrel?"

"Yes, ma'am, I sure did. The little face looking outta that car. I guess I just wanted to get something down, case anything come of it. And the barrel was new and needed some beautifying."

Easy. Don't spook him.

"Did you happen to recall the date?"

"Yes, ma'am, I put that right on there, real small, down by her chin. It happened further back than I thought." I heard movement, as though the phone was being shifted from hand to hand. "The year was 2013. I'm guessing it was probably in the fall, 'cause the month starts with a one. And I recall the leaves was changing."

"And the day?" Pulse quickstepping.

"The rest of the numbers is rusted away. Surprised any of it lasted. Tell the truth, I used some paint that weren't in its prime. That help you any?"

"A great deal. Would it be all right if someone came to look at your barrel? To shoot a few pictures?"

"Warn 'em it smells like a shitpot and watch out for snakes."

"I'll do that."

We disconnected. I didn't have to check.

Jahaan Cole disappeared in October of 2013.

I spent a moment calming my nerves, then dialed Slidell again. This time, he answered.

"Christ Almighty. Can't you get the hint I'm tied up?"

I relayed what I'd just learned from Keesing. "You should send someone out to photograph that barrel and take his statement."

"As soon as I can."

"He said the barrel was relatively new. Maybe you can pinpoint the exact date of purchase. Even if that's impossible, what he witnessed might still be enough for a warrant."

"You're a lawyer now?"

I ignored that. "Are you getting anywhere with the list of missing kids?"

"Can't talk now." Lots of commotion in the background. Voices. Bleating phones. I figured Slidell was in the squad room and it was hopping. "Gimme Ryan."

"Too late. He's making his way back to France. We need to grill Yuriev."

A weary sigh.

"Vodyanov didn't go to the ashram to be treated for taphophobia," I said. "That was a cover—"

"I gotta cut you loose for a while."

"What?" I couldn't believe I'd heard correctly.

No response at the other end of the line. I sensed Slidell weighing options. Finally, "There's another one."

"Another one what?" I snapped.

"Missing kid. An eight-year-old girl. It's not my case. Obviously. But the lead asked me to pitch in."

"My phone didn't sound an Amber Alert."

"Being issued as we speak."

"What happened?" Skin feeling suddenly cold.

There was some shuffling as Slidell flipped pages. "April Siler, blond hair, green eyes, eighty-two pounds, fifty-six inches tall. Last seen wearing white shorts and a red-and-white-striped top. Disappeared from the athletic fields behind Carmel Middle School. The mother was watching the younger brother play baseball. The area was crawling with parents, siblings, lots of teams playing at the time, so the kid was allowed to roam unsupervised. When the game ended, she was nowhere to be found."

"When was this?"

"Call came in at sixteen thirty yesterday afternoon."

"Why the delayed alert?"

"Looked like a probable noncustodial parental abduction. Turns out that's not the case. The father's in Denver, been there since Wednesday."

"A zillion people around, and someone snatches a kid in broad daylight?" Way too harsh. Slidell wasn't to blame. As the bearer, he was taking the hit.

I listened to more silence. Longer this time. Much longer.

"Gotta go." Gruff.

"Keep me updated," I said, more controlled.

"Right."

"You have to find this kid."

"I know that."

After disconnecting, I got a glass of iced tea. Store-bought, not steeped on the porch. Downed it. Breathed deeply several times to clear the old noggin. Slow the old ticker.

The noggin counseled restraint.

The ticker urged otherwise.

Sparkling Waters Ashram looked as summer-camp-monasterial as it had two weeks earlier. Same security fence. Same cameras. Same guardhouse. I skipped all that and went straight to the squat pink box housing administration.

E. Desai's replacement looked up when I came through the door. Blond hair, not from a bottle, the real deal, aquamarine eyes, skin so pale it was almost translucent. The name bar on the desk now said *Z. Kantzler*.

"Welcome to Sparkling Waters." Kantzler beamed a smile that would have made her predecessor proud. "May I assist you?"

"I'm here to see Dr. Yuriev."

"I'm so sorry." Looking impressively blue. "The director isn't here at the moment. Is there something I can help you with?"

"When do you expect him?"

"Do you have an appointment?"

I turned. Yuriev's door was closed. I crossed to it and tried the knob. The office was locked.

Kantzler pushed away from her desk, the wheels

on her chair protesting the sudden backward thrust. It was a soft sound but hostile in its own way.

"You mustn't go in there."

I pivoted. Kantzler was on her feet and no longer smiling.

"Is he gone for the day?" I asked.

Her eyes cut to the front window. "His car is still here."

"The white Mercedes?" Following her sightline.

The aquamarines snapped back, clouded by worry at leaking classified info. "Is Dr. Yuriev aware of your visit?"

"No."

"Perhaps you'd like to schedule an appointment?"

"No."

"May I give him your name?"

"No."

My blasting out the door obliterated Kantzler's next question.

It was maybe two degrees cooler than on my previous visit. Which put the mercury at a bump south of 98°F. Waiting al fresco wasn't an option.

I got into my car and started the engine. The gas gauge indicated a half-full tank. Uncertain how long that much fuel would last, I turned the AC to low, rolled to a spot beside the Mercedes, and settled in to wait.

Twenty minutes later, Yuriev came striding up the path. He was carrying a briefcase and had a fawn linen jacket finger-hooked over one shoulder. His pants were tan, his shirt so white it threatened to trigger snow blindness. Scrunching low, I tracked his progress.

Instead of continuing toward the pink box, Yuriev veered from the path and angled toward the Mercedes. Five yards out, he *wheep-wheeped* the locks, then popped the trunk.

It was then I realized I had no plan. Confront him on the pavement? He might get into his car and drive away. Follow him? Then what?

Yuriev circled to the rear to deposit the briefcase and jacket. The raised trunk lid blocked his view of my car. Without further thought, I acted.

Moving with as much speed and stealth as possible, I eased open my door, crouch-walked the gap between vehicles, and slipped into the Mercedes's passenger seat.

The good doctor entered butt-first and sideways, then swiveled to position his feet by the pedals. Catching a glimpse of me in his peripheral vision, he gave a small squeak. His shoulders jumped, and both hands shot into the air. They were trembling.

"Take the car!" Never looking my way.

"I don't want the car." Not quite true. It beat the hell out of mine.

"Take my wallet. My watch."

"It's me," I said.

Nothing but quick, hiccupy breathing.

"Look at me."

"If I do, you'll have to kill me."

"If you don't, I'll shoot your ass."

Yuriev's head rotated so slowly I thought it might be stuck on his neck. His chin was canted and showed decidedly less attitude than on our first meeting.

I waggled my fingers, demonstrating I was unarmed.

Yuriev seemed unsure, just for a moment. Then his shoulders and hands dropped, and his eyes went stone-hard.

"You," he said.

I smiled in confirmation.

"You were with that rude detective. The one asking about someone he claimed had been a guest at this facility." Yuriev looked different somehow. Not just the chin. A trick of the lighting?

"Felix Vodyanov," I said. "Aka F. Vance."

"As I have explained, doctor-patient privilege prohibits discussion of any guest under my care. Had that ever been the case." His face was more symmetrical than I recalled, the nose more centered over the upper lip.

"Vodyanov is dead," I said.

"I do not know the man." Enunciating every syllable by moving his mouth in exaggerated slo-mo. Exposing the very bad gums.

Snapshot memory.

Sudden insight. Like nuclear fusion—two separate atoms coming together to form something new.

"I think you do," I said.

"I am going to ask you to—"

"I think the two of you shared a fondness for snus."

Yuriev said nothing, but an overly forceful hiccup suggested surprise.

"Göteborgs Rapé? Is that your preferred brand?"

The stone eyes narrowed.

"Vodyanov died with a canister of Göteborgs Rapé in his pocket. Also a thumb drive recording your name."

"What is it you want?"

"The truth."

"That a man used snus?"

"Felix Vodyanov died from a fentanyl overdose."

A woman appeared on the path. She wore teal scrubs and looked like she'd been up for a month. We both watched her trudge the pavement, face lowered and flushed with the heat. A moment of fumbling in a shoulder bag, then she entered a battered Camry and drove toward the exit.

"I think Vodyanov killed himself," I said. "And I think you know why."

Yuriev's eyes remained stubbornly fixed on the windshield. His face gave away nothing.

"He wasn't being treated for taphophobia, was he?"

"What are you suggesting?"

"Felix Vodyanov had Huntington's."

Huntington's disease is a progressive brain disorder. Typically, signs of HD first appear in midlife. Weight loss. Changes in coordination. Fidgety movements that can't be controlled. Slowness or stiffness. Trouble thinking through problems. Depression or irritability.

As the disease advances, often over a span of decades, symptoms worsen. Sufferers may drop things, fall, experience difficulty speaking or swallowing. Many have trouble staying organized.

"Here's my take. Vodyanov's HD was beginning to interfere with his day-to-day life. He was exhibiting abnormal movements he could no longer hide. Stumbling or banging into things. Having memory issues."

"How could you know this?" Yuriev's tone had softened a notch.

"I studied autopsy photos. Vodyanov's body had

bruises in varying stages of healing. I've seen notes he wrote to himself. Information he feared he might forget."

"Such a condition is never the patient's fault. Why hide it?"

"My take, again. And admittedly, this part is speculation. Vodyanov worked for his brother, Nick Body. I suspect you're aware of him?"

Yuriev's jaw muscles bulged, but he said nothing.

"Given your training, I'm sure you know that HD is caused by a mutation in either of an individual's two copies of a gene called HTT or huntingtin. That while some spontaneous mutations do occur, in most cases, HD is passed on from a parent. That since the gene is dominant, the child of an affected person has a fifty-fifty chance of inheriting the disease."

"I am quite cognizant of the hereditary nature of Huntington's. What does this have to do with Felix and his brother?"

"For years, Body's been hawking the theory that HD is caused by a microbe. That it's contagious and can pass between people."

"That's preposterous. You can't catch HD from another person."

"Of course it's preposterous. But Body and his confederacy of wackos insist that the answer to solving HD is to study it like an infectious disease. They say other scientists know this and are hiding the information."

"To what end?" Somewhat less vehement.

"Either out of embarrassment that their theories are wrong or for various more nefarious reasons."

"Nick Body is an unusual man."

"Let me take my speculation one step further. I think Body wanted proper care for his brother but couldn't let it be known that he was following accepted medical protocol. If that came out, he'd look like a fraud. Now, here's where you come in."

Yuriev still refused to make eye contact.

"I'm guessing Vodyanov checked in at Sparkling Waters periodically under the alias F. Vance. Not for taphophobia, for Huntington's. My question to you. Why agree to a cover-up?"

"Celebrities often check into hospitals and hotels under assumed names. It safeguards their privacy. It is not illegal."

"Is that it? Compassionate confidentiality? Or were your motives slightly less pious?"

"How dare you?" Finally swiveling to face me.

"In the course of our investigation, the rude detective and I found evidence suggesting Vodyanov was harming children. Perhaps at the direction of his brother."

"For what purpose?"

"To inflame fear and drive followers to Body's podcasts and blogs. Maybe you knew about it. Maybe—"

"No!"

"Did you know that Vodyanov tried to contact several people before he died? He stalked a man demanding info on kids who'd vanished or been murdered. He pursued me, perhaps to share information about a missing child. He may have visited an old lady, posing as a cop. I think he was feeling terrible guilt. I think the HD was making his life unbearable. He knew that it would only get worse. I think before committing suicide, he wanted to make amends."

Silence crammed the small space.

After a very long moment, Yuriev spoke.

"You have it all wrong."

It was then he produced the missing piece of the jigsaw.

32

"It wasn't Felix."

The sun was skimming the horizon, painting the car's interior a soft tangerine. "It was the brother."

"Body had Huntington's?"

"No. No. You were correct on that point." Yuriev's face looked like a sandstone mask. "But then, I don't care about Nick Body."

"Very compassionate."

"May I indulge?" Tapping a finger to his upper lip. "It calms me."

I shrugged.

Withdrawing the familiar blue tin from the center console, he pinched a little white packet and thumbed the snus up against his gum.

"I won't apologize. It is my sole addiction."

Yuriev closed his eyes and concentrated on controlling his breathing. I sensed an easing of anxiety. When he resumed speaking, his voice sounded steadier.

"You were also correct that Felix took his own life. His symptoms had become so severe that he no longer wished to live. Upon his last visit to the ashram, he asked that I assist him with suicide. I refused. He asked that I prescribe drugs to enable him to overdose. I refused that request also."

I nodded, wondering how much of this I could trust.

"You are an astute woman, Dr. Brennan. It is Brennan?"

"The rude detective helped a lot. His name is Slidell."

"Felix was employed doing research for his brother. He traveled the world finding unconventional ideas and looking for evidence to support them."

"Unconventional?"

Yuriev tipped his head, acknowledging a valid point. "Some concepts were more controversial than others."

"Such as?"

For the next ten minutes Yuriev relayed material I already knew from the blogs and podcasts. I listened, mostly to evaluate his candor.

As he spoke, his gaze remained fixed on the windshield. Not once did he again make eye contact. Not once did he show even a nodding acquaintance with sentiment. Not once did he touch on the topic of kids.

"And Body's crackpot theories about the abduction of children?" I asked when he'd finished.

"I reject them."

"As does anyone with an IQ higher than a mushroom. But Vodyanov had no qualms about supporting his brother's lunatic ravings. Body's hate and fear mongering."

"Call it weak, call it flawed. Felix was devoted."

"Most people love their siblings. But most place limits on what they will do for them."

"I will share a few facts Felix revealed concerning his childhood. He is dead now. Ethically, I'm allowed to do so. And I believe he would approve, as the story may provide insight into his character. Perhaps into his brother's."

Yuriev took a moment to collect his thoughts. Or sift through ethics.

"Felix and Nick were born four years apart to a woman named Tatiana Yanova. Tatiana fled Petropavlovsk, Kamchatka, in the late sixties after being abandoned by her lover following the stillbirth of a child. Though uneducated, unskilled, and speaking no English, Tatiana managed to get herself across the Bering Sea and to a tiny community called the Russian Old Believers in Nikolaevsk, on Alaska's Kenai Peninsula.

"How did she manage that?"

"According to Felix, his mother was a large woman. She buzz-cut her hair, wore men's clothing, and hired on as crew to a fishing vessel. I suppose border control was less stringent back then.

"In Nikolaevsk, Tatiana met an unemployed miner named Aleksandr Vodyanov. The couple married and, after Felix came along, made their way south to the lower forty-eight, hoping to find employment. On May 2, 1972, Aleksandr was one of ninety-one miners killed in a fire at the Sunshine Mine in Kellogg, Idaho. Alone, impoverished, and pregnant a third time, Tatiana was once again forced to rely on her own wits.

"I forget the details, probably not pertinent, but in Idaho, Tatiana threw in with another miner, a Russian, of course, and the family eventually ended up somewhere in West Virginia. I don't know the man's name or his fate, only that he drank, was violent, and eventually left."

When Yuriev didn't continue. "What happened to Tatiana?"

"Felix said she's alive and in some sort of assisted-living facility near Morgantown, West Virginia."

"I understand how difficult life must have been for Tatiana and her children. But how is this relevant?"

"Throughout their childhood, Tatiana ingrained an old Russian proverb into her boys' thinking."

Yuriev reached into his pocket, withdrew pen and paper, jotted, and handed the note to me. I read: всевозможное.

I looked a question at Yuriev.

"Do whatever it takes," he translated. "For Felix, that meant he was to do anything necessary to protect his little brother. He took the mandate literally, interpreted it to mean total loyalty and devotion."

"Detective Slidell and I suspect Felix's support of Nick went far beyond brotherly support."

"Lest you judge Felix too harshly, know that Tatiana's approach to parenting was nothing short of brutal. She kept a large wooden spoon on a hook in her kitchen, threatened its use constantly. And followed through. Some examples. When Nick broke a vase at age three, both he and Felix were beaten, then made to kneel on the shards. When Nick wet his bed at age four, the spoon was applied, then the brothers were forced to wear the urine-soaked pajamas around their necks for days. When, at age six, Nick returned home from a playground with a bloodied nose, Tatiana beat Felix, then ordered him to stand under a freezing shower for hours. When the brothers snuck a stray kitten into the house, they were beaten—"

"I get the picture."

"—then required to watch as Tatiana boiled the young cat alive. Felix was forced to wear the corpse around his neck, as he had the pajamas."

I was too appalled to speak.

Yuriev went silent. Maybe assessing the impact of what he was saying. Maybe enjoying the snus. Then, "It is my professional opinion that Felix was incapable of hurting a child."

"Why reach out to strangers before killing himself?"

"Most people have regrets at the end of their lives."

"Most talk to a rabbi or priest."

"Felix was not an evil man. He wished to die with a clear conscience." Yuriev drew a breath as if to add something, changed his mind, and closed his lips.

"Go on."

He didn't.

"Detective Slidell can compel you to talk," I said.

"No. He cannot."

He had me there. I didn't like it.

"Who paid for Vodyanov's stays at Sparkling Waters?"

"Mr. Body."

"Did he come to visit his brother?"

"Never."

"Did Vodyanov mention Hardin Symes? Jahaan Cole? Timothy Horshauser?"

"No."

A tightening at the corners of the hard little eyes. There, then gone. I suspected Yuriev was lying.

"They are kids who were murdered or who vanished without a trace. Their parents have no idea what happened to them."

"I'm very sorry—"

"Vodyanov supported his brother in exploiting those tragedies."

Yuriev sat stiffly. His features were fast receding into shadow.

"Detective Slidell and I suspect Felix's support went beyond mere exploitation."

"Is that a question?"

"Here's one. Ever hear of Holly Kimrey?"

"No."

"Yates Timmer?"

"No."

More lies?

"Another child disappeared yesterday." No reason to bring that up, but the arrogant bastard was pissing me off. "Her name is April Siler. She's eight. Know anything about her?"

Yuriev's fingers tightened on the wheel. "Why are you badgering me in this way?"

"Because I think you're a lying sack of shit."

Deep sigh. Slight wag of the head. Then, "Felix was a very circumspect man. That he revealed anything about his childhood, even in counseling, was surprising to me. Normally, he spoke little of his personal affairs or acquaintances. But there was one name he mentioned occasionally. Another of his brother's employees. Floy Unger."

Not the answer I'd expected. "Unger was employed to do what?"

"As I understand it, he would receive the podcasts as audio files, encrypt them, decrypt them, whatever one does, then set them up for broadcast. Besides Felix, I believe he was one of the few people to interact face-to-face with Mr. Body."

"And?" Sensing that Yuriev was again holding back.

"I have only Felix's version. His personal view. I've never met Mr. Unger."

"Go on."

"From Felix's comments, I must conclude that the man is odious."

"Odious?"

"Dishonest and capable of violence."

"Your point?"

"If anyone harmed children, it was Unger."

"Can you be more specific?"

"Any further comments would be pure speculation." Another pause as Yuriev sat staring through the glass. Or at it. "Read Mr. Body's blogs."

"I've done that."

"His most recent ones. Listen to his latest podcasts."

I studied the side of Yuriev's face. He was right, of course. As Vodyanov's treating physician, he was bound by confidentiality. Still, I was pissed.

"One question," I said. "In your professional opinion, what drives Body?"

A long moment, then, "I suspect Mr. Body applies his mother's directive in a very different way."

"Meaning?"

"He does whatever it takes to succeed and make money."

"Do you know where I can find Floy Unger?" Unable to think of further questions to pose.

Yuriev slowly nodded.

Driving away, I wondered. Why so little emotion? Was Yuriev cold by nature? Or had years of dealing with the disturbed and depressed totally drained the man?

I phoned Slidell while waiting for my takeout order at Baoding. Of course, he didn't answer.

Once home, while sharing cashew chicken and Hunan beef with my feline companion, I did as Yuriev suggested. The experience left me feeling like I'd swum through raw sewage.

Slidell called as I was stashing the little white cartons in the fridge. He listened as I briefed him on my conversation with Yuriev.

"A bad gene that makes a bad protein that makes you sick and wastes your brain cells."

"Yes." Way to go, Skinny. I'd never heard a more concise definition of Huntington's.

"And you get it from a parent."

"Usually."

"And it kills you."

"It does."

"That sucks."

"Very much."

I described Body's latest tantrums.

"So the world's about to end."

"Nuclear war, natural disaster, pandemic. Pick your calamity. And a new twist. The bastard's saying his brother was murdered."

"Why?"

"Felix had uncovered secret information about the government kidnapping kids."

"That's bullshit." Slidell sounded as repulsed as I felt.

"It is."

"But I meant, why go there at all?"

"Typical media ploy. Get out ahead of a scandal."

"But *why*?" Added hours without sleep hadn't improved Slidell's disposition.

"How the hell would I know?" Or mine. We were both edging toward shrill. "Maybe he thinks we're closing in. Maybe he thinks Heavner's about to release the tox report."

"Is she?"

"You think she'd tell me?" Hearing my tone, I brought it down a level. "Whatever Body's provocation, these tirades make his earlier ones sound like yogic meditation."

"What's your read on Yuriev?" Also more controlled.

"The bastard knew those kids' names."

"He admitted that?"

"No. But I could sense it."

"Uh-huh."

"Look, it all ties together. Cole. Horshauser. Maybe this new one."

"That's going a stretch."

"Body renews his crusade about child abductions. Voilà! Another kid disappears in his own backyard."

"You're really liking Vodyanov for these disappearances?"

"I don't know what to think."

"He definitely didn't snatch April Siler."

"No. Yuriev fingered a guy named Floy Unger."

"Hold on."

I heard protesting springs, then the slow, two-fingered clicking of keys.

"Unger's in the system. The FBI investigated him for running an investment-pool scam. Hold on." More keys. "He was collecting money to build apartments in storm-ravaged areas, assuring a twenty-two percent return. The first wave of investors were getting paid, but off the backs of later victims."

"Sounds like a Ponzi scheme."

"Then there's something about an impersonation and advance-fee scheme—"

"The Nigerian email-type crap?"

"Yeah. Not much stuck. He did a nickel at Butner for a pump-and-dump securities fraud."

"Sounds like Unger is strictly white-collar."

"Well hell-*o*. Floy Unger was charged with assault in '09. Pleaded out to a lesser." Another, longer pause. "Nothing since then."

I heard the whir of a printer. The unhappy springs. Wondered at the absence of background noise.

"Any progress on April Siler?"

"Got one solid lead. A witness claims he saw the kid leaving the athletic fields with a woman in a ball cap. Another says she saw the kid getting into a van. Same description."

"Anyone get the plate?"

"No." Leaden with fatigue. "I been helping with the tip line. Which don't make for heart-pumping action. The kid's snatched by gypsies. Locked away by nuns up in Boone. Transported to Roswell so aliens can study her innards. There are some freakin' loons out there."

"Indeed."

"But I did score some intel on that property. You were dead-on. There's an underground Atlas F missile silo inside that fence."

"Wait. Are you talking about Cleveland County?"

"No. The convent in Boone."

"Hilarious. Owned by whom?"

"Originally, Uncle Sam. In '08, the property sold through something called—let me get this right." More squeaking springs. "The Formerly Used Defense Site program. FUDS. Can't beat the military for alphabet soup."

"Who bought it?"

"A holding company called DeepHaven Ventures, LLC."

"Who owns the holding company?" Heart spiking hard.

"The thing has a shit ton of subsidiary LCs, LPs, LLPs, SOBs, but only two principal investors. You ready for this?"

I wanted to reach across the line and strangle Slidell with his Kmart tie. Instead, I waited.

"Nick Body and Yates Timmer."

"Sonofabitch."

"Sonofabitch."

"I'm telling you, everything circles back."

All I heard was air whistling in and out of Slidell's nose. Finally, "There's no PO listed for Unger, and his LKA dates to '09." Cop code for parole officer and last-known address. "You got any idea where to find this mutt?"

"Yuriev gave me an address. Could be a misdirect."

"Let me have it."

I did.

"I'll send a unit to haul his ass to the bag."

"For what?"

"Pissing in public. Failure to register his pet iguana."

"It's going on midnight."

"I'll think of something."

"You'll let me know if you get him?"

"Sure."

"Then what?"

"Unger cooks overnight, enjoys Sunday-morning pancakes. Then I open him like a can of sardines."

"What time tomorrow?"

"Eleven."

I vowed to be at headquarters by ten.

I'm a pragmatist. Karma, fate, destiny, call it what you will. It's not my thing. But lying in bed, restless and tense, I couldn't shake the feeling that my future was barreling at me like a wrecking ball. Two contradictory premonitions fought for dominance.

The first was—the faceless man's suicide was the act of a soul guilty of nothing more than fraternal loyalty and possession of a malicious gene. All the rest was the product of my overcharged imagination. Vodyanov and Body were shameless cons but not criminals. My career in Charlotte would soon end.

The second was—Slidell and I would reveal the name of the faceless man, lay bare the web of evil emanating from Vodyanov and his brother, find answers for parents, maybe rescue April Siler, and expose Margot Heavner as the self-aggrandizing charlatan I knew her to be. The zombie ant's reign would soon end, and I'd return from exile.

33

A hush hung over the violent crimes division. Partly Sunday morning. Partly the fact that everyone was pounding the pavement to find April Siler and the woman in the baseball cap. It's a cliché, but clichés exist for good reason. In child abductions, the first forty-eight hours are critical. The clock was ticking toward forty-two.

Slidell wasn't in the squad room. I sat at his desk, drinking my Starbucks and fidgeting impatiently. He showed up at ten twenty, looking like he'd spent the night in a dumpster. I assumed he'd slept a bit without leaving the building.

Slidell had already ordered Unger brought up from holding. Together we walked to the same interrogation room occupied by Vince Aiello the previous Wednesday. On the way, he explained that Unger thought they were looking at him for defrauding seniors with a reverse-mortgage scam. He carried a legal pad and what I assumed was Unger's file. He also carried a dummy folder similar to the one he'd employed with the kiddie-porn patent lawyer. I hoped the prop worked better with this guy.

I went to the same room I'd used to observe Aiello, stood by the same mirror.

Cue the lights. The audio. It was like watching take two of a movie shoot. Today the camera's little eye was glowing red. And the male lead looked very different.

Floy Unger was built along the lines of dental floss—tall and skeletal, with skin the color of a toilet bowl. His scalp was covered with greasy brown hair whose longevity didn't look promising, his body with a polo shirt, baggy shorts, and flip-flops.

Unger also wore handcuffs. I wondered if Slidell would have them removed. He didn't. Nice touch. The guy looked cocky as hell. Make him nervous.

Slidell had Unger sign some sort of form. Tucked it into the fake folder.

"Should I have a lawyer?" Unger asked.

"Do you need a lawyer?"

"I've done nothing wrong."

Slidell spit-thumbed through the papers in his folder, pretended to consult one. "You know an old lady named Mary Ellen Hopper?"

"No. Who is she?"

"Sandra Sarah Lee?"

"No." Hiking both shoulders as if to enhance his credibility.

"Carl Prendergast?"

"Look, I'm clean. I've been out of the game for years."

Unger's voice made me think of the bottom of an abandoned well. Dark and dank and hollow. It sounded wrong coming from such a scrawny man.

"Uh-huh." Slidell, light-years beyond dubious.

"I've got a job now. New skills."

"Skills."

"I work with the internet."

"We all work with the internet."

"I'm employed by a media celebrity."

"Tell me about that."

Unger's eyes dropped to his hands, lying flat on the table. His wrists looked like two pale twigs rising out of the manacles.

"I can't go into details."

"Yeah? What's this big star gonna do when you're a no-show because your ass is in the can?"

The bony fingers reached for each other. Intertwined. My skin crawled at the thought of them grabbing a child.

Slidell flipped through Unger's jacket, perused his arrest record.

"Tell me about Penelope Koster." Unlike the aforementioned, a real person.

"What about her?" Grip tightening.

"In '09, Koster said you broke into her place, fractured her nose and two of her ribs."

"She's a lying bitch."

"You pleaded guilty."

"To a misdemeanor. I was defending myself."

"She claimed you were stalking her."

"She also claimed she was going to be the next Taylor Swift."

Slidell waited a long moment before going on.

"You're a con man, Floy. I think you're trying to con me now."

"I'm telling you, you've got the wrong guy for this mortgage thing."

"Maybe yes, maybe no. But I can jam you up for a very long time."

Unger lifted his hands, spread them as wide as the cuffs would allow. "What do you want from me, detective?"

Slidell picked up his pen and pulled the pad close. "Tell me about Nick Body."

If Unger was surprised, he hid it well. "Who?"

Slidell leaned forward, and his voice dropped lower. "I've dealt with a lot of con artists, Floy. Most of 'em a whole lot smarter than you. They waste my time. I don't like people wasting my time."

"I—"

"You've got exactly one minute to give it to me straight. Then I'm going to send you back to lockup and think long and slow on what charges I'll use to book you."

The cuffs made a soft *clunk* as they reconnected with the table. Unger stared down at them. Or his hands. Through the glass, I studied the top of his oily scalp, wondering if maybe Yuriev had scammed *me*.

Slidell waited as seconds of silence ticked by. Finally, he turned and reached for the phone.

"Send someone to collect the asshole in room three."

"No. Wait!" Unger's palms rose, pointed at Slidell in surrender.

Slidell stood. "I'm done pissing away time on you, Floy."

"OK. I work for Nick Body."

"I'm listening."

"Mr. Body is obsessive about his privacy. Anything I say here must be kept in strict confidence."

"Uh-huh."

Slidell again dialed and spoke into the phone. "Hold off on that pickup." Then he pulled out his chair and sat back down.

"Before I talk, can I get some sort of deal? Immunity or something?"

"Immunity for what?"

"I'm just saying."

"Here's your deal. You level with me, I let you walk out of here." A somewhat hollow threat. Slidell had to charge Unger within forty-eight hours or let him go. I was surprised the dope didn't know this.

Unger raised his arms. "Can I get these off?"

"No." Slidell went right for the heart. "Do you help Body snatch kids to drive business to his site?"

"What? That's insane!" Genuinely shocked or an Oscar-level delivery.

"Did his brother?"

"No."

"Do you know Felix Vodyanov?"

"Yes. No." The hands dropped. "I mean, I met him a few—"

"Did *he*?" Slidell began a shotgun barrage meant to keep Unger off balance.

"Did he what?"

"Kidnap kids."

"No."

"Who does?"

"I have no idea."

"Why?"

"Why what?"

"Why are they grabbing kids?"

"I don't know."

"You don't know why they're grabbing them?"

"I don't know that they are!"

"Does Body live at an abandoned Atlas missile silo in Cleveland County?"

This time, Unger couldn't hide his surprise. "He has an improvised apartment there. Stays in it off and on. The place creeps me out."

"Why?"

"It's a million miles underground. You have to go down—"

"Why does he stay there?"

"His brother has some disease. Body's afraid he might have it, too."

"Does he?"

"I'll lose my job if any of this gets out." No longer smug. Now worried as hell.

"Does he?" Dagger-sharp.

"I don't know."

"Is that why he hides from the public?"

Unger shrugged.

"Why do you go there?"

"When Body's in bunker mode, he records underground. Occasionally, he has issues."

"Have you ever spotted kids on the property?"

"Once."

"Girl or boy?"

"Girl."

"Describe her."

"I don't know. She was on the grounds. I didn't get close enough to really see her."

"Toddler? Teenager?"

"Middle size. Maybe seven, eight. I'm not good with kids."

I felt my fingers curl into fists.

Slidell continued hammering. "What exactly do you do for Body?"

"Organize his podcasts."

"That it?"

"Help with IT. A few business affairs."

"What the shit does that mean?"

"I assist with some investments."

"Sounds like giving a drunk the keys to the bar."

"It's all legal."

"Talk about DeepHaven Ventures."

Unger stiffened. A beat, then, "My being here has nothing to do with scamming seniors, does it?"

"I'm asking the questions."

Unger sat mute, weighing his options.

Slidell looked at him a long moment, then pushed back his chair.

Unger decided on the old tried-and-true. Save your own ass. "DeepHaven Ventures, LLC, is a holding company. Its structure is complicated."

Slidell picked up and poised the pen over the pad.

Unger paused a moment to collect his thoughts. "Body and a fellow investor—"

"Yates Timmer."

Tight nod. No longer astonished at anything. "Body and Timmer have invested in the construction of underground condo complexes."

"In abandoned missile silos?"

"They're called survival homes. It's a booming market."

"The sky's falling. I get it. How's the scheme work?"

"Body and Timmer had little of their own money, so they created a holding company, DeepHaven Ventures. Do you want actual figures?"

"Later."

"They each put up a small sum, then got investors to contribute much larger amounts in exchange for part ownerships in the project. They got a bank to provide additional money via a secured nonrecourse mortgage. Do you follow?"

Slidell scribbled, nodded. I doubted he did.

"A percentage derived from the sale of each unit is paid to businesses called DeepHaven I, LLC, and Deep-Haven II, LLC, two subsidiary holding companies."

Unger interpreted Slidell's expression as confusion.

"Look at it this way. The holding company allows Body and Timmer to tie up peanuts for a controlling interest in a multimillion-dollar project."

"You cooked this up?"

"I did not invent the concept of the holding company."

"Where are these 'homes'?"

"DeepHaven I is in a converted Atlas missile silo in West Virginia."

"Describe it."

Unger kicked into what sounded like a sales pitch.

Which made me wonder if he'd been at Lake Wylie the night Slidell and I crashed Timmer's party.

"In addition to eleven floors of living units and one penthouse, the complex includes a swimming pool, dog park, theater, general store, classroom, arcade, library, shooting range, rock-climbing wall, and aquaponic farm."

Slidell didn't interrupt.

"The complex has redundant infrastructure for power, water, air, and food—everything needed for comfortable and extended off-grid survival."

"It's safe living where they used to stash nuclear warheads?" Despite himself, Slidell was intrigued.

"Before construction began, the site was examined by the State of West Virginia, the Army Corps of Engineers, and the Environmental Protection Agency and was declared fit for development."

"So how's this money train rolling?"

"DeepHaven I is complete and fully sold out. Deep-Haven II is ready for conversion."

"What's the holdup?"

"Some investors have withdrawn, and presales are sluggish."

"Sluggish."

"They've only managed to sell a single half-floor unit."

"Timmer and Body feeling the squeeze?"

"Big-time," Unger said.

Quick change of direction. "Is Body staying at the Cleveland County property now?"

"No."

"Where's he living?"

"No clue." Unger's eyes slid down and left, a sure sign of deception.

"Got a phone number?"

"No. I receive the files electronically. If he needs to talk, which is rare, he contacts me."

"Who's Holly Kimrey?" Slidell veered again.

Unger leaned back. Picked at one thumbnail with the other.

"I'm waiting," Slidell said.

"Holly Kimrey is Body's gopher." Mirthless snort. "And dealer."

"Body's on the junk?"

"The guy's nose burns more bread than his Deep-Haven project."

Slidell sat very still, considering, I assumed, what Unger had told him. Then he did exactly what I would have done.

A few misleading questions. Then Slidell picked up the phone and ordered Unger's release.

34

The next three hours seemed to last three days. Then the whole bloody mess ended with a whimper.

Slidell phoned to ask that Unger's release be delayed until he could position himself for a tail. Then he requested backup. After disconnecting, you guessed it, he ordered me to sit tight. I told him not a chance. He blustered all the way down to ground level.

Two uniforms were waiting in the lobby, a guy who could have passed for Ice-T and a woman who must have been born lifting weights. Torrance and Spano.

When a rough plan was in place, Torrance and Spano exited and climbed into their cruiser. As Slidell and I hurried to his 4Runner, he called upstairs to give the go-ahead. Twelve minutes later, Unger appeared, cell phone to one ear. Six minutes after that, a red Ford Fiesta pulled into the lot. I heard Unger ask the driver if his name was Olaf.

"Shit-looking taxi," Slidell mumbled.

"It's probably an Uber."

Two bloodshot eyes cut sideways to me. "I'm not a moron. I know about Uber."

Half right, I thought.

Unger got in, and Olaf pulled out into traffic. Slidell waited ten seconds, then followed. Torrance and Spano were right on our bumper.

It was early afternoon on the Lord's Day in Dixie, so uptown traffic was sparse. To avoid notice, Slidell held back several car lengths. No problem. The Fiesta stood out like a maraschino cherry on wheels.

Passenger and driver were visible as overlapping silhouettes through the rear window. The body movement suggested animated conversation, Unger's head bobbing a full foot higher than Olaf's.

Slidell drove in silence, either sulking or concentrating on the road. Maybe running logistics in his head.

Olaf exited uptown on Central Avenue, eventually made a left onto the Plaza, then a right onto Belvedere, heading into the Plaza-Midwood neighborhood.

"Sonofabitch." Slidell palm-slapped the wheel.

"What?"

"The toad's going home."

"How do you know?"

"We busted him there last night."

"Maybe he wants to pick up his car." Or maybe we're wrong, and Unger won't lead us to Body. I didn't add that.

Slidell said nothing.

The Fiesta made several more turns, weaving through streets lined with frame-and-brick bungalows built a century ago to create Charlotte's first streetcar burb. Prices are modest, so many university faculty live in the hood. I'd been to the occasional party but hadn't recognized the address Yuriev provided.

A quarter hour after leaving the Law Enforcement Center, Olaf pulled in at one of the larger homes on the street, a two-story number with a wide front porch bordered by desperately thirsty azalea bushes. A silver Jaguar XF sat in the gravel drive.

Slidell stopped twenty yards short of Unger's house. Torrance and Spano drove past us and eased to the curb far up the block.

Unger got out of the Fiesta and went inside. Olaf drove off.

"Goddammit." Slidell again smacked the wheel.

"Will you please stop that," I said, equaling Skinny's testiness.

Shortly after entering, Unger reemerged. He'd swapped khakis for the shorts, deck shoes for the flip-flops. His hair was still greasy. I watched him cross to the Jag and, limb by limb, fold himself in. Made me think of a walking stick.

A quick glance in the rearview mirror, then Unger backed down the drive and *vroomed* up the street. Slidell threw the 4Runner into gear and gunned off in his wake. I braced against the dash, watching the world come at me way too fast. Hoping no kid or beagle got in our way.

Unger retraced the path we'd taken from uptown, eventually got onto Freedom Drive, which, with a slight apologetic bend, became Moores Chapel Road. Several miles, then he cut onto Sullins and made another quick right. When Slidell rounded the corner, the Jag was hooking a left.

Crap! Had he spotted us?

Slidell made the turn.

The Jag was halfway up the block, traveling more slowly, not being evasive. Relieved, I leaned back and surveyed my surroundings through the passenger-side window.

We were weaving through another residential area, this one of more recent vintage than the one we'd just left. The homes were all one-story and variations on a very limited, very artless theme. Siding in dingy pastels. Painted versus stained front doors. Carports to the left or to the right. As developments go, it seemed the bottom of the architectural food chain.

Unger turned again. As before, Slidell held back, then followed. A hundred yards up, the Jag veered onto a street cutting in from the right, a spur that ended in a cul-de-sac.

We rolled to a stop just short of the corner and surveyed the scene. Two homes faced off across a concrete circle, each flanked by empty lots. One house was pea-green and had a bay window, detached garage, and small front stoop with a Kmart bench holding a black-and-red racing bike tight to one wall. The other was gray and had none of those niceties.

The Jag was parked in front of the pea. A curbside mailbox said *Schneller*. The neighbor's said *Russak*. Unger got out of the Jag and strode to Schneller's front door. A thumb to the bell, it opened, he disappeared inside.

Slidell punched keys, then spoke into his phone.

"Pull this up." He gave the address. 4 Pine Lily Court.

The response was deadened by Slidell's head. I heard muted sputtering. More sputtering. The voice again, high, probably Spano, a lengthy report.

"What's behind it?"

I couldn't make out a word of the reply.

"No street access?"

Clipped answer. No, I assumed.

"Holding position."

"What?" I asked when Slidell had disconnected.

"Title's been in the name Otto Schneller since the house was built in '97. No record of any calls to the address. No complaints from the neighbors. Schneller's got no history, no jacket."

Though the day was heavy and humid, Slidell felt the need for outside air. We sat with his window half open, breathing the strong smells of rotting garbage, charcoal briquettes, and chlorine losing out to stagnant pool water. Of Slidell's failing Right Guard and sweat-soaked shirt.

Five minutes. Ten.

As Slidell would say, stakeouts don't make for heart-pumping action. My eyes roved the property, logging detail.

Trees muscled up to the edge of the backyard, maybe twenty yards distant from the house. A huge wasp's nest hung below one eave. A door stood ajar at the rear of the garage. Beside the door, a wheelbarrow held a jumbled green blanket. A garden spade lay crosswise atop the bowl, fresh soil on the blade.

That seemed wrong.

I widened my scope.

Neither the street we were on nor Pine Lily Court

was seeing any action. No kids riding bikes or scooters. No neighbors washing cars, pushing mowers, or pulling weeds. The only sounds were Slidell's thumbs drumming on the wheel and a persistent locust hum.

Then, over the drumming and humming, a muted purr.

I was about to comment when Slidell's mobile buzzed. This time, he didn't mash the thing so tight to his ear. I caught most of the exchange.

"Motorcycle approach . . . oving fast. If . . . your location, ETA . . . ess than two minutes."

"Copy that."

Slidell moved fast. In seconds, the 4Runner was backed into a driveway across from and facing the cul-de-sac.

The purr sharpened into a whine. The same whine I'd heard at the bunker? Shortly, a motorcycle slalomed up the block, swerved onto Pine Lily, and angled up the walkway leading to number 4. The rider wore faded cutoffs, a yellow tee, cowboy boots, and a shiny blue helmet.

I watched the rider kill the engine and heel the kickstand into place. My jaw tightened. The boots were tan with a green floral overlay and turquoise studs.

"It's Holly Kimrey," I said.

"You're sure?"

"Yes."

Kimrey dismounted and removed the helmet. His hair was the color of old beets, spiky on top and slicked back on the sides with some sort of oil. From my vantage point, it was impossible to see his features.

Moving with a coiled energy I found unsettling,

Kimrey balanced the helmet on the seat, then hurried up the walk and let himself into number 4. Staring at the drab suburban ranch, I couldn't wrap my mind around the thought that this was Nick Body's home. Could the vainglorious firebrand really live in such a mundane setting?

And an even more grim possibility. Might April Siler be in that house? Buried in the yard or the woods beyond? Were we about to confront a monster? Or was this all a ghastly mistake?

Again, Slidell reached for his phone.

"I'm going in. You and Torrance cover the back in case anyone decides to take a runner."

Mumbled whatever.

"Roger." To me. "Let's go squeeze this jackass. I do the talking, got it?"

"Is it OK if I breathe?"

While crossing the cul-de-sac, I noticed Slidell reach down to adjust his holster. The precaution suggested a tension level equal to mine.

Slidell's knock was answered by a flicking drape in the bay window. No one came to the door. He pounded again, harder, fingers curled into a fist.

"Beat it." A warbly voice said, probably Kimrey.

"Police. Open up."

"Go away."

"Not happening."

"What is this shit?"

"A little party I call open the fucking door."

"Why should I?"

Slidell lifted his badge and waggled it in front of a tiny window at eye level.

"How about we talk warrant?" Kimrey said.

"How about we talk murder?"

"What the fuck?"

"I'm not getting any cooler standing out here."

The door opened the length of a security chain, enough to allow Kimrey to eyeball Slidell. Apparently, what he saw made an impression. Acting with the enthusiasm of a dead man walking, he closed and liberated the door, then withdrew, leaving a gap large enough for us to pass through.

Friends tell me the annex needs a makeover. The decor here was so outdated it should have been wearing vinyl boots and a pillbox. The L-shaped space was small but crammed with an abundance of furniture way past its shelf life. Swag lamps hung from the corners of the ceiling. Olive shag carpet covered the floor.

Straight ahead, up the back of the L, was a dining alcove containing a sideboard, table, and chairs, all pretending to be maple. Metal shelving ran below a window at the far end. A drone-sized fly was sluggishly buzzing one of the panes. A walking cane leaned in one corner, wood, with a derby handle and leather wrist loop.

The living room was directly to the right, in the foot of the L. Gold floral paper covered one wall. The others were bare save for warehouse imitations of great works. Van Gogh's *Starry Night*. Monet's *Sunrise*. Botticelli's *Birth of Venus*.

A flat-screened Sony obscured most of the bay window. Opposite the TV, against the flowery paper, was a grouping upholstered in beige brocade. A matching armchair squatted to either side of a sofa, a faux chrome-and-glass coffee table cowered in front. Identical end tables held identical lamps composed of peony ceramic bases crowned with bubblegum-pink tasseled shades.

Except for the TV, the whole place looked like it was frozen in time. Being generous, I'd say the sixties.

A green bakery box gaped open on the coffee table. A crumb and sugar scatter on the glass suggested the recent ingestion of doughnuts.

Floy Unger was on the sofa, bony knees winging, hands clasped and hanging between them. He looked tired. And something else. Scared?

Holly Kimrey slouched in the chair facing our way, legs outstretched, ankles crossed. Eyes focused on a remnant of chocolate glazed. A man sat opposite, motionless, his back to us. I saw thick black hair and a sunbaked neck suggesting future melanoma.

A fist tightened in my belly.

Was I about to meet the notorious Nick Body?

35

"Anyone else attending this little freak show?" Slidell, gaze bouncing the room and the trio in it.

Unger continued staring at a point in space somewhere beyond his knees. Kimrey remained fixated on the pastry. The black-haired man said nothing.

"I'm talking here, people." Almost a snarl.

Unger flinched. No one else reacted.

Slidell shot me a *stay put* look, then, hand hovering at his Glock, moved off to make a sweep of the house. I watched him pass through the dining alcove into what I assumed was a kitchen, then reverse down a hall into what I assumed were bedrooms and baths. In seconds, he was back. A quick nod to me, then he strode across the nasty shag toward the unfortunate brocade, every sense on high alert.

I joined Slidell and got my first glimpse of the guy whose back had been to us. Despite the added years, leatherized tan, and leaner physique, I recognized him as the third person in the MKUltra conference photo. The man with Felix Vodyanov and Yates Timmer. Nick Body.

"Holly tells me you're quite the pair." Gravelly words escaping from somewhere far back in Body's throat.

I glanced sideways toward Kimrey. Up close, he looked older than I'd imagined. I noted broken veins in his cheeks, starbursts around his eyes and at the corners of his lips. A faint stubble shadow.

"We do what we can." Sarcasm coating Slidell's tone.

"I know you're a cop." Body raised his chin in my direction. "Who the hell's she?"

"Your worst nightmare." The taut shoulders and harsh tone told me Slidell had his full Chuck Norris on.

"Amusing." Body's whole affect was arrogance.

"Why'd you order your flunky to set fire to her townhouse?" Glancing at Kimrey.

"I've no idea what you're talking about."

"I think you do."

"Holly is my assistant, nothing more."

"I checked. Your assistant's got a long, crowded sheet."

Body shrugged, an awkward hitch of one beefy shoulder.

"The dumb shit left prints."

"What the fuck?" Apparently, Kimrey wasn't as fixated on the doughnut as he looked.

"Cops plant evidence," Body said. "They're famous for it."

"Hard to plant fingerprints."

"Tell that to Johnnie Cochran." Body draped a casual arm over his chairback, unconcerned.

The feigned indifference triggered a repugnance so powerful it overrode my resolve to stay silent. "Why have people I questioned about you left town or stopped talking?"

"You noticed."

"I did."

"I paid them off."

"Why?"

"To shut down the meddling."

"What did you hope to gain?"

"What do *you* hope to gain?"

"The truth."

When Body smirked, his lips went tight to his front teeth, down at the far reaches. It was the kind of smirk a viper would make, if a viper could smirk.

"Did you murder your brother?" I asked.

Utter silence.

"These questions too tough for you, Nick? I could use shorter sentences." Adrenaline had me wired to the far side of the galaxy.

"I loved my brother."

"You love his Huntington's?"

"You are thorough." Icy.

"I am." Icier.

"I begged Felix not to do it. He wouldn't listen."

Beside me, Slidell was radiating agitation from every pore.

"Still, it must have been a relief." I pressed on, sensing a weak spot. "His disease could have been embarrassing. Cost you followers. Maybe investors in your missile-silo scam."

More silence. No smirk.

"Hogs ate him, you know." Cruel, but the adrenaline was in full command.

"Don't talk about my brother like that, you bitch." Body's jaw tightened all the way down to his throat.

"Yuriev camouflaged the Huntington's," I hammered on. "Is Heavner on board to sugarcoat the death?"

"Who?"

"Margot Heavner. Your pal, Dr. Morgue."

Unger seemed to return from his point in space. His gaze went to Body, some inner conflict playing out on his face. Body's eyes narrowed in warning. Unger turned away.

"Dr. Heavner is an investor in one of my projects," Body said. "Nothing more."

"We know all about DeepHaven," I said evenly, forcing my face blank to mask my repugnance. And shock.

Out of patience, Slidell retook control. He moved a step closer to Body. "You use that show of yours to spread lies and sell your worthless safe houses. You spew any horseshit that enters your head."

"Yes." Again the viper smirk. "I do."

Slidell was through screwing around. "Where's the kid, Body?"

"What kid?"

"Should I say kids?"

"You're nuts."

"Jahaan Cole. Timmy Horshauser. You want I should go on?"

"I'm aware of those children. I've discussed their disappearances publicly. Beyond that, I know nothing."

"I think you do."

"Have you one shred of evidence to support these ridiculous allegations?"

Slidell glared with such hatred I thought of a gargoyle.

"No, detective," Body sang out. "And you never will."

"That's it. You're stringing me, and it's wasting my time. I'm booking every one of you dipshits."

"For what?" Kimrey asked, equal parts indignation and outrage.

Slidell yanked a plush pink unicorn from his pocket and tossed it at Body. The sight sent Freon out through my veins.

"You get your rocks off on kiddie toys, Nicky boy?" Not bothering to tamp down the savage edge of revulsion. "You like stroking your willy on fuzzy stuffed animals?"

"How dare you!" Cheeks flaming.

"You been doing some grave digging lately? We gonna find some kid in your garden?"

"What the fuck!" Apparently, Kimrey's vocabulary was less than expansive.

"You're all going down." Slidell glowered from one to the next. "Drugs. Fraud. Breaking and entering. Arson. Kidnapping. How does attempted murder sound?"

That's when things went sideways.

Kimrey shot from his chair and bolted across the room. Being directly in his path, I took the hit. An elbow to the ribs knocked me into the Sony. The screen shattered. Numbed by the blow, I stood gasping, lungs knotted in spasm. In my peripheral vision, Unger sat frozen, paralyzed by indecision.

Not so Body. In the same instant, he pushed to his feet and began skirting the coffee table to slip past Slidell.

"I'm on him!" I croaked, stumble-charging after Kimrey.

Behind me, I heard Slidell lunge. An expulsion of breath as Body was rammed in the chest. Flesh slamming brocade. Bone striking plaster. Splintering ceramics.

Kimrey raced to the entrance and yanked the door wide. It banged the wall hard and ricocheted inward.

At my back, an animal grunt, a wheezing whimper, the *snick* of handcuffs locking into place. Startled movement, a barked command from Slidell. A high-pitched squeal from Unger. A crash, probably the second lamp joining its colleague.

Reopening the door cost Kimrey precious time. As I dashed outside, he was just reaching his cycle. I closed in and struck, leading with my hips and following through with my shoulders, all my weight and fury behind the attack.

The helmet flew, and the bike toppled. Kimrey face-dived onto the lawn, my body wrapping his like a leech on a frog. Going down, I caught a flash of Spano's cruiser at the curb. Empty.

Scrabbling to break free, Kimrey elbow-clawed forward while twisting and kicking backward with his fancy boots. I gripped so tightly I felt the strain of his sinewy muscles, the hardness of his bones beneath. Inch by inch, he dragged us across the grass. Arms burning with the effort, I held on, face pressed to his back.

One foot. Two. Kimrey outweighed me by a little, but his desperation was fueling murderous strength. Slowly, my arms slipped downward along the bony spine.

The blistering sunlight, the sweltering humidity, the bucking ride across the scorched grass. The torturous funhouse seemed to go on forever. Then Kimrey's right shoulder dropped as his arm stretched out. I heard a scrape, his throat sucking air as his upper body twisted.

The impact of the helmet told me what my ears had been trying to explain. Stars exploded in my vision. Pain roared from my forehead down through my vertebrae.

I must have loosened my grasp. Kimrey bounced up as though spring-loaded. I scrambled after, unsteady but dogged.

Kimrey had two options. Crank up the cycle. Run for the trees. The woods would do him little good. He had to rely on his wheels.

He was muscling the bike upright when I leveled him with his own trick. Using all the power I could muster, I swung the helmet by its chin strap and roundhouse-clocked him on the side of the head. He dropped and lay still, stunned but conscious.

I felt blood, hot and thick, trickle down my face.

Through the open door, I heard Slidell barking into his phone.

"Need help here!" I bellowed.

I was about to call out again when Spano rounded the corner of the house, barreling fast. With one efficient move, she rolled Kimrey to his stomach and cuffed his wrists.

"Can you understand my words?" Spano asked.

"Fuck you," Kimrey replied.

"Are you in need of medical attention?" Less warmly.

"Kiss my ass."

Disgusted, I turned away. My eyes fell on the open garage door. On the wheelbarrow with its blanket and dirt-crusted spade. I gazed toward the backyard and the woods beyond, overcome with sadness, facing one thought. April Siler could be out there. Other missing kids.

I was backhanding blood and sweat from my face when Slidell appeared in the doorway, an odd look crimping his wildly flushed features. Eyes locking onto mine, he shook his head slowly.

What? I raised both palms.

Slidell crossed to me.

"Just got a call about April Siler." A deep breath. A pause filled with the confusion of contradictory emotions. "They found her."

Despite the heat, my body went cold. I must have faltered. Taking one arm, Slidell led me up to the Kmart bench.

"You need water," he said.

Before I could protest, he hurried into the house. Buying time before having to say the unthinkable?

Minutes passed. My pulse and breathing eased toward normal.

Slidell was crossing the stoop, plastic tumbler in one hand, when a CMPD transport vehicle pulled into the cul-de-sac. Two uniforms got out, one tall, one short. As Tall opened the rear door, Slidell strode to them.

Spano walked Kimrey to the van and helped him climb in. Short disappeared into the house, emerged moments later with a manacled Unger, left eye swelling shut, and added him to the cage.

Torrance was escorting Body across the lawn, hands cuffed behind him, when a burgundy Kia Optima turned into Pine Lily and pulled to a stop behind Unger's Jag. Everyone present went to DEFCON 1.

The Optima's passenger door opened, and a girl hopped out. She wore sandals, a yellow dress dotted with smiling suns, silver seahorse earrings. Her hair was black, her lips glossy pink, her eyes cornflower-blue. I put her age at twelve or thirteen.

I looked at Slidell. His attention was laser-focused on the kid.

The girl was beaming, revealing teeth only possible in the very young. Pressed to her chest was a plastic trophy topped with a swimmer poised to go off the block.

The girl began skipping, sunny dress swinging to the rhythm of her gait. As the scene registered, she slowed. The van. The cops. The handcuffed man in urine-stained pants.

The cornflower eyes widened as the day's joy turned to nightmare. She stopped. The glossy lips trembled. Reshaped to form one word.

"Daddy?"

36

I thought and read a lot about the human brain that summer. About the complex three-pound organ containing a hundred billion neurons branching out to more than a hundred trillion synapse points. About the brain's one hundred thousand miles of blood vessels. Neuroanatomists have named the fissures and sulci and lobes: cerebrum, cerebellum, hypothalamus, medulla oblongata. They've dissected the parts, traced the neural pathways, analyzed the electrical and chemical properties. Still, no one fully understands how the sucker works. I was definitely at a loss concerning mine.

The skirmish at Body's house exists in my memory as a hodgepodge of sensory input. Sight. Sound. Smell. Pain. Lots of pain.

And one crystal-clear snapshot.

A child's terrified cry. *Daddy!* Body turning on the

beat of that word, a look of devastation on his face. The same look mirrored on hers.

At the station, Body, Unger, and Kimrey were allowed to see that Yates Timmer was also enjoying the hospitality of the CMPD. Each was hosted in a separate interview room. All that day and the next, I observed the questioning, shifting from window to window as Slidell moved up and down the hall.

The four "persons of interest" stonewalled briefly, eventually turned on one another. But gently, not with the save-your-ass savagery we'd expected. More like playground snitches sharing benign crumbs. Some info came out. Not what we'd hoped.

The child with the trophy was Body's daughter, AvaLeigh Tayman. AvaLeigh's mother had left Body years earlier, subsequently remarried. Needless to say, the divorce decree included a monster nondisclosure clause. Thus, their names never surfaced in any of my online searches.

AvaLeigh made occasional visits to the fenced property in Cleveland County. The teeth and pink sneaker were hers. She was probably the child Duncan Keesing saw driven through the gate. The child whose face he'd painted on his barrel.

The house at Lake Wylie was a sales office for Timmer's inventory of abandoned military silos and bunkers. And a clubhouse for local "homeowners" in his two underground condo complexes. Rah-rah promotional pitches were made there. Social events were held. Movie night. Steaks on the grill. Cocktails cruising the lake.

According to Body, his motive for investing with

Timmer was purely financial. According to Timmer, his partner's reasons were more complex. Fearing he carried the mutation for Huntington's, Body planned to retreat underground if symptoms appeared.

DeepHaven I was a legitimate success. As Unger had stated in his earlier interview, the twelve-story subterranean complex was complete and fully sold out. Timmer told the same story. Documents confirmed it was true.

And an unexpected zinger. Six years back, during her series of on-air conversations on *Body Language*, Margot Heavner purchased a small unit, the million and a half price significantly discounted in exchange for inside morgue information, especially on cases involving kids.

To me, an underground getaway seemed out of character for Heavner. I'd have guessed her spare bucks would go for Botox or Jimmy Choos. Struck Slidell that way, too. When he questioned her, Dr. Morgue admitted that money, not survival, was her motivator. She planned to flip the unit for a profit but to date had found no taker.

Guess Heavner's ethics were even lower than I suspected. Her desire for wealth even stronger.

DeepHaven II was a different situation. The project was hemorrhaging money, and no one was buying. According to both Timmer and Unger, propaganda about missing kids had worked with phase I. Unclear why. People purchase bunkers for a lot of reasons: fear of financial collapse, a race war, a nuke strike, a plague. A survival home is an option that remains empty most of the time. When the big one comes, you can head underground. So why acquire one out of fear of losing your children?

Rightly or wrongly, Body believed the trend was real, so a similar campaign was implemented to boost sales for phase II. Body was using his blogs and podcasts to create panic among his reading and listening public. His defense was repulsive. What the hell? No law against spreading a little alarm.

Each time I listened to a session with the loudmouthed carnival barker, I had to fight back my incredulity. And revulsion. Body wasn't a defender of the little guy, as he portrayed himself. The blustering bully was in reality a middle-aged cokehead up to his eyeballs in debt. He didn't live in the little cookie-cutter house on Pine Lily but in a sprawling estate in an area of sprawling estates near Weddington, south of Charlotte. A property titled to another holding company and mortgaged far beyond its value. Not as heinous or dangerous a profile as I'd suspected. Still, the great Oz was a fraud on so many levels my instincts still insisted there was something else there.

Over the years, Felix Vodyanov had been tasked with researching many topics, the *Estonia* tragedy and missing and murdered children being but two. Nothing sinister. Nothing violent. No kid was ever harmed by anyone involved with *Body Language* or DeepHaven. On that point, all four held firm.

ITO was the brand name of a tie sold in Japan in the mid-nineties. The company, started by an entrepreneurial high school kid, manufactured a very limited run before going bankrupt. The ties, quite rare, were now worth a fortune. Vodyanov had scored one, liked the name, and used it for one of his many aliases.

The apartment in Ramos's building was leased primarily for storage of files Body wanted kept off-site and hidden. Felix had lived in the house on Pine Lily Court. Otto Schneller was a Vodyanov cousin. Wanting to safeguard his and his brother's anonymity, Body had gotten Schneller to agree to put the title in his name in exchange for a trip to the States. Little risk, it seemed. Otto was eighty-seven and living in Minsk.

Again, my gut told me there was more to it. Why such security? Such secrecy? Something reeked like week-old trout.

Everyone agreed that Vodyanov had left the Hyundai at Art's garage. That he'd written the directions to help locate the car, probably as a reminder to himself. He'd jotted the message in code, as was his habit. Perhaps he'd visited the area several times while planning his final goodbye.

One of the numbers indented into the notebook was for a burner briefly owned by Holly Kimrey. None of the four knew why Vodyanov had listed my mobile on the same page. Or the reference to Jahaan Cole. So they said.

That unconnected dot came from Yuriev. And an explanation of his reaction upon hearing Jahaan Cole's name during our conversation in his car. When pressed, the good doctor admitted that Vodyanov had once spoken of an interview given by a forensic anthropologist named Temperance Brennan on the fourth anniversary of Cole's disappearance. Hence, Vodyanov's choice of me as the person to contact.

Yuriev's link to Body and Vodyanov was through a chess club favored by Russian expats. The doctor had nothing to do with Vodyanov's suicide, had tried to argue his patient back from the edge. In the end, he gave up, knowing Felix's future held nothing but misery. He'd supplied no drugs. Though Kimrey denied it, Body and Unger both implied the fentanyl came from him.

Why taphophobia? Yuriev and Vodyanov found the paradox amusing.

Kimrey was doing a drug run to the bunker the day I found the folder. He was sure Vodyanov had chucked it in the dumpster, speculated Felix was cleaning house before offing himself. He'd seen Vodyanov burning the contents of other boxes, probably those he'd kept at Ramos's building. Not knowing who I was or what I intended to do with the file or the teeth pouch, Kimrey nicked both. Plus, he was freaked that I'd breached security due to his carelessness, didn't want his boss to learn he'd left the gate unlocked.

Based on details grudgingly pried loose from all four interviewees, a picture of Vodyanov slowly emerged. A man devoted to Nick Body yet always in his younger brother's shadow. A man crafting the appearance of a lifestyle he couldn't afford—secondhand clothes, imitation art. A man facing his own physical and mental decline, stumbling, falling, writing notes to himself to keep his thoughts organized. To access passcodes he couldn't remember. A man tortured by some of his actions, seeking to make amends before ending his life.

But no one was involved in harming kids. No way. Never. Inconceivable. Either the four were telling the truth, or their performances were superb.

By Monday afternoon, Body, Unger, and Timmer had all lawyered up. Simultaneous with Slidell's interrogation, slowed now by endless interruptions from counsel, searches of the Pine Lily house and Body's home in Weddington were carried out, and another was begun at the bunker. All day, Slidell's mobile buzzed. Each time, he grabbed it and stepped out of the room. Each time, the news was discouraging. Nothing was turning up to tie any of the men to any missing or murdered child.

Slidell also ordered an investigation into Body Language. Although the site generated some revenue via advertising, he was curious about how Body earned sufficient income to maintain his lifestyle. As expected, records were convoluted and far from transparent.

By Monday night, neither the tossing nor the grilling nor the financial digging had produced evidence of any criminal activity. Rising up like a small swarm of angry wasps, the lawyers demanded that Slidell release their clients.

My fingers curled into fists as I watched the smarmy trio walk free. The little voice in my hindbrain bellowed hopeless opposition.

Holly Kimrey wasn't so lucky. The tail bag on his bike had yielded a full catalog of pharmaceuticals, so Body's dealer would continue as a guest of Mecklenburg

County. In addition, the district attorney was preparing charges related to the B&E and fire at my townhouse. A search of Kimrey's apartment had produced items suggestive of arson, not sure what that means. And my phone. No confusion there. Enough to convict, but the DA hoped Kimrey would flip and finger Body as the person behind the plot.

At seven thirty, tired and discouraged, I headed home.

A few hours with the Pasquerault file, then I fell into bed. Of course, I didn't sleep.

The faceless man refused to let go of my mind.

Why had Felix Vodyanov sought me out? Phoned my mobile? He'd seen the interview, knew my role in the Jahaan Cole case, but how had he learned where I live? Found my number? What was it he'd wanted to say or ask before dying?

He'd written Jahaan Cole's name in his notebook. Maybe posed as a cop to talk to Cootie Clanahan. Clipped and saved articles on Cole and Timothy Horshauser. Did he have information on one or both? Had he been involved in harming them?

Why had Vodyanov written that one Russian word? *Finished. Ended.* To what was he referring? The Latvian book from which the scrap had been torn? His complicity in trafficking his brother's hateful vitriol? In harming kids? His life?

Pete had skimmed the volume, reported that it was published in 2003 to promote the theory that the *Estonia* was purposefully sunk.

Felix Vodyanov. A spy? An assassin's target? Crazy as a bag of rats?

A child molester? A killer?

What was real? What was not?

In 1983, the mutation for Huntington's was mapped to a location on chromosome 4. Diagnosis is now possible via submission of a small blood sample. Body refuses to be tested.

Nick Body. A blowhard and scammer? An HD sufferer? A man needlessly living with dread?

A child molester? A killer?

What was real? What was not?

Had I really made a trip to that underground bunker? Or was the experience simply a migraine-induced hallucination? Had my own three-pound arrangement of electricity, chemicals, circuitry, and cells conspired to take me down? Had my unruly arteries sent my own blood thundering against me?

Had I been drugged? Had Kimrey laced my tea with Molly or LSD?

What was real? What was not?

Had Kimrey torched my home? He denied any involvement. Was the fire simply the result of a faulty wire delivering just enough spark to a chemical-soaked rag? If so, why the print by my window?

What was real? What was not?

I slept badly all night. Repeatedly woke, checked the clock. I tried deep-breathing exercises, inhaling slowly, then spreading the warm harmony into my fingers and toes. Nothing worked. I really suck at letting the peace in.

When I was awake, a movie titled *Vodyanov and Body* played in my head. Or on the ceiling. Or in the darkness between. Again and again, the scenes led me back to the same conclusion. Body had to be dirty. Otherwise, why such security? Why order the fire at the annex? If it had been arson. Why discourage witnesses from talking to me? If not child abduction, what was his sin? I was convinced Body was into something far more sinister than simply gaslighting the public.

Body's podcasts also looped in my brain, increasing my agitation. My anger at seeing the bastard walk free, the viper smile on his face.

By dawn, I was convinced there had to be some clue buried somewhere in all of those histrionics. Vowing to find it before leaving town, I got up and headed downstairs.

A mug of coffee and a bowl of Raisin Bran later, I booted my laptop. Once online, I went directly to Body Language and, as before, paid the required fee, this time with an untraceable prepaid card purchased in a *Spy vs. Spy* moment with cash at a Walmart. Then I answered the nonoptional profile questions, presenting not as myself but as a forty-two-year-old white male. Not sure why. To assure myself I could be cyber-sneaky, too?

The page opened. There were the tabs offering links to podcasts, blogs, the general store. All as I remembered. I decided to go with the archived audio files. Started plowing through, beginning with the most recent and working my way back in time.

By ten, my head was ready to explode. Much as I wanted to nail the oily prick, I needed a break. A fill-up on coffee, then I returned to Body's home page and, lacking a better idea, linked over to check out the merchandise for sale.

Stared.

Blinked.

Blinked again.

The page looked, what? Off?

I felt the familiar adrenaline-fueled dread. Were the irksome cranial vessels conspiring for action? Was a headache barreling in?

Take the meds?

No. Not yet.

I closed my eyes. Waited. Opened them. Focused on the screen.

This wasn't the usual aura—the flashing-fizzing-black-hole optical display heralding an upcoming migraine. My vision was fine. The page was sharp and clear. It just looked wrong.

I clicked on the "aisle" offering podcasts for sale. Noted nothing different from my last visit. I was thinking about that when frenzied knocking managed to seep into my concentration.

Mama was peering through the back door, face anxious, nose pressed to the glass. I got up to let her in.

"What's wrong, sweet pea? I can tell by those lines creasing your lovely brows that something's amiss. Are you having a spell?" she asked, parking a covered casserole dish on the counter and reaching a hand to my forehead in one deft move.

"I'm fine, Mama. Really. Where's Sinitch?"

"Doing some serious introspection."

"You've quarreled?"

Sniff. "The gentleman has lost all playground privileges for a while, let's just leave it at that."

Totally in agreement.

"I brought you my spinach and Gruyère quiche. Given your condition, it's imperative that you eat properly." Noting the laptop. "What are you working on? Does it have to do with that poor man got gnawed by the hogs?"

"Indirectly." Then, wanting to divert from the topic of my "condition," "Let me ask you something."

"Shoot."

"What might cause a website to look slightly off?"

"That question is about as clear as mushroom soup. Be more specific."

"I've visited the site recently. Now when I go back, it doesn't appear the page has been updated or redesigned. It just doesn't look right."

"Show me." Setting her Louis Vuitton tote on the table and repositioning a chair beside mine.

I did. And described the connection between Vodyanov and Nick Body. Kept it vague. Like the soup.

"How'd you log in each time?"

I told her.

Pulling a MacAir from her bag, she brought up Body's site and, fingers flying as fast as any teen hacker on the planet, explained what she was doing.

"I'm profiling myself as a seventy-seven-year-old female."

"Why?"

"Because that's what I am, sweet pea. But more important, if your perception is accurate and my hunch is correct, I'll explain the relevance."

"I'm happy to pay the subscription fee."

"Done."

"How?"

"Cyber-currency."

I didn't ask.

When Mama was in and had linked over to the general store, we both studied the images, eyes ping-ponging between our two side-by-side screens.

"There," I said, pointing. Those bundled sets of archived podcasts. They're offered on my laptop but not on yours."

"Huh." Fingers dancing. Firing through the inventory presented on her screen. "Let me see your laptop." A few key combinations. Then, "Malware."

"Malware?" I knew what it was but wasn't sure where she was going.

"They're using some sort of malicious virus, something like DNSChanger, to infect the computers of certain visitors to the site."

"DNSChanger?"

"I'll back up. But you really must educate yourself more about the World Wide Web, sweat pea." Pause. "DNS, the Domain Name System, is an internet service that converts user-friendly names, for example, Body Language.com or ESPN.com, into numerical addresses that allow computers to talk to each other. Without DNS and the DNS servers operated by internet service providers, computer users wouldn't be able to browse websites or send email."

"Got it." I did.

"A malware program like DNSChanger redirects an unsuspecting user to a rogue server, allowing a hacker to manipulate that user's web activity."

"Let me get this straight. When the user of an infected computer clicks on the link for some website, say, BodyLanguage.com or ESPN.com, because of the malware, they are taken to a different website instead."

"Close enough. A few years back, the FBI busted an internet-fraud ring operating out of the Baltics that had infected millions of computers worldwide."

"Why?"

"It allowed the hackers to manipulate the multi-billion-dollar internet advertising industry. It's fascinating. Do you want to hear the details?"

"Later. So why infect my computer and not yours?"

"They must be using an algorithm that selects only certain visitors. If the designated profile logs in, that computer is infected and redirected."

"To a rogue server they control."

"Yes."

I considered that.

"A forty-two-year-old man is rerouted but not a seventy-seven-year-old woman."

Mama finished the thought. "To a modified site offering bundled podcasts. At very high prices, I might add. Who would pay that amount to listen to such drivel?"

My mind was going a billion miles a second.

"What type of audio files are those podcasts?" I asked.

A series of keystrokes. "MP3 files."

Several beats as we both stared at our screens. Then Mama gasped, sharp and quick. I turned. Her eyes were like hubcaps. Wearing mascara.

"What?"

"I believe I know what deviltry Body is up to."

37

Thirty minutes later, Slidell was swiping us through security and into the crime lab. Mittie Peppers met us outside the QD section. Nods all around. No pleasantries. The tension was enough to revive the DOA Mars rover.

Peppers led us through the door, past the marvelous ESDA machine, to a village of computers glowing along a back wall.

"You think it's nuts?" I asked. "What I said on the phone?"

"Not at all."

"You're familiar with the process my mother referred to?"

"Steganography. Definitely."

"You're on board with her malware theory?"

"Let's see your computer."

I entered my password and handed Peppers my

Mac. She settled by one of her screens and began working my keyboard. I sat beside her. Slidell stood behind, taut as a patient awaiting a root canal.

Seconds passed. A full five minutes. I chewed a thumbnail, as agitated as when I'd come to Peppers about the indented writing.

"Oh, yeah. You've got a nasty little bugger."

"Sonofabitch."

"This machine seems brand new."

"I bought it last Friday." After my old one was incinerated due to my own stupidity. I didn't add that.

"Have you visited Body's site using this Mac?"

I nodded, anger sparking so hot I didn't trust my voice.

"I can remove the malware when we're done."

"I'll owe you. Go to BodyLanguage.com."

She did.

"I've joined as a forty-two-year-old male. Use that profile, then link over to the general store, and enter the podcast aisle."

She did. I pointed to the bundled podcasts. Explained how they'd appeared on my Mac earlier and not on Mama's. Peppers logged onto one of the lab's computers, joined Body Language as a thirty-three-year-old female, promising to bill Slidell at the CCU for reimbursement, and navigated to the proper aisle in the general store. No bundled podcasts. Peppers agreed that an algorithm in the malware was sending some users to a rogue server, then to a modified version of the page, which was hawking the bundles to what the site's operators perceived as a specialized slice of the market.

"Roll me through steganography," I said. "How does it work?"

"Stick to the King's English, ladies?" Slidell, churlish.

The ladies shared an eye roll.

"You've heard of encryption, right?" Peppers began.

"Coding," I said.

Peppers nodded. "When we talk about encrypting, we mean making something indecipherable. It's obvious the secret code is there, but no one can read it without knowing the key. Steganography is all about hiding a message so that no one even knows it's present."

"Like writing with invisible ink." Mama had used that analogy.

"Exactly. Say you want to hide some info in another document, maybe in an image. You do it by subtly adjusting individual pixels . . ."

Peppers stopped mid-sentence. Turned from the screen to see if we were following.

"Pixels are the tiny squares that make up a digital image." Hearing Slidell grunt, I let it go at that.

"A pixel is barely noticeable to the human eye but easily detected by a computer," Peppers continued. "By making very subtle adjustments, you can hide whole strings of text. For example, change the color or brightness values of three successive pixels, and you could invisibly code the word CAB. I am greatly oversimplifying."

"You're talking about hiding text," I said. "Could you also conceal one image inside another?"

"Yes. Since the intensity values are changed only slightly, the steganography creates deviations so subtle they can't usually be detected by the naked eye. Typically, the only way you could say that one pic is a steg would be to compare two seemingly identical images. Even then, if you suspect one may be modified, there's no quick way to tell which is the innocent and which is the carrier."

"Come on, come on." Slidell flicked a hand at the screen. "If Body's dirty, I got to nail his ass fast."

"Can you hide text or images in audio files?" I asked, feeling the same blunt-force dread as when Mama first proposed the idea.

"Yes. You take advantage of the way the algorithm for MP3—that's code for mathematical process—converts and compresses analog audio into digital form. Your secret information would not only be hidden, it would be encrypted as well, so very hard to detect and decrypt."

"There are programs that do this?" I was so pumped I was asking dumb questions.

"The web is lousy with apps. For example, MP3Stego hides things in music files. SkyDe is a steganographic add-on for Skype. There's COAGULA—"

Slidell cut us off. "Brennan's thinking this jerkweed Body might be floating kiddie porn in stuff he sells on his site. Maybe hiding it in these podcasts." Jabbing a thumb at the monitor.

"Is that possible?" I asked, wanting confirmation. Not wanting confirmation.

"A lot of steganography is done with apps on mobile devices. What you're suggesting would require computers on both ends. The buyer would download the podcast—the MP3 file, one of the most common audio files out there, by the way. Normally, he or she would play it using an audio player on his or her computer, iTunes on Mac, for example. But instead, with the setup I'm picturing, the buyer would open the file in a special program that is shared by the bad guy and the buyer, let's call it Play Inside."

"Which Body has used to hide images or videos."

"Yes. The buyer opens Play Inside and selects the downloaded podcast from within that program. Play Inside then decodes the hidden porn, or whatever it is. Additional security might be to require the use of a password to open the file from within the special program."

"Body's got tech people could figure shit like that." Slidell was pressing way too close to my back. "Maybe that freak Unger."

"A savvy undergrad could set it up." Peppers turned raised brows to me, then swiveled them to Slidell. "You in a spending mood, detective? Shall we put one of these in our shopping basket?"

"Fuckin' A."

We cruised the inventory, chose a podcast collection labeled "Our Children Are in Danger," the only suggestive title of the half dozen offered. Peppers purchased and downloaded the bundle to one of the lab's computers. Then, with a flurry of typing I couldn't begin to follow, she launched a program and opened the first MP3.

"The DSSS steg-hiding algorithm—" she began.

"DSSS?" Wanting to be sure I understood.

"Direct sequence spread spectrum. It's a technical method used for cell phones and other digital signals, which can also modify MP3 files to hide bits of a message."

"Because an MP3 file is nothing more than a digital signal."

"Exactly. The DSSS steg-hiding algorithm can enter random noises into audio files." More keystrokes. "The software I'm using now analyzes sound, checking for extremely subtle variations, random noises like blips, barely detectable, but clues that might suggest a steg version of an original file."

Lots of readouts and sliding bars and flashing lights on the screen. Peppers watched them as she listened for indicators of manipulation. Shook her head slowly.

"I'm going to reduce the speed. Slowing can reveal sounds incongruous to the flow of the music or the voice, or whatever, distortions that would be missed when playing at regular speeds."

She typed in the command. A few seconds, then, "There. Do you hear that?" Raising an index finger, eyes now closed for better concentration.

Unconsciously, I leaned in. Behind me, I felt Slidell mash closer to my chair. Bend lower, so his breath was hot on my neck.

At first, nothing. Then I caught it. Tiny hitches in Body's gravelly voice. A quick note here and there of higher or lower pitch.

"Yes." Heart pumping fast. "What is it? Are you able to decode what's been hidden?"

"Unfortunately, no. I can say this file demands more analysis to determine if something else is there, but without a lot more digging, I can't tell you what it is." Peppers leaned back and turned to face me. Instead of elated, she seemed wary.

"What?" I asked.

"The problem is, the whole thing seems unwieldy."

"Unwieldy."

"I'm not sure an audio file like this would have enough space"—she hooked air quotes around the last word—"to contain a whole image, much less a video. An image could be spread across several MP3 files, I suppose . . ." She didn't sound convinced.

"Go on."

"OK, say a buyer forks over for a bundle of podcasts. They're expensive but not crazy. How much could Body make off this type of operation? As a distribution system for child porn, it would be reasonably secure and keep him at arm's length. And the images would be hard to detect. But profitable?"

Though my mind was in hyperdrive, my thoughts were tracking along the same lines.

"Holy bleeding Jesus." Slidell straightened like a marionette yanked up by strings. Shot a hand through his hair. "So you're sayin' we still got nothing on this bastard?"

"I'll keep at it," Peppers said, tipping both palms in a gesture meant to calm.

It didn't. With one final growl, Slidell turned and thundered out, nostrils flaring, looking ready to dog-dare anyone to get in his way.

Exiting police headquarters, I was overwhelmed with feelings of anger and self-blame. Body was going to skate, and that was partly my fault. What if I'd done more? Been smarter? Confronted Heavner earlier? Pushed Duncan Keesing harder? Been more conscientious about backing up my laptop? Spotted something in one of those lost images? Hadn't been so damn preoccupied with the state of my brain? A million what-ifs.

And I was running out of time. In a few short hours, I had to board a flight to Montreal. Driving toward home, I felt myself clawing for sanity with ten ragged nails.

Mittie Peppers rang at twelve past five. I recall noting the time on my phone. Trepidation must have seared the glowing digits into my memory.

I'd just finished packing, which took ten minutes. Lacking enthusiasm for couture or maquillage, I'd simply tossed random items into a Rollaboard. Business suit for court. Beyond that, whatever.

"I've got it." Unlike earlier, Peppers now sounded jazzed.

"You managed to open an image?"

"Not exactly. Can you come back uptown?"

"You bet your ass."

Slidell arrived as I did. We ascended together. He smelled extra-ripe, even for Skinny. The reek of frustration and sleep deprivation.

Once in her lab, Peppers wasted no time. As we reconvened at the same computer, she said, "Body's not hiding images. He's hiding links and passwords."

We both stared at the back of her head.

"It's a double-layered setup. The message hidden in the steg podcast is a URL, many fewer bytes than an image." Pointing to a string of text displayed on the screen. "Once the buyer uses the special program to decode and display the link on his or her computer, he or she copies or clicks on it, and the browser loops to another window."

"You're unbelievable. How did you—"

"Open it." Slidell's barked command was like a slap, quick and painful.

"Not that simple," Peppers said. "For added security, Body requires a password to access the URL."

"Sonofafreakinbitch."

"Fear not, detective. After attempting *beaucoup* manipulations—I won't burden you with the fine points—I cracked the bastard."

Returning to the Body Language homepage, Peppers pointed to the tab labeled "Support Our Efforts." "I won't go into detail now, but the buyer gets to decode the password, also hidden in the podcast, by making a five-thousand-dollar donation here."

"That explains profitability." My mouth and throat felt rough and dry.

"It does."

"So what do these maggots get for their money?"

Peppers returned to the original screen and indicated a second string of text that I hadn't noticed before. "That's our password. Alert your boss, detective. My department will be billing yours."

"Do it!" Slidell snapped.

Peppers clicked on the link. The screen shifted to the new URL. A rectangular box demanded a password. She entered the $5,000 string of text.

Again, the screen morphed. A video began to play. No, not a video. A livestreamed image, broadcast in real time.

I couldn't move, couldn't breathe, couldn't blink.

Adrenaline surged through every vessel in my body.

38

I never took the stand. As I was climbing the steps of the Palais de Justice, Dorothée Pasquerault's killer pleaded guilty to manslaughter, and the trial was adjourned. I would later learn that the scumbag got fifteen years. A shorter time than Dorothée was allowed to breathe air on the planet.

I was out of the courthouse by ten, rode the Métro to Papineau, then walked the remaining half mile to the Édifice Wilfrid-Derome. The weather was cool and rainy. A pleasant change from the hothouse I'd left behind in Charlotte.

My intent was to erase the stress of the past two weeks by diving straight into my Quebec life. Into whatever awaited me at the Laboratoire de sciences judiciaires et de médecine légale. That didn't go well.

My Quebec life was there and happy to welcome

me back. My desk with its squeaky file drawer and gouged wood. My view of rue Parthenais and the Fleuve Saint-Laurent twelve stories below. Cases as familiar as the back of my hand. Weathered cemetery bones. A partial skeleton unearthed in an abandoned septic tank. I resolved to focus on the dead in need of my attention.

Try as I might, I couldn't concentrate. Partly fatigue. My flight had landed late, of course. By the time I'd made it through customs and immigration, gotten an Uber, and ridden from Pierre Elliott Trudeau into Centreville, it was well past midnight.

At one thirty, I gave up and headed home. To my new Quebec digs.

Knowing the larder was bare, I made a quick stop at a noodle shop near the Peel Métro and was back at my condo building by two. Our condo building. Though Ryan wouldn't be in it. He'd called late Tuesday to say that his return to Montreal would be on Friday. Neville had been reunited with his very grateful mistress, a vineyard worker was behind bars, and a guy in Marseille was stuck with a whole lot of oats.

After winging up in the unfamiliar elevator, I let myself in and dumped my briefcase on the unfamiliar counter in the shiny state-of-the-art kitchen. Lots of marble and stainless steel.

The place was blissfully quiet. Vowing to stay awake at least until sundown, I peeled off my go-to-court suit, pulled on sweats, then ate my pad thai while checking my iPad for news from Charlotte. Found the follow-up coverage I wanted.

April Siler was alive and well. I knew that. Slidell had gotten word just as Kimrey tripped the wire at the Pine Lily Court house. The father's girlfriend had lured April into her van on a day when Daddy was in Denver, thus providing him with an alibi. They planned to transport the child by private jet to Costa Rica, where the girlfriend owned property.

I learned that Papa and his honey were now in custody, and April was home with her mother.

Hallelujah. One happy ending.

Two, actually.

On Monday and Tuesday, while Slidell was firing questions at his suspects, a CSU unit had been scouring Pine Lily Court, running cadaver dogs over the property and through the surrounding woods. Stoking expectations, a golden retriever named Hilda had grown agitated on approaching a suspicious depression. Unfortunately, excavation revealed that the depression was, in fact, a shallow grave holding only a recently deceased opossum.

Punchy with exhaustion, posttrial letdown, and the metabolic effort of digesting my body weight in carbs, I gave up on my vow to stay up until dusk. After trudging down the hall to the unfamiliar bedroom, I closed the unfamiliar curtains, then fell into the unfamiliar hundred-acre bed. And slept a sleep as secluded and still as the dead I'd left behind in my lab.

I awoke to the chimes of incoming texts. Groggy and confused, I picked up and tapped my phone. 5:52. I'd been asleep barely two hours.

Both messages were from Slidell. In the first, he

reported that the search of the Cleveland County bunker was still under way. He included a few photos. The place looked like the before shots of Timmer's World's End House.

The second was composed of three words. *Nailed Body. Call.*

I hit speed dial.

"Where'd you get him?" Jumping right in, Slidell style.

"The shit-for-brains was gophered into one of the back tunnels in his underground Shangri-la. Guess Atlas Acres wasn't all that foolproof after all."

"Timmer?"

"There's nothing to tie him to what Peppers uncovered. Besides, I know where to find him. His lawyer's assured me his client is going nowhere."

"Unger?"

"Oh, yeah, given his history, I'll bet my ass he's dirty. I'm letting Body and Unger simmer a while. From what they've let drop so far, each is going to turn on the other like a bobcat on prey."

"What more has Peppers learned?" Burning ice below my sternum at recollection of the abhorrent scene that had played on her screen.

"It worked pretty much as she said. They weren't hiding steg images in the audio files. It was passwords and hookups to a site showing video in real time." Slidell's voice darkened with loathing. "You download the link, you buy the password, you get to watch footage of kids being abused live and in color. The buyers are thousands of miles away, so no skin off their noses.

No guilt. Also, the sick twists can pursue their sport without actually storing files on their computers. Keep your browser history clean, you're golden. Or so the morons thought."

"Livestreaming from where?"

"The Philippines. Some town north of Manila. I gotta say, the vice boys over there jumped right on this when we made contact. Issued warrants, busted the guy running the webcam outta his home. So far, they've ID'd a dozen kids between the ages of six and fifteen."

"The children are OK?"

"Who the hell knows? They're with social services, or whatever it is the Philippines got. Here's the part tears your heart out. My contact says a lot of those being arrested are family members."

"Seriously?"

"He says the parents live in poverty. They got no jobs, no hopes of scoring nothing in life. For a couple hundred bucks, they allow their kids to be sexually abused for the entertainment of pervs all over the globe."

"It's that widespread?" The heat-chill expanding across my chest.

"Yeah. The feds are taking over. And Uncle Sam will have lots of help smoking out this pond scum. Britain, Australia, and Germany are already on board."

"Unger orchestrated the IT for Body?" Pleased with the calm tone of my voice.

"No doubt."

"What are they facing?"

"For now, possession and distribution of child pornography and exploitation of a minor related to child pornography. The DA is busting ass to make sure these dirtbags get the max possible."

"Whatever the sentence, it won't be enough." If they serve any time at all, I thought, remembering how Aiello had skated.

"Never is," Slidell agreed.

"Anything on Jahaan Cole or Timmy Horshauser? On any of our kids?" I knew the answer but couldn't help asking.

"No."

A long, heavy silence filled the line. Then, "Heavner's out."

"Good riddance." I'd already discovered that via another news feed. In light of the scandal and her connection to Body, Dr. Morgue had resigned as Mecklenburg County's chief medical examiner. The search for her replacement had begun.

"Here's a nugget you'll find rich. You know those pics you got by text? The ones kicked this whole thing off?"

"Yes." I didn't recall telling Slidell about the images, but apparently, I had. Or maybe he'd learned of them from Ryan.

"Heavner sent them."

"What? No way. Why? How do you know?" So shocked I was babbling.

"Because of the Body fiasco, a search was run on Heavner's computer. Seems she was using a special email account to communicate with a reporter named Breugger."

"Gerry." The lizard. The only journalist addressed by name at her presser.

"Whatever. She shared intel with Breugger, probably hoping to see her name in the papers."

"I'll bet the farm she hit Brennan instead of Breugger when both names came up as auto-suggested recipients for the text."

"Ain't that the kickass of irony? Heavner shares pics hoping for glory and brings a simmering shitpot down on her head."

Snippets of a conversation floated back from the past. Paulette Youngman, designer light glinting off one unfashionable lens. *Morality hijacked by a need for fame and public adulation.*

Another happy ending. At least, for me. Hopefully, my exile would soon be at an end.

"What now?" I asked.

"Peppers and the IT guys are going through Body's computers. Ditto Unger's. I'm looking at a cell phone turned up when I was with CSU at the Weddington crib. Looks like Body used it strictly for personal stuff. The thing's not even password protected. No surprises in the contacts, no photos, emails, or text messages. Little in the call history—mostly his kid."

"Any unusual software?"

"There's a couple programs I don't know what the fuck they are. Soon as I hang up, I'll shoot the device up to Peppers."

"Text me screen shots of the apps?" Not particularly hopeful, but what the hell? I had nothing else pressing, and a smartphone can tell a lot about a person.

"How do I do that?"

I explained the key combo and how to send the images. A few more exchanges of info, then we disconnected.

I sat a while cross-legged on the bed, thinking about our conversation. I fervently hoped the DA would succeed in bringing the house down on Unger and his boss. For me, taking a snake like Body off the street and off the internet and airways would be as satisfying as locking up a homicidal felon. I knew Slidell felt the same. Still, I couldn't shake the feeling that we were missing something. That Body was guilty of an offense more sinister than child porn. Why buy off witnesses? Why take the risk of ordering Kimrey to torch my home? To poison me?

Nevertheless, I was pleased with Slidell's update. And with the fact that he was still digging and had taken the time to brief me. Unanswered questions swirled in my brain for only a few minutes before I drifted back to sleep.

The next morning, after logging nearly twelve hours with the covers drawn close, I was up and making coffee in the kitchen when I heard more texts chime on my phone. Additional bulletins from Slidell? I walked to the living room and gazed through the floor-to-ceiling window forming one wall. The sun was just clearing the gray skyline in the east, turning the high-rise towers and brownstones lining rue Sherbrooke a misty reddish bronze. Dawn, and Skinny was already awake and revved?

I took my mug to one of two white leather armchairs facing the glass. Traffic on Sherbrooke was light at that hour. I stared out, watching vehicles stream toward me, then away. A lone cyclist was pedaling slowly along the empty sidewalk. Up and down the street, windows winked crimson, reflecting the extraordinarily colorful antics of *le soleil*. Lights were on in some of the rooms. I sat sipping, wondering fleetingly at the lives filling each.

A little more caffeine to fuel up, then I lifted my phone, confirmed that it was indeed Slidell who'd pinged me, and opened his text.

A pair of screenshots showed the apps on Body's mobile. All but two were standard issue—settings, calendar, contacts, phone, text messages, and so on. One of the oddballs was a program designed to intercept telemarketers. I had the same blocker on mine.

The other unique app was orange with two teepees, one upright and white, one inverted and peach. I stared at the icon, feeling that little tingle deep down in my id. I'd seen it before. Where?

I made a visit to the App Store. Scrolled. Didn't find it. The app wasn't trending. I had no keyword or suggestive phrase with which to search.

My eyes drifted to the scene far below. The cyclist had stopped outside the Musée des Beaux-Arts gift shop. He was squatting by his rear wheel, adjusting something only cyclists understand.

The tingle released random bytes into the wilds of my brain. Keesing's reference to "places that lit up bright on some kind of maps." Body Language rants about a fitness app revealing the location of secret military bases. A bent bicycle wheel shadowed under camo netting. A racing bike pressed to a wall at Pine Lily. Body's sunbaked neck.

Acceleration.

Supercollision at one of those trillion cerebral synapse points.

Barely breathing, I went back to the App Store and searched using the keyword *biking*.

I recognized the icon instantly. Strava, a mobile fitness app used by cyclers and runners to keep track of their distances, speeds, and routes. Larabee had relied on it to log his runs.

Easy, Brennan. It could be nothing.

I bolted for my laptop.

Two hours later, I was punch-dialing Slidell.

39

"Will you please stop barking and listen?"

"I'm listening. You ain't making sense."

"Do you have your computer open to the Strava website?" Between Skinny's churlishness and my own excitement, I was finding it hard to stay civil.

"Yeah. But I—"

"The user logs on with a smartphone, or Apple Watch, or Fitbit, or whatever." I explained the application once more. Slowly. "As he bikes or—"

"You're sayin' Body did this?"

"He has a verified account." Resolutely controlled. "As Body bikes, GPS tracks his location and draws a line following his path." Out of habit with Skinny, keeping it simple.

"He don't have a million privacy settings hiding where he goes?"

"Strava allows access for any registered user, so information on routes is publicly available." To clarify.

"Profiles are public by default. Though privacy settings are offered, Body set none."

No response. I assumed Slidell was studying the screen on his end.

"I created an account, made up a profile—"

"This Agnes Pipehead dame."

"Yes."

"Why the hell'd you pick the name Agnes—"

"Then I went outside and walked around, to test the program for accuracy. What you're seeing is the publicly accessible route report generated by Strava on my account."

"That squiggly red line."

"Yes. Now, do this." I gave instructions on how to get to Body's profile. Then on how to bring up stored routes. I waited out the slow clicking of keys.

Then, "Body's had an account since 2013."

"At least that long."

"He's stored a shitload of outings."

"He has. Open this one." I provided more guidance, then waited, confident Slidell would grasp the import. He did.

"Sonofafreakinbitch."

The route map included a neighborhood painfully familiar to both Skinny and me. A segment of street. A corner with a library stand once offering a copy of Laura Ingalls Wilder's *Little House on the Prairie*.

"Body pedaled his skanky ass through Jahaan Cole's hood." Simmering rage in his voice.

"He did."

I waited out a long stretch of agitated breathing. "DA'll say his being there don't mean squat."

"Check the date."

"October 6, 2013. Fuckin' hell."

"Four days *before* Jahaan Cole disappeared."

"So even if the DA drags ass about charges, I maybe could use the info to get one of these turds to junk his jeans."

"Exactly."

"Vodyanov registered the Hyundai in West Virginia, right down the road from where the Horshauser kid went missing. You find anything tying Body to him?"

"Not with Strava." I'd looked.

"I'm on it."

And Skinny was gone.

At nine that night, he called again, sounding like a bundle of jolting nerves.

"I been alternating working Unger and Body, letting one sweat while grilling the other. You know the deal, find the weak link, push for the flip. At first, I low-keyed it, then I turned the screws hard, asking about Jahaan Cole, dropping hints on this Strava joy, mentioning little things like the death penalty and the longevity of child killers inside the can."

"And?" Wanting new info, not a review of Slidell's interrogation tactics.

"Hot-fuckin-diggety."

"You got a confession?"

"By the time their windbag lawyers showed up, both were looking to deal. I made no promises but implied things might go better if one of their clients had something to trade."

I waited out a pause while Slidell performed some complicated maneuver, probably rotating his head to relieve tension in his neck.

"Bottom line. According to Unger, Body grabbed Cole, intending to hold her for a few days, then free her. Things went south, and the kid died. Like we thought, Body wanted the publicity to drive audiences to his shitpods, generate distrust in the government, and goose the sale of his underground crash pads. Unger admits to setting up the kiddie-porn op but says he had nothing to do with snatching any kid.

"Body's version differs on a few key points." Oozing sarcasm. "He says he made an innocent off-the-cuff remark to the effect that wouldn't it be perfect if some kid disappeared and the public went apeshit. He claims Unger, being a dolt, took him at his word and followed through, an outcome he never intended. He claims Unger told him what he'd done, that the kid had died, and that he'd disposed of her body. Body claims he was unaware of the kidnapping until after the fact."

"Who do you believe?" My impatience leaking through.

"Your Strava stuff seems to back Unger's version. At this point, who the hell knows?"

"Timothy Horshauser?"

"Both deny knowing anything about him."

A sensation of strobing emotions, shutter-quick feelings vying for ascendancy. Abhorrence. Relief. Anger. Sadness.

"Do you think either can be persuaded to reveal the location of Jahaan's body?"

"Both claim they know zip. I think there's some

lawyerly advice operating there. Hold back that intel to score a sweeter deal. But don't worry. I'll pry it loose. Before I'm done, this case will be wrapped tighter than a mummy's dick."

"Good job, detective. The Cole family may finally get some closure."

"Yeah." Dejected. "Trust me, doc. At least one of these shitstains is going away for the whole ride. Maybe both."

After a brief pause, I asked, "Was Timmer involved?"

"No."

"What about Vodyanov?"

"According to Unger, Vodyanov wasn't looped in on the kiddie-porn op or Jahaan Cole. The guy was just a stooge, chasing down crap for Body's shows. Then, sometime last fall, he stumbled onto something, Unger wasn't sure what it was or how he got it. Vodyanov started poking around, confronting people—"

"Vince Aiello."

"Vodyanov always had Body's back, never asked questions. But messing with kids crossed some kinda line. Shitting his jockeys with guilt, he decided to blood-hound what he could, unload on you, then off himself."

"Why'd he give up before talking to me?"

"In the end, maybe he just couldn't bring himself to burn little brother."

Unbidden, a phrase winged into my thoughts. *Do whatever it takes*. How differently that dictum had been interpreted by Tatiana's two sons. Felix became the compassionate nurturer for his sibling. Nick became the egomaniacal psychopath.

A long, melancholy silence hung between Slidell

and me. I suspected Skinny's thoughts were traveling the same path as mine, imagining the upcoming conversation with Jahaan Cole's mother. Though heartbreaking, we both knew Skinny's news would be welcomed. Knowledge concerning the fate of a missing child, no matter how bleak, is always better than the agony of not knowing.

Slidell spoke first. "That's it. I'm going back at these squirrels, starting with Body. He's been off the blow long enough now sweat's pushing out of him like guts from a roach. I'm betting he'll soon be begging to trade it all."

"Thanks for keeping me apprised. It means a lot."

"Eeyuh."

After disconnecting, I moved to the chair by the window. Sat and closed my eyes. Did some deep breathing to check my roiling emotions. Eventually, my pulse slowed sufficiently to consider retiring.

I knew I wouldn't sleep as ferociously as I had the day before for a long time to come. That most nights, racing thoughts, fragmented memories, and disjointed scenes would replay in my mind. That I'd again see Heavner, Body, Timmer, and the others. Vodyanov with his mangled face and eviscerated belly. The fenced property, the underground bunker.

I knew the headaches would continue to plague me. Worries about the aneurysm. But I would come out the winner. My doctors would help. Together we'd find the proper combo of meds and lifestyle adjustments.

I knew I'd struggle with my recall of the grotesque characters and events associated with the faceless man. To objectively sort reality from illusion.

What was real? What was not?

My eyes drifted over the things Ryan and I had chosen together. The acrylic bar cart. The chrome lamp curving overhead. The Chihuly lithograph hanging on the wall. I pictured the annex, where repair of the incinerated study was already under way.

Rising, I went to the bedroom, dug an item from my suitcase, and returned to the window. The warm ginger sunset wrapped the little elephant-headed deity lying in my palm. Ganesha, the remover of obstacles. The god of beginnings. Even with one tusk. For a very long moment, I just gazed at him. He gazed back. Challenging me?

OK, old friend. I accept. I will blend my life with Ryan's and set forth on a new course. Leading to a strengthened bond? To a sad ending? Hard to know.

A horn honked far below on Sherbrooke. Another answered.

My thoughts drifted back to Body. He claimed he was free to spew any cockamamie theories or toxic falsehoods he chose. Sadly, he was right. And the world was worse for it. But he wasn't free to pander the abuse of children for the sick pleasure of pedophiles. To line his pockets by exploiting the vulnerability of people living in poverty. To harm kids. Happily, Slidell and I had helped shut him down.

Jahaan Cole was dead, the location of her body as yet unknown. Unger or Body was responsible. Perhaps both. I had confidence Slidell would sort that out and that justice would finally be served.

Timothy Horshauser remained missing. Others. Body and his cronies claimed to know nothing about their disappearances. Maybe they didn't. Maybe they did. We might never find out.

So many unknowns. But one thing was certain. Slidell and I wouldn't stop looking. Despite his bluster and bullying and bad suits, Skinny was one of the good guys.

I'd continue to search for clarity, for answers. For health. For happiness with Ryan.

And, always, I would search for the missing children.

A Conspiracy of Bones provides a peek into the field of forensic entomology via a fleeting reference to *Ophio-cordyceps camponoti-balzani.* Zombie ants. (Seriously. Check them out.) Why mention ants here? Because I'm a bit like the wee buggers, my feelers always out and sniffing for fresh booty, be it from a case at the lab, a newspaper or journal article, or an incident related to me by a colleague. Anything I do, read, hear, or see can be grist for the next Temperance Brennan novel.

My writing process unfolds in three phases. First comes the ant phase, when my mind collects and stashes tidbits. Some info is so timely and compelling that a book practically writes itself. Other items must germinate a while, intermingling and cross-pollinating until an idea for a plot line arises from the cerebral mix. Then I move to the paper phase, making lists, drawing charts, scribbling outlines, and testing whether the potential story has the muscle to grow into a book. What if *this* occurs? I ask myself. What if *that*? What setting? What contemporaneous happenings in our heroine's life? When all the weaving and twisting and juxtaposing are done, and questions of plausibility have been considered and potential winners selected, it's on to the computer phase. Bum to the chair, eyes to the screen, fingers to the keyboard.

A Conspiracy of Bones was no exception. The ant gathering began years ago when a friend shared her misgivings concerning the sinking of the ferry *Estonia*. Too busy with a new job to continue studying the tragedy, she offered me her trove of research materials. Intrigued, but unable to find that all-important engine to drive a plot line, I let the idea lie dormant for almost a decade.

Also sleeping in my gray matter was an article I'd read about Somerton Man, a real-life death investigation and now a very cold case. Somerton Man's body was discovered on a beach near Adelaide in the winter of 1948, and the case is described as one of Australia's "most profound mysteries." All labels had been cut from his clothing. A pants pocket held a scrap bearing a Persian phrase meaning "it is ended." Investigators tracked the scrap to a book containing indented writing— phone numbers and encrypted script. Theories were wide-ranging. Was Somerton Man a postwar refugee? An assassinated cold war spy? An eccentric local who'd overdosed or taken his own life? To this day the gentleman's name and cause of death remain unknown.

Great starters. I could imagine sinister links to the *Estonia* incident. But Somerton Man had a face and teeth and fingers. A corpse arriving in Tempe's lab could very well lack such identifiers.

A third tidbit slumbering in the old noggin, as Skinny Slidell would say, was a homicide case I worked on in the mid-nineties. The remains, found in a heavily forested area, were badly decomposed and scattered due to scavenging by bears. My skeletal autopsy suggested a white female in her forties. The profile matched that of a local woman missing several months. The victim's boyfriend, a recently paroled felon, was eventually convicted of her murder.

Though far from my sole case involving animal damage to bone, the circumstances of this woman's death touched me deeply. Every murder is wrong, but hers seemed doubly so. She'd fought for her killer's release from prison. He'd thanked her by taking her life.

The bear-scavenged remains offered useful elements for a Temperance Brennan case: no features, no dentals, no prints. But for this novel I wanted our heroine in Dixie, not the northern woods or South Australia. While we have bears, feral hogs are a real nuisance in parts of North Carolina.

I envisioned a tragedy around which swirled theories of treachery. A body bearing ominous clues. A corpse lacking identifiers. This trio could work. But what about context? What is going on with our heroine?

In the novella *First Bones*, readers learned of the death of Tim Larabee, Mecklenburg County's longtime medical examiner. Why not follow up on this misfortune and create a story arc in the manner that we relied on in the *Bones* writers' room? How has this loss affected Tempe? Is the new boss an ally? Does the new boss appreciate Tempe's expertise? Or, to the contrary, does this new person wish her ill? Good stuff. Next.

I began the nineteenth Brennan book at a time when bloggers and extremist talk show hosts were polluting the internet and the airways with hateful dialogue, unfounded conspiracy theories, and dangerous misinformation. When mainstream journalists felt compelled to fact-check the utterances of powerful figures. When the terms "fake news" and "alternate facts" had become common lingo. When listeners and readers were constantly forced to question the reliability of both the media and the media critics.

A national atmosphere of suspicion and doubt prevailed. What is real and what is not? It was a timely backdrop. But I also wanted to bring this sense of uncertainty down to a personal level.

That's when I made a difficult decision. Like Tempe, I am a private person, reluctant to divulge my secrets or express my feelings. I would break that pattern. I would share with my readers a challenge that I recently faced. I would make an aspect of this story my own.

As some of you may know, I didn't release a book last year. There is a reason I took time off.

Not long ago I was diagnosed with an unruptured cerebral aneurysm. Following its serendipitous discovery, my doctors monitored my brain like NASA tracks asteroids. There have been annual MRAs and the occasional MRI, simple procedures to check for signs of change. For a while all was dandy, everything in place. Then the little bubble decided to do some shape-shifting. I underwent an embolization, a procedure in which miniature metal coils are injected to block blood flow through the arterial wall. Since the surgery, I experience the occasional migraine, but otherwise all is well.

Bottom line. I have a brain oddity and headaches,

so our heroine also has the dastardly duo. Do I worry about the aneurysm? Not much. Does Tempe? A bit more. And her fears about the state of her mind parallel the central theme of *Conspiracy*. What is real and what is not? What happens when the reliability of one's judgment is questioned?

In Tempe's case, what ensues when all hard data— her stock and trade—are taken from her? In Chapter 27, she thinks, "I am a scientist. I test hypotheses based on items I can observe, measure, weigh, and photograph. I'd been left with none. Could I rely on my stored perceptions? Could I sort what was real from what was not?"

So. Take a maritime disaster, two separate forensic cases, an atmosphere of hate-mongering propaganda and faux news, a stressful work situation, and a personal medical calamity. Add a computer crash involving a nonfunctioning backup drive and a creepy guy prowling my daughter's yard at midnight. Mix thoroughly. Ta-da! *A Conspiracy of Bones*.

Acknowledgments

An army of people is involved in the production of any book—and at least a platoon in the creation of the story. As usual, I owe thanks to many for their contributions to *A Conspiracy of Bones*.

Andra Purkalitis alerted me to controversies surrounding the sinking of the ferry *Estonia* and graciously bequeathed to me all her research materials on the topic. Credit to Juta Rābe's *Estonia: Kuga nogrimšanas traģēdija* and to Drew Wilson's *The Hole*.

Dr. Jennifer Newman was my go-to expert on the topic of steganalysis.

Captain Harold W. Henson and Detective W. C. Hastings, Charlotte-Mecklenburg Police Department, provided information on Hispanic gangs in Charlotte. Thanks, Two Chucks!

In the U.S., much appreciation to those who work so hard for me at Scribner: Nan Graham, Roz Lippel, Brian Belfiglio, Abigail Novak, Katie Rizzo, Kyle Kabel, and Beckett Rueda. And, above all, to my tireless editor, Rick Horgan.

In Canada, I am indebted to Kevin Hanson, Laurie Grassi, and Felicia Quon.

In the UK, Team Reichs is composed of Ian Chapman, Suzanne Baboneau, Gill Richardson, Polly Osborn, Pip Watkins, Richard Vlietstra, and Harriett Collins.

Gratitude to Dan Ruffino in Australia, and to Rahul Srivastava in India.

I would also like to thank my representatives, Deneen Howell and Robert Barnett, for their wise advice.

Paul Reichs offered valuable suggestions when the manuscript was in its infancy.

Last, but light-years from least, I want to thank my returning readers for their loyalty and patience during my gap year. And a big, warm welcome to any first-timers to Tempe's lab! I love you all, and hope to see each and every one of you in the very near future.

FIRST BONES

An origin story. That sounded like fun.

As I began to write about Tempe's start in the lab, it made me think of my own beginnings in forensics. In the early 1980s, I was on faculty at the University of North Carolina–Charlotte, focusing on bioarchaeology. The ancient dead. One day, a Charlotte-Mecklenburg PD detective asked me to examine bones discovered beneath a house. I was teaching courses on human evolution and skeletal biology, but had never worked with law enforcement. It sounded intriguing. I agreed to do the evaluation.

The remains were those of a dog. Case closed. The police brought me other skeletal material from time to time and I told them what they had. Then I got a call that would change my life. The detective spoke of a missing five-year-old girl. He wanted me to visit the scene. To determine if the small bones could be human. If they could be those of the child.

They were. Her murder hit me hard. She'd been the same age as one of my daughters. I wanted justice. Didn't get it. The prime suspect, an eighth-grade drop-out, was never charged. He later died while serving a life sentence for eight counts of child molestation and the murder of a ten-year-old girl who'd lived one block from my victim.

The lack of closure was frustrating. I resolved to contribute what skills I had toward the resolution of such crimes. After retraining and earning certification by the American Board of Forensic Anthropology, I began consulting for law enforcement, coroners, and medical examiners. ID. Manner of death. Postmortem interval. Anything to provide answers for families and to help nail the guilty.

People in towns that have suffered crimes against children remember the names of those victims for years. Charlotte, North Carolina; Soham, England; Praia da Luz, Portugal. All have been scarred by violence against the helpless. The innocent.

A sad but true fact is that, unlike in fiction, not every killer is caught. In my early case, the child's remains were identified, but her aggressor was not charged. I carry the names of several such children in my memory, and I am burdened by the knowledge that there will always be new murders, not all of which will be solved.

While this little girl's murder helped propel me into forensics, the majority of deaths I investigate are not those of children. The victims in *First Bones* are adult males. Their murders take place in the 1980s, a time when the country was facing a different type of killer. The AIDS/HIV epidemic. For those of us working with the dead, AIDS and HIV posed a new and real danger.

The human immunodeficiency virus (HIV) and related acquired immunodeficiency syndrome (AIDS) were little understood in the early 1980s. The disease was initially thought to affect only gay men. Few preventive public health measures were in force. The medical community was slow to appreciate the widespread danger and did little to guard against it. But as evidence about the deadly nature of AIDS accumulated, drastic changes in procedure were introduced.

Medical examiners, forensic anthropologists, and laboratory technicians donned special masks and aprons and goggles and gloves. We avoided unsafe contact with the bodily fluids of corpses. We followed strict new guidelines for the handling and disposal of blades and needles. The threat was real and we were taking it seriously.

Improved medical methodology has slowed the spread of the disease. Education of at-risk populations. Better pharmaceuticals—drugs a long time coming.

Though much progress has been made, we still haven't "removed the pump handle," as Tempe says to Pete in *First Bones*. In 2019, for the first time in decades, a new strain of HIV was identified. According to the Centers for Disease Control and Prevention, in 2017, 38,739 people received an HIV diagnosis in the United States. That same year, Health Canada reported 2,402 cases. Statistics from the World Health Organization suggest 36.7 million people are affected worldwide.

In 1985, a small group of people conceived a project to commemorate those who had died of AIDS. Known as the Names Project AIDS Memorial Quilt, the blanket is a patchwork of three-by-six-foot panels, each recording the name of a decedent.

I first saw the quilt in the early 1990s, during a visit to Washington, D.C., to see my daughter. It stretched from the Capitol Building to the Washington Monument, inviting us to sit down and learn about the disease.

When I saw it again in 1996, rectangles representing over seventy thousand people covered the entire Washington Mall. Today the quilt has more than fifty thousand panels containing names from all fifty U.S. states and forty-three countries. If laid end to end, they would stretch for miles.

It is the storm of illness-related emotions that drives *First Bones*. The daily anxiety of those with HIV. Their fear that the condition will progress to AIDS. Their worry that they may have transmitted the sickness to others. Their struggle with the duty to disclose. Far worse is the agony of those diagnosed with full-blown AIDS. Their heartbreaking knowledge that the virus will kill them. That the death will not be pretty. In my story, these feelings grow strong enough to result in murder.

I sometimes think of my own "quilt." The bones to which I could not put names. The victims of violence whose perpetrators remain unknown. Or unpunished. I try to keep my work separate from my personal life. Try to leave the stories at the morgue. Still, in unguarded moments, the unsolved cases break into my thoughts.

I take satisfaction in knowing that most Jane and John Does go home to their families. That most killers are caught. I believe in the power of science. To battle disease. To solve crime. I will continue to apply my expertise in forensic anthropology toward the pursuit of justice.

For more information on the Names Project AIDS Memorial Quilt, visit aidsquilt.org/about/the-aids -memorial-quilt.

1

I sat with my chair drawn close to him, an icy heat hovering below my sternum. Fear.

Through the sliding glass door came muted hospital sounds. An arriving elevator. A rattling gurney or cart. A paged code or name. In the room, only the soft rhythmic pinging of sensors monitoring vital signs.

His face looked gaunt and greenish gray in the glow of machines tracking his pulse and respirations. Every now and then I glanced at a screen. Watching the lines jump their erratic zigzag patterns. Willing the pinging and jumping to continue.

Surgical Trauma Intensive Care Unit. So cold. So sterile. Yet a human touch: a stain shaped like Mickey's ears on one rail of the overcomplicated bed. Funny what you notice when under stress.

A sheet covered him from the neck down, leaving only his arms exposed. A pronged tube delivered oxygen to his nostrils. A needle infused liquids into a vein in his right wrist. The arm with the IV lay tucked to his torso. The other rested on his chest, elbow flexed at an obtuse angle.

I watched his sheet-clad chest rise and fall. Somehow his body looked smaller than normal. Shrunken. Or was it an illusion created by the fish-tank illumination?

He didn't move, didn't blink. In the eerie light, his lids appeared translucent purple, like the thinly peeled skin of a Bermuda onion. His eyeballs had receded deep into their orbits.

Hollywood's dramatic death scenes are a scam. A slug to the body destroys roughly two ounces of tissue, no more. A bullet doesn't necessarily drop a man on the spot. To kill instantly, you have to shoot into the brain or high up in the spinal cord, or cause hemorrhage by hitting a main vessel or the heart. None of those things had happened to him. He'd survived until a late-night dog walker stumbled upon him, unconscious and bleeding but still showing a pulse.

The wee-hours call had roused me from a deep sleep. Adrenaline rush. Shaky clawing up of the phone. Then the heart-hammering drive across town. The argument to talk myself into the STICU. I hadn't bothered with polite.

Death by firearm depends on multiple factors: bullet penetration deep enough to reach vital organs, permanent cavity formation along the bullet's path, temporary cavity formation due to transfer of the bullet's kinetic energy, bullet and bone fragmentation. All of those things had happened to him.

The surgeons had done what they could. They'd spoken gently, voices calm through the fatigue, eyes soft with compassion. The internal damage was too severe. He was dying.

How could that be? Men his age didn't die. But they did. We all did. America was armed to the teeth and no one was safe.

I felt a tremor in my chest. Fought it down.

Uncaring death was about to punch a hole in my life. I didn't want to consider the coming weeks. Months. We had done so much together. Fed off each other physically, emotionally. Despite the occasional aloofness, abruptness. The arguments. The unexplained retreats. The exchanges weren't always pleasant, but they spurred the process, helped us accomplish more than either of us would have managed solo. Now the future looked bleak. Unbearable sadness wrapped me like a shroud.

He'd been a good man. Capable. Devoted to his work. Always busy, but willing to listen, to provide feedback, sometimes outrageous, sometimes sage. Forever in motion.

I thought of the hours we'd spent together. The shared challenges. The identification of issues and approaches toward solutions. The painstaking attention to detail that could knit together a comprehensible whole from fragments. The shared sense of accomplishment in uncovering answers to perplexing questions. The mutual frustration and disappointment when no solution emerged.

I'd seen so much death. Corpses whole and partial, known and unknown. Lives ended in every conceivable manner. From the very old to the very young, male and female. At times cause was apparent, at others a puzzle requiring prolonged assessment and all my acuity. He was my greatest resource.

Throughout my career I was often the bearer of heartbreaking news. The changer of lives, informing anxious next of kin that their loved ones were dead. He'd been there. Or listened to my telling. Death was a constant in my work, and now death would put an end to this cherished partnership.

I looked again at the man in the bed. All was past. There would be no future.

The door opened and a nurse entered, rubber soles noiseless on the immaculate tile. She was short and round with ebony skin that gleamed in the monitors' reflected light. A badge on her scrubs said V. SULE.

Nurse V. Sule smiled, a quick upward flick of her lips, then patted my hand.

"He is having morphine." Accented English. Rich, lilting. "He will sleep long. You go, hon. You have a coffee."

"I'm good," I said.

Another pat, then Nurse V. Sule began checking fluid levels and dials and tracings. I scooched my chair to the wall and sat back down. I'd been in it for hours. Ever since he was wheeled into that room.

I watched Nurse V. Sule. Her movements were quick and efficient, but at the same time strangely graceful. I thanked her when she left.

The chair was uncommonly comfortable as hospital furnishings go, armed, padded, willing to tilt slightly if I leaned back. I wondered if seating of this type was specially selected for rooms hosting those facing vigils of long duration. For visitors helping usher in death.

I gazed at the rising and falling sheet. My vision blurred. The final breath would soon be drawn.

Exhausted, and overwhelmed by sorrow, I stretched my legs, angled my head back, and closed my eyes.

Just for a moment.

2

The knob rattles. I feel a subtle pull of air, note the time, and look up, curious. It's winter break and the building is deserted. The entire campus is deserted. Who could be coming into my lab?

The door wings back and two men stride in. Uninvited. Both are tall, maybe six feet. One is thin. The other is not thin. Both are in their mid-thirties.

I'm annoyed at the interruption. I've been on the anthropology faculty at the University of North Carolina–Charlotte a single semester, my employment contingent upon having a PhD. The junior member of my doctoral committee has recently informed me that he won't be signing off on my dissertation. Not only did the jackass refuse to read my opus during summer break, now that he has read it he's demanding the inclusion of another trait in the statistical treatment.

The borrowed collection I'm examining is due to be returned in three weeks. Spring term looms and course outlines, lectures, and exercises must be prepared. I've yet to hang tinsel or purchase a single gift. So, yes. I'm not in a ho-ho-ho mood.

The heavy man has cop stamped on his forehead. Which, being greasy, matches his hair. Brown corduroy jacket, butt-shiny polyester pants, Kmart tie, kiss-my-ass swagger.

The thin man looks like an antonym in more ways than weight. Designer suit, silk tie, custom shirt, Italian leather shoes gleaming like soup. His hair is artfully arranged to disguise its erosion from his scalp.

I lower my mask but don't rise. The men cross to my work table. Kiss My Ass takes the lead.

"Where's Doc Becknell?"

"I'm Dr. Brennan." Premature on the title, but soon enough. If I can shake this pair and get back to scoring foramina. "Can I help you?"

"We need the doc."

"And you gentlemen would be?" Laying down my magnifier.

Kiss My Ass yanks a badge from his belt and holds it out for inspection. The leather fob is so new it still smells of cow.

"Congratulations on the promotion, Detective Slidell."

Slidell's chin cocks up and his lower lids crimp.

"Fresh off the press," I respond to his unasked question, then turn to his partner.

"Detective Eddie Rinaldi. We're sorry for the intrusion, ma'am."

"Where's Becknell?" Slidell demands.

"Unavailable."

"How 'bout we get her on the horn and make her available."

"That would be difficult."

"We live in difficult times."

"Dr. Becknell is on sabbatical," I say.

"Meaning?"

"She's away." I suspect this Slidell is oblivious to the ways of academia.

"Away where?"

"North Azraq, Jordan."

"Doing what?"

"Excavating. The site is Epipaleolithic, early Kebaran down to Acheulean. Also some lower Levallois-Mousterian layers." Half making it up, knowing the guy's clueless. Bitchy. But Slidell's arrogance isn't playing well with me.

"Dandy."

"Indeed."

Slidell's eyes hold on mine, then drop to the table. "What's that?"

"Prehistoric cremains."

The eyes roll up, still irritated over my newbie crack. Maybe the archaeo-jargon.

"Burned bone," I explain.

"Who's the vic?"

"A girl who died in her teens."

"How?"

"Her heart stopped beating."

"You're funny."

"I try."

"So you do the same bone-whispering mojo as Doc Becknell?"

"What is it you want, Detective?" The clock is ticking. And I don't like this man.

"I've got a crisper needs a name."

"Excuse me?"

Hearing the disgust in my tone, Rinaldi jumps in.

"Let me explain, please. A physician named Keith Millikin vanished about a week ago. Dr. Millikin ran a street clinic off Wilkinson Boulevard, a one-man operation providing low-cost health services for indigents, the homeless, street kids—"

"Junkies and deadbeats."

I ignore Slidell. So does Rinaldi.

"When Dr. Millikin failed to open his office for five days running, one of his patients, a gentleman named Louis Grimm, filed a missing persons report."

I wait. Rinaldi doesn't continue.

"Go on." Guarded. I suspect where this is headed.

Slidell opens his mouth, but his partner hushes him gently with a raised palm. I notice that Rinaldi's fingers are long and graceful, his nails buffed, his cuticles neatly trimmed.

"Dr. Millikin lived in an Airstream off Highway 49, down near the South Carolina line. Yesterday, getting no response from the police, Mr. Grimm persuaded his brother to drive him to Dr. Millikin's home. To make a long story short—"

"Which you ain't."

"—Mr. Grimm observed smoke damage to the rear of the trailer, found the door unlocked, and entered." Rinaldi sounds like he's reading from an incident report. "The trailer's interior was gutted by fire. Spotting remains among the debris, and feeling the authorities might once again ignore him—"

"Grimm bagged the bones and hauled ass to the morgue. Apparently he and his brother watch a lot of *Quincy*."

Though I know little about death-scene recovery, that doesn't sound good. I say nothing.

"The arson team will be heading there soon. From Mr. Grimm's account, a kerosene heater may be involved."

"Corpses ain't sausage. Smoking don't improve 'em." Slidell thinks he's quite a wordsmith. Again, I ignore him.

"I'm a bioarchaeologist. I don't do forensic work." Not admitting to the tiny skeleton I once examined at the request of an anthro grad student who is also a cop. Those images still haunt me.

"A charred stiff's a charred stiff," Slidell says.

"This 'charred stiff'"—hooking air quotes around Slidell's callous turn of phrase—"died two thousand years ago. A medical examiner won't be issuing a death certificate. An insurance company won't be paying beneficiaries."

"So why bother?"

"Archaeologists work to piece together humanity's past." Now I'm defensive and spouting boilerplate. "To reconstruct the complexit—"

"And a few eggheads in ivory towers give a shit."

"I believe interest in human evolution is much more widespread than that." Cool. How could I explain my love of bioarchaeology to this dolt? My passion for understanding people who inhabited the earth long before my birth? For learning of their accomplishments, their failures, the minutiae of their lives? The connectedness I felt when touching their bones?

Slidell shoots me a brief, pitying glance. Then he tries a different tack. A good one.

"Doc Becknell ain't so wrapped up in the past she don't care about the living."

That hits home. Still, I can't spare the time. But is work pressure the sole reason for my reluctance? Or is something else operating? Fear of inadequacy?

"Dr. Becknell has training in areas that I do not," I say.

Slidell laughs, a mirthless little snort. "Horseshit."

Heat flames my cheeks. I bite back a retort.

Rinaldi tries to defuse my anger. "That didn't come out the way my partner intended."

I say nothing. I think, Horseshit.

"Skinny means he's confident you possess the skill set required to ID this man."

"Skinny?" Slidell is far from that.

"Erskine."

Slidell glares. I store the nickname for future use.

"Dr. Millikin has family?" Against my will, I feel myself drawn in.

"A son. In Wisconsin." Rinaldi pauses, cop instincts triaging what is safe from what must be withheld. "Dr. Millikin was a loner. And, by all accounts, an odd duck. But his patients say he was a kind and generous man."

"You speak of him in the past tense."

"Dr. Millikin's patients insist that he would never willingly abandon them. A burned body has been found in his home." Rinaldi's brows float up. What remains to be said?

"Millikin was a whack-job, Millikin was a saint. It don't matter." Slidell, caring only about closing a file. "Until someone says otherwise, I got a John Doe in a cooler with a tag on his toe. If he still has a toe."

"Once more, with feeling. I don't do police work."

"You could."

Easy, Brennan.

"I'm very sorry. But I haven't the time right now."

"You got time for people haven't breathed since John the Baptist was handing out towels."

"Colorful image."

"I try." Slidell fires back my own quip. Though obnoxious, the man isn't dumb.

Slidell crosses his arms and gives me a hard green stare. I give it back. His fingers drum an impatient staccato on one brown corduroy sleeve. Several nails wear dark crescent caps. I refuse to consider the nature of the grime.

Around us, things hum quietly. The overhead fluorescents. The HVAC. The motor in the ancient storage fridge.

"If you'll excuse me." I rise.

The fingers drum faster. It's clear Skinny is used to getting his way.

Seconds pass. No one moves. No one speaks. Then Slidell fires one last volley.

"Guess the little lady ain't ready for prime time."

"Really, Detective." Calm. I want to reach out and stuff the Kmart tie down his chauvinist throat. "You can do better than that."

A bell trills, dismissing students far away on beaches and slopes.

Slidell's arms drop to his sides. His shoulders roll back. His lips part, but Rinaldi jumps in

"May I say one last thing?"

I nod.

"Keith Millikin was an educated man. A physician. Had he chosen, he could have led a very different life. Taken cruises, driven Porsches, played golf at the club. He did none of those things. He lived in a trailer and treated the people whom society has kicked to the curb. The poor and forgotten. Should we forget him?"

Sonofabitch.

I make a decision that changes my life.

3

The Mecklenburg County Medical Examiner facility is located in uptown Charlotte. The drive takes twenty-two minutes. That's where my mind is. Tallying lost time like a taximeter tallies up miles.

Using Rinaldi's directions, I find the place, a brick box with all the architectural whimsy of a Stalinist bunker. Signs tell me the MCME is at one end, satellite offices of the Charlotte-Mecklenburg Police Department are at the other. Parking is easy. The building is surrounded by enough asphalt to pave Orlando.

I kill the engine and get out of my VW Bug. The sky is clotted with clouds that are serious about rain. The wind is sharp.

I mount a few stairs and approach a window to the left of double glass doors. A woman is behind it. She is blond and probably living on a high-carb diet. Her cardigan is a shade of yellow that nails the daisies in her shirtwaist dress. A chain loops her chest, connecting the button to the buttonhole side.

I press my faculty ID to the window. The woman studies it so long I think she's memorizing the content. Finally satisfied, she gives me a big wide smile. Her teeth aren't great.

The lock buzzes. I enter a small vestibule and continue through a second set of doors. To the left stretch Cardigan's command post and four work carrels. To the right, groupings of upholstered furniture and wooden tables. Magazines. Plastic plants. The universal waiting room motif. Today, no one is waiting.

Cardigan greets me. She's younger than I thought. Too young for the severe perm and sweater clip.

"Welcome, Dr. Brennan." Vowels broader than juleps and grits. "I'm Mrs. Flowers."

We shake hands. Mrs. Flowers's grip could maybe crumple a tissue.

"Dr. Larabee is expecting you. I'll let him know you've arrived."

"Thank you." I assume Larabee is the ME.

"Please make yourself comfortable."

I sit facing the carrels. Only one shows evidence of use. Stapler, pens, stacked folders. A framed picture of Joe DiMaggio.

Behind Mrs. Flowers's desk is a mountain range of gray filing cabinets. Opposite the cabinets, on the far wall, is an erasable board divided into a grid. Numbers and dates fill some of the cells. Abbreviations I don't understand.

I assume the digit-letter combinations represent cases. Suicides, homicides, accidents, flukes. Deaths that have earned tickets to Y incisions. One entry has been designated ME1207. The code also incorporates the year. The letters *Sk-b* have been penned into one of the squares. I suspect this is the man I am here to inspect.

The meter ticks a long ten minutes. I wonder if Slidell is having success acquiring the antemortem records I've asked him to gather. If he's found a forensic dentist to look at them. I wonder if Rinaldi is learning anything from Millikin's neighbors.

Finally, a man hurries toward me with long, lopey strides. His limbs are sinewy, his torso lean inside blue surgical scrubs. I stand.

"Dr. Tim Larabee." He doesn't offer a hand. Fine with me. The bloodstains on his chest aren't reassuring.

"Temperance Brennan."

"I apologize for the delay. I have a gunshot case open on the table."

"No problem."

"Thanks for agreeing to pitch in." Larabee's gaze is intense. There's an air of coiled energy about the man.

"I don't know how helpful I'll be."

"You'll outperform me. My knowledge of bone is minimal. Ready?"

I nod. Pick up my purse and backpack.

Larabee leads me to the secure side of the operation. The "dirty" side. His Nikes make little squeaks when we cross from the carpet onto tile. My heels click softly. We turn down a corridor, pass several doors, stop at one with a plaque that says AUTOPSY.

"You're set up in here. I'll be over there." Indicating an identical door with an equally grim plaque. "This one's outfitted with special ventilation." In case I miss the meaning, he adds, "For odor. Joe Hawkins calls it the stinky room. He's my death investigator."

I can think of no response.

"I doubt you'll need it. There's almost no soft tissue." Larabee points to a door farther down the hall. No signage. "The locker room's there. We don't have women's scrubs, but a man's small should fit."

"Sexy."

Larabee looks at me, uncertain if I'm serious.

"Joe is away on a pickup, so I'm afraid you're on your own. He's set out forms, cameras, Dr. Becknell's kit. X-rays are on the counter. If you need anything, just ask."

With that he's gone.

I go to the locker room and change out of my street clothes. By rolling the cuffs and cinching the waist string I make it work. Pant legs flapping, I cross to the stinky room.

ME1207's intake form contains little information. A case number. A brief description of the remains, of the circumstances surrounding their arrival at the morgue. Slidell and Rinaldi are listed as investigators.

The room has one autopsy table, which is outfitted with an adjustable overhead light. Counters with cabinets above and below, a sink, a scale, a dissecting scope. Lots of gleaming tile, glass, and stainless steel.

A Nikon and a Polaroid sit on the counter. I check. Both are loaded.

Next to the cameras is a small metal suitcase with butterfly hasp locks. Assuming this is Becknell's "kit," I thumb the clips and lift the lid. Inside are the familiar tools of my trade: calipers, brushes, magnifiers, a diagram of sub-adult dental development, a list of equations for calculating height from long bones.

I search drawers, eventually find items to accessorize my fetching ensemble. Paper apron and mask. Latex gloves. I pass on the plastic goggles.

The cardboard carton on the table once held cornflakes. The number written on its lid matches that on the form and on the erasable board.

I shoot 35-millimeter prints, backups with the Polaroid, then pop the X-rays onto wall-mounted light boxes. Each film makes a sound like a tiny thunder roll.

I hit the switches and, plate by plate, study the images. See a skull, other glowing white shapes I recognize as bones and teeth. Densely opaque blobs that could be dental restorations. I haven't a clue about the nature of the gray matrix.

I find a plastic sheet and spread it across the autopsy table, don my protective gear, and open the carton. My heart sinks.

The brothers Grimm have done a good job of separating decedent from Airstream. The box, half-full, holds mostly bone, little debris. The gray jumble turns out to be bits of charred carpet and fabric not easily detachable from the remains.

The brothers Grimm have done a lousy job of estimating the volume of a burned human being. And a lousy job of keeping that human being intact. Accompanying the skull are limb bones, all broken, the left half of a mandible, and a hunk of pelvis. Discoloration ranges from black to gray to white, suggesting varying degrees of exposure to flame. Eyeing the paltry postcranial assemblage, I know major parts are missing.

Slowly, gingerly, I begin transferring elements. Some are brittle and leave scatters of ash on the blue plastic sheeting. A few retain remnants of tendon or muscle cooked hard and leathery as beef jerky. A smell like cinders and charred meat permeates the air.

Eventually, a patchwork skeleton lies with arms and legs spread, torso sparse, hands and feet unrepresented. Though the skull has survived relatively intact, the face is badly damaged, and every dental crown is missing from the maxilla and mandible.

I center the skull on a rubber ring for stability. It stares at me with empty black orbits.

I begin my examination. My pulse settles. Grudgingly, I admit that Slidell is right. My skill set is dead-on.

I observe the orbital ridges and rims, the nuchal crest on the occiput, the hunk of pelvis, which includes the right pubic and sacroiliac areas. I measure the diameter of a decapitated femoral head. I record gender as male in my notes.

Enough of the right pubic symphysis remains to observe the articular surface. Two fragments of rib are complete to their sternal ends. Two isolated molar crowns, each showing moderate wear on its occlusal surface. I check the X-ray, see completed molar roots in the mandibular fragment. I record age as thirty-five to fifty.

With my ancient dead I don't address the question of race. But I know the markers. I observe a narrow nasal opening and tight cheekbones. Little projection of the lower face. A parabolic dental arcade. I write *Caucasoid* in my notes. Add a question mark. Erase it.

There is sufficient femoral shaft to calculate height. I measure, do the math, add the estimate to my profile. Five eight to six one. The range is broad and I anticipate

Slidell's scorn. But the bone is incomplete and I'm unsure of the amount of shrinkage due to burning.

Still, Slidell will be pleased. The remains are compatible with what he and Rinaldi have told me about Keith Millikin.

But something bothers me. I know cremation of a human corpse takes an hour and a half at a thousand degrees Fahrenheit. Ballpark. The Grimm brothers reported minimal damage to the outside of the trailer. Yet Millikin is toast. I wonder how long the fire burned undetected. I know body fat can provide fuel after other combustibles have been depleted. I make a note to ask if Millikin was obese.

And something else is not right. The brain is roughly 75 percent water. With temperatures high enough and exposure long enough, that water turns to steam. The steam expands, causing separation along the sutures, cracking, sometimes explosion of the skull.

Millikin's head shows no thermal fracturing. Why?

I rotate the skull on its ring, studying every detail with a magnifying lens. Melted gunk coats the crown in back. Scrap by scrap, I tweeze it free. When the area is clean, I retrieve the magnifier. And feel an irrational flip in my gut.

I stare, breathing in the smell of ash and soot. I'm still staring, nose inches from the glass, when Slidell shoulder-barges through the door. His hair is flattened and separated into wet clumps. The corduroy jacket is mottled with dark splotches.

I glance at the clock: 12:14. The rain has started.

I set down the lens. "Detective."

No response. Slidell is seeing nothing but the burned man on the blue plastic sheeting.

"Did you obtain Dr. Millikin's dental records?"

He pulls an envelope from a pocket and tosses it onto the counter.

"Originals?" I have instructed him that copies are unacceptable.

"Yeah. Dr. Steiner's a real peach of a guy."

I imagine the conversation. Feel empathy for Steiner.

"Did you contact a forensic dentist?"

"None to be had."

"I'm not qualified—"

"So what's up here?" Hooking a thumb at the table.

I tell Slidell that the bioprofile is compatible with the descriptors he's provided for Keith Millikin.

He rolls that around.

"The victim is a white middle-aged male." I add this, thinking he doesn't understand.

Slidell gives me a pained look, like I've said frogs can croak. Then the cop notebook comes out. A stub of pencil. He licks, then poises the lead.

"Shoot."

I outline my findings. He jots them quickly in some kind of shorthand.

"What else?" Without looking up.

I give him my height estimate.

"That narrows it to half the population."

"It's the best I can do with so much missing."

"What do you mean, missing?"

"Gone. Absent. AWOL."

"Burned up?"

"Or not collected."

"Like what?"

"His hands and feet. Most of his dentition."

"There enough to get a positive with those?" Jabbing the notebook toward Dr. Steiner's envelope.

"It's iffy."

"Iffy?"

"I have a total of three crowns."

"You know burned teeth when you see 'em?"

"Yes." Guarded.

A fraction of a pause, then the notebook slaps shut and disappears into a pocket. "You gotta go out there."

"No. I don't." I almost say "gotta."

"Doc Becknell would."

"I'm not Doc Becknell."

A moment of standoff silence. I break it.

"I have found something disturbing." Positioning the magnifier over the posterior right parietal, I gesture him to me.

Slidell circles the table, takes the lens, and brings the skull into focus. Up close, I see oily strips of scalp between the rain-parted hair. Smell drugstore cologne and stale cigarette smoke.

When Slidell finally speaks, I'm not sure what I hear in his tone. I know it's not good.

4

"That what I'm thinking?" Slidell is sparking energy that wasn't there before.

"It is."

"You're sure?"

"Yes, Detective. It's a bullet entrance."

"How do you know?" He flips to a clean page in the spiral.

"The round shape, the radiating fractures, the beveling on the endocranial border."

Slidell's eyes come up and narrow in warning.

"On the inside of the skull."

"Where's the exit?"

"I don't know."

"Where's the slug?" The questions fire pepper-hot. I wonder if this could be Slidell's first homicide.

"It may have exited through an orbit, maybe the mouth or nasal opening. The face is too damaged to tell."

"Any way Millikin could have popped himself?"

"It's possible, but unlikely." I demonstrate by winging an elbow to point a finger to the back of my head.

"What else?"

"It puzzled me why Millikin's skull stayed intact. The bullet hole explains it."

Slidell twirls the pencil stub, impatient.

"It must have been an oven in that Airstream. At temperatures that high, liquids in the brain expand and the increased intracranial pressure leads to cracking, even explosion." An oversimplification, but good enough.

"The hole acted like a steam vent."

"Yes." Not bad, Skinny.

"So you're telling me some fuckbucket capped Millikin, then fricasseed his ass?"

"I'm telling you Millikin suffered a gunshot wound to the head. I don't know what killed him. If it *is* Millikin."

"What about those?" Indicating Dr. Steiner's envelope.

"I'm not a forensic dentist."

"I'm gutted. Just take a look."

Slidell watches as I remove a set of tiny X-rays and arrange them in anatomical order on an illuminator.

"Crap."

"What?"

"Millikin's dental work is all on the lower right. I don't have that half of the jaw."

"You think it's still out there?"

I shrug. Who knows?

Slidell makes a sound in his throat I cannot interpret. Shoots a cuff to check his watch. "Rinaldi radioed while I was on my way here. In twenty minutes, the arson boys start tossing that trailer."

I know that's a death sentence for fragile bone. Knowing I know it, Slidell hammers harder.

"By all accounts, this guy Millikin was Charlotte's answer to Mother Teresa. You don't want to help catch the bastard that killed him?"

"That's your job."

"One day ain't gonna derail your life."

I know Slidell is playing me. I also know he's right. Conscience already booking a guilt trip, I cross to the phone. Check a list of extensions. Dial the other autopsy room. When Larabee answers, I explain the situation.

"We'll have to be careful with this."

We?

"How much are you missing?"

I tell him, then wait out a long, gaping pause.

"You think more teeth may have survived?"

"It's possible."

"Will you go out there?"

"I've never worked a fire scene."

"Suppose we do it together?"

I rearrange things in my mind. Take a look at priorities. Make another decision.

Millikin's Airstream is off Highway 49, almost at the South Carolina border. Too far south of Charlotte and too far north of Lake Wylie. Real estate that is cheap and untrendy. I pass few other homes along that stretch of two-lane.

I find the turnoff and make a right down a narrow track cutting through hickory, chestnut oak, and short-leaf pine. My wipers slap the windshield, fighting off rain. My tires spit gravel, struggling for traction. My radio pumps songs about angels and reindeer.

A quarter mile, then I reach barbed-wire fencing. Signs warn NO TRESPASSING in bold orange on black. The gate is open. I drive through and across a clearing.

The Airstream is a motor home, not the small bubble I'm expecting, silver with a bright blue stripe. The entrance is outfitted with an awning and makeshift wooden porch. On the porch is a green La-Z-Boy, stuffing sprouting from the seams like over-yeasted dough. The door has a square window with blinds covering the inside. Like the gate, someone has left it wide open.

I take a moment to assess. Behind the Airstream is a shed. Opposite the shed is a rectangle of dirt fenced in the same barbed wire that encloses the clearing. A triangle connects the three through soggy brown grass, gravel paths neatly edged with rock.

In the garden, stakes project from parallel mounds now devoid of vegetation. Rain pools between the mounds in long, skinny canals, brown-black and pock-marked by the deluge.

A truck is parked beside the Airstream, CHARLOTTE-MECKLENBURG PD CRIME LAB written on one side. A white Crown Victoria is parked beside the truck, a black Pontiac Bonneville beside that. I assume the cars belong to Slidell and Rinaldi. Not sure why. The Airstream must be towed by a vehicle. I ponder the whereabouts of Millikin's car or truck.

I pull in beside the Pontiac, kill the engine, and get

out. Somewhere, a startled creature squeals. I glance around, banjos dueling in my brain. Seeing nothing sinister, I retrieve Becknell's case and the camera bag from the backseat, lower my head, and scurry to the trailer.

I enter what was once a kitchen. The air is damp and smells of smoke, scorched metal, and melted plastic. Everything wears a thick coat of soot.

My mind continues logging input. I note the burned-out hulks of a sink, stove, and fridge. Warped cabinetry. A blackened tube that probably supported a table. Pipes twisting inward from their points of attachment.

Slidell and Rinaldi are to my right, in what I assume is the living room. Wires dangle from the ceiling. Unrecognizable objects cover the floor and lie angled against walls or the denuded frames of built-in sofas or chairs.

Two arson investigators are present. One is taking photos. The other is down on all fours, making notes as he advances along a wall. I assume Slidell has told them the trailer is now a crime scene.

I set down the case and camera bag and start picking my way forward. Hearing movement, Slidell turns.

"Bedroom." Pointing toward the opposite end of the trailer. "Have at it. They've already shot pics."

I reverse, grab the equipment, and duck under toppled metal shelving, boots crunching on complicated stratigraphy involving a lot of broken glass. At the burned-out doorframe, a noxious element enters the olfactory mix. Gas or kerosene.

I stop dead, adrenaline zinging. Not the smell. The sight.

The room is small, maybe six by nine. Almost filling it is a jumble of charred rubble, blackened mattress coils peeking through. All that remains of a bed and bedding. To the right of the bed sits a scorched metal box, I assume the suspect space heater. Beside the box, a grotesquely distorted lamp. No bulb. No cord. No shade.

High up, on the trailer's rear wall, is another window covered with aluminum blinds. Bleak, rainy-day light oozes through the disfigured slats.

I make out footprints. Ash trails leading to objects stacked along the baseboards. The handiwork of the brothers Grimm. I realize it is pointless to try to reconstruct body position. To recapture information forever lost.

I step forward. Squat. See a chalky-white metacarpal. A talus. Moving ever so calmly, I open the case, pull on latex gloves, and drag my fingers through the ash. A molar crown rolls into the track, enamel brittle and checked by a latticework of spidery cracks.

I stare at the tooth, a funhouse of emotion whirling inside me. Can I do this? Unbidden, Slidell's taunt sounds in my head. *A charred stiff's a charred stiff.* Crude wording. But this morning I've learned it is true.

I shout, "I need light in here!"

Minutes later two battery-operated LEDs have the room blazing like a Hollywood set. Becknell's tools are laid out: trowels, brushes, strainers, tweezers, pipettes. I have marked the date, the location, and my initials on vials and evidence bags. I have prepared Vinac, a solution of polyvinyl acetate resin and methanol useful for preserving calcined bone.

I mask and go to work. Larabee arrives thirty minutes later. I explain the grid system I have devised for mapping the location of finds, then continue searching the east side of the room. He takes the west. We work in silence. I lose all track of time.

I'm dripping Vinac onto a crumbling incisor when I hear raised voices. Male. The words are muffled, but the cadence is clear. Both men are angry.

I look to Larabee. He shrugs, a bony move that makes me think of a turtle.

Cold and needing a break, I creak to an upright position. My knees are not happy with the new arrangement. I flex and straighten each to encourage circulation. Behind me I hear Larabee doing the same.

We are about to worm our way toward the kitchen when Slidell appears in the doorway. He is tense as a cobra poised to strike. His face is the color of claret.

"You ain't gonna believe this."

"We've found most of the missing dentition." I think good news might prevent a cardiac event.

"We're busting our chops out here and who strolls in?"

"I'm not following." Larabee speaks for us both.

"The asshole himself."

Nothing.

"Jesus Christ. Do I have to spell it out? The dumbshit doc."

"Millikin?" Simultaneous.

"No. Hawkeye Pierce."

Neither Larabee nor I appreciates the sarcasm.

"Turns out Mother Teresa's been partying south of the border."

"Millikin was in Mexico?" This is making no sense to me.

Slidell nods.

"Doing what?" Larabee asks.

"Muchachas and margaritas. Ain't they famous for it?"

"So who's this?" I arc an arm at the evidence bags lining one wall.

"Beats me." The LEDs cause a collision of shadows on Slidell's face. "But he took a bullet to the head and there's a shooter out there who's going down."

5

It's after eight when I pull to the curb in a neighborhood just south of uptown. Like Millikin's rural patch, Elizabeth is far from hip. But rent is cheap and the quartier has a certain je ne sais quoi.

I kill the engine, hear the wail of an ambulance not far off. After six months, the sirens barely register. Presbyterian Hospital stands at the end of the block.

The rain has stopped, but water drips from live oaks spreading their branches from the parkway out over the street. The drops beat fat and erratic on the roof of my Bug.

Up and down both sides of Kenmore, primary colors twinkle on homes, shrubs, lawns, and trees. Here and there, electric icicles frame a window or door. At mid-block, a neon-blue palm beams its renegade Noel.

I'm cold, my clothes are sooty, and I smell like I've spent the day in a smoker. Though I've cleaned my hands as best I can, my nails are as grime-encrusted as Slidell's. My thoughts are focused on Pinot and a long, hot bath.

I lock the car and climb to the porch. Am triaging keys when my common-wall neighbor's front door opens. Artemis prances out. Mr. Speliopoulos follows on the other end of a leash. Artemis is a dachshund. Mr. Speliopoulos is a barber. We exchange Christmas greetings. Neither comments on my appearance.

I ease out of my jacket, drop it onto the stoop, and let myself in. A hammered tin mirror on the foyer wall reflects me dimly. My hair is a mess, my face speckled with ash.

Bowie and Jagger are singing about dancing in the street. I'm pleased to be spared more Magi or drummer boys.

Straight ahead, a no-nonsense staircase shoots to the second floor. The living room is to my right, the fireplace, mantel, and woodwork that seduced us into signing a lease. The dining room is toward the back, through a wide arch whose sliding oak doors are forever jammed in their eighty-year-old pockets.

Pete is at the table, a sea of law books and documents flowing around him. The Zamzow case. A limb lost as a result of a bungled diagnosis. So claims the plaintiff. At breakfast we discussed defense strategies. Mostly I listened. Breakfast seems a lifetime away.

"The archaeo-warrior home from the hill." Pete speaks without looking up.

"Sorry I'm so late."

"Long day."

"It was."

Pete's nose and upper lip crimp. I know the face.

He's sniffed rot that must be tracked to a Ziploc or bin. Inserting a placeholder finger in the file, he looks up.

"Christ on a cracker."

I hang my purse on the newel post.

"What happened to you?"

"Bath first."

Pete gives me the full-on lawyer stare. I give him the full-on don't-ask-now stare back.

"Need a hug?" Sincere as a bookie at an audit.

"Many. After I've soaked."

The bath is all I hoped it would be. Bubbles. Lavender-peach shampoo and conditioner. The old claw-foot tub was also a draw.

Thirty minutes later, I descend smelling of Jo Malone Pomegranate Noir body lotion. I wear a long-sleeved T and flannel pajama pants, pink with sheep and white clouds. The sheep are either drowsy or drunk.

Wynton Marsalis is now playing low and cool, and Mount Legal has been relocated to the sideboard. A pizza box sits center stage on the table. Two places have been set, including mats, plates, utensils, napkins, and goblets. Pete is being thoughtful, even by Pete standards.

My husband and I agree on many things. The hilarity of *Catch-22* and *A Confederacy of Dunces.* Beaches over mountains. Woody Allen. Politics. Pizza is not among them. I like everything on my pie but blubber and ants. Pete is a purist—tomato and cheese.

I take my seat and open the box. Half-gloppy, half-plain. I relax a bit. Pete fills my glass with Pinot. I sip. I relax a bit more.

Though curious, Pete waits, all caring eyes and

reassuring pats. He assumes something has gone very wrong at the university.

We talk of other things. His malpractice suit. Last night's Tar Heels victory. The latest happenings on *Cheers*. Mr. Speliopoulos's taste in music. My comments tend toward the monosyllabic.

When finished, we uncork a second bottle and move to the living room. Pete lights a fire, then joins me on the couch. Wrapping my shoulders with one arm, he pulls me close. I lean into his chest.

As the logs catch, we sit in a quiet made up of a hundred small sounds. The ticking of my grandmother's mantel clock. The muted *whoosh* of tires on wet pavement. Artemis's whining on the far side of the wall.

Despite the calming metronome of Pete's heart, the fire is a mistake. The crackling and popping trigger images in my overstimulated brain. Jarring, like slivers knifing under my nails. Sensing my disquiet, Pete doesn't push. Finally, three Pinots down, I unload.

Slidell and Rinaldi at UNCC. Keith Millikin, his street clinic, his mysterious disappearance. The fire at the Airstream. The discovery of remains by Louis Grimm and his brother. My finding of skeletal compatibility with Millikin's profile. The bullet hole. The missing dentition. My recovery efforts with Larabee. The startling appearance of Millikin himself.

Pete asks the obvious. "So who died in the Airstream?"

"A white male, five eight to six one in height, thirty-five to fifty years old."

"That rules out Tina Turner."

I smack Pete's arm.

He feigns hurt, then refills my glass. "This Slidell sounds like quite the character."

"He's an arrogant prick."

"Still, you liked it."

"Liked what?"

"Maybe *like* isn't the best word." Pete thinks, shakes his head. "I don't know. There was something in your voice."

"Pinot?"

"Not that." Again he hesitates, perhaps unsure, perhaps not wanting to offend. "An excitement I don't hear when you talk about your research. About archaeology."

"What you're hearing is terror."

"Temperance Brennan fears nothing."

I raise my glass in acknowledgment. He clinks my rim with his.

No one speaks as we consider what he has said. What I have said. Then he asks, "Terror of what?"

"Being wrong."

"You're never wrong."

"There was that one time. I thought I was wrong, but it turned out I wasn't."

Another clink. Another thoughtful pause.

"You're right," I say. "I was reluctant to get involved. But once in, I kept thinking about the victim. About who he was. Who he leaves behind him—kids, a wife, a girlfriend. I kept remembering that somewhere someone is missing him. And somewhere his killer is walking around free."

"And the terror?"

All day, I asked myself that.

"In archaeology I work with anonymous populations. I think in terms of demographics: males, females; juveniles, adults. No names or personal stories. My findings are discussed in print and at conferences—"

"Or ignored."

"My point is"—this time he gets an elbow to the ribs—"praised or disputed, my theories about the ancient dead impact no one's life. The opposite is true with forensic work. Evidence can be recovered or lost due to the competence of scene processing. An innocent person can be falsely accused. A guilty person can go free. Based on lab analysis, a family can find closure or continue to search. Based on court testimony, a suspect can be convicted or acquitted. It's a huge responsibility."

"No one reads a skeleton better than you."

"True. But knowledge of archaeology and osteology isn't enough for the cops or the coroner. I'm a rookie. I'd need to retrain big-time."

"Why do I sense that decision has already been made?"

"Even then. What if I screw up?"

"I'll represent you."

I roll my eyes. Which feel loose. "I'd need to work toward board certification."

"How long would that take?"

"The rest of my life." The Pinot is weighing in.

"We survived the bar exam."

"I'd need to apply for membership in the American Academy of Forensic Sciences."

"And finish your dissertation."

"And that."

Pete sets his glass on the table. Collects mine and

places it beside his. Leans close and breathes hot in my ear.

I lean back and close my eyes, traveling with the sleepy-drunk pajama sheep. The fire is glowing warm somewhere behind Pete's back. I hook my arms around his neck.

The phone shrills. We both startle like kids caught in the backseat.

My eyes flick to Gran's clock: 10:42.

"Ignore her," Pete whispers.

"She could be in trouble." We both suspect my sister, who often calls in the wee hours. Or at dawn.

"Harry's always in trouble." Sighing, Pete draws back. "More wine?"

"Definitely not." I lift the handset and click on. "This better be good."

A short, startled pause. "For me or the guy got whacked?"

Now I'm the one taken off guard. Then the voice registers. "Excuse me, Detective. I was expecting a call from my sister."

"Sorry to disappoint." Clearly, Slidell isn't.

I say nothing. Pete rises to gather the glasses.

"Doc Larabee says you done okay out there today. So I got something for you." In a voice that kicks the apprehension back into gear.

Pete's cleanup has gone quiet. I know he's listening.

"Eddie and I got shit running our own MPs, so we spread out, floated some queries. Got a response from Gastonia." I hear rustling, picture Slidell checking his notes. "Russell Ingram. The wife reported him missing this morning. Apparently Ingram left for work two days ago, never came home. No one's been answering his office phone. When she went to check, it looked like hubby never made it in. You're gonna love this. The guy was a dentist."

"The nurse said nothing about his absence? The receptionist?"

"Ingram ran a one-man operation. Guess his patients weren't kicking up a stink about not getting drilled."

"How old is he?"

"Forty-two."

"White?"

"Yes."

"The height fits?"

"Yeah. He wasn't a hamster."

I ignore that. "Antemortem records?"

"We're about to roll one lucky dentist out of the rack."

6

The next morning I rise at six, a move not popular with my frontal lobe. Pete is gone but has made coffee. I down a quart and eat a bowl of raisin bran. After filling my travel mug, I palm two aspirin and head to UNCC.

While driving, I realize that Slidell said zip about Millikin the night before. I wonder where the good doctor is now. If Slidell has questioned him. His story. His relationship to Russell Ingram.

I've been observing cremains for over two hours when the phone rings. Slidell has Ingram's dental records and will meet me at the MCME at nine-thirty.

I check my watch: 8:55.

I secure the collection and the lab and race uptown. Mrs. Flowers buzzes me in, and I hurry to the stinky room. It is empty. It stays empty for the next twenty minutes. Frustrated, I look for Larabee. He is nowhere to be found. I decide to make use of the time I'm losing by writing a report on ME1207.

After collecting my notes, I walk to the front, explain my intention, and ask Mrs. Flowers if a spare office and typewriter might be available. She fires from her chair as though on a spring-loaded hinge.

"You just come with me." Beaming like an over-permed deranged clown.

I follow her to a room beyond Larabee's office. It is small and claustrophobic and contains a single desk and chair. Beside the desk are shelves holding nothing but unused folders.

On the desk is a keyboard attached to a computer monitor. Between the two is a pair of cubes labeled DRIVE 1 and DRIVE 2. Each drive has a slot and a small red bulb marked IN USE. Neither bulb is lit.

On the keyboard is a brightly striped logo shaped like an apple, with **apple**][inserted into a missing bite. I'm pleased. Though far from experienced, during my grad training I've brushed elbows with Steve Wozniak's genius creation.

Mrs. Flowers explains the obvious. "It's a personal computer. New to us. Dr. Larabee hasn't even tried it."

"Do you need it right now?"

"Oh my heavens, no." She actually takes a step back in her little gray pumps. "I prefer my Selectric."

I thank her. She leaves, promising notification the instant Slidell arrives.

I press a button to the upper right of the screen. Drop into the chair. The processor whirs and the screen lights up. I'm relieved to see an icon for WordStar, a software program I recognize.

In the desk's long center drawer, I find a pack of five-and-a-quarter-inch floppy disks. I insert one into a drive, open a file, and begin transferring information from my notes.

I've almost finished when Slidell shows up. It is ten forty-five. I ask Mrs. Flowers to send him to the stinky room, consider lingering to let him cool his heels. Reluctantly admit that such behavior would be petty.

Slidell is checking his watch when I push through the door. Seriously?

"Detective," I greet him.

He hands me a brown envelope, not big but larger than the one produced by Millikin's dentist. *Dr. Allison Martin* is scribbled across the flap. I wonder if being in the trade translates into better care. Or if Martin is merely more meticulous than Steiner about covering her ass.

I don't squabble about lack of qualification. To placate Detective Delightful, I agree to render a preliminary opinion but insist that a forensic dentist sign off on a positive ID. Or Larabee.

This time I use a tabletop illuminator that I've found in a cabinet. I plug it in, flip the switch, and arrange Ingram's bitewings on the top half of the glass. Below them, I do the same with the postmortem X-rays Hawkins has shot for the charred remains recovered from the Airstream.

The action is all on the lower right, and includes the following. An unerupted third molar sitting sideways in its socket. A root canal and crown in the second molar. Restorations in the first molar and first premolar shaped like Montana and Ireland, respectively.

The white blobs and spicules on the antemortem films superimpose perfectly atop those on the postmortem films. Every root shape is identical.

I have no doubt. The dead man in Millikin's trailer is Russell Ingram. Still, I take my time. Slidell's arrogance annoys me almost as much as his tardiness. Childish, I know. I'm not perfect.

Finally, I straighten and turn. "You'll need a forensic—"

"Yeah, yeah." He wiggles impatient fingers.

"*Unofficially,* it looks like a match."

Slidell is about to respond when the pager on his belt erupts in a series of jarring beeps. He yanks it free and reads the message. Crosses to the phone and dials. I hear his end of the conversation.

"Slidell."

Pause.

"Sonofabitch. When?"

Longer pause.

"Where?"

I collect Ingram's X-rays and return them to their envelope.

"Any chance of a visual?"

I do the same with the postmortem films.

"They need help out there? I'm with the anthropologist."

I pivot. Slidell's eyes are on me. I glare and shake my head.

"She ain't gonna like that," he says.

She? Me? Like what?

"Yeah. We'll hold tight."

Slidell cradles the receiver. "It's your lucky week, Doc. 'Tis the season for crispers."

"I don't work here," I say.

"Doc Larabee's at another scene, says he and

Hawkins can handle recovery. He wants you to hang here and help with ID."

I picture the cremains in my lab. Know they're fated not to return to the lender institution on time.

"You want particulars?" Slidell asks.

"Sure. The suspense is killing me."

"This one's a car fire. Toyota Corolla, probably 1980."

I don't ask where or how. Or why the make of vehicle is important.

"They're peeling the driver off the wheel as we speak. It ain't going well."

"Just one body?"

"Yeah. The dumbshit hit a tree, then *blammo*." Explosion of fingers.

"There may be a medical explanation for losing control." I sound pompous, don't care.

"Yeah." Slidell snorts. "Or a pint of Jim B. rolling around on the floor."

Hawkins arrives at the morgue shortly past noon. That's when I get my first look at the "crisper."

When exposed to fire, muscles shrink and joints bend. In humans, this results in the pugilistic posture, or boxer's pose. This has happened to the ill-fated driver of the Corolla. Though baked and blackened, a shroud of soft tissue holds the skeleton together. The fingers, wrists, elbows, and knees are tightly flexed.

The body is lying supine, limbs up. Unbidden, my mind pops an image. A puppy rolled onto its back to play dead.

I understand why Larabee has requested my help. The face is a featureless mass above a mouth stretched wide in a hideous grin. No nose, ears, lips, or hair remain. The eyes rest like shriveled raisins in the lidless orbits. The genitals are toast.

I return to the wondrous Apple II to finish my report on ME1207. Hawkins completes full body X-rays and photographs by one and wheels the remains to the stinky room. They have been assigned case number ME1211. I spend the next two hours tweezing off remnants of clothing, soaking and stripping flesh, sawing free bone specimens needed to construct a bioprofile.

By three I've finished with everything but the two heaps of charred rubble that accompanied or came off the body. My head is pounding. Maybe wine, maybe lack of lunch. Maybe the unsettling truth I have found yet again.

I'm jotting my final note when Larabee comes through the door. He holds a small pink paper in one hand.

"Rinaldi called." The scrubs tell me Larabee has gone from recovery of the fire victim straight into an autopsy. From death to death. I wonder if I want any part of this world.

"The car was registered to a Mark Wong." Larabee sounds exhausted. "Chinese American male, age twenty-seven, height five foot six."

There's no need to consult my notes. "That fits."

"I'll have Slidell collect antemorts."

"Where is he?"

"Questioning Millikin. At headquarters. I think. I'm not sure."

"What's Wong's story?"

"He's an acupuncturist. Was. That's all I know."

"Look at this."

It unfolds as a replay of the previous day. I step away from the table and hand Larabee the lens. He studies the defect I've found at the back of the skull.

"That's a bullet hole." He turns to me, worry lines creasing his brow.

"It is."

"Like Russell Ingram."

"Yes."

"Same MO. Cap the vic, torch the body. Any link between the two?"

"Both are men. Both were shot in the head."

"That should crack the case wide open. I'll call Slidell."

When Larabee leaves I start examining debris. The pile on the counter contains the shreds of scorched clothing I've removed from the corpse. The pile on the gurney came in lying beside him.

Much is burned beyond recognition. Not all. I start with the gurney. Find the vestige of a leather sole. A lump of melted vinyl, probably from the car. A key. Not sure of the protocol, I begin an evidence log.

I'm working through the clothing when I notice a patch of denim with several metal studs. The thing is maybe two inches square. I figure it's a portion of the victim's jeans, from the area of the seat protected by his bum.

The denim seems thick. Too thick. I look closer, realize I'm holding two pieces stuck together. A remnant of a pocket?

Using tweezers, I gently tug the top layer. Grudgingly, it lifts. When I peel it back, my heart throws in a few extra beats. A fragment of something thin and pale clings to the underside.

The fragment is stained and charred on the edges. It appears to be paper. The paper appears to have writing.

I raise and lower the magnifier. The letters are faint and refuse to focus. Except for a few. When I read them my skin goes cold. What I see can't be correct.

Barely breathing, I try to decipher more. Fail. The ink is too faded.

I'm still trying when the phone shrills.

7

"Whaddya got?" No salutation. I am learning the breadth of Slidell's charm.

"The bioprofile of the victim is consistent with that of Mark Wong. But you'll need—"

"Yeah, yeah. Wong's antemorts are on the way. I ain't spent this much time with dentists since I was nine. Anything else?"

"The victim was shot in the back of the head."

"Holy shit."

That summed it up well, so I said nothing.

"That what killed him?"

"Now that I've finished my analysis, Dr. Larabee will try an autopsy." Given the state of the body, I hold little optimism. I don't say that.

"You get the bullet?"

"None showed up on X-ray." Again, I mention the upcoming attempt at a Y incision.

"That it?"

"There is one other thing. I found a scrap of paper

in what I think was the back pocket of Wong's jeans." Realizing my error, I correct myself. "The victim's jeans."

"Doc, I got a zillion—"

"The ink is faded, but I can make out some writing."

"What kind of writing?"

I tell him what I think I've read.

"You sure?" His tone says he's skeptical. But interested.

"No."

Slidell thinks about that for a moment.

"You got the thing?"

"Yes."

"You know how to get to headquarters?"

I tell him I don't. He gives me directions.

"Be in the lobby in half an hour. I'll call the document guy."

"I have to get back to campus, so please—"

Dial tone.

The Charlotte-Mecklenburg PD is headquartered in a big stone fortress at the corner of Fourth and McDowell. Though just blocks from the MCME, I drive, hoping to continue on to UNCC.

To my astonishment, Slidell is waiting as promised. Same corduroy jacket, but today the shirt is green and the tie is blue. On it is something that could be an emu.

We ride the elevator in silence, pointlessly watching each digit light up. Slidell stands with feet spread, thumbs hooked in his belt. Twice, he sighs deeply.

We exit on the fourth floor, turn right, and proceed

to what appears to be the crime lab's administrative area. Doors bear plaques: CASE AND ADMINISTRATIVE FILES; CONFERENCE ROOM; DIRECTOR.

Beyond the director's office is a door labeled DOC-UMENTS SECTION. We enter a room that is small and furnished with a standard government-issued metal desk, chair, and file cabinet. A small table holds equipment I assume is used for optic analysis and measurement.

Seated at the desk is a man on the shy side of medium. Five six, wiry, hair neither long nor short, blond nor brown. He holds an ear by one finger in a way that makes me think he's just been probing.

On seeing us, the man rises. He's wearing a lab coat with a neatly knotted tie in the V at his neck. We approach. Slidell greets the man as George. I'm unsure if that's his first name or his last.

Slidell introduces me as the anthropologist, nothing more. I hope George won't feel compelled to shake hands. He doesn't.

Slidell has explained in advance the purpose of our visit. George is expecting us and asks if I have the spec-imen. I produce the vial containing the illegible scrap.

George leads us out of the front area and down a corridor I find surprisingly quiet. I've envisioned lab-coated scientists hurrying to and fro.

We enter what is identified as the Photography Section and walk to the back of the room. A long table holds a setup that includes a desktop computer, cameras, a display screen, and gizmos about whose functions I'm clueless.

"Ever seen a Video Spectral Comparator?" George's vowels stretch even wider than Mrs. Flowers's.

I shake my head. Slidell says nothing.

"She's a pip."

Slidell and I look appropriately impressed.

"Know much about light?"

"High school physics." I suspect I'm about to learn more than I want.

"Light is a form of radiant energy that occupies the four-hundred-through-seven-hundred-nanometer range of the electromagnetic spectrum and travels in different wavelengths. When you see colors, your eye is actually perceiving those wavelengths. You with me?"

I nod. Slidell doesn't bother.

"When light is directed toward an object, one of five things can happen."

Slidell starts to speak. George raises and waggles a finger.

"All or most of the light can be reflected, making the object appear white or lighter. All or most of the light can be absorbed, making the object appear black or darker." He ticks points off on his fingers. "Part of the light can be reflected and part absorbed, producing colors in the visible portion of the spectrum."

Slidell clears his throat. George lectures on, oblivious.

"Light can be transmitted through the object." Pinky finger. "Light can strike the object, be absorbed, and then be reemitted at a longer wavelength, an event called luminescence."

George gestures at the VSC. "This baby uses a combo of cameras, lights, and filters to allow the examiner, *moi*"—tenting the fingers of one hand on his chest—"to produce each of these effects."

"We just want to eyeball some script."

"Some wavelengths of radiant energy aren't visible to the human eye." Clearly, George has his own agenda.

"Infrared and ultraviolet," I say, hoping to hurry that agenda along.

"Exactly. The effects I've just listed occur in both the visible *and* IR and UV portions of the spectrum. But there can be big differences. The same object that absorbed light in the visible spectrum and appeared black can transmit radiant energy in the IR spectrum and appear clear as glass."

Sensing Slidell's irritation, I try again. "So ink that's faded to invisibility can leave traces viewable using UV or IR."

"Precisely." Proud teacher to bright pupil.

"Can we just do this?" Slidell is out of patience.

Lips crimped in displeasure, George gloves, removes the scrap, and positions it in the VSC. A white rectangle fills the screen. I still can't read the writing.

George takes a seat at the table. "You're seeing what the camera sees. I'll now apply an IR filter to block all visible light. Only radiation longer than six hundred forty-five nanometers will be seen by the camera."

Slidell sighs and thumb-hooks his pants. Though the visit is his idea, it's clear he thinks the effort is a waste of his time.

The monitor goes green. The letters on the scrap luminesce like glowworms in an underground cave.

Slidell and I lean in, lime pixels highlighting our frowns.

A short, shocked pause.

"It's ballpoint." No one listens to George.

"What the fuck?" Slidell explodes. Straightens.

"Language," George admonishes.

Legible on the scrap are letters and digits. *K Mil ik AZ 364 8111*

"Where's the phone?" Slidell's eyes are bouncing around the room.

George points to a side counter. Slidell beelines, snatches the receiver, jabs keys, listens, face moving through a series of grimaces and scowls. Thirty seconds, then he slams home the handset.

"I need a copy of that." Hooking a thumb at the message shimmering on the screen.

"Of course."

George gives Slidell the original denim scrap and makes a print of the enhanced version. I say thank you as we hurry off. Skinny does not.

It's five. The lab-coated experts I'd imagined now crowd the floor. The wait for an elevator seems interminable. Inanely, Slidell thumbs the button again and again.

I don't expect Slidell to share intel on the investigation; still, I'm offended. Standing beside him, I seethe quietly.

Finally, I can hold back no longer. "It's the phone number at Millikin's clinic, right?" I keep my voice low and discreet.

Slidell adjusts his emu tie. Says nothing.

"Is AZ an abbreviation for Arizona?"

Slidell lets out a clip of a snort. "Yeah. The guy was a Suns fan."

I ignore the sarcasm. "Larabee thought you had Millikin here. Is he still in the building?"

Slidell's eyes flick to me. No response.

"You're heading downstairs to interrogate him."

Slidell jabs the button.

"I want to observe."

"No way."

"I'm an anthropologist. I have training in the sub-tleties of human behavior." Bullshit. But suddenly I'm on fire to see Millikin questioned.

"Look, Doc. I appreciate—"

"Ingram and Wong were both shot in the head, then burned. Ingram died in Millikin's trailer. I found the evidence you need to tie Millikin to Wong."

"What I need is for you to keep out of my way."

"So that's my response the next time you come begging for help?"

The elevator doors slide open. We enter. Are body-packed to the rear wall.

"Well?" I whisper.

"Jesus, Mary, and the Mousketeers."

The elevator stops on two. Slidell elbows his way out. I follow in his wake, heart plowing my ribs.

I wonder what the hell I'm doing.

8

Slidell legs it so fast I find it hard to keep up. We blow by doors, signs showing the hornets' nest logo of the Charlotte-Mecklenburg PD.

Men move along the corridor in both directions, most in shirtsleeves and ties, one in khaki pants and a navy golf shirt featuring the intrepid wasp symbol. Some carry mugs or vending machine snacks. All pack a lot of firepower. I assume they are detectives.

Slidell thunders into a room marked VIOLENT CRIMES DIVISION. I thunder behind. The space is large and divided into cubicles housing desks, some solo, some in pairs. Each desk holds a phone, in- and out-baskets, the usual office paraphernalia. Flying by, I grab quick peeks of photos, sports memorabilia, sun-starved plants.

Some cubicles are occupied. From one floats a fragment of an argument about ballistics. From another, unrestrained snoring.

Greeting no one, Slidell weaves to a work space

with two desks shoved together so the occupants sit face-to-face. Rinaldi is at one, receiver pressed to his ear with one hunched shoulder. He glances up. Looks mildly surprised.

Slidell half-turns, sees me. Something flickers deep in his eyes. Wordlessly, he drops into his chair.

I stand as Slidell ignores me and Rinaldi talks on the phone. It's awkward. I would rather be with my ancient cremains.

Slidell leans back, toes free a bottom drawer, rests one foot on it, and ankle-crosses the other on top. His socks are orange. I wonder if the choice is a fashion statement or simply bad taste.

Rinaldi wraps up his conversation and unfolds to get me a chair. I thank him and sit. He directs subtly lifted brows at Slidell. A poorly camouflaged question.

Slidell shrugs. "She tailed me from four."

My cheeks flame. He makes me sound like a puppy.

Rinaldi asks about our visit to the crime lab. Slidell describes the note in Wong's pocket. Maybe Wong. I don't correct him. He doesn't mention my role in finding it.

"So Wong knew Millikin. And Ingram was killed in Millikin's crib."

"Booyah," Slidell says. I don't know what that means.

"Finding Ingram's body in the trailer doesn't mean Millikin knew him," I toss out. "Or that he died there."

Rinaldi nods. Slidell asks him, "You get a prelim from the arson boys?"

"Both the trailer and the car fire were deliberately set. They found accelerants at both. Want to see the report?"

"No. What'd you dig up on Ingram?"

"Not much." Rinaldi looks down at his notes. "Ingram's office was shut down three years ago for failing to comply with health regulations. Got nailed on a random inspection."

"The state yank his license?"

The licensing body would be a dental board, but I say nothing.

Rinaldi shakes his head. "He was fined and reprimanded. But the media hopped on the allure of unsanitary conditions, ran the story a few days."

"Slime and drool always boost ratings," Slidell says.

Rinaldi digs a photo from a folder and hands it to me. "You asked about Ingram's weight?"

The man looks like an orange grove with legs. His hair, lashes, and brows are carrot, his skin, behind a blizzard of freckles, sunburn-pink. He is seated in a leather chair, which he dwarfs, belly overhanging his belt and forcing his thighs wide. He holds a book low to divert attention from the unglamorous crotch. Or maybe he was actually caught reading.

"Ingram was a big guy," I say.

"Three twenty." Rinaldi returns the pic to its folder.

"Wife got motive? Insurance?" Slidell.

Rinaldi shakes his head. "She gets nothing. And without his income she'll have to sell their home. Ingram was in debt to his eyebrows."

"Tell me about Wong."

"Acupuncturist. His office shares space on East Boulevard with a couple of massage therapists and a hair salon."

"No one reported the guy missing?"

"He wasn't gone that long. A masseuse saw him leave his office around noon the day before yesterday. He said Wong bunched his appointments to avoid working daily."

"The home front?"

"Wong was single, lived in Dilworth with a roommate." Rinaldi flips a page in his notebook. "Derrek Hull. Hull sells hospital equipment and claims he's been in Florida the past five days. Says he has a list of clients can put him there. I talked to the employer and his story tracks."

"Any issues between Hull and Wong?"

"I checked for 911 calls to the address, complaints about noise, that sort of thing. Found zip. Canvassed. None of the neighbors ever heard yelling or saw them fighting."

I think this amount of digging is premature without a positive ID on Wong, keep it to myself. Less than a minute later, I'm glad. While Slidell is gone getting coffee, Rinaldi's phone rings. It's Larabee. He has the dental file and will be signing off on Wong.

When Slidell returns, Rinaldi gives him the news. Skinny shoots me an "I told you so" look. I think. Hard to tell since he's focused on unwrapping a Mounds bar.

"Either of these yaks have a jacket?" Slidell asks through chocolate and coconut.

"No," Rinaldi says.

A full minute crawls by. Around us, male voices, sporadic laughter, ringing phones. Finally, Slidell folds the candy wrapper and uses an edge to probe a molar.

"How 'bout you keep digging while I go at him?" he asks Rinaldi after irrigating the irritant tooth with coffee.

"Sounds like a plan."

Both detectives consider me. I feel my stomach tighten, my jaw clench.

Rinaldi shrugs. "She found the link to Wong."

Slidell eyes me so long I'm certain I'm about to get booted. Then his mug hits the desktop with a sharp crack. Not bothering to mop the spillage, he dials an extension and asks that an interrogation room be set up pronto. That Millikin be brought to it.

After downing the dregs of his coffee, Slidell glares in my direction. "You sit and say nothing."

I follow Slidell out of the squad room, down the hall, and into a tiny cell containing a metal table, two folding chairs, a speaker, and a phone. The floor is dull and scuffed, the walls cinder block painted puke beige. Centered on one is a rectangular window made of one-way glass.

Slidell motions me to a chair and leaves. When the door clicks shut my jaw relaxes. My gut doesn't buy in. I take a seat and place my purse on the table.

In minutes, the audio sparks to life in a symphony of hollow sounds. A rattling door. Footsteps. A scraping chair. The window lights up.

Millikin is at a table identical to mine. Behind him is a wall similar to those surrounding me. He's a skinny white guy wearing a cranberry sweater, plaid shirt, and baggy jeans. His hair is dull brown, side-parted and thin. Deep dark hollows underline his eyes.

Slidell sits opposite Millikin, looking like someone who eats kittens for lunch. An unopened folder lies before him on the table.

"Why am I here? A man died in my home. I've lost

all my possessions. I should be under medical care for traumatic stress."

"Damn shame. How'd it happen?"

"What can I say? I was out of the country. I authorized no one to enter my trailer. I've no idea why Dr. Ingram was there. Or how he got in."

"You expect me to buy that?"

"It's true!"

"Why the junket to Mexico?"

"I needed a break."

"So you split without so much as an adios to your patients?"

Millikin's hands are tightly clasped on the tabletop. He stares at them.

"Tell me about Ingram." Slidell isn't even trying for good cop.

"I treated him. We weren't close."

"Why would a dentist from Gastonia visit a street clinic in Charlotte?"

"I'm not at liberty to share that information."

"You gonna pull that patient-doctor crap on me?"

"Hardly crap. It's the law. And a physician's duty."

"Uh-huh." Slidell flips open the folder and studies a paper. I know it's a ruse. "Tell me about Mark Wong."

Millikin's face blanches and his fingers tighten. I notice they are trembling. I notice something else. A feature heightened by the newly paled skin.

A tumbling split second as the detail beyond the window collides with a recently stored image slapping into my forebrain. *AZ.*

"Holy crap!"

I fire to the adjacent room and pound on the door.

As expected, Slidell is not pleased with the interruption. Before he can bluster, I pull him out into the hall.

"Millikin has AIDS."

"What the Christ are you—"

"The lesion on his nose."

"He's got purple crud. So what?"

"It's Kaposi's sarcoma. Millikin has AIDS."

Slidell looks at me like I'm batshit crazy.

"Even under infrared, the note in Wong's pocket wasn't fully legible. I think *AZ* was part of AZT, a drug for treating AIDS. AZT isn't available in the U.S. yet."

It sinks in slowly.

"Can you get it in Mexico?"

"Yes." I overnod.

"Millikin was treating Ingram and Wong for AIDS. That's why Ingram hauled ass from Gastonia to Charlotte."

"It makes sense."

"Millikin was running AZT from Mexico. You think the sonofabitch was dealing through his clinic?"

"His lifestyle doesn't suggest that he was in it for the money. *If* he was in it."

A tight jerk of his head, then Slidell whips around and storms back in to the interview. When I return to my window, he's already grilling Millikin.

"—know you went south of the border to score AZT. How much were you nailing these poor bastards? A three hundred percent markup? Four? Five? Or am I thinking too small?"

Millikin doesn't respond.

"Or were you hoarding the stuff for yourself?"

"It wasn't like that." Barely audible.

"Yeah? What was it like?"

"These men live in shame. No one wants to treat them." All Adam's apple and black-sun pupils. "I try to help."

Millikin's next words make my heart rate gallop.

9

"Dr. Ingram and Mr. Wong were both under my care. As I've stated, information pertaining to their medical histories is privileged."

Slidell starts to erupt. Millikin raises a hand.

"What I can tell you is that I am also treating a patient who detests both of those men."

"Why?"

"He believes that his"—Millikin searches for a word—"issues are due to interactions with Dr. Ingram and Mr. Wong."

"What issues?"

"I can't say."

"What's his name?"

"I can't say."

Slidell looks like he's about to throttle the guy. Instead he leans back, crosses his arms, and speaks in a voice made of steel. "You know I'm gonna get it."

"I do," Millikin says. "But not from me."

"I can make your life hell."

"You can."

"This patient. Is he heated enough to kill?"

"I'm not a psychologist."

Slidell draws a deep breath. Exhales. Pooches out his lips and rolls his eyes to the ceiling. Then he leans forward, elbows on the table. "Look. I want to help you, Doc. But you gotta give me something."

Millikin meets his gaze. His conscience allows, "This gentleman was also furious with a third party. For similar reasons."

"A patient?"

"No."

"Then a name's no problem."

"Nero Height. He goes by Nehi."

Slidell jots it on the file folder. "What's Height's story?"

"He's just a kid, a corner boy who also turns tricks."

"What's he deal?"

"Crack, H, speed, the usual."

"Where's he live?"

"I have no idea."

Slidell tosses down his pen and glares.

This time, Millikin glares back.

Thirty minutes later I'm in my lab at UNCC. Slidell has dismissed me and, grudgingly, agreed to keep me updated. I don't believe him.

I find it hard to stay focused on my thousand-year dead, I'm so jazzed on the events of the past two days. The fires in the Airstream and Corolla. The gunshot wounds to the skulls of Ingram and Wong. Millikin's

AIDS. His excursion to Mexico to buy AZT. His story of an angry patient. Of the street kid, Nehi Height. Shortly after seven I give up and head out.

On the way home, I divert to Reid's and buy marinated flank steak, sweet potatoes, and asparagus. Pete's favorites. On guilty impulse, I grab a miniature spruce trimmed with spiffy red bows and candy canes. Christmas is just a week away and our townhouse wears zip that is festive.

Surprisingly, Pete is home when I arrive. His case has settled. He has placed a plastic Santa on the mantel and hung mistletoe from the dining room arch. I show him my tree. We both laugh. I realize it's been a while since I've done that.

We vow to keep dinner a work-free zone. While cooking, we discuss our upcoming Yuletide plans with Harry and her new squeeze. Pete thinks he's Arturo. I go with Alejandro. We agree that the name is unimportant, since the poor chump will be gone by year's end.

The plates have barely hit the table when I mention my trip to police headquarters. Pete asks about Slidell. I tell him Skinny and I may run off together. He gives me a faux sad face, queries other developments. I fill him in on the day's progress. I think he'll comment on Wong's murder. He doesn't.

"Millikin's right. People with AIDS take a double hit. Not only are they sick, they're stigmatized."

I start to agree, but Pete hasn't finished.

"An AIDS diagnosis is a death sentence. There's no support system, no effective treatment, and society just turns its back on these people. Why? The public sees AIDS as a gay disease. There's an attitude that scum like homosexuals—"

"And IV drug users."

"—don't deserve special attention. Everyone wishes the poor bastards would shut up and die in private."

"Not everyone." I'm surprised by Pete's vehemence.

"True. But there's that element. Some say AIDS is what homosexuals deserve. Can you imagine how it must feel? No one will kiss you on the cheek or let you hold their baby?"

"It must be truly awful."

"The problem is we don't know the cause."

"Ever heard of a nineteenth-century physician named John Snow? In the 1850s, Londoners were dying of cholera and no one knew why. Snow discovered that all the sick had drunk water from the same well. He didn't grasp the underlying mechanism but knew that pump was the link."

"And?" Pete, not seeing the relevance.

"He removed the pump handle."

"That stopped the outbreak?"

"It did."

"Your point?"

"Eventually the handle will come off the AIDS pump."

As we clear the dishes, attorney Pete hits the talking points for a theory coagulating in my brain.

"Wong and Ingram were Millikin's patients. Do you suppose he was treating them for AIDS?"

"Could be."

"Wong does acupuncture, a procedure involving needles. Ingram's a dentist nailed for running a dirty practice. Dentists also use needles and come in contact with blood."

"Yes."

"Millikin treats people with AIDS. Maybe his angry patient also has AIDS. Maybe he believes Wong or Ingram infected him."

"Ergo, the killings are about revenge." I finish the thread.

A beat.

Pete asks, "Nehi Height is a prostitute?"

I nod. We both understand the implication.

"Shouldn't someone warn the kid?" Pete asks.

"They're trying to figure out where he lives."

We finish our wine, watch the news, and retire. We don't go right to sleep.

Five days pass. I hear nothing from Slidell or Rinaldi. Nothing from Larabee.

On the sixth morning, the phone rings as I'm preparing to head to the university. I answer.

"The guy's name is Terry Flynn."

It takes me a moment to dial in. "The patient Millikin refused to name."

"Yeah." Slidell coughs, hawks something unimaginable, spits, I hope, into a hanky. "Flynn's a banker, which narrows it to half the suits in Charlotte. Lives in Eastover, which means he excels at his job."

I hear voices, maybe drawers being opened and closed. "Where are you?"

"Millikin's office. I've been going through files. Dull reading unless you're into diarrhea and shit."

I doubt Slidell is aware of his pun. "You obtained a warrant?"

"Nah, I'm going rogue. Think a little entrepreneurial zest might play well with a jury."

I muster the willpower to bite back a snarky retort.

"CSU found a boatload of AZT in the shed behind Millikin's trailer. The doc was selling to his patients, but charging only nickels and dimes. Except for one lucky customer."

"Terry Flynn."

"Bingo. The fat cat was paying through the nose."

"Where's Millikin?"

"We had to kick him."

"Did you confront him with all this?"

"Yeah. He rolled. Admitted he piped the money to the clinic, used some to finance his trips south. Looks like his story's gonna have legs."

I wait out another cough. Then I share the theory Pete and I discussed a few nights ago.

There's a long moment of background noise.

"I'm going to talk to this fuckwit Flynn. Maybe you want to be there."

That astounds me. "Where's Rinaldi?"

"Height's sister lives in the Southside Homes. Nashawna." He elongates the second syllable unnecessarily. "Eddie's watching for Nehi, wants to give the kid a heads-up if he shows."

"Dumb question, but why are you inviting me along on this interview?"

Slidell does something in his throat I can't begin to interpret.

"Sorry?"

"You spotted Wong's memo, Millikin's gay cancer."

I let the latter slide and wait for further explanation. Slidell offers none.

"So, what the hell? Am I picking you up?"

"Sure." I give him my address. What the hell?

❋   ❋   ❋

Slidell's Crown Vic is a rolling recycle bin. The day is cold, and a filthy sky promises it's going to get wet. The heater is pumping and the car's interior is overripe with smells. Old food. Sweat. Bad cologne. Stale cigarette smoke.

The drive seems endless. It lasts ten minutes.

Flynn's home is on Colville Road in one of Charlotte's caviar-and-Cadillac hoods. Circle drive, manicured lawn, house definitely not trying for subtle. The place is lit like a cruise ship on a holiday sail.

Slidell drives to the top of the circle. We get out and climb to a veranda spanning the entire first floor. Propped by the door is a toboggan that says MERRY CHRISTMAS, Y'ALL!

Slidell thumbs the bell. I hear a muffled chime that goes on longer than Wagner's *Ring Cycle*.

No one appears. No voice crackles from the little intercom box.

Slidell rings again.

No response.

Slidell resorts to the same battering tactic he employed with the elevator button.

Still nothing.

A window to our right throws slashes of light onto the brick at our feet. I step to it, lean close, and peer through the plantation shutters covering the inside of the glass.

The room is a library with floor-to-ceiling shelves holding hundreds of books. Carved mahogany desk. Large, angular sofas and chairs. A globe. Photos of sports figures on the mantel over a fieldstone fireplace.

Behind me, Slidell curses. As I turn, he kicks out at the sled. It sails, hits the wall, and ricochets onto the steps. The Y'ALL greeting wings off into a bush.

I cock a brow but don't comment.

We're walking toward the Crown Vic when the radio sputters. Slidell hasn't brought his portable, so he bolts for the car. By the time I slide in he's rehooking the speaker mic. He looks like he's just had a kick to the nuts.

"What?" I ask.

Slidell shifts and pounds the accelerator. We reverse so quickly my head snaps forward. He throws the engine into gear, guns down the drive, and cuts a fast left. I brace myself on the dash with both hands.

"What the crap?" I say with more feeling.

"A patrol unit spotted Flynn's Bimmer on Baltimore Avenue."

"And?" I don't know the street, the significance.

"It's parked opposite Nashawna Height's unit."

10

The Southside Homes feel suburban to the extent that public housing can ever feel suburban—one-and two-story brick duplexes with small windows, small porches, and small front lawns that bleed into one another. Some units are fronted by shrubs, others by ragged dirt strips. Here and there, a window is edged with jingle bell lights. Not Chestnut Hill, but not the usual "government-bleak efficient" mode either.

Dumpsters sit at intervals along Baltimore Avenue. At one, a cat paws trash that has fallen or been tossed to the base. Its calico fur is matted and dull, its body cadaver-thin. As we pass, the cat's head whips up and it crouches so low its belly touches the ground.

Rinaldi's Bonneville is parked across from unit 8A, a short distance below the intersection with Griffith Street. He's in it. Slidell noses to the Pontiac's rear bumper and we both get out.

"Where's Flynn's ride?" Slidell asks.

"Gone when I got here."

"You talk to the sister?"

"Nashawna. She's not receptive."

"You clue her that Nehi's ass is in serious jeopardy?" Slidell is eyeing 8A. I'm sure Nashawna is similarly assessing us from behind the blue sheet draping the dingy front window. Suspect others are doing the same.

"I told her I was here to help."

"You say you're a cop?"

"No need. The lady's been through the system."

"She probably thinks you came to bust her brother." Both detectives look at me.

Rinaldi says, "A unit's cruising, looking for Flynn."

"How 'bout you hang here while I chat with Nashawna?" This time Slidell has brought his handheld radio. Not awaiting Rinaldi's blessing, he strides toward 8A. The Motorola looks like a brick in his hand.

I watch him climb the steps, ring the bell, wait. Open the screen and fist-bang the inner door. A series of dull thuds carries in the wintry air.

I notice a Weber grill beside the neighboring unit. A ceramic pot on a rusty tripod. A section of ankle-high picket fencing protecting both.

Thud. Thud. Thud.

I watch two small children coax a kite skyward in the area of common grass running behind the buildings. An old woman walking a pit bull that looks even older than she. Two geezers arguing, too far away for me to hear the point of contention.

I feel my fingertips turning blue. Think about gloves. Slip my hands inside my pockets.

Finally, Slidell pauses and his upraised hand drops. Though his back is to us, I see his shoulders angle downward and his head move in a way suggesting conversation. I assume Nashawna is listening to him through the smallest of cracks.

Slidell takes something from inside his trench coat. A beat, then he pivots and hurries to rejoin us.

"Christ. There's a brain trust."

"What did she say?" Rinaldi asks.

"She and Nehi ain't close. She hasn't seen him. Kiss my bony black ass."

"What do you think?"

"I think the kid probably has product stashed in her bedsprings."

"Now what?"

"Dispatch knows the situation with Flynn?" Slidell is scanning the block, not looking at his partner or me.

"Yeah."

"Tell them to find the dirtbag." Slidell's voice has that buzz again. "I'm going to drop the doc off, then swing back to Flynn's pad."

I don't protest. I'm not properly dressed and my toes are going numb.

We've gotten off I-77 south onto the John Belk Freeway and are approaching the Fourth Street exit when the radio spits something that snags Slidell's attention. He grabs the hand mic. As he thumbs and releases the button, I hear both ends of the exchange. Flynn's car, a black BMW 735i with tinted windows and North Carolina plate NNX-43, has been spotted heading south on Tryon Street toward Griffith.

"Tell them to stay on it."

"The unit is no longer in visual contact."

"Sonofabitch!"

We spin a U-ey sharp enough to launch me sideways into the passenger-side door. Slidell activates flashing headlights and a *whup-whup* siren and bulls his way across Fourth and onto Third. We're barreling back the way we came when dispatch again summons him.

"What?" Barked.

"A Nashawna Height just dialed 911 asking for you."

"What's she saying?"

"A man is parked across the street watching her place."

"What's he look like?"

Pause.

"He's white."

"Jesus on a jump rope. What's wrong with people? Old, young? Tall, short?"

Pause.

"She says he's a tall skinny white guy."

Slidell's scowl tells me the description fits Terry Flynn.

"Height calling from home?"

"A neighbor's phone."

"Tell her I'll be there in less than five. Keep her on the line."

"I'll try. She's pretty agitated."

I feel my heart beating way too fast.

Dispatch keys in again. "Height says she's watching the guy from the neighbor's kitchen window. Says he's out of the car and walking toward her building."

"Is her brother with her?"

Short pause.

"The brother is in the home."

"You got a unit en route?"

"Yes. Hold on."

Long pause.

"Height thinks the guy's armed."

"Tell her to stay where she is. I'm three minutes out, max."

Slidell runs a stop sign at the Remount Road exit. Drivers hit their brakes and their horns.

The dispatcher's voice reemerges from the static. "The caller says she's leaving to help her brother."

"Order her to stay put! I'm almost there!"

My heart is now racing as fast as the Crown Vic. I know we can't reach Nashawna or Nehi before Flynn gets to the door.

No response.

"What's happening?" Slidell demands.

"I lost her."

"What do you mean you lost her?"

"She hung up."

At Baltimore Avenue, Slidell makes a high-speed right turn and mashes the gas pedal. Halfway up the block a white panel truck pulls from the curb. Slidell slows a hair, swerves around it, and accelerates. In the side mirror, I see the receding driver wave a one-finger salute.

"Where's Rinaldi?"

"On his way."

In moments we squeal up behind Flynn's BMW. Slidell throws the gearshift into park. My whole body lurches forward. He is out before I can right myself.

"Ass on the leather!" he shouts, finger jabbing at me. He starts toward 8A, gun drawn and held low by his thigh.

My fingers are white on the dash. I push myself back. Realize I'm not breathing, and inhale deeply.

I look around. See the Pontiac but not Rinaldi. No cruiser. No Flynn. No Nehi. No bony black ass.

The kids are gone from the grass. The pit bull granny. The bickering men. I'm glad. Every instinct in me is howling danger. Adrenaline is pumping hard.

I lower my window and listen. Except for distant vehicles, all is still. Just traffic and my hammering pulse.

Seconds pass. A full minute. I hear a scrape followed by a crash. My mind offers no picture to accompany the soundtrack. Then recognition. The tripod-urn has been upended and shattered.

I'm digesting that when a gunshot rips the cold morning air. Another follows. A third.

An image explodes in my forebrain. Slidell ambushed, bleeding out on the icy lawn. Maybe Rinaldi.

A man bellows. Another bellows back. The voices come from behind 8A. I can't make out the words.

I'm not good at taking orders. Never have been. I know I should stay where I am. That I'm untrained. That I shouldn't put myself at risk.

But I need to find out what's happening. And hiding in the car isn't going to help a damn.

I take a few calming breaths and slip from the Crown Vic. Do a three-sixty sweep, then, moving as discreetly as possible, diagonal toward the gap between 8A and its neighbor.

I see them as soon as I round the house. Slidell. Nashawna. Nehi. Flynn. I assume Rinaldi is near but out of sight. All are locked in a tableau of horror and shock.

Flynn has Nehi at gunpoint, barrel pressed tight to his throat, forcing his chin up at a painful angle. They are on the back stoop. The door has flown inward and is no longer hanging square on its hinges. Muddy footprints suggest Flynn has kicked it in. Most are at odd angles, suggesting lousy balance or poor muscle control. A trio of small holes explains the gunfire.

Nashawna is at the rear of the neighboring unit, hands pressed to her mouth, hunkered behind the Weber. Slidell is beside her, gun held two-handed and pointed at Flynn.

Flynn's body is little more than a skeleton shrink-wrapped in bruised flesh.

"You didn't tell me, you twisted little prick!" Flynn's voice trembles with rage.

"Tell you what, man?" Nehi's words are choked due to pressure on his trachea and the unnatural thrust of his jaw.

"You killed me, now I kill you. Eye for an eye, *man*. Justice, *man*? The Bible tells me so."

"What the fuck you talking about?" Nehi is small and wiry with eyes like those of a terrified dog, deep brown and rimmed with way too much white.

"You signed my death certificate, you sick little bastard."

"You talking that gay immune shit? I ain't got that, man."

I hear an engine, tires, car doors opening behind us on Baltimore Avenue. The sputter of a radio.

"You deserve it. You sell heroin and crack. You sell yourself. You're scum. I had so much to live for and you took it all away."

"I said drop your weapon!" Slidell shouts. I know he isn't firing, for fear of hitting Nehi.

Flynn jams the muzzle deeper into Nehi's flesh.

Tightens his grip on the handle. Though Flynn is far taller than his prey, his posture is so stooped their heads are almost level.

Feet pound in our direction. I note the rhythm. Four.

"I'm telling you one more time!" Slidell yells. "Drop the gun."

Nehi is a scrapper. A survivor. And afraid for his life. What happens next is a testimonial to that powerful trifecta.

Flynn's eyes cut to the sound of the approaching footsteps for a sliver of a second. Sensing the shift, Nehi twists, hooks one leg around the back of Flynn's knees, shoulder-shoves his chest, and strikes at the gun hand. Flynn goes down with a sound like logs striking a hearth. The gun flies free.

"Height! Back away!"

Ignoring Slidell, Nehi straddles Flynn's chest and presses both his wrists to the ground. It's no contest. Teenage street fighter versus middle-aged invalid. Though Flynn struggles, Nehi has him pinned.

The choreography is spontaneous and fast. Slidell closes in. Rinaldi steps from behind the unit to the north, gun straight out and aimed at Flynn. Two uniforms round the house, see the action, and draw their weapons. Nehi jumps free and scuttles sideways. Rinaldi scoops Flynn's gun from the grass. It is over in seconds.

Nashawna scrambles from behind the Weber. I run forward and wrap her shoulders with one arm. Tears stream down her cheeks. She is shaking and allows me to restrain her.

"He's okay," I say. "Everything will be all right."

"That man crazy," she says. "Nehi don't got no AIDS. His girlfriend made him get hisself tested."

Over her shoulder, I see that Flynn is on his feet. One of the uniforms cuffs him, reads him his rights. Nashawna and I watch him and his partner lead Flynn away. He walks between them, wobbly, limping.

I try but feel little sympathy for Flynn. He is dying, but murdered two men and tried to kill a third. I can forgive that he is angry. Confused. Distraught. I cannot forgive that he is vengeful.

And I cannot forgive that he is self-righteously judgmental. That he views himself as superior to Nehi Height. That his life is more valuable.

Terry Flynn is an arrogant ass.

"Thank you," Nashawna says.

"Thank them." I indicate Slidell and Rinaldi. The cops who are folding Flynn into the backseat of their cruiser.

Nashawna lifts one shoulder in a noncommittal shrug.

Slidell is talking to Nehi, his bearing haughty, his tone brusque.

I think, You are arrogant, Skinny Slidell. But far from an ass.

Flakes are now swirling in indifferent eddies, not snow, not rain. I watch a few settle and dissolve on the grass.

Nashawna says something I fail to catch.

"I'm sorry?"

"Happy holidays," she repeats quietly.

I have forgotten.

It is Christmas Eve.

11

Something brushed my shoulder, spiderweb-soft. I opened my eyes.

A silhouette blocked my view of the screens, a dark cutout against the aquamarine glow.

"How are you doing?" Whispered, voice filled with compassion.

"I'm good," I lied.

Andrew Ryan smiled encouragement. I tried to smile back. Managed only a melancholy tightening of the corners of my mouth.

"You need a break?"

I shook my head.

"How's he doing?"

I shook it again, more slowly, not trusting my voice.

"Want company?"

"Sure."

Ryan disappeared, returned from the corridor

with a second chair. Dropping into it, he reached out a hand. I took it. Held tight, overcome with a tangle of emotions.

Time passed.

The monitors paraded their bloodless peaks and valleys. Sounded their impartial pinging.

And then they screamed. And the lines went flat.

Ryan's eyes met mine, too blue, too wide.

Adrenaline snapped through every cell in my body.

No!

The door winged open and Nurse V. Sule charged in and grabbed the crash cart, all stainless steel and bright red drawers. On top were a defibrillator and what looked like a tackle box.

Others raced in with her, color-coded in their scrubs. Faces grim, focused.

I got to my feet. Sensed rather than saw Ryan rise beside me. My eyes were fixed on the man in the bed.

Nurse V. Sule threw back the sheet, now motionless as the sea after a wild storm. Ripped open the gown covering his chest. Her eyes skidded to me as she positioned her palms, one atop the other, for CPR.

"Please." Tipping her head toward the open door. Arms already pumping.

Ryan and I hurried out into the corridor. Stood, not knowing what to say. What to do.

Feeling helpless, and needing to move, I crossed to the window and looked at the city spreading out eleven floors below. The day's first pale light was tickling the horizon. The skyline of uptown rose out of the gray, a grainy black-and-white version of its daytime self.

A barrage of memories unspooled in my brain,

some immediate, some distant. His voice on the phone.
His form bent over a shallow grave. His eyes taking in
a ghostly white newborn. His hands traveling over a
mummified corpse.

Guilt swirled in the mix. A sister was coming from Fort
Worth. What else did I know of his personal life? There
were no children. Had there ever been a spouse? Partners
had come and gone. I remembered no names.

I pictured his goodbye wave the evening before.
Casual. Unaware he was living his last day on earth.

The onslaught was dizzying. The recognition that
we would have no final parting. That words left unsaid
between us would remain unsaid forever.

It couldn't be true.

Footsteps sounded, heels sharp on the tile. Not the
soft-soled tread of the hospital staff.

I turned.

Two men were hurrying in our direction. One was
dressed all in black, save for a small white rectangle at
his throat. The other wore a plaid sport jacket over a
grease-stained apricot shirt. Polyester pants.

Slidell's hangdog gaze met mine. Our mutual stare
lasted what seemed a very long time. Then, eyes down-
cast, he veered toward Ryan.

The priest took a chair, laced his fingers in his lap,
and closed his eyes.

It was true.

Tim Larabee was dying.

I felt tears burn my lids. Fought them back.

Behind Ryan and Slidell, through the open door, I
saw a nurse slide a clear plastic mat under Larabee's
back as V. Sule tore paper packets, withdrew pads, and

attached them to his chest. When she'd finished, both women glanced at the defibrillator screen. V. Sule's lips formed a single word.

"Clear."

Everyone stepped back from the bed. Larabee's body arched. Arched again. Lay still. The other blue-clad nurse placed two fingers on his carotid. Checked the pulse in his wrist. The screens. Shook her head.

V. Sule began a second round of chest compressions.

Ryan and Slidell were speaking in hushed tones, heads bowed and close. I swallowed, inhaled deeply, and crossed to them.

"—hopped up on crank. The sonofabitch—"

Slidell stopped abruptly when I drew near.

"Larabee was out for a late run?" My voice was calmer than I'd dared hope.

Slidell nodded, sorrow making his face look older than its legitimate claim. And exhaustion. I knew he'd been working all night, searching for Larabee's assailant.

"He was a random victim?"

"Wrong place, wrong time."

How often we'd talked of the fickleness of life. Larabee had coined a phrase for its sudden, unpredictable cessation. Death by acute numerical assumption. The victim's number was up.

A casual goodbye wave. A late-night jog in Freedom Park.

Behind the men, a nurse in green injected meds into an IV line. A bubble of space opened around the bed. Larabeee lurched, lurched again. Then a nurse in blue checked for a pulse. A man in white made notes in a file.

"Who's the doer?" Ryan was in cop mode. Keeping his emotions buckled down.

Ditto Slidell. "A street kid name of Garret Hearst. A real piece of work."

"Meaning what?" I asked.

"Hearst's a tweaker with too few brain cells left to wipe his own ass." Angry. Harsh. "Who the hell mugs a jogger? What's he gonna do? Carry a wad in his shorts?"

"You're sure he's the shooter?" Ryan asked.

"Surveillance video puts him in the park around the time a wit recalls hearing shots. The dumbshit left the gun at the scene. His prints are all over it. Ballistics will show a match."

To the bullets that ripped through Larabee's belly.

"When was that?" I had to know.

"Eleven-fifteen."

"The dog walker discovered him just past midnight?"

"Yeah."

Our little group fell silent, appalled by the ghastly image. Horrified by the possibility that quicker intervention might have saved Larabee's life.

"Where's Hearst now?"

"In the can."

V. Sule was again pumping Larabee's chest. My mind had done the math. Two minutes of CPR, then a vitals check, followed by defib. I glanced at my watch. Thirty minutes had passed since Larabee flatlined. I wondered how long the lifesaving efforts would continue.

"Have you interviewed the kid?" Ryan.

"The little prick's too fried to know his own name."

As suddenly as it began, the desperate dance stopped. In the room at our backs, everyone froze.

Larabee lay unmoving. Like the mourned and unmourned dead he'd tended to so gently for so many years.

The man in white looked at the clock. Spoke aloud. Entered time of death in his file.

The priest rose.

V. Sule circled the bed and drew the sheet up over Larabee's face.

Goodbye, old friend.

And then the tears had their way.

Seeing my distress, Slidell stepped forward and wrapped me in a crushing bear hug. Our cheeks touched. To my shock, his were salty-wet like mine.

Standing awkwardly, off-balance, I realized something for the first time. Through all the years—the triumphs and failures, the sorrows and joys, the harrowing rescues and the heartbreaking deaths—Skinny and I had never once embraced.

I leaned against him and wept on the apricot shirt.

ACKNOWLEDGMENTS FOR
FIRST BONES

I owe huge thanks to Roger Thompson, the former director of the Charlotte-Mecklenburg Police Department crime laboratory. Together, we reconstructed how it was "back in the day."

READ AN EXCERPT FROM
#1 *New York Times*
BESTSELLING AUTHOR
KATHY REICHS'S NEW BOOK

THE BONE CODE

AVAILABLE SUMMER 2021

I awoke to pitch-black.

Groggy, I rose to a crouch and groped for the chain on the overhead fixture. Pulled. Nothing.

Great. Still no electricity.

Dropping back onto the improvised bed, I located my phone. The screen showed the time to be 6:22.

Morning?

I opened my hurricane-tracking app.

Inara had made landfall as a Cat 2 hurricane between Savannah and Charleston around nine the previous night. After a five-hour tantrum, she'd moved offshore and was now Virginia's problem.

Good news. Charlotte had caught only her western edge.

I opened the closet door. Pearl-gray light was seeping between the closed slats of the plantation shutters, throwing off-angle slashes onto the floor.

I crawled out into the hall. Birdie, ever cautious, remained huddled in the blankets.

Inside the annex, all was quiet. No humming refrigerator or blowing AC. Outside, bird chatter high above and the staccato barking of a distant dog.

Using my iPhone as illumination, I made a quick tour of both floors. Save for a torn screen on one bedroom window, everything appeared to be intact.

Coffee was impossible, so I got a Diet Coke from the slumbering fridge, then crossed the kitchen. Despite much forceful shoving and shouldering, the back door wouldn't budge. Encountering no such impediment in front, I stepped out onto the stoop.

As is typical following hurricanes, the air seemed extraordinarily clear and crisp. The sky, slowly brightening, was unmarred by even the tiniest of clouds.

Sharon Hall looked like a bomb had gone off. Trees were down and debris and vegetation covered the grounds. Uprooted shrubs lay jumbled along the manor house foundation and a trash can hung wedged between its pillars. Two concrete urns lay shattered on the porch, soil and begonias spewing from them like innards from a squashed roach.

Slowly, my neighbors began to emerge, hesitant but game, like survivors of some B-movie apocalypse. Most were already suited up for yard work. A few pushed wheelbarrows. Many carried garden tools.

I went inside, brushed my teeth, and changed into jeans and a sweatshirt. After locating a pair of old work gloves, I joined the recovery effort, doing my bit with a very questionable rake.

Shortly after nine, word spread that the power had been restored. I took a break to return to the annex to plug in my mobile. And to rejoice. I have to admit, I'm a huge fan of electricity.

Birdie had ventured forth, startled awake when the bare bulb in his haven lit up. He was calmer, but still needed a couple milligrams of something to restore him to normal.

I was heading back outside when my newly

connected mobile warbled. The first of three calls that day. Not the one that would send my life off-kilter.

Recognizing the number, I steeled myself. Previous conversations had shown that—I'm being kind here—Lloyd Thorn lacked certain interpersonal skills.

"Good morning, Mr. Thorn."

"I wasn't sure I'd get through. A real pisser, this storm."

"We've just started to clean up the mess."

"My clients are shitting their shorts waiting for your take."

"I understand."

"Don't misread me. Tereza's death is a freakin' tragedy. But my clients did nothing wrong. It's an outrage they're sitting in jail."

When he'd hired me, Thorn had explained that he represented parents who claimed that their adopted child, Tereza, was far older than initially represented to them by Bulgarian adoption officials. According to the parents, Tereza had waged a campaign of fraudulent—and even psychopathic—behavior for years, culminating, tragically, in her accidently drinking herself to death while they were out of state. Now the parents were facing multiple charges—child abandonment, child endangerment, and negligent homicide—and their only chance at exoneration rested on their "child" not being a child at all, but an adult.

"Please hold while I get my notes."

Resuming the conversation, I placed Thorn on speaker. I could hear him fidgeting impatiently, probably clicking a ballpoint pen.

"I'm somewhat limited having never examined

Tereza or viewed a photo of her. But I did spend several hours with the X-rays."

"Let's cut to the chase."

"In my opinion, Tereza at the time of her death was in her early to mid-twenties. I believe she had a condition called Silver-Russell syndrome."

"What's that?" The clicking stopped. Paper rustled.

"A congenital growth disorder tha—"

"I went to law school, not med school. For now, just the basics."

"SRS can explain the stunted growth."

"Stunted?"

"Children with SRS tend to have high foreheads, small jaws, and triangular faces. But those features become less obvious with age."

"Uh-huh."

"There's no specific radiological indicator of SRS. However, delayed bone age, clinodactyly, and 5th middle or distal phalangeal hypoplasia have been reported as suggestive of the syndrome." Speaking über slowly and purposely using medical jargon.

"What the hell's that mean?"

"They are features that can be seen on X-rays. Which is what I had to work with and which is objective evidence. Clinodactyly refers to the abnormal curvature of a digit. Hypoplasia refers to the underdevelopment of a body part, in this case, of portions of the little finger."

"Tereza had all that?"

"She did."

"How's this relevant?"

"It can explain her extremely short stature."

"Short stature in adults?"

"Yes. Especially if growth abnormalities aren't treated postnatally."

"Like *that* would have happened in Bulgaria. How common is this SRS?"

"Stats put the occurrence somewhere between one in three thousand and one in one hundred thousand births."

"That's about as useful as a tit on a nun."

Unable to disagree, I didn't respond.

"You said congenital. This thing's inherited?"

"Yes. But the genetics are unclear. Autosomal-dominant, autosomal-recessive, and X-linked inheritance models have been reported, but without going into—"

"Yeah, don't."

Having had my fill of Thorn's abrasive manner, I did.

"It's thought that loci—think genes—on chromosome 11 play a major role in SRS. But chromosome 7 may also—"

"You're saying Tereza was a dwarf because of wonky genes."

"I wouldn't put it in quite those words." Wondering precisely where this jerk *did* go to law school.

"So she was an adult, not a kid. In her twenties."

"Yes."

"Not fuckin' fifteen."

Definitely not Harvard.

"You're gonna put all this on paper?"

"I'll send a full report."

"When?"

"When it's finished."

"You know, one time this little psycho drowned the family puppy. Another, she set fire to the house. I could go on." Info added to spur me to quicker action? "Anyway, great stuff, doc. I'm gonna get this asshole prosecutor on the horn right now."

I didn't envy the hapless DA whose phone was about to ring.

Despite the gloves, I developed an epic assortment of blisters. At noon, I returned to the annex to treat them.

My mobile lay on the counter, fully charged at last. The little green icon showed one voice message. My best friend, Anne Turnip.

The second call of the day after Thorn. This one not the world-tilter, either.

I listened to the directive, delivered with typical Anne melodrama.

"Call me ASAP. Like, now! As soon as you hear this."

A few words about my BFF.

Anne has emerald eyes and long blond hair, its color now maintained through the magic of chemistry. She is leggy-tall and, despite an aversion to exercise and all forms of sport, has remained as thin as the day we met. A very long time ago.

After downing a somewhat warm peach yogurt, I hit call-back.

"Oh, God, Tempe! You've got to come!" Anne's tone made Birdie seem tranquil in comparison.

"Where are you?"

"At the beach house. Now that the weenie boy-cop at the connector finally let me onto the island." Vowels reflecting her Alabama birth and Mississippi schooling, broadened further by the moment's indignation. "You wouldn't believe the Gestapo—"

"How does it look?"

"Devastated! I need help!"

"Take a deep breath."

Long pause. Then, "Right. You're absolutely right. I'm sounding eighty-proof bonkers."

"The house is still standing?"

"Yes."

"Your roof is still on?"

"Yes."

"The roads are open?"

"Yes."

"Do you have power?"

"Not yet. Jesus, Lord, nothing's working. The damn commode won't flush!"

"It'll flush. The seat just won't light up. Besides, you have six others."

"I can't charge the car. I'm trapped here!"

Sounded similar to my morning. Except for the TOTO toilet and Tesla.

"Where is TT?" I asked.

"Who the flipping flamingo knows?"

For years Anne was married to an attorney named Tom Turnip. Decades back, when Tom was a second-year associate, a senior partner at his firm addressed him as Ted for an entire month. We'd called him Tom-Ted ever since. TT.

The marriage eventually ended. Long, unoriginal

story. Anne walked away with a handsome settlement, including property at the Isle of Palms, South Carolina. Despite the financial spanking, she and TT remain friends. With benefits. Apparently, post-storm restoration was not among them.

"Anne, I can't—"

"They've reversed the eastbound lanes on I-26 back to normal. You won't have any problem getting here."

"It's not that."

"Did you have much damage at your place?"

"No. But—"

"Are you working on any *humongous* cases?"

"No. But—"

"If your boss needs you, Charlotte is just three hours away."

She had me there. And, were the situation reversed, I knew Anne would drop everything to rush to my aid. She had in the past. More than once.

I looked at the clock.

"Fine." Unnecessarily dramatic sigh. "It'll take me at least an hour to secure the annex and pack a few things."

"Hallelujah, Harry! I'll mix us a whole passel of drinks with those little paper umbrellas in 'em. Virgin for you, of course. Thank God, I've got Fritos in the pantry."

I promised an infusion of provisions and disconnected.

Turning, I saw Birdie watching me intently.

"Ready for a road trip?"

Totally noncommittal stare.

A quick call to Nguyen, minimal packing, a go at the tree limb jamming the back door, then we were off.

Driving across town was an experience I don't wish to repeat. Broken branches and downed trees littered the streets, requiring U-turns and rerouting at several points. Traffic lights were malfunctioning at many intersections, forcing drivers to figure things out for themselves. Some were better at that than others.

Normally it's twenty minutes from the annex to I-77. That morning it took sixty. With Birdie yowling the whole way.

Three hours after leaving Charlotte, I'd exited I-26 and gone several miles along I-526, when my phone rang for the third time that day.

Area code 843.

The call that would send my life off-kilter for weeks and alter my worldview forever.

"Temperance Brennan." I answered using speaker-phone.

"Dr. Brennan. My name is Ebony Herrin." The voice was gravelly, neither high nor low. Based on pitch and cadence, I thought the caller might be Black and male. Wasn't sure on either. "I'm the newly elected Charleston County coroner."

"How can I help you, Dr. Herrin?"

"No need for titles. I'm an RN."

"How can I be of help?" Sir? Madam?

"I called your office in Charlotte, got forwarded to Dr. Nguyen. She told me you were heading to Charleston."

A little backstory.

With one short and unpleasant hiatus, I've served for decades as forensic anthropologist for the Mecklenburg County Medical Examiner in Charlotte, North Carolina. The MCME is the decoder of death for the region, and I'm the specialist who analyzes remains unfit for a pathologist's scalpel: the decomposed, dismembered, burned, mummified, mutilated, and skeletal.

Throughout my career my boss was Dr. Tim Larabee, a brilliant pathologist, amateur marathoner, and all-around good guy. Larabee ran the office until a hopped-up junkie took him out with two bullets to the gut in a mindless mugging.

After Larabee's murder, Dr. Margot Heavner was hired. In her spare time, the new chief authored tell-all books on forensics that earned her the label Dr. Morgue. To boost sales, Dr. Morgue appeared on any media platform that would have her and sensationalized her work. I didn't like many of her comments. And said so. As a result, there was history between us.

Case in point. I publicly criticized Heavner for a series of interviews she did with a tinfoil-hat blogger and conspiracy theorist named Nick Body. Heavner was incensed. And held a grudge. Thus, the hiatus. During Dr. Morgue's tenure, I was exiled from the MCME.

Fortunately, that tenure was short. Within months of assuming her duties, Heavner was exposed as corrupt and forced to resign in disgrace. Dr. Samantha Nguyen was chosen as her replacement.

Unlike Heavner, Nguyen had no trouble directing outside callers to me.

"Yes." Tires humming as I rolled across the bridge spanning the Wando River. Glancing south, I saw the quayside cranes at the Wando harbor, dark and bony against the pinks and yellows of the fading day.

"As I'm sure you're aware, we've had no resident forensic anthropologist in South Carolina for many years. But I noted from old reports that you've done consults for my predecessor."

"Yes." Wary.

"I have a situation that requires your expertise."

"I'm listening." Not wanting to.

"Last night's hurricane tossed a container ashore down near the battery. I won't burden you with details on the phone, but a couple of kayakers found the thing early this morning, pried off the lid, and spotted what they thought was a body. They called the cops, the cops called me.

"My investigator collected the container and transported it to the MUSC morgue. There are actually two people inside. Just eyeballing the bulk, it looks to be one adult and one kid."

"Any possibility of visual IDs?" Seriously, Brennan? If that were the case, why would Herrin be contacting you?

"The amount of mass tells me decomp will be too advanced."

"Any personal effects, clothing, jewelry, etc.?"

"Both bodies were wrapped in plastic sheeting secured with electrical wire. I didn't want to do too much poking around, but I peeled back enough to see that at least the one is nude."

From nowhere, a flashback image. A woman. A child. A plastic container washed from the sea.

My gut clenched and my mouth went dry.

I swallowed.

"Any clues as to cause of death?"

"I caught a better glimpse of the one body, because of the kids pulling on the wrapping and me tugging it a bit more. Looks to be a single bullet to the head. Also, the hands and teeth are gone."

It can't be.

"You'll need a pathologist." Sounding calmer than I felt.

"I like a guy named Klopp. I've left him a message suggesting y'all meet at the hospital tomorrow. I'll text you the time he's available."

"Fine."

"A detective named Vislosky came to the scene. Not sure about her stomach for autopsies." A brief pause, then, "Tell me what you need."

I did, then we disconnected.

Moments later, I crossed the bridge connecting Mount Pleasant to the Isle of Palms. Salt marsh stretched to the horizon on both sides, tranquil and still. Here and there I saw a wink of white, an ibis or egret, fading into shadow along with the spartina grass in which it stood.

I turned onto Palm Boulevard, a single phrase ricocheting in my head, a mantra born of foreboding.

It can't be.

It can't be.